The Shepherd of Salisbury Plain and Other Tales by Hannah More

Hannah More was born on February 2nd, 1745 at Fishponds in the parish of Stapleton, near Bristol. She was the fourth of five daughters.

The City of Bristol, at that time, was a centre for slave-trading and Hannah would, over time, become one of its staunchest critics.

She was keen to learn, possessed a sharp intellect and was assiduous in studying. Hannah first wrote in 1762 with The Search after Happiness (by the mid 1780s some 10,000 copies had been sold).

In 1767 Hannah became engaged to William Turner. After six years, with no wedding in sight, the engagement was broken off. Turner then bestowed upon her an annual annuity of £200. This was enough to meet her needs and set her free to pursue a literary career.

Her first play, The Inflexible Captive, was staged at Bath in 1775. The famous David Garrick himself produced her next play, Percy, in 1777 as well as writing both the Prologue and Epilogue for it. It was a great success when performed at Covent Garden in December of that year.

Hannah turned to religious writing with Sacred Dramas in 1782; it rapidly ran through nineteen editions. These and the poems Bas-Bleu and Florio (1786) mark her gradual transition to a more serious and considered view of life.

Hannah contributed much to the newly-founded Abolition Society including, in February 1788, her publication of Slavery, a Poem recognised as one of the most important of the abolition period.

Her work now became more evangelical. In the 1790s she wrote several Cheap Repository Tracts which covered moral, religious and political topics and were both for sale or distributed to literate poor people. The most famous is, perhaps, The Shepherd of Salisbury Plain, describing a family of incredible frugality and contentment. Two million copies of these were circulated, in one year.

In 1789, she purchased a small house at Cowslip Green in Somerset. She was instrumental in setting up twelve schools in the area by 1800.

She continued to oppose slavery throughout her life, but at the time of the Abolition Bill of 1807, her health did not permit her to take as active a role in the movement as she had done in the late 1780s, although she maintained a correspondence with Wilberforce and others.

In July 1833, the Bill to abolish slavery throughout the British Empire passed in the House of Commons, followed by the House of Lords on August 1st.

Hannah More died on September 7th, 1833.

Index of Contents

The Shepherd of Salisbury Plain
The Two Shoemakers
The History of Tom White, the Post Boy
The Sunday School
The History of Hester Wilmot, being the sequel to the Sunday School
The History of Betty Brown, the St. Giles's Orange Girl
Black Giles the Poacher
Tawney Rachel, or the Fortune-Teller; with some account of   Dreams, Omens, and Conjurers
Stories for Persons of Middle Rank
The History of Mr. Fantom (the new-fashioned Philosopher), and his man William
The Two Wealthy Farmers; or the History of Mr. Bragwell
'Tis all for the best
A Cure for Melancholy
Allegories
The Pilgrims
The Valley of Tears
The Strait Gate and the Broad Way
Parley the Porter
The Grand Assizes; or General Jail Delivery
The Servant Man turned Soldier, or the Fair-weather Christian
Hannah More – A Short Biography

TALES FOR THE COMMON PEOPLE

"Religion is for the man in humble life, and to raise his nature, and to put him in mind of a state in which the privileges of opulence will cease, when he will be equal by nature, and may be more than equal by virtue."—Burke on the French Revolution.

ADVERTISEMENT

To improve the habits, and raise the principles of the common people, at a time when their dangers and temptations, moral and political, were multiplied beyond the example of any former period, was the motive which impelled the author of these volumes to devise and prosecute the institution of the "Cheap Repository." This plan was established with an humble wish not only to counteract vice and profligacy on the one hand, but error, discontent, and false religion on the other. And as an appetite for reading had, from a variety of causes, been increased among the inferior ranks in this country, it was judged expedient, at this critical period, to supply such wholesome aliment as might give a new direction to their taste, and abate their relish for those corrupt and inflammatory publications which the consequences of the French Revolution have been so fatally pouring in upon us.

The success of the plan exceeded the most sanguine expectations of its projector. Above two millions of the tracts were sold within the first year, besides very large numbers in Ireland; and they continue to be very extensively circulated, in their original form of single tracts, as well as in three bound volumes.

As these stories, though principally, are not calculated exclusively for the middle and lower classes of society, the author has, at the desire of her friends, selected those which were written by herself, and presented them to the public in this collection of her works, in an enlarged and improved form.

THE SHEPHERD OF SALISBURY PLAIN

PART I

Mr. Johnson, a very worthy charitable gentleman, was traveling some time ago across one of those vast plains which are well known in Wiltshire. It was a fine summer's evening, and he rode slowly that he might have leisure to admire God in the works of his creation. For this gentleman was of opinion, that a walk or a ride was as proper a time as any to think about good things: for which reason, on such occasions he seldom thought so much about his money or his trade, or public news, as at other times, that he might with more ease and satisfaction enjoy the pious thoughts which the wonderful works of the great Maker of heaven and earth are intended to raise in the mind.

As this serene contemplation of the visible heavens insensibly lifted up his mind from the works of God in nature to the same God as he is seen in revelation, it occurred to him that this very connexion was clearly intimated by the royal prophet in the nineteenth Psalm—that most beautiful description of the greatness and power of God exhibited in the former part, plainly seeming intended to introduce, illustrate, and unfold the operations of the word and Spirit of God on the heart in the latter. And he began to run a parallel in his own mind between the effects of that highly poetical and glowing picture of the material sun in searching and warming the earth, in the first six verses, and the spiritual operation attributed to the "law of God," which fills up the remaining part of the Psalm. And he persuaded himself that the divine Spirit which dictated this fine hymn, had left it as a kind of general intimation to what use we were to convert our admiration of created things; namely, that we might be led by a sight of them to raise our views from the kingdom of nature to that of grace, and that the contemplation of God in his works might draw us to contemplate him in his word.

In the midst of these reflections, Mr. Johnson's attention was all of a sudden called off by the barking of a shepherd's dog, and looking up, he spied one of those little huts which are here and there to be seen on those great downs; and near it was the shepherd himself busily employed with his dog in collecting together his vast flock of sheep. As he drew nearer, he perceived him to be a clean, well-looking, poor man, near fifty years of age. His coat, though at first it had probably been of one dark color, had been in a long course of years so often patched with different sorts of cloth, that it was now become hard to say which had been the original color. But this, while it gave a plain proof of the shepherd's poverty, equally proved the exceeding neatness, industry, and good management of his wife. His stockings no less proved her good housewifery, for they were entirely covered with darns of different colored worsteds, but had not a hole in them; and his shirt, though nearly as coarse as the sails of a ship, was as white as the drifted snow, and was neatly mended where time had either made a rent, or worn it thin. This furnishes a rule of judging, by which one shall seldom be deceived. If I meet with a laborer, hedging, ditching, or mending the highways, with his stockings and shirt tight and whole, however mean and bad his other garments are, I have seldom failed, on visiting his cottage, to find that also clean and well ordered, and his wife notable, and worthy of encouragement. Whereas, a poor woman, who will be lying a-bed, or gossiping with her neighbors when she ought to be fitting out her husband in a cleanly manner, will seldom be found to be very good in other respects.

This was not the case with our shepherd: and Mr. Johnson was not more struck with the decency of his mean and frugal dress, than with his open honest countenance, which bore strong marks of health, cheerfulness, and spirit.

Mr. Johnson, who was on a journey, and somewhat fearful from the appearance of the sky, that rain was at no great distance, accosted the shepherd with asking what sort of weather he thought it would be on the morrow. "It will be such weather as pleases me," answered the shepherd. Though the answer was delivered in the mildest and most civil tone that could be imagined, the gentleman thought the words themselves rather rude and surly, and asked him how that could be. "Because," replied the shepherd, "it will be such weather as shall please God, and whatever pleases him always pleases me."

Mr. Johnson, who delighted in good men and good things, was very well satisfied with his reply. For he justly thought that though a hypocrite may easily contrive to appear better than he really is to a stranger; and that no one should be too soon trusted, merely for having a few good words in his mouth; yet as he knew that out of the abundance of the heart the mouth speaketh, he always accustomed himself to judge favorably of those who had a serious deportment and solid manner of speaking. It looks as if it proceeded from a good habit, said he, and though I may now and then be deceived by it, yet it has not often happened to me to be so. Whereas if a man accosts me with an idle, dissolute, vulgar, indecent, or profane expression, I have never been deceived in him, but have generally on inquiry, found his character to be as bad as his language gave me room to expect.

He entered into conversation with the shepherd in the following manner: "Yours is a troublesome life, honest friend," said he. "To be sure, sir," replied the shepherd, "'tis not a very lazy life; but 'tis not near so toilsome as that which my GREAT MASTER led for my sake; and he had every state and condition of life at his choice, and chose a hard one; while I only submit to the lot that is appointed to me." "You are exposed to great cold and heat," said the gentleman. "True, sir," said the shepherd; "but then I am not exposed to great temptations; and so, throwing one thing against another, God is pleased to contrive to make things more equal than we poor, ignorant, short-sighted creatures are apt to think. David was happier when he kept his father's sheep on such a plain as this, and employed in singing some of his own Psalms perhaps, than ever he was when he became king of Israel and Judah. And I dare say we should never have had some of the most beautiful texts in all those fine Psalms, if he had not been a shepherd, which enabled him to make so many fine comparisons and similitudes, as one may say, from country life, flocks of sheep, hills, and valleys, fields of corn, and fountains of water."

"You think, then," said the gentleman, "that a laborious life is a happy one." "I do, sir; and more so especially, as it exposes a man to fewer sins. If king Saul had continued a poor laborious man to the end of his days, he might have lived happy and honest, and died a natural death in his bed at last, which you know, sir, was more than he did. But I speak with reverence, for it was divine Providence overruled all that, you know, sir, and I do not presume to make comparisons. Besides, sir, my employment has been particularly honored: Moses was a shepherd on the plains of Midian. It was to 'shepherds keeping their flocks by night,' that the angels appeared in Bethlehem, to tell the best news, the gladdest tidings, that ever were revealed to poor sinful men; often and often has the thought warmed my poor heart in the coldest night, and filled me with more joy and thankfulness than the best supper could have done."

Here the shepherd stopped, for he began to feel that he had made too free, and talked too long. But Mr. Johnson was so well pleased with what he said, and with the cheerful contented manner in which he said it, that he desired him to go on freely, for it was a pleasure to him to meet with a plain man, who, without any kind of learning but what he had got from the Bible, was able to talk so well on a subject in which all men, high and low, rich and poor, are equally concerned.

"Indeed I am afraid I make too bold, sir, for it better becomes me to listen to such a gentleman as you seem to be, than to talk in my poor way: but as I was saying, sir, I wonder all working men do not derive as great joy and delight as I do from thinking how God has honored poverty! Oh! sir, what great, or rich, or mighty men have had such honor put on them, or their condition, as shepherds, tentmakers, fishermen, and carpenters have had! Besides, it seems as if God honored industry also. The way of duty is not only the way of safety, but it is remarkable how many, in the exercise of the common duties of their calling, humbly and rightly performed, as we may suppose, have found honors, preferment, and blessing: while it does not occur to me that the whole sacred volume presents a single instance of a like blessing conferred on idleness. Rebekah, Rachel, and Jethro's daughters, were diligently employed in the lowest occupations of a country life, when Providence, by means of those very occupations, raised them up husbands so famous in history, as Isaac, Jacob, and the prophet Moses. The shepherds were neither playing, nor sleeping, but 'watching their flocks,' when they received the news of a Saviour's birth; and the woman of Samaria, by the laborious office of drawing water, was brought to the knowledge of him who gave her to drink of 'living water.'"

"My honest friend," said the gentleman, "I perceive you are well acquainted with Scripture." "Yes, sir, pretty well, blessed be God! Through his mercy I learned to read when I was a little boy; though reading was not so common when I was a child, as, I am told, through the goodness of Providence and the generosity of the rich, it is likely to become now-a-days. I believe there is no day, for the last thirty years, that I have not peeped at my Bible. If we can't find time to read a chapter, I defy any man to say he can't find time to read a verse; and a single text, sir, well followed, and put in practice every day, would make no bad figure at the year's end: three hundred and sixty-five texts, without the loss of a moment's time, would make a pretty stock, a little golden treasury, as one may say, from new-year's day to new-year's day; and if children were brought up to it, they would come to look for their text as naturally as they do for their breakfast. No laboring man, 'tis true, has so much leisure as a shepherd, for while the flock is feeding I am obliged to be still, and at such times I can now and then tap a shoe for my children or myself, which is a great saving to us, and while I am doing that I repeat a chapter or a Psalm, which makes the time pass pleasantly in this wild solitary place. I can say the best part of the New Testament by heart: I believe I should not say the best part, for every part is good, but I mean the greatest part. I have led but a lonely life, and have often had but little to eat, but my Bible has been meat, drink, and company to me, as I may say, and when want and trouble have come upon me, I don't know what I should have done indeed, sir, if I had not had the promises of this book for my stay and support."

"You have had great difficulties then?" said Mr. Johnson. "Why, as to that, sir, not more than neighbors' fare; I have but little cause to complain, and much to be thankful; but I have had some little struggles, as I will leave you to judge. I have a wife and eight children, whom I bred up in that little cottage which you see under the hill, about half a mile off." "What, that with the smoke coming out of the chimney?" said the gentleman. "Oh no, sir," replied the shepherd, smiling, "we have seldom smoke in the evening, for we have little to cook, and firing is very dear in these parts. 'Tis that cottage which you see on the left hand of the church, near that little tuft of hawthorns." "What, that hovel with only one room above and below, with scarcely any chimney? how is it possible that you can live there with such a family?" "Oh, it is very possible, and very certain too," cried the shepherd. "How many better men have been worse lodged! how many good Christians have perished in prisons and dungeons, in comparison of which my cottage is a palace! The house is very well, sir; and if the rain did not sometimes beat down upon us through the thatch when we are a-bed, I should not desire a better; for I have health, peace, and liberty, and no man maketh me afraid."

"Well, I will certainly call on you before it be long; but how can you contrive to lodge so many children?" "We do the best we can, sir. My poor wife is a very sickly woman, or we should always have done tolerably well. There are no gentry in the parish, so that she has not met with any great assistance in her sickness. The good curate of the parish, who lives in that pretty parsonage in the valley, is very willing, but not very able to assist us on these trying occasions, for he has little enough for himself, and a large family into the bargain. Yet he does what he can, and more than many other men do, and more than he can well afford. Besides that, his prayers and good advice we are always sure of, and we are truly thankful for that, for a man must give, you know, sir, according to what he hath, and not according to what he hath not."

"I am afraid," said Mr. Johnson, "that your difficulties may sometimes lead you to repine."

"No, sir," replied the shepherd, "it pleases God to give me two ways of bearing up under them. I pray that they may be either removed or sanctified to me. Besides, if my road be right, I am contented, though it be rough and uneven. I do not so much stagger at hardships in the right way, as I dread a false security, and a hollow peace, while I may be walking in a more smooth, but less safe way. Besides, sir, I strengthen my faith by recollecting what the best men have suffered, and my hope, with the view of the shortness of all suffering. It is a good hint, sir, of the vanity of all earthly possessions, that though the whole Land of Promise was his, yet the first bit of ground which Abraham, the father of the faithful, got possession of, in the land of Canaan, was a grave."

"Are you in any distress at present?" said Mr. Johnson. "No, sir, thank God," replied the shepherd, "I get my shilling a-day, and most of my children will soon be able to earn something; for we have only three under five years old." "Only!" said the gentleman, "that is a heavy burden." "Not at all; God fits the back to it. Though my wife is not able to do any out-of-door work, yet she breeds up our children to such habits of industry, that our little maids, before they are six years old, can first get a half-penny, and then a penny a day by knitting. The boys, who are too little to do hard work, get a trifle by keeping the birds off the corn; for this the farmers will give them a penny or two pence, and now and then a bit of bread and cheese into the bargain. When the season of crow-keeping is over, then they glean or pick stones; any thing is better than idleness, sir, and if they did not get a farthing by it, I would make them do it just the same, for the sake of giving them early habits of labor.

"So you see sir, I am not so badly off as many are; nay, if it were not that it costs me so much in 'pothecary's stuff for my poor wife, I should reckon myself well off; nay I do reckon myself well off, for blessed be God, he has granted her life to my prayers, and I would work myself to a 'natomy, and live on one meal a day, to add any comfort to her valuable life; indeed I have often done the last, and thought it no great matter neither."

While they were in this part of the discourse, a fine plump cherry-cheek little girl ran up out of breath, with a smile on her young happy face, and without taking any notice of the gentleman, cried out with great joy—"Look here, father, only see how much I have got!" Mr. Johnson was much struck with her simplicity, but puzzled to know what was the occasion of this great joy. On looking at her he perceived a small quantity of coarse wool, some of which had found its way through the holes of her clean, but scanty and ragged woolen apron. The father said, "This has been a successful day indeed, Molly, but don't you see the gentleman?" Molly now made a courtesy down to the very ground; while Mr. Johnson inquired into the cause of mutual satisfaction which both father and daughter had expressed, at the unusual good fortune of the day.

"Sir," said the shepherd, "poverty is a great sharpener of the wits. My wife and I can not endure to see our children (poor as they are) without shoes and stockings, not only on account of the pinching cold which cramps their poor little limbs, but because it degrades and debases them; and poor people who have but little regard to appearances, will seldom be found to have any great regard for honesty and goodness; I don't say this is always the case; but I am sure it is too often. Now shoes and stockings being very dear, we could never afford to get them without a little contrivance. I must show you how I manage about the shoes when you condescend to call at our cottage, sir; as to stockings, this is one way we take to help to get them. My young ones, who are too little to do much work, sometimes wander at odd hours over the hills for the chance of finding what little wool the sheep may drop when they rub themselves, as they are apt to do, against the bushes.[1] These scattered bits of wool the children pick out of the brambles, which I see have torn sad holes in Molly's apron to-day; they carry this wool home, and when they have got a pretty parcel together, their mother cards it; for she can sit and card in the chimney corner, when she is not able to wash or work about the house. The biggest girl then spins it; it does very well for us without dyeing, for poor people must not stand for the color of their stockings. After this our little boys knit it for themselves, while they are employed in keeping cows in the fields, and after they get home at night. As for the knitting which the girls and their mother do, that is chiefly for sale, which helps to pay our rent."

[1] This piece of frugal industry is not imaginary, but a real fact, as is the character of the shepherd, and his uncommon knowledge of the Scriptures.

Mr. Johnson lifted up his eyes in silent astonishment at the shifts which honest poverty can make rather than beg or steal; and was surprised to think how many ways of subsisting there are, which those who live at their ease little suspect. He secretly resolved to be more attentive to his own petty expenses than he had hitherto been; and to be more watchful that nothing was wasted in his family.

But to return to the shepherd. Mr. Johnson told him that as he must needs be at his friend's house, who lived many miles off, that night, he could not, as he wished to do, make a visit to his cottage at present. "But I will certainly do it," said he, "on my return, for I long to see your wife and her nice little family, and to be an eye-witness of her neatness and good management." The poor man's tears started into his eyes on hearing the commendation bestowed on his wife; and wiping them off with the sleeve of his coat, for he was not worth a handkerchief in the world, he said, "Oh, sir, you just now, I am afraid, called me an humble man, but indeed I am a very proud one." "Proud!" exclaimed Mr. Johnson, "I hope not. Pride is a great sin, and as the poor are liable to it as well as the rich, so good a man as you seem to be ought to guard against it." "Sir," said he, "you're right, but I am not proud of myself, God knows I have nothing to be proud of. I am a poor sinner; but indeed, sir, I am proud of my wife: she is not only the most tidy, notable woman on the plain, but she is the kindest wife and mother, and the most contented, thankful Christian that I know. Last year I thought I should have lost her in a violent fit of the rheumatism, caught by going to work too soon after her lying-in, I fear; for 'tis but a bleak, coldish place, as you may see, sir, in winter, and sometimes the snow lies so long under the hill, that I can hardly make myself a path to get out and buy a few necessaries in the village; and we are afraid to send out the children, for fear they should be lost when the snow is deep. So, as I was saying, the poor soul was very bad indeed, and for several weeks lost the use of all her limbs except her hands; a merciful Providence spared her the use of these, so that when she could not turn in her bed, she could contrive to patch a rag or two for her family. She was always saying, had it not been for the great goodness of God, she might have her hands lame as well as her feet, or the palsy instead of the rheumatism, and then she could have done nothing—but, nobody had so many mercies as she had.

"I will not tell you what we suffered during the bitter weather, sir, but my wife's faith and patience during that trying time, were as good a lesson to me as any sermon I could hear, and yet Mr. Jenkins gave us very comfortable ones too, that helped to keep up my spirits."

"I fear, shepherd," said Mr. Johnson, "you have found this to be but a bad world."

"Yes, sir," replied the shepherd, "but it is governed by a good God. And though my trials have now and then been sharp, why then, sir, as the saying is, if the pain be violent, it is seldom lasting, and if he but moderate, why then we can bear it the longer, and when it is quite taken away, ease is the more precious, and gratitude is quickened by the remembrance; thus every way, and in every case, I can always find out a reason for vindicating Providence."

"But," said Mr. Johnson, "how do you do to support yourself under the pressure of actual want. Is not hunger a great weakener of your faith?"

"Sir," replied the shepherd, "I endeavor to live upon the promises. You, who abound in the good things of this world, are apt to set too high a value on them. Suppose, sir, the king, seeing me at hard work, were to say to me, that if I would patiently work on till Christmas, a fine palace and a great estate should be the reward of my labors. Do you think, sir, that a little hunger, or a little wet, would make me flinch, when I was sure that a few months would put me in possession! Should I not say to myself frequently—cheer up, shepherd, 'tis but till Christmas! Now is there not much less difference between this supposed day and Christmas, when I should take possession of the estate and palace, than there is between time and eternity, when I am sure of entering on a kingdom not made with hands? There is some comparison between a moment and a thousand years, because a thousand years are made up of moments, all time being made up of the same sort of stuff, as I may say; while there is no sort of comparison between the longest portion of time and eternity. You know, sir, there is no way of measuring two things, one of which has length and breadth, which shows it must have an end somewhere, and another thing, which being eternal, is without end and without measure."

"But," said Mr. Johnson, "is not the fear of death sometimes too strong for your faith?"

"Blessed be God, sir," replied the shepherd, "the dark passage through the valley of the shadow of death is made safe by the power of him who conquered death. I know, indeed, we shall go as naked out of this world as we came into it, but an humble penitent will not be found naked in the other world, sir. My Bible tells me of garments of praise and robes of righteousness. And is it not a support, sir, under any of the petty difficulties and distresses here, to be assured by the word of him who can not lie, that those who were in white robes came out of tribulation? But, sir, I beg your pardon for being so talkative. Indeed you great folks can hardly imagine how it raises and cheers a poor man's heart when such as you condescend to talk familiarly to him on religious subjects. It seems to be a practical comment on that text which says, the rich and the poor meet together, the Lord is the maker of them all. And so far from creating disrespect, sir, and that nonsensical wicked notion about equality, it rather prevents it. But to turn to my wife. One Sunday afternoon when she was at the worst, as I was coming out of church, for I went one part of the day, and my eldest daughter the other, so my poor wife was never left alone; as I was coming out of church, I say, Mr. Jenkins, the minister, called out to me and asked me how my wife did, saying he had been kept from coming to see her by the deep fall of snow, and indeed from the parsonage-house to my hovel it was quite impassable. I gave him all the particulars he asked, and I am afraid a good many more, for my heart was quite full. He kindly gave me a shilling, and said he would certainly try to pick out his way and come and see her in a day or two.

"While he was talking to me a plain farmer-looking gentleman in boots, who stood by listened to all I said, but seemed to take no notice. It was Mr. Jenkins's wife's father, who was come to pass the Christmas-holidays at the parsonage-house. I had always heard him spoken of as a plain frugal man, who lived close himself, but was remarked to give away more than any of his show-away neighbors.

"Well! I went home with great spirits at this seasonable and unexpected supply; for we had tapped our last sixpence, and there was little work to be had on account of the weather, I told my wife I had not come back empty-handed. 'No, I dare say not,' says she, 'you have been serving a master who filleth the hungry with good things, though he sendeth the rich empty away.' True, Mary, says I, we seldom fail to get good spiritual food from Mr. Jenkins, but to-day he has kindly supplied our bodily wants. She was more thankful when I showed her the shilling, than, I dare say, some of your great people are when they get a hundred pounds."

Mr. Johnson's heart smote him when he heard such a value set upon a shilling; surely, said he to himself, I will never waste another; but he said nothing to the shepherd, who thus pursued his story:

"Next morning before I went out, I sent part of the money to buy a little ale and brown sugar to put into her water-gruel; which you know, sir, made it nice and nourishing. I went out to cleave wood in a farm-yard, for there was no standing out on the plain, after such snow as had fallen in the night. I went with a lighter heart than usual, because I had left my poor wife a little better, and comfortably supplied for this day, and I now resolved more than ever to trust God for the supplies of the next. When I came back at night, my wife fell a crying as soon as she saw me. This, I own, I thought but a bad return for the blessings she had so lately received, and so I told her,—'Oh,' said she, 'it is too much, we are too rich; I am now frightened, not lest we should have no portion in this world, but for fear we should have our whole portion in it. Look here, John!' So saying, she uncovered the bed whereon she lay, and showed me two warm, thick, new blankets. I could not believe my own eyes, sir, because when I went out in the morning, I had left her with no other covering than our little old thin blue rug. I was still more amazed when she put half a crown into my hand, telling me, she had had a visit from Mr. Jenkins, and Mr. Jones, the latter of whom had bestowed all these good things upon us. Thus, sir, have our lives been crowned with mercies. My wife got about again, and I do believe, under Providence, it was owing to these comforts; for the rheumatism, sir, without blankets by night, and flannel by day, is but a baddish job, especially to people who have little or no fire. She will always be a weakly body; but thank God her soul prospers and is in health. But I beg your pardon, sir, for talking on at this rate." "Not at all, not at all," said Mr. Johnson; "I am much pleased with your story; you shall certainly see me in a few days. Good night." So saying, he slipped a crown into his hand and rode off. Surely, said the shepherd, goodness and mercy have followed me all the days of my life, as he gave the money to his wife when he got home at night.

As to Mr. Johnson, he found abundant matter for his thoughts during the rest of his journey. On the whole, he was more disposed to envy than to pity the shepherd. I have seldom seen, said he, so happy a man. It is a sort of happiness which the world could not give, and which, I plainly see, it has not been able to take away. This must be the true spirit of religion. I see more and more, that true goodness is not merely a thing of words and opinions, but a living principle brought into every common action of a man's life. What else could have supported this poor couple under every bitter trial of want and sickness? No, my honest shepherd, I do not pity, but I respect and even honor thee; and I will visit thy poor hovel on my return to Salisbury, with as much pleasure as I am now going to the house of my friend.

If Mr. Johnson keeps his word in sending me an account of his visit to the shepherd's cottage, I will be very glad to entertain my readers with it.

PART II

I am willing to hope that my readers will not be sorry to hear some further particulars of their old acquaintance, the Shepherd of Salisbury Plain. They will call to mind that at the end of the first part, he was returning home full of gratitude for the favors he had received from Mr. Johnson, whom we left pursuing his journey, after having promised to make a visit to the shepherd's cottage.

Mr. Johnson, after having passed some time with his friend, set out on his return to Salisbury, and on the Saturday evening reached a very small inn, a mile or two distant from the shepherd's village; for he never traveled on a Sunday without such a reason as he might be able to produce at the day of judgment. He went the next morning to the church nearest the house where he had passed the night, and after taking such refreshment as he could get at that house, he walked on to find out the shepherd's cottage. His reason for visiting him on a Sunday was chiefly because he supposed it to be the only day which the shepherd's employment allowed him to pass at home with his family; and as Mr. Johnson had been struck with his talk, he thought it would be neither unpleasant nor unprofitable to observe how a man who carried such an appearance of piety spent his Sunday: for though he was so low in the world, this gentleman was not above entering very closely into his character, of which he thought he should be able to form a better judgment, by seeing whether his practice at home kept pace with his professions abroad: for it is not so much by observing how people talk, as how they live, that we ought to judge of their characters.

After a pleasant walk, Mr. Johnson got within sight of the cottage, to which he was directed by the clump of hawthorns and the broken chimney. He wished to take the family by surprise; and walking gently up to the house he stood awhile to listen. The door being half open, he saw the shepherd (who looked so respectable in his Sunday coat that he should hardly have known him), his wife, and their numerous young family, drawing round their little table, which was covered with a clean, though very coarse cloth.

There stood on it a large dish of potatoes, a brown pitcher, and a piece of a coarse loaf. The wife and children stood in silent attention, while the shepherd, with uplifted hands and eyes, devoutly begged the blessing of heaven on their homely fare. Mr. Johnson could not help sighing to reflect, that he had sometimes seen better dinners eaten with less appearance of thankfulness.

The shepherd and his wife sat down with great seeming cheerfulness, but the children stood; and while the mother was helping them, little fresh-colored Molly, who had picked the wool from the bushes with so much delight, cried out, "Father, I wish I was big enough to say grace, I am sure I should say it very heartily to-day, for I was thinking what must poor people do who have no salt to their potatoes; and do but look, our dish is quite full." "That is the true way of thinking, Molly," said the father; "in whatever concerns bodily wants and bodily comforts, it is our duty to compare our own lot with the lot of those who are worse off, and will keep us thankful: on the other hand, whenever we are tempted to set up our own wisdom or goodness, we must compare ourselves with those who are wiser and better, and that will keep us humble." Molly was now so hungry, and found the potatoes so good, that she had no time to make any more remarks; but was devouring her dinner very heartily, when the barking of the great dog drew her attention from her trencher to the door, and spying the stranger, she cried out, "Look, father, see here, if yonder is not the good gentleman!" Mr. Johnson finding himself discovered, immediately walked in, and was heartily welcomed by the honest shepherd, who told his wife that this was the gentleman to whom they were so much obliged.

The good woman began, as some very neat people are rather apt to do, with making many apologies that her house was not cleaner, and that things were not in a fitter order to receive such a gentleman. Mr. Johnson, however, on looking round, could discover nothing but the most perfect neatness. The trenchers on which they were eating were almost as white as their linen; and notwithstanding the number and smallness of the children, there was not the least appearance of dirt or litter. The furniture was very simple and poor, hardly indeed amounting to bare necessaries. It consisted of four brown wooden chairs, which by constant rubbing, were become as bright as a looking-glass; an iron pot and kettle; a poor old grate, which scarcely held a handful of coal, and out of which the little fire that had been in it appeared to have been taken, as soon as it had answered the end for which it had been lighted—that of boiling their potatoes. Over the chimney stood an old-fashioned broad bright candlestick, and a still brighter spit; it was pretty clear that this last was kept rather for ornament than use. An old carved elbow chair, and a chest of the same date, which stood in the corner, were considered the most valuable part of the shepherd's goods, having been in his family for three generations. But all these were lightly esteemed by him in comparison of another possession, which, added to the above, made up the whole of what he had inherited from his father: and which last he would not have parted with, if no other could have been had, for the king's ransom: this was a large old Bible, which lay on the window-seat, neatly covered with brown cloth, variously patched. This sacred book was most reverently preserved from dog's ears, dirt, and every other injury but such as time and much use had made it suffer in spite of care. On the clean white walls were pasted a hymn on the Crucifixion of our Saviour, a print of the Prodigal Son, the Shepherd's hymn, a New History of a True Book, an Patient Joe, or the Newcastle Collier.[2]

[2] Printed for the Cheap Repository.

After the first salutations were over, Mr. Johnson said that if they would go on with their dinner he would sit down. Though a good deal ashamed, they thought it more respectful to obey the gentleman, who having cast his eye on their slender provisions, gently rebuked the shepherd for not having indulged himself, as it was Sunday, with a morsel of bacon to relish his potatoes. The shepherd said nothing, but poor Mary colored and hung down her head, saying, "Indeed, sir, it is not my fault; I did beg my husband to allow himself a bit of meat to-day out of your honor's bounty; but he was too good to do it, and it is all for my sake." The shepherd seemed unwilling to come to an explanation, but Mr. Johnson desired Mary to go on. So she continued: "You must know, sir, that both of us, next to a sin, dread a debt, and indeed in some cases a debt is a sin; but with all our care and pains, we have never been able quite to pay off the doctor's bill for that bad fit of rheumatism which I had last winter. Now when you were pleased to give my husband that kind present the other day, I heartily desired him to buy a bit of meat for Sunday, as I said before, that he might have a little refreshment for himself out of your kindness. 'But,' answered he, 'Mary, it is never out of my mind long together that we still owe a few shillings to the doctor (and thank God it is all we did owe in the world). Now if I carry him his money directly it will not only show him our honesty and our good-will, but it will be an encouragement to him to come to you another time in case you should be taken once more in such a bad fit; for I must own,' added my poor husband, 'that the thought of your being so terribly ill without any help, is the only misfortune that I want courage to face.'"

Here the grateful woman's tears ran down so fast that she could not go on. She wiped them with the corner of her apron, and humbly begged pardon for making so free. "Indeed, sir," said the shepherd, "though my wife is full as unwilling to be in debt as myself, yet I could hardly prevail on her to consent to my paying this money just then, because she said it was hard I should not have a taste of the gentleman's bounty myself. But for once, sir, I would have my own way. For you must know, as I pass the best part of my time alone, tending my sheep, 'tis a great point with me, sir, to get comfortable matter for my own thoughts; so that 'tis rather self-interest in me to allow myself in no pleasures and no practices that won't bear thinking on over and over. For when one is a good deal alone, you know, sir, all one's bad deeds do so rush in upon one, as I may say, and so torment one, that there is no true comfort to be had but in keeping clear of wrong doings and false pleasures; and that I suppose may be one reason why so many folks hate to stay a bit by themselves. But as I was saying—when I came to think the matter over on the hill yonder, said I to myself, a good dinner is a good thing, I grant, and yet it will be but cold comfort to me a week after, to be able to say—to be sure I had a nice shoulder of mutton last Sunday for dinner, thanks to the good gentleman! but then I am in debt. I had a rare dinner, that's certain, but the pleasure of that has long been over, and the debt still remains. I have spent the crown; and now if my poor wife should be taken in one of those fits again, die she must, unless God work a miracle to prevent it, for I can get no help for her. This thought settled all; and I set off directly and paid the crown to the doctor with as much cheerfulness as I should have felt on sitting down to the fattest shoulder of mutton that ever was roasted. And if I was contented at the time, think how much more happy I have been at the remembrance! O, sir, there are no pleasures worth the name but such as bring no plague or penitence after them."

Mr. Johnson was satisfied with the shepherd's reasons, and agreed that though a good dinner was not to be despised, yet it was not worthy to be compared with a contented mind, which (as the Bible truly says) is a continual feast. "But come," said the good gentleman, "what have we got in this brown mug?" "As good water," said the shepherd, "as any in the king's dominions. I have heard of countries beyond sea, in which there is no wholesome water; nay, I have been myself in a great town not far off, where they are obliged to buy all the water which they get, while a good Providence sends to my very door a spring as clear and fine as Jacob's well. When I am tempted to repine that I have often no other drink, I call to mind that it was nothing better than a cup of cold water which the woman at the well of Sychar drew for the greatest guest that ever visited this world."

"Very well," replied Mr. Johnson; "but as your honesty has made you prefer a poor meal to being in debt, I will at least send and get something for you to drink. I saw a little public house just by the church, as I came along. Let that little rosy-faced fellow fetch a mug of beer." So saying, he looked full at the boy, who did not offer to stir; but cast an eye at his father to know what he was to do. "Sir," said the shepherd, "I hope we shall not appear ungrateful if we seem to refuse your favor; my little boy would, I am sure, fly to serve you on any other occasion. But, good sir, it is Sunday; and should any of my family be seen at a public house on a Sabbath-day, it would be a much greater grief to me than to drink water all my life. I am often talking against these doing to others; and if I should say one thing and do another, you can't think what an advantage it would give many of my neighbors over me, who would be glad enough to report that they had caught the shepherd's son at the alehouse without explaining how it happened. Christians, you know, sir, must be doubly watchful; or they will not only bring disgrace on themselves, but what is much worse, on that holy name by which they are called."

"Are you not a little too cautious, my honest friend?" said Mr. Johnson. "I humbly ask your pardon, sir," replied the shepherd, "if I think that is impossible. In my poor notion, I no more understand how a man can be too cautious, than how he can be too strong, or too healthy."

"You are right indeed," said Mr. Johnson, "as a general principle, but this struck me as a very small thing." "Sir," said the shepherd, "I am afraid you will think me very bold, but you encourage me to speak out." "'Tis what I wish," said the gentleman. "Then, sir," resumed the shepherd, "I doubt if, where there is a frequent temptation to do wrong, any fault can be called small; that is, in short, if there is any such thing as a small willful sin. A poor man like me is seldom called out to do great things, so that it is not by a few striking deeds his character can be judged by his neighbors, but by the little round of daily customs he allows himself in."

"I should like," said Mr. Johnson, "to know how you manage in this respect."

"I am but a poor scholar, sir," replied the shepherd, "but I have made myself a little sort of rule. I always avoid, as I am an ignorant man, picking out any one single difficult text to distress my mind about, or to go and build opinions upon, because I know that puzzles and injures poor unlearned Christians. But I endeavor to collect what is the general spirit or meaning of Scripture on any particular subject, by putting a few texts together, which though I find them dispersed up and down, yet all seem to look the same way, to prove the same truth, or hold out the same comfort. So when I am tried or tempted, or any thing happens in which I am at a loss what to do, I apply to my rule—to the law and the testimony. To be sure I can't always find a particular direction as to the very case, because then the Bible must have been bigger than all those great books I once saw in the library at Salisbury palace, which the butler told me were acts of Parliament; and had that been the case, a poor man would never have had money to buy, nor a working man time to read the Bible; and so Christianity could only have been a religion for the rich, for those who had money and leisure; which, blessed be God! is so far from being the truth, that in all that fine discourse of our Saviour to John's disciples, it is enough to reconcile any poor man in the world to his low condition, to observe, when Christ reckons up the things for which he came on earth, to observe, I say, what he keeps for last. Go tell John, says he, those things which ye do hear and see: the blind receive their sight, and the lame walk, the lepers are cleansed, and the deaf hear, and the dead are raised up. Now, sir, all these are wonders to be sure, but they are nothing to what follows. They are but like the lower rounds of a ladder, as I may say, by which you mount to the top—and the poor have the Gospel preached to them. I dare say, if John had any doubts before, this part of the message must have cleared them up at once. For it must have made him certain sure at once, that a religion which placed preaching salvation to the poor above healing the sick, which ranked the soul above the body, and set heaven above health, must have come from God."

"But," said Mr. Johnson, "you say you can generally pick out your particular duty from the Bible, though that immediate duty be not fully explained."

"Indeed, sir," replied the shepherd, "I think I can find out the principle at least, if I bring but a willing mind. The want of that is the great hinderance. Whosoever doeth my will, he shall know of the doctrine. You know that text, sir. I believe a stubborn will makes the Bible harder to be understood than any want of learning. 'Tis corrupt affections which blind the understanding, sir. The more a man hates sin, the clearer he will see his way, and the more he loves holiness, the better he will understand his Bible—the more practical conviction will he get of that pleasant truth, that the secret of the Lord is with them that fear him. Now, sir, suppose I had time and learning, and possessed of all the books I saw at the bishop's, where could I find out a surer way to lay the axe to the root of all covetousness, selfishness, and injustice, than the plain and ready rule, to do unto all men as I would they should do unto me. If my neighbor does me an injury, can I be at any loss how to proceed with him, when I recollect the parable of the unforgiving steward, who refused to pardon a debt of a hundred pence, when his own ten thousand talents had been remitted to him? I defy any man to retain habitual selfishness, hardness of heart, or any other allowed sin, who daily and conscientiously tries his own heart by this touchstone. The straight rule will show the crooked practice to every one who honestly tries the one by the other."

"Why you seem to make Scripture a thing of general application," said Mr. Johnson, "in cases in which many, I fear, do not apply."

"It applies to every thing, sir," replied the shepherd. "When those men who are now disturbing the peace of the world, and trying to destroy the confidence of God's children in their Maker and their Saviour; when those men, I say, came to my poor hovel with their new doctrines and their new books, I would never look into one of them; for I remember it was the first sin of the first pair to lose their innocence for the sake of a little wicked knowledge; besides, my own book told me—To fear God and honor the king—To meddle not with them who are given to change—Not to speak evil of dignities—To render honor to whom honor is due. So that I was furnished with a little coat of mail, as I may say, which preserved me, while those who had no such armor fell into the snare."

While they were thus talking, the children who had stood very quietly behind, and had not stirred a foot, now began to scamper about all at once, and in a moment ran to the window-seat to pick up their little old hats. Mr. Johnson looked surprised at this disturbance; the shepherd asked his pardon, telling him it was the sound of the church-bell which had been the cause of their rudeness; for their mother had brought them up with such a fear of being too late for church, that it was but who could catch the first stroke of the bell, and be first ready. He had always taught them to think that nothing was more indecent than to get into church after it was begun; for as the service opened with an exhortation to repentance, and a confession of sin, it looked very presumptuous not to feel ready to join it; it looked as if people did not feel themselves to be sinners. And though such as lived at a great distance might plead difference of clocks as an excuse, yet those who lived within the sound of the bell, could pretend neither ignorance nor mistake.

Mary and her children set forward. Mr. Johnson and the shepherd followed, taking care to talk the whole way on such subjects as might fit them for the solemn duties of the place to which they were going. "I have often been sorry to observe," said Mr. Johnson, "that many who are reckoned decent, good kind of people, and who would on no account neglect going to church, yet seem to care but little in what frame or temper of mind they go thither. They will talk of their worldly concerns till they get within the door, and then take them up again the very minute the sermon is over, which makes me ready to fear they lay too much stress on the mere form of going to a place of worship. Now, for my part, I always find that it requires a little time to bring my mind into a state fit to do any common business well, much more this great and most necessary business of all." "Yes, sir," replied the shepherd; "and then I think too how busy I should be in preparing my mind, if I were going into the presence of a great gentleman, or a lord, or the king; and shall the King of kings be treated with less respect? Besides, one likes to see people feel as if going to church was a thing of choice and pleasure, as well as a duty, and that they were as desirous not to be the last there, as they would be if they were going to a feast or a fair."

After service, Mr. Jenkins, the clergyman, who was well acquainted with the character of Mr. Johnson, and had a great respect for him, accosted him with much civility; expressing his concern that he could not enjoy just now so much of his conversation as he wished, as he was obliged to visit a sick person at a distance, but hoped to have a little talk with him before he left the village. As they walked along together, Mr. Johnson made such inquiries about the shepherd, as served to confirm him in the high opinion he entertained of his piety, good sense, industry, and self-denial. They parted; the clergyman promising to call in at the cottage in his way home.

The shepherd, who took it for granted that Mr. Johnson was gone to the parsonage, walked home with his wife and children, and was beginning in his usual way to catechise and instruct his family, when Mr. Johnson came in, and insisted that the shepherd should go on with his instruction just as if he were not there. This gentleman, who was very desirous of being useful to his own servants and workmen in the way of instruction, was sometimes sorry to find that though he took a good deal of pains, they now and then did not quite understand him; for though his meaning was very good, his language was not always very plain; and though the things he said were not hard to be understood, yet the words were, especially to such as were very ignorant. And he now began to find out that if people were ever so wise and good, yet if they had not a simple, agreeable, and familiar way of expressing themselves, some of their plain hearers would not be much the better for them. For this reason he was not above listening to the plain, humble way in which this honest man taught his family; for though he knew that he himself had many advantages over the shepherd, had more learning, and could teach him many things, yet he was not too proud to learn even of so poor a man, in any point where he thought the shepherd might have the advantage of him.

This gentleman was much pleased with the knowledge and piety which he discovered in the answers of the children: and desired the shepherd to tell him how he contrived to keep up a sense of divine things in his own mind, and in that of his family, with so little leisure, and so little reading. "Oh! as to that, sir," said the shepherd, "we do not read much except in one book, to be sure; but with my hearty prayer for God's blessing on the use of that book, what little knowledge is needful seems to come of course, as it were. And my chief study has been to bring the fruits of the Sunday reading into the week's business, and to keep up the same sense of God in the heart, when the Bible is in the cupboard as when it is in the hand. In short, to apply what I read in the book to what I meet with in the field."

"I don't quite understand you," said Mr. Johnson. "Sir," replied the shepherd, "I have but a poor gift at conveying these things to others, though I have much comfort from them in my own mind; but I am sure that the most ignorant and hard-working people, who are in earnest about their salvation, may help to keep up devout thoughts and good affections during the week, though they have had hardly any time to look at a book; and it will help them to keep out bad thoughts too; which is no small matter. But then they must know the Bible; they must have read the word of God diligently, that is a kind of stock in trade for a Christian to set up with; and it is this which makes me so careful in teaching it to my children; and even in storing their memories with Psalms and chapters. This is a great help to a poor hard-working man, who will scarcely meet with any thing in them but what he may turn to some good account. If one lives in the fear and love of God, almost every thing one sees abroad will teach one to adore his power and goodness, and bring to mind some text of Scripture, which shall fill his heart with thankfulness, and his mouth with praise. When I look upward the Heavens declare the glory of God, and shall I be silent and ungrateful? If I look round and see the valleys standing thick with corn, how can I help blessing that Power who giveth me all things richly to enjoy? I may learn gratitude from the beasts of the field, for the ox knoweth his master, and the ass his master's crib, and shall a Christian not know, shall a Christian not consider what great things God has done for him? I, who am a shepherd, endeavor to fill my soul with a constant remembrance of that good shepherd, who feedeth me in green pastures and maketh me to lie down beside the still waters, and whose rod and staff comfort me. A religion, sir, which has its seat in the heart, and its fruits in the life, takes up little time in the study, and yet in another sense, true religion, which from sound principles brings forth right practice, fills up the whole time and life too as one may say."

"You are happy," said Mr. Johnson, "in this retired life, by which you escape the corruptions of the world." "Sir," replied the shepherd, "I do not escape the corruptions of my own evil nature. Even there, on that wild solitary hill, I can find out that my heart is prone to evil thoughts. I suppose, sir, that different states have different temptations. You great folks that live in the world, perhaps, are exposed to some of which such a poor man as I am, knows nothing. But to one who leads a lonely life like me, evil thoughts are a chief besetting sin; and I can no more withstand these without the grace of God, than a rich gentleman can withstand the snares of evil company, without the same grace. And I find that I stand in need of God's help continually, and if he should give me up to my own evil heart I should be lost."

Mr. Johnson approved of the shepherd's sincerity, for he had always observed, that where there was no humility, and no watchfulness against sin, there was no religion, and he said that the man who did not feel himself to be a sinner, in his opinion could not be a Christian.

Just as they were in this part of their discourse, Mr. Jenkins, the clergyman, came in. After the usual salutations, he said, "Well, shepherd, I wish you joy; I know you will be sorry to gain any advantage by the death of a neighbor; but old Wilson, my clerk, was so infirm, and I trust so well prepared, that there is no reason to be sorry for his death. I have been to pray by him, but he died while I staid. I have always intended you should succeed to his place: it is no great matter of profit, but every little is something."

"No great matter, sir," cried the shepherd; "indeed it is a great thing to me, it will more than pay my rent. Blessed be God for all his goodness." Mary said nothing, but lifted up her eyes full of tears in silent gratitude.

"I am glad of this little circumstance," said Mr. Jenkins, "not only for your sake but for the sake of the office itself. I so heartily reverence every religious institution, that I would never have the amen added to the excellent prayers of our church, by vain or profane lips, and if it depended on me, there should be no such thing in the land as an idle, drunken, or irreligious parish clerk. Sorry I am to say that this matter is not always sufficiently attended to, and that I know some of a very indifferent character."

Mr. Johnson now inquired of the clergyman whether there were many children in the parish. "More than you would expect," replied he, "from the seeming smallness of it; but there are some little hamlets which you do not see." "I think," returned Mr. Johnson, "I recollect that in the conversation I had with the shepherd on the hill yonder, he told me you had no Sunday School." "I am sorry to say we have none," said the minister. "I do what I can to remedy this misfortune by public catechising; but having two or three churches to serve, I can not give so much time as I wish to private instruction; and having a large family of my own, and no assistance from others, I have never been able to establish a school."

"There is an excellent institution in London," said Mr. Johnson, "called the Sunday School Society, which kindly gives books and other helps, on the application of such pious clergymen as stand in need of their aid, and which I am sure would have assisted you, but I think we shall be able to do something ourselves. Shepherd," continued he, "if I were a king, and had it in my power to make you a rich and a great man, with a word speaking, I would not do it. Those who are raised by some sudden stroke, much above the station in which divine Providence had placed them, seldom turn out very good, or very happy. I have never had any great things in my power, but as far as I have been able, I have been always glad to assist the worthy. I have however, never attempted or desired to set any poor man much above his natural condition, but it is a pleasure to me to lend him such assistance as may make that condition more easy to himself, and put him in a way which shall call him to the performance of more duties than perhaps he could have performed without my help, and of performing them in a better manner to others, and with more comfort to himself. What rent do you pay for this cottage?"

"Fifty shillings a year, sir."

"It is in a sad tattered condition; is there not a better to be had in the village?"

"That in which the poor clerk lived," said the clergyman, "is not only more light and whole, but has two decent chambers, and a very large light kitchen." "That will be very convenient," replied Mr. Johnson; "pray what is the rent?" "I think," said the shepherd, "poor neighbor Wilson gave somewhat about four pounds a year, or it might be guineas." "Very well," said Mr. Johnson, "and what will the clerk's place be worth, think you?" "About three pounds," was the answer.

"Now," continued Mr. Johnson, "my plan is, that the shepherd should take that house immediately; for as the poor man is dead, there will be no need of waiting till quarter-day, if I make up the difference." "True, sir," said Mr. Jenkins, "and I am sure my wife's father, whom I expect to-morrow, will willingly assist a little toward buying some of the clerk's old goods. And the sooner they remove the better, for poor Mary caught that bad rheumatism by sleeping under a leaky thatch." The shepherd was too much moved to speak, and Mary could hardly sob out, "Oh, sir! you are too good; indeed this house will do very well." "It may do very well for you and your children, Mary," said Mr. Johnson, gravely, "but it will not do for a school; the kitchen is neither large nor light enough. Shepherd," continued he, "with your good minister's leave, and kind assistance, I propose to set up in this parish a Sunday School, and to make you the master. It will not at all interfere with your weekly calling, and it is the only lawful way in which you could turn the Sabbath into a day of some little profit to your family, by doing, as I hope, a great deal of good to the souls of others. The rest of the week you will work as usual. The difference of rent between this house and the clerk's I shall pay myself, for to put you in a better house at your own expense would be no great act of kindness. As for honest Mary, who is not fit for hard labor, or any other out-of-door work, I propose to endow a small weekly school, of which she shall be the mistress, and employ her notable turn to good account, by teaching ten or a dozen girls to knit, sew, spin, card, or any other useful way of getting their bread; for all this I shall only pay her the usual price, for I am not going to make you rich, but useful."

"Not rich, sir?" cried the shepherd; "How can I ever be thankful enough for such blessings? And will my poor Mary have a dry thatch over her head? and shall I be able to send for the doctor when I am like to lose her? Indeed my cup runs over with blessings; I hope God will give me humility." Here he and Mary looked at each other and burst into tears. The gentlemen saw their distress, and kindly walked out upon the little green before the door, that these honest people might give vent to their feelings. As soon as they were alone they crept into one corner of the room, where they thought they could not be seen, and fell on their knees, devoutly blessing and praising God for his mercies. Never were more hearty prayers presented, than this grateful couple offered up for their benefactors. The warmth of their gratitude could only be equaled by the earnestness with which they besought the blessing of God on the work in which they were going to engage.

The two gentlemen now left this happy family, and walked to the parsonage, where the evening was spent in a manner very edifying to Mr. Johnson, who the next day took all proper measures for putting the shepherd in immediate possession of his now comfortable habitation. Mr. Jenkins's father-in-law, the worthy gentleman who gave the shepherd's wife the blankets, in the first part of this history, arrived at the parsonage before Mr. Johnson left it, and assisted in fitting up the clerk's cottage.

Mr. Johnson took his leave, promising to call on the worthy minister and his new clerk once a year, in his summer's journey over the plain, as long as it should please God to spare his life. He had every reason to be satisfied with the objects of his bounty. The shepherd's zeal and piety made him a blessing to the rising generation. The old resorted to his school for the benefit of hearing the young instructed; and the clergyman had the pleasure of seeing that he was rewarded for the protection he gave the school by the great increase in his congregation. The shepherd not only exhorted both parents and children to the indispensable duty of a regular attendance at church, but by his pious counsels he drew them thither, and by his plain and prudent instructions enabled them to understand, and of course to delight in the public worship of God.

THE TWO SHOEMAKERS

PART I

Jack Brown and James Stock, were two lads apprenticed at nearly the same time, to Mr. Williams, a shoemaker, in a small town in Oxfordshire: they were pretty near the same age, but of very different characters and dispositions.

Brown was eldest son to a farmer in good circumstances, who gave the usual apprentice fee with him. Being a wild, giddy boy, whom his father could not well manage or instruct in farming, he thought it better to send him out to learn a trade at a distance, than to let him idle about at home; for Jack always preferred bird's-nesting and marbles to any other employment; he would trifle away the day, when his father thought he was at school, with any boys he could meet with, who were as idle as himself; and he could never be prevailed upon to do, or to learn any thing, while a game at taw could be had for love or money. All this time his little brothers, much younger than himself, were beginning to follow the plow, or to carry the corn to the mill as soon as they were able to mount a cart-horse.

Jack, however, who was a lively boy, and did not naturally want either sense or good-nature, might have turned out well enough, if he had not had the misfortune to be his mother's favorite. She concealed and forgave all his faults. To be sure he was a little wild, she would say, but he would not make the worse man for that, for Jack had a good spirit of his own, and she would not have it broke, and so make a mope of the boy. The farmer, for a quiet life, as it is called, gave up all these points to his wife, and, with them, gave up the future virtue and happiness of his child. He was a laborious and industrious man, but had no religion; he thought only of the gains and advantages of the present day, and never took the future into the account. His wife managed him entirely, and as she was really notable, he did not trouble his head about any thing further. If she had been careless in her dairy, he would have stormed and sworn; but as she only ruined one child by indulgence, and almost broke the heart of the rest by unkindness, he gave himself little concern about the matter. The cheese, certainly was good, and that indeed is a great point; but she was neglectful of her children, and a tyrant to her servants. Her husband's substance, indeed, was not wasted, but his happiness was not consulted. His house, it is true, was not dirty, but it was the abode of fury, ill-temper, and covetousness. And the farmer, though he did not care for liquor, was too often driven to the public-house in the evening, because his own was neither quiet nor comfortable. The mother was always scolding, and the children were always crying.

Jack, however, notwithstanding his idleness, picked up a little reading and writing, but never would learn to cast an account: that was too much labor. His mother was desirous he should continue at school, not so much for the sake of his learning, which she had not sense enough to value, but to save her darling from the fatigue of labor: for if he had not gone to school, she knew he must have gone to work, and she thought the former was the least tiresome of the two. Indeed, this foolish woman had such an opinion of his genius, that she used, from a child, to think he was too wise for any thing but a parson, and hoped she would live to see him one. She did not wish to see her son a minister because she loved either learning or piety, but because she thought it would make Jack a gentleman, and set him above his brothers.

Farmer Brown still hoped that though Jack was likely to make but an idle and ignorant farmer, yet he might make no bad tradesman, when he should be removed from the indulgences of a father's house, and from a silly mother, whose fondness kept him back in every thing. This woman was enraged when she found that so fine a scholar, as she took Jack to be, was to be put apprentice to a shoemaker. The farmer, however, for the first time in his life, would have his own way, and too apt to mind only what is falsely called the main chance, instead of being careful to look out for a sober, prudent, and religious master for his son, he left all that to accident, as if it had been a thing of little or no consequence. This is a very common fault; and fathers who are guilty of it, are in a great measure answerable for the future sins and errors of their children, when they come out into the world, and set up for themselves. If a man gives his son a good education, a good example, and a good master, it is indeed possible that the son may not turn out well, but it does not often happen; and when it does, the father has no blame resting on him, and it is a great point toward a man's comfort to have his conscience quiet in that respect, however God may think fit to overrule events.

The farmer, however, took care to desire his friends to inquire for a shoemaker who had good business, and was a good workman; and the mother did not forget to put in her word, and desired that it might be one who was not too strict, for Jack had been brought up tenderly, was a meek boy, and could not bear to be contradicted in any thing. And this is the common notion of meekness among people who do not take up their notions on rational and Christian grounds.

Mr. Williams was recommended to the farmer as being the best shoemaker in the town in which he lived, and far from a strict master, and, without further inquiries, to Mr. Williams he went.

James Stock, who was the son of an honest laborer in the next village, was bound out by the parish in consideration of his father having so numerous a family, that he was not able to put him out himself. James was in every thing the very reverse of his new companion. He was a modest, industrious, pious youth, and though so poor, and the child of a laborer, was a much better scholar than Jack, who was a wealthy farmer's son. His father had, it is true, been able to give him but very little schooling, for he was obliged to be put to work when quite a child. When very young, he used to run of errands for Mr. Thomas, the curate of the parish; a very kind-hearted young gentleman, who boarded next door to his father's cottage. He used also to rub down and saddle his horse, and do any other little job for him, in the most civil, obliging manner. All this so recommended him to the clergyman, that he would often send for him of an evening, after he had done his day's work in the field, and condescend to teach him himself to write and cast accounts, as well as to instruct him in the principles of his religion. It was not merely out of kindness for the little good-natured services James did him, that he showed him this favor, but also for his readiness in the catechism, and his devout behavior at church.

The first thing that drew the minister's attention to this boy, was the following: he had frequently given him half-pence and pence for holding his horse and carrying him to water before he was big enough to be further useful to him. On Christmas day he was surprised to see James at church, reading out of a handsome new prayer-book; he wondered how he came by it, for he knew there was nobody in the parish likely to have given it to him, for at that time there were no Sunday Schools; and the father could not afford it, he was sure.

"Well, James," said he, as he saw him when they came out, "you made a good figure at church to-day: it made you look like a man and a Christian, not only to have so handsome a book, but to be so ready in all parts of the service. How can you buy that book?" James owned modestly that he had been a whole year saving up the money by single half-pence, all of which had been of the minister's own giving, and that in all that time he had not spent a single farthing on his own diversions. "My dear boy," said the good Mr. Thomas, "I am much mistaken if thou dost not turn out well in the world, for two reasons:— first, from thy saving turn and self-denying temper; and next, because thou didst devote the first eighteen-pence thou wast ever worth in the world to so good a purpose."

James bowed and blushed, and from that time Mr. Thomas began to take more notice of him, and to instruct him as I said above. As James soon grew able to do him more considerable service, he would now and then give him a sixpence. This he constantly saved till it became a little sum, with which he bought shoes and stockings; well knowing that his poor father, with a large family and low wages, could not buy them for him. As to what little money he earned himself by his daily labor in the field, he constantly carried it to his mother every Saturday night, to buy bread for the family, which was a pretty help to them.

As James was not overstout in his make, his father thankfully accepted the offer of the parish officers to bind out his son to a trade. This good man, however, had not, like farmer Brown, the liberty of choosing a master for his son; or he would carefully have inquired if he was a proper man to have the care of youth; but Williams the shoemaker was already fixed on, by those who were to put the boy out, who told him if he wanted a master it must be him or none; for the overseers had a better opinion of Williams than he deserved, and thought it would be the making of the boy to go to him. The father knew that beggars must not be choosers, so he fitted out James for his new place, having indeed little to give him besides his blessing.

The worthy Mr. Thomas, however, kindly gave him an old coat and waistcoat, which his mother, who was a neat and notable woman, contrived to make up for him herself without a farthing expense, and when it was turned and made fit for his size, it made a very handsome suit for Sundays, and lasted him a couple of years.

And here let me stop to remark what a pity it is, that poor women so seldom are able or willing to do these sort of little handy jobs themselves; and that they do not oftener bring up their daughters to be more useful in family work. They are great losers by it every way, not only as they are disqualifying their girls from making good wives hereafter but they are losers in point of present advantage; for gentry could much oftener afford to give a poor boy a jacket or a waistcoat, if it was not for the expense of making it, which adds very much to the cost. To my certain knowledge, many poor women would often get an old coat, or a bit of coarse new cloth given to them to fit out a boy, if the mother or sisters were known to be able to cut out to advantage, and to make it up decently themselves. But half a crown for the making a bit of kersey, which costs but a few shillings, is more than many very charitable gentry can afford to give—so they often give nothing at all, when they see the mothers so little able to turn it to advantage. It is hoped they will take this hint kindly, as it is meant for their good.

But to return to our two young shoemakers. They were both now settled, at Mr. Williams's who, as he was known to be a good workman had plenty of business—he had sometimes two or three journeymen, but no apprentices but Jack and James.

Jack, who, with all his faults, was a keen, smart boy, took to learn the trade quick enough, but the difficulty was to make him stick two hours together to his work. At every noise he heard in the street down went the work—the last one way, the upper leather another; the sole dropped on the ground, and the thread dragged after him, all the way up the street. If a blind fiddler, a ballad singer, a mountebank, a dancing bear, or a drum were heard at a distance out ran Jack, nothing could stop him, and not a stitch more could he be prevailed on to do that day. Every duty, every promise was forgotten for the present pleasure—he could not resist the smallest temptation—he never stopped for a moment to consider whether a thing was right or wrong, but whether he liked or disliked it. And as his ill-judging mother took care to send him privately a good supply of pocket-money, that deadly bane to all youthful virtue, he had generally a few pence ready to spend, and to indulge in the present diversion, whatever it was. And what was still worse even than spending his money, he spent his time too, or rather his master's time. Of this he was continually reminded by James, to whom he always answered, "What have you to complain about? It is nothing to you or any one else; I spend nobody's money but my own." "That may be," replied the other, "but you can not say it is your own time that you spend." He insisted upon it, that it was; but James fetched down their indentures, and there showed him that he had solemnly bound himself by that instrument, not to waste his master's property. "Now," quoth James, "thy own time is a very valuable part of thy master's property." To this he replied, "every one's time was his own, and he should not sit moping all day over his last—for his part, he thanked God he was no parish 'prentice."

James did not resent this piece of foolish impertinence, as some silly lads would have done; nor fly out into a violent passion: for even at this early age he had begun to learn of Him who was meek and lowly of heart; and therefore when he was reviled, he reviled not again. On the contrary he was so very kind and gentle, that even Jack, vain and idle as he was, could not help loving him, though he took care never to follow his advice.

Jack's fondness for his boyish and silly diversions in the street, soon produced the effects which might naturally be expected; and the same idleness which led him to fly out into the town at the sound of a fiddle or the sight of a puppet-show soon led him to those places to which all these fiddles and shows naturally led; I mean the ale-house. The acquaintance picked up in the street was carried on at the Grayhound; and the idle pastimes of the boy soon led to the destructive vices of the man.

As he was not an ill-tempered youth, nor naturally much given to drink, a sober and prudent master, who had been steady in his management and regular in his own conduct, who would have recommended good advice by a good example, might have made something of Jack. But I am sorry to say, that Mr. Williams, though a good workman, and not a very hard or severe master, was neither a sober nor a steady man—so far from it that he spent much more time at the Grayhound than at home. There was no order either in his shop or family, he left the chief care of his business to his two young apprentices; and being but a worldly man, he was at first disposed to show favor to Jack, much more than to James, because he had more money, and his father was better in the world than the father of poor James.

At first, therefore, he was disposed to consider James as a sort of drudge; who was to do all the menial work of the family, and he did not care how little he taught him of his trade. With Mrs. Williams the matter was still worse; she constantly called him away from the business of his trade to wash the house, nurse the child, turn the spit, or run of errands. And here I must remark, that though parish apprentices are bound in duty to be submissive to both master and mistress, and always to make themselves as useful as they can in the family, and to be civil and humble; yet on the other hand, it is the duty of masters always to remember, that if they are paid for instructing them in their trade, they ought conscientiously to instruct them in it, and not to employ them the greater part of their time in such household or other drudgery, as to deprive them of the opportunity of acquiring their trade. This practice is not the less unjust because it is common.

Mr. Williams soon found out that his favorite Jack would be of little use to him in the shop; for though he worked well enough, he did not care how little he did. Nor could he be of the least use to his master in keeping an account, or writing out a bill upon occasion, for, as he never could be made to learn to cipher, he did not know addition from multiplication.

One day one of the customers called at the shop in a great hurry, and desired his bill might be made out that minute. Mr. Williams, having taken a cup too much, made several attempts to put down a clear account, but the more he tried, the less he found himself able to do it. James, who was sitting at his last, rose up, and with great modesty asked his master if he would please give him leave to make out the bill, saying, that though but a poor scholar, he would do his best, rather than keep the gentleman waiting. Williams gladly accepted his offer, and confused as his head was with liquor, he yet was able to observe with what neatness, dispatch, and exactness, the account was drawn out. From that time he no longer considered James as a drudge, but as one fitted for the high departments of the trade, and he was now regularly employed to manage the accounts, with which all the customers were so well pleased, that it contributed greatly to raise him in his master's esteem; for there were now never any of those blunders of false charges for which the shop had before been so famous.

James went on in a regular course of industry, and soon became the best workman Mr. Williams had; but there were many things in the family which he greatly disapproved. Some of the journeymen used to swear, drink, and sing very licentious songs. All these things were a great grief to his sober mind; he complained to his master, who only laughed at him; and, indeed, as Williams did the same himself, he put it out of his power to correct his servants, if he had been so disposed. James, however, used always to reprove them, with great mildness indeed, but with great seriousness also. This, but still more his own excellent example, produced at length very good effects on such of the men as were not quite hardened in sin.

What grieved him most, was the manner in which the Sunday was spent. The master lay in bed all the morning; nor did the mother or her children ever go to church, except there was some new finery to be shown, or a christening to be attended. The town's-people were coming to the shop all the morning, for work which should have been sent home the night before, had not the master been at the ale-house. And what wounded James to the very soul was, that the master expected the two apprentices to carry home shoes to the country customers on the Sunday morning; which he wickedly thought was a saving of time, as it prevented their hindering their work on the Saturday. These shameful practices greatly afflicted poor James; he begged his master with tears in his eyes, to excuse him, but he only laughed at his squeamish conscience, as he called it.

Jack did not dislike this part of the business, and generally after he had delivered his parcel, wasted good part of the day in nutting, playing at fives, or dropping in at the public house: any thing was better to Jack than going to church.

James, on the other hand, when he was compelled, sorely against his conscience, to carry home any goods on a Sunday morning, always got up as soon as it was light, knelt down and prayed heartily to God to forgive him a sin which it was not in his power to avoid; he took care not to lose a moment by the way, but as he was taking his walk with the utmost speed, to leave his shoes with the customers, he spent his time in endeavoring to keep up good thoughts in his mind, and praying that the day might come when his conscience might be delivered from this grievous burden. He was now particularly thankful that Mr. Thomas had formerly taught him so many psalms and chapters, which he used to repeat in these walks with great devotion.

He always got home before the rest of the family were up, dressed himself very clean, and went twice to church; as he greatly disliked the company and practices of his master's house, particularly on the Sabbath-day; he preferred spending his evening alone, reading the Bible, which I had forgot to say the worthy clergyman had given him when he left his native village. Sunday evening, which is to some people such a burden, was to James the highest holiday. He had formerly learned a little how to sing a psalm of the clerk of his own parish, and this was now become a very delightful part of his evening exercise. And as Will Simpson, one of the journeymen, by James's advice and example, was now beginning to be of a more serious way of thinking, he often asked him to sit an hour with him, when they read the Bible, and talked it over together in a manner very pleasant and improving; and as Will was a famous singer, a psalm or two sung together was a very innocent pleasure.

James's good manners and civility to the customers drew much business to the shop; and his skill as a workman was so great, that every one desired that his shoes might be made by James. Williams grew so very idle and negligent, that he now totally neglected his affairs, and to hard drinking added deep gaming. All James's care, both of the shop and the accounts, could not keep things in any tolerable order: he represented to his master that they were growing worse and worse, and exhorted him, if he valued his credit as a tradesman, his comfort as a husband and father, his character as a master, and his soul as a Christian, to turn over a new leaf. Williams swore a great oath, that he would not be restrained in his pleasures to please a canting parish 'prentice, nor to humor a parcel of squalling brats—that let people say what they would of him, they should never say he was a hypocrite, and as long as they could not call him that, he did not care what else they called him.

In a violent passion he immediately went to the Grayhound, where he now spent not only every evening, which he had long done, but good part of the day and night also. His wife was very dressy, extravagant, and fond of company, and wasted at home as fast as her husband spent abroad, so that all the neighbors said, if it had not been for James, his master must have been a bankrupt long ago, but they were sure he could not hold it much longer.

As Jack Brown sung a good song, and played many diverting tricks, Williams liked his company; and often allowed him to make one at the Grayhound, where he would laugh heartily at his stories; so that every one thought Jack was much the greater favorite—so he was as a companion in frolic, and foolery, and pleasure, as it is called; but he would not trust him with an inch of leather or sixpence in money: No, no—when business was to be done, or trust was to be reposed, James was the man: the idle and the drunken never trust one another, if they have common sense. They like to laugh, and sing, and riot, and drink together, but when they want a friend, a counselor, a helper in business or in trouble, they go further afield; and Williams, while he would drink with Jack, would trust James with untold gold; and even was foolishly tempted to neglect his business the more from knowing that he had one at home who was taking care of it.

In spite of all James's care and diligence, however, things were growing worse and worse; the more James saved, the more his master and mistress spent. One morning, just as the shop was opened, and James had set every body to their respective work, and he himself was settling the business for the day, he found that his master was not yet come from the Grayhound. As this was now become a common case, he only grieved but did not wonder at it. While he was indulging sad thoughts on what would be the end of all this, in ran the tapster from the Grayhound out of breath, and with a look of terror and dismay, desired James would step over to the public house with him that moment, for that his master wanted him.

James went immediately, surprised at this unusual message. When he got into the kitchen of the public house, which he now entered for the first time in his life, though it was just opposite to the house in which he lived, he was shocked at the beastly disgusting appearance of every thing he beheld. There was a table covered with tankards, punch-bowls, broken glasses, pipes, and dirty greasy packs of cards, and all over wet with liquor; the floor was strewed with broken earthen cups, old cards, and an EO table which had been shivered to pieces in a quarrel; behind the table stood a crowd of dirty fellows, with matted locks, hollow eyes, and faces smeared with tobacco; James made his way after the tapster, through this wretched looking crew, to a settle which stood in the chimney-corner. Not a word was uttered, but the silent horror seemed to denote something more than a mere common drunken bout.

What was the dismay of James, when he saw his miserable master stretched out on the settle, in all the agonies of death! He had fallen into a fit; after having drunk hard best part of the night, and seemed to have but a few minutes to live. In his frightful countenance, was displayed the dreadful picture of sin and death, for he struggled at once under the guilt of intoxication, and the pangs of a dying man. He recovered his senses for a few moments, and called out to ask if his faithful servant was come. James went up to him, took him by his cold hand, but was too much moved to speak. "Oh! James, James," cried he in a broken voice, "pray for me, comfort me." James spoke kindly to him, but was too honest to give him false comfort, as it is too often done by mistaken friends in these dreadful moments.

"James," said he, "I have been a bad master to you—you would have saved me, soul and body, but I would not let you—I have ruined my wife, my children, and my own soul. Take warning, oh, take warning by my miserable end," said he to his stupefied companions: but none were able to attend to him but James, who bid him lift up his heart to God, and prayed heartily for him himself. "Oh!" said the dying man, "it is too late, too late for me—but you have still time," said he to the half-drunken, terrified crew around him. "Where is Jack?" Jack Brown came forward, but was too much frightened to speak. "Oh, wretched boy!" said he, "I fear I shall have the ruin of thy soul, as well as my own to answer for. Stop short! Take warning—now in the days of thy youth. O James, James, thou dost not pray for me. Death is dreadful to the wicked—Oh, the sting of death to a guilty conscience!" Here he lifted up his ghastly eyes in speechless horror, grasped hard at the hand of James, gave a deep hollow groan, and closed his eyes, never to open them but in an awful eternity.

This was death in all its horrors! The gay companions of his sinful pleasures could not stand the sight; all slunk away like guilty thieves from their late favorite friend—no one was left to assist him, but his two apprentices. Brown was not so hardened but that he shed many tears for his unhappy master; and even made some hasty resolutions of amendment, which were too soon forgotten.

While Brown stepped home to call the workmen to come and assist in removing their poor master, James staid alone with the corpse, and employed these awful moments in indulging the most serious thoughts, and praying heartily to God, that so terrible a lesson might not be thrown away upon him; but that he might be enabled to live in a constant state of preparation for death. The resolutions he made at this moment, as they were not made in his own strength, but in an humble reliance on God's gracious help, were of use to him as long as he lived, and if ever he was for a moment tempted to say, or do a wrong thing, the remembrance of his poor dying master's long agonies, and the dreadful words he uttered, always operated as an instant check upon him.

When Williams was buried, and his affairs came to be inquired into, they were found to be in a sad condition. His wife, indeed, was the less to be pitied, as she had contributed her full share to the common ruin. James, however, did pity her, and by his skill in accounts, his known honesty, and the trust the creditors put in his word, things came to be settled rather better than Mrs. Williams had expected.

Both Brown and James were now within a month or two of being out of their time. The creditors, as we said before, employed James to settle his late master's accounts, which he did in a manner so creditable to his abilities, and his honesty, that they proposed to him to take the shop himself. He assured them it was utterly out of his power for want of money. As the creditors had not the least fear of being repaid, if it should please God to spare his life, they generously agreed among themselves to advance him a small sum of money without any security but his bond; for this he was to pay a very reasonable interest, and to return the whole in a given number of years. James shed tears of gratitude at this testimony to his character, and could hardly be prevailed on to accept their kindness, so great was his dread of being in debt.

He took the remainder of the lease from his mistress; and in settling affairs with her, took care to make every thing as advantageous to her as possible. He never once allowed himself to think how unkind she had been to him; he only saw in her the needy widow of his deceased master, and the distressed mother of an infant family; and was heartily sorry it was not in his power to contribute to their support; it was not only James's duty, but his delight, to return good for evil—for he was a Christian.

James Stock was now, by the blessing of God, on his own earnest endeavors, master of a considerable shop, and was respected by the whole town for his prudence, honesty, and piety. How he behaved in his new station, and also what befell his comrade Brown, must be the subject of another book; and I hope my readers will look forward with some impatience for some further account of this worthy young man. In the mean time, other apprentices will do well to follow so praiseworthy an example, and to remember that the respectable master of a large shop, and of a profitable business, was raised to that creditable situation, without money, friends, or connections, from the low beginning of a parish apprentice, by sobriety, industry, the fear of God, and an obedience to the divine principles of the Christian religion.

PART II

THE APPRENTICE TURNED MASTER

The first part of this history left off with the dreadful sudden death of Williams, the idle shoemaker, who died in a drunken fit at the Grayhound. It also showed how James Stock, his faithful apprentice, by his honest and upright behavior, so gained the love and respect of his late master's creditors, that they set him up in business, though he was not worth a shilling of his own—such is the power of a good character! And when we last parted from him he had just got possession of his master's shop.

This sudden prosperity was a time of trial for James, who, as he was now become a creditable tradesman, I shall hereafter think proper to call Mr. James Stock. I say, this sudden rise in life was a time of trial; for we hardly know what we are ourselves till we become our own masters. There is indeed always a reasonable hope that a good servant will not make a bad master, and that a faithful apprentice will prove an honest tradesman. But the heart of man is deceitful, and some folks who seem to behave very well while they are under subjection, no sooner get a little power than their heads are turned, and they grow prouder than those who are gentlemen born. They forget at once that they were lately poor and dependent themselves, so that one would think that with their poverty they had lost their memory too. I have known some who had suffered most hardships in their early days, become the most hard and oppressive in their turn: so that they seem to forget that fine considerate reason, which God gives to the children of Israel why they should be merciful to their servants, remembering, said he, that thou thyself wast a bond-man.

Young Mr. Stock did not so forget himself. He had indeed the only sure guard from falling into this error. It was not from any easiness in his natural disposition, for that only just serves to make folks good-natured when they are pleased, and patient when they have nothing to vex them. James went upon higher ground. He brought his religion into all his actions; he did not give way to abusive language, because he knew it was a sin. He did not use his apprentices ill, because he knew he had himself a Master in heaven.

He knew he owed his present happy situation to the kindness of the creditors. But did he grow easy and careless because he knew he had such friends? No indeed. He worked with double diligence in order to get out of debt, and to let these friends see he did not abuse their kindness. Such behavior as this is the greatest encouragement in the world to rich people to lend a little money. It creates friends, and it keeps them.

His shoes and boots were made in the best manner; this got him business; he set out with a rule to tell no lies, and deceive no customers; this secured his business. He had two reasons for not promising to send home goods when he knew he should not be able to keep his word. The first, because he knew a lie was a sin, the next, because it was a folly. There is no credit sooner worn out than that which is gained by false pretenses. After a little while no one is deceived by them. Falsehood is so soon detected, that I believe most tradesmen are the poorer for it in the long run. Deceit is the worst part of a shopkeeper's stock in trade.

James was now at the head of a family. This is a serious situation (said he to himself, one fine summer's evening, as he stood leaning over the half-door of his shop to enjoy a little fresh air); I am now master of a family. My cares are doubled, and so are my duties. I see the higher one gets in life the more one has to answer for. Let me now call to mind the sorrow I used to feel when I was made to carry work home on a Sunday by an ungodly master: and let me now keep the resolution I then formed.

So what his heart found right to do, he resolved to do quickly; and he set out at first as he meant to go on. The Sunday was truly a day of rest at Mr. Stock's. He would not allow a pair of shoes to be given out on that day, to oblige the best customer he had. And what did he lose by it? Why, nothing. For when the people were once used to it, they liked Saturday night just as well. But had it been otherwise, he would have given up his gains to his conscience.

SHOWING HOW MR. STOCK BEHAVED TO HIS APPRENTICES.

When he got up in the world so far as to have apprentices, he thought himself as accountable for their behavior as if they had been his children. He was very kind to them, and had a cheerful merry way of talking to them, so that the lads who had seen too much of swearing, reprobate masters, were fond of him. They were never afraid of speaking to him; they told him all their little troubles, and considered their master as their best friend, for they said they would do any thing for a good word and a kind look. As he did not swear at them when they had been guilty of a fault, they did not lie to him to conceal it, and thereby make one fault two. But though he was very kind, he was very watchful also, for he did not think neglect any part of kindness. He brought them to adopt one very pretty method, which was, on a Sunday evening to divert themselves with writing out half a dozen texts of Scripture in a neat copy-book with gilt covers. You have the same at any of the stationers; they do not cost above fourpence and will last nearly a year.

When the boys carried him their books, he justly commended him whose texts were written in the fairest hand. "And now, my boys," said he, "let us see which of you will learn your texts best in the course of the week; he who does this shall choose for next Sunday." Thus the boys soon got many psalms and chapters by heart, almost without knowing how they came by them. He taught them how to make a practical use of what they learned: "for," said he, "it will answer little purpose to learn texts if we do not try to live up to them." One of the boys being apt to play in his absence, and to run back again to his work when he heard his master's step, he brought him to a sense of his fault by the last Sunday's text, which happened to be the sixth of Ephesians. He showed him what was meant by being obedient to his master in singleness of heart as unto Christ, and explained to him with so much kindness what it was, not to work with eye-service as men-pleasers, but doing the will of God from the heart, that the lad said he should never forget it, and it did more toward curing him of idleness than the soundest horse-whipping would have done.

HOW MR. STOCK GOT OUT OF DEBT

Stock's behavior was very regular, and he was much beloved for his kind and peaceable temper. He had also a good reputation for skill in his trade, and his industry was talked of through the whole town, so that he had soon more work than he could possibly do. He paid all his dealers to the very day, and took care to carry his interest money to the creditors the moment it became due. In two or three years he was able to begin to pay off a small part of the principal. His reason for being so eager to pay money as soon as it became due, was this: he had observed tradesmen, and especially his old master, put off the day of payment as long as they could, even though they had the means of paying in their power. This deceived them: for having money in their pockets they forgot it belonged to the creditor, and not to themselves, and so got to fancy they were rich when they were really poor. This false notion led them to indulge in idle expenses, whereas, if they had paid regularly, they would have had this one temptation the less: a young tradesman, when he is going to spend money, should at least ask himself, "Whether this money is his own or his creditors'?" This little question might help to prevent many a bankruptcy.

A true Christian always goes heartily to work to find out what is his besetting sin; and when he has found it (which he easily may if he looks sharp), against this sin he watches narrowly. Now I know it is the fashion among some folks (and a bad fashion it is), to fancy that good people have no sin; but this only shows their ignorance. It is not true. That good man, St. Paul, knew better.[3] And when men do not own their sins, it is not because there is no sin in their hearts, but because they are not anxious to search for it, nor humble to confess it, nor penitent to mourn over it. But this was not the case with James Stock. "Examine yourselves truly," said he, "is no bad part of the catechism." He began to be afraid that his desire of living creditably, and without being a burden to any one, might, under the mask of honesty and independence, lead him into pride and covetousness. He feared that the bias of his heart lay that way. So instead of being proud of his sobriety; instead of bragging that he never spent his money idly, nor went to the ale-house; instead of boasting how hard he worked and how he denied himself, he strove in secret that even these good qualities might not grow out of a wrong root. The following event was of use to him in the way of indulging any disposition to covetousness.

[3] See Romans, vii.

One evening as he was standing at the door of his shop, a poor dirty boy, without stockings and shoes, came up and asked him for a bit of broken victuals, for he had eaten nothing all day. In spite of his dirt and rags he was a very pretty, lively, civil spoken boy, and Mr. Stock could not help thinking he knew something of his face. He fetched him out a good piece of bread and cheese, and while the boy was devouring it, asked him if he had no parents, and why he went about in that vagabond manner? "Daddy has been dead some years," said the boy; "he died in a fit over at the Grayhound. Mammy says he used to live at this shop, and then we did not want for clothes nor victuals neither." Stock was melted almost to tears on finding that this dirty beggar boy was Tommy Williams, the son of his old master. He blessed God on comparing his own happy condition with that of this poor destitute child, but he was not prouder at the comparison; and while he was thankful for his own prosperity, he pitied the helpless boy. "Where have you been living of late?" said he to him, "for I understand you all went home to your mother's friends." "So we did, sir," said the boy, "but they are grown tired of maintaining us, because they said that mammy spent all the money which should have gone to buy victuals for us, on snuff and drams. And so they have sent us back to this place, which is daddy's parish."

"And where do you live here?" said Mr. Stock. "O, sir, we were all put into the parish poor-house." "And does your mother do any thing to help to maintain you?" "No, sir, for mammy says she was not brought up to work like poor folks, and she would rather starve than spin or knit; so she lies a-bed all the morning, and sends us about to pick up what we can, a bit of victuals or a few half-pence." "And have you any money in your pocket now?" "Yes, sir, I have got three half-pence which I have begged to-day." "Then, as you were so very hungry, how came you not to buy a roll at that baker's over the way?" "Because, sir, I was going to lay it out in tea for mammy, for I never lay out a farthing for myself. Indeed mammy says she will have her tea twice a-day if we beg or starve for it." "Can you read, my boy?" said Mr. Stock: "A little, sir, and say my prayers too." "And can you say your catechism?" "I have almost forgotten it all, sir, though I remember something about honoring my father and mother, and that makes me still carry the half-pence home to mammy instead of buying cakes." "Who taught you these good things?" "One Jemmy Stock, sir, who was a parish 'prentice to my daddy. He taught me one question out of the catechism every night, and always made me say my prayers to him before I went to bed. He told me I should go to the wicked place if I did not fear God, so I am still afraid to tell lies like the other boys. Poor Jemmy gave me a piece of ginger bread every time I learnt well; but I have no friend now; Jemmy was very good to me, though mammy did nothing but beat him."

Mr. Stock was too much moved to carry on the discourse; he did not make himself known to the boy, but took him over to the baker's shop; as they walked along he could not help repeating aloud a verse or two of that beautiful hymn so deservedly the favorite of all children:

"Not more than others I deserve,
Yet God hath given me more;
For I have food while others starve,
Or beg from door to door."

The little boy looked up in his face, saying, "Why, sir, that's the very hymn which Jemmy Stock gave me a penny for learning." Stock made no answer, but put a couple of threepenny loaves into his hand to carry home, and told him to call on him again at such a time in the following week.

HOW MR. STOCK CONTRIVED TO BE CHARITABLE WITHOUT ANY EXPENSE

Stock had abundant subject for meditation that night. He was puzzled what to do with the boy. While he was carrying on his trade upon borrowed money, he did not think it right to give any part of that money, to assist the idle, or even help the distressed. "I must be just," said he, "before I am generous." Still he could not bear to see this fine boy given up to a certain ruin. He did not think it safe to take him into his shop in his present ignorant, unprincipled state. At last he hit upon this thought: I work for myself twelve hours in the day. Why shall I not work one hour or two for this boy in the evening? It will be but for a year, and I shall then have more right to do what I please. My money will then be my own: I shall have paid my debts.

So he began to put his resolution in practice that very night, sticking to his old notion of not putting off till to-morrow what should be done to-day: and it was thought he owed much of his success in life, as well as his growth in goodness, to this little saying: "I am young and healthy," said he, "one hour's work more will do me no harm; I will set aside all I get by these over-hours, and put the boy to school. I have not only no right to punish this child for the sins of his father, but I consider that though God hated those sins, he has made them to be instrumental to my advancement."

Tommy Williams called at the time appointed. In the mean time Mr. Stock's maid had made him a neat little suit of clothes of an old coat of her master's. She had also knit him a pair of stockings, and Mr. Stock made him sit down in the shop, while he fitted him with a pair of new shoes. The maid having washed and dressed him, Stock took him by the hand, and walked along with him to the parish poor-house to find his mother. They found her dressed in ragged, filthy finery, standing at the door, where she passed most of her time, quarreling with half a dozen women as idle and dirty as herself. When she saw Tommy so neat and well-dressed, she fell a crying for joy. She said "it put her in mind of old times, for Tommy always used to be dressed like a gentleman." "So much the worse," said Mr. Stock; "if you had not begun by making him look like a gentleman, you needed not have ended by making him look like a beggar." "Oh Jem!" said she (for though it was four years since she had seen him she soon recollected him), "fine times for you! Set a beggar on horseback—you know the proverb. I shall beat Tommy well for finding you out and exposing me to you."

Instead of entering into a dispute with this bad woman, or praising himself at her expense; instead of putting her in mind of her past ill behavior to him, or reproaching her with the bad use she had made of her prosperity, he mildly said to her, "Mrs. Williams I am sorry for your misfortunes; I am come to relieve you of part of your burden. I will take Tommy off your hands. I will give him a year's board and schooling, and by that time I shall see what he is fit for. I will promise nothing, but if the boy turns out well, I will never forsake him. I shall make but one bargain with you, which is, that he must not come to this place to hear all this railing and swearing, nor shall he keep company with these pilfering, idle children. You are welcome to go and see him when you please, but here he must not come."

The foolish woman burst out a crying, saying, "she should lose her poor dear Tommy forever. Mr. Stock might give her the money he intended to pay at the school, for nobody could do so well by him, as his own mother." The truth was, she wanted to get these new clothes into her clutches, which would have been pawned at the dramshop before the week was out. This Mr. Stock well knew. From crying she fell to scolding and swearing. She told him he was an unnatural wretch, that wanted to make a child despise his own mother because she was poor. She even went so far as to say she would not part from him; she said she hated your godly people, they had no bowels of compassion, but tried to set men, women, and children against their own flesh and blood.

Mr. Stock now almost lost his patience, and for one moment a thought came across him, to strip the boy, carry back the clothes, and leave him to his unnatural mother. "Why," said he, "should I work over-hours, and wear out my strength for this wicked woman?" But soon he checked this thought, by reflecting on the patience and long-suffering of God with rebellious sinners. This cured his anger in a moment, and he mildly reasoned with her on her folly and blindness in opposing the good of her child.

One of the neighbors who stood by said, "What a fine thing it was for the boy! but some people were born to be lucky. She wished Mr. Stock would take a fancy to her child, he should have him soon enough." Mrs. Williams now began to be frightened lest Mr. Stock should take the woman at her word, and sullenly consented to let the boy go, from envy and malice, not from prudence and gratitude; and Tommy was sent to school that very night, his mother crying and roaring instead of thanking God for such a blessing.

And here I can not forbear telling a very good-natured thing of Will Simpson, one of the workmen. By the by, it was that very young fellow who was reformed by Stock's good example, when he was an apprentice, and who used to sing psalms with him on a Sunday evening, when they got out of the way of Williams's junketing. Will coming home early one evening was surprised to find his master at work by himself, long after the usual time. He begged so heartily to know the reason, that Stock owned the truth. Will was so struck with this piece of kindness, that he snatched up a last, crying out, "Well, master, you shall not work by yourself, however; we will go snacks in maintaining Tommy: it shall never be said that Will Simpson was idling about when his master was working for charity." This made the hour pass cheerfully, and doubled the profits.

In a year or two Mr. Stock, by God's blessing on his labors, became quite clear of the world. He now paid off his creditors, but he never forgot his obligation to them, and found many opportunities of showing kindness to them, and to their children after them. He now cast about for a proper wife, and as he was thought a prosperous man, and was very well looking besides, most of the smart girls of the place, with their tawdry finery, used to be often parading before the shop, and would even go to church in order to put themselves in his way. But Mr. Stock when he went to church, had other things in his head; and if ever he thought about these gay damsels at all, it was with concern in seeing them so improperly tricked out, so that the very means they took to please him made him dislike them.

There was one Betsy West, a young woman of excellent character, and very modest appearance. He had seldom seen her out, as she was employed night and day in waiting on an aged, widowed mother, who was both lame and blind. This good girl was almost literally eyes and feet to her helpless parent, and Mr. Stock used to see her, through the little casement window, lifting her up, and feeding her with a tenderness which greatly raised his esteem for her. He used to tell Will Simpson, as they sat at work, that such a dutiful daughter could hardly help to make a faithful wife. He had not, however, the heart to try to draw her off from the care of her sick mother. The poor woman declined very fast. Betsy was much employed in reading or praying by her, while she was awake, and passed a good part of the night while she slept, in doing some fine works to sell, in order to supply her sick mother with little delicacies which their poor pittance could not afford, while she herself lived on a crust.

Mr. Stock knew that Betsy would have little or nothing after her mother's death, as she had only a life income. On the other hand, Mr. Thompson, the tanner, had offered him two hundred pounds with his daughter Nancy; but he was almost sorry that he had not in this case an opportunity of resisting his natural bias, which rather lay on the side of loving money. "For," said he, "putting principle and putting affection out of the question, I shall do a more prudent thing by marrying Betsy West, who will conform to her station, and is a religious, humble, industrious girl, without a shilling, than by having an idle dressy lass, who will neglect my family and fill my house with company, though she should have twice the fortune which Nancy Thompson would bring."

At length poor old Mrs. West was released from all her sufferings. At a proper time Mr. Stock proposed marriage to Betsy, and was accepted. All the disappointed girls in the town wondered what any body could like in such a dowdy as that. Had the man no eyes? They thought Mr. Stock had more taste. Oh! how it did provoke all the vain, idle things to find, that staying at home, dressing plainly, serving God, and nursing a blind mother, should do that for Betsy West, which all their contrivances, flaunting, and dancing, could not do for them.

He was not disappointed in his hope of meeting with a good wife in Betsy, as indeed those who marry on right grounds seldom are. But if religious persons will, for the sake of money, choose partners for life who have no religion, do not let them complain that they are unhappy: they might have known that beforehand.

Tommy Williams was now taken home to Mr. Stock's house and bound apprentice. He was always kind and attentive to his mother; and every penny which Will Simpson or his master gave him for learning a chapter, he would save to buy a bit of tea and sugar for her. When the other boys laughed at him for being so foolish as to deny himself cakes and apples to give his money to her who was so bad a woman, he would answer, "It may be so, but she is my mother for all that."

Mr. Stock was much moved at the change in this boy, who turned out a very good youth. He resolved, as God should prosper him, that he would try to snatch other helpless creatures from sin and ruin. "For," said he, "it is owing to God's blessing on the instructions of my good minister when I was a child, that I have been saved from the broad way of destruction." He still gave God the glory of every thing he did aright: and when Will Simpson one day said to him, "Master, I wish I were half as good as you are." "Hold, William," answered he gravely, "I once read in a book, that the devil is willing enough we should appear to do good actions, if he can but make us proud of them."

But we must not forget our other old acquaintance, Mr. Stock's fellow 'prentice. So next month you may expect a full account of the many tricks and frolics of idle Jade Brown.

PART III

SOME ACCOUNT OF THE FROLICS OF IDLE JACK BROWN

You shall now hear what befell idle Jack Brown, who, being a farmer's son, had many advantages to begin life with. But he who wants prudence may be said to want every thing, because he turns all his advantages to no account.

Jack Brown was just out of his time when his master Williams died in that terrible drunken fit at the Grayhound. You know already how Stock succeeded to his master's business, and prospered in it. Jack wished very much to enter into partnership with him. His father and mother too were desirous of it, and offered to advance a hundred pounds with him. Here is a fresh proof of the power of character! The old farmer, with all his covetousness, was eager to get his son into partnership with Stock, though the latter was not worth a shilling; and even Jack's mother, with all her pride, was eager for it, for they had both sense enough to see it would be the making of Jack. The father knew that Stock would look to the main chance; and the mother that he would take the laboring oar, and so her darling would have little to do. The ruling passion operated in both. One parent wished to secure the son a life of pleasure, the other a profitable trade. Both were equally indifferent to whatever related to his eternal good.

Stock, however, young as he was, was too old a bird to be caught with chaff. His wisdom was an overmatch for their cunning. He had a kindness for Brown, but would on no account enter into business with him. "One of these three things," said he, "I am sure will happen if I do; he will either hurt my principles, my character, or my trade; perhaps all." And here by-the-by, let me drop a hint to other young men who are about to enter into partnership. Let them not do that in haste which they may repent at leisure. Next to marriage it is a tie the hardest to break; and next to that it is an engagement which ought to be entered into with the most caution. Many things go to the making such a connection suitable, safe, and pleasant. There is many a rich merchant need not be above taking a hint in this respect, from James Stock the shoemaker.

Brown was still unwilling to part from him; indeed he was too idle to look out for business, so he offered Stock to work with him as a journeyman, but this he also mildly refused. It hurt his good nature to do so; but he reflected that a young man who has his way to make in the world, must not only be good-natured, he must be prudent also. "I am resolved," said he, "to employ none but the most sober, regular young men I can get. Evil communications corrupt good manners, and I should be answerable for all the disorders of my house, if I knowingly took a wild, drinking young fellow into it. That which might be kindness to one, would be injustice to many, and therefore a sin in myself."

Brown's mother was in a great rage when she heard that her son had stooped so low as to make this offer. She valued herself on being proud, for she thought pride was a grand thing. Poor woman! She did not know that it is the meanest thing in the world. It was her ignorance which made her proud, as is apt to be the case. "You mean-spirited rascal," she said to Jack, "I had rather follow you to your grave, as well as I love you, than see you disgrace your family by working under Jem Stock, the parish apprentice."

She forgot already what pains she had taken about the partnership, but pride and passion have bad memories.

It is hard to say which was now uppermost in her mind, her desire to be revenged on Stock, or to see her son make a figure. She raised every shilling she could get from her husband, and all she could crib from the dairy to set up Jack in a showy way. So the very next market day she came herself, and took for him the new white house, with the two little sash windows painted blue, and blue posts before the door. It is that house which has the old cross just before it, as you turn down between the church and the Grayhound. Its being so near the church to be sure was no recommendation to Jack, but its being so near the Grayhound was, and so taking one thing with the other it was to be sure no bad situation; but what weighed most with the mother was, that it was a much more showy shop than Stock's; and the house, though not half so convenient, was far more smart.

In order to draw custom, his foolish mother advised him to undersell his neighbors just at first; to buy ordinary but showy goods, and to employ cheap workmen. In short she charged him to leave no stone unturned to ruin his old comrade Stock. Indeed she always thought with double satisfaction of Jack's prosperity, because she always joined to it the hope that his success would be the ruin of Stock, for she owned it would be the joy of her heart to bring that proud upstart to a morsel of bread. She did not understand, for her part, why such beggars must become tradesmen; it was making a velvet purse of a sow's ear.

Stock, however, set out on quite another set of principles. He did not allow himself to square his own behavior to others by theirs to him. He seldom asked himself what he should like to do: but he had a mighty way of saying, "I wonder now what is my duty to do?" And when he was once clear in that matter he generally did it, always begging God's blessing and direction. So instead of setting Brown at defiance; instead of all that vulgar selfishness, of catch he that catch can—and two of a trade can never agree—he resolved to be friendly toward him. Instead of joining in the laugh against Brown for making his house so fine, he was sorry for him, because he feared he would never be able to pay such a rent. He very kindly called upon him, told him there was business enough for them both, and gave him many useful hints for his going on. He warned him to go oftener to church and seldomer to the Grayhound: put him in mind how following the one and forsaking the other had been the ruin of their poor master, and added the following

ADVICE TO YOUNG TRADESMEN

Buy the best goods; cut the work out yourself; let the eye of the master be everywhere; employ the soberest men; avoid all the low deceits of trade; never lower the credit of another to raise your own; make short payments; keep exact accounts; avoid idle company, and be very strict to your word.

For a short time things went on swimmingly. Brown was merry and civil. The shop was well situated for gossip; and every one who had something to say, and nothing to do was welcome. Every idle story was first spread, and every idle song first sung, in Brown's shop. Every customer who came to be measured was promised that his shoes should be done first. But the misfortune was, if twenty came in a day the same promise was made to all, so that nineteen were disappointed, and of course affronted. He never said no to any one. It is indeed a word which it requires some honesty to pronounce. By all these false promises he was thought the most obliging fellow that ever made a shoe. And as he set out on the principle of underselling, people took a mighty fancy to the cheap shop. And it was agreed among all the young and giddy, that he would beat Stock all hollow, and that the old shop would be knocked up.

ALL IS NOT GOLD THAT GLISTENS

After a few months, however, folks began to be not quite so fond of the cheap shop; one found out that the leather was bad, another that the work was slight. Those who liked substantial goods went all of them to Stock's, for they said Brown's heel-taps did not last a week; his new boots let in water; and they believed he made his soles of brown paper. Besides, it was thought by most, that this promising all, and keeping his word with none, hurt his business as much as any thing. Indeed, I question, putting religion out of the question, if lying ever answers, even in a political view.

Brown had what is commonly called a good heart; that is, he had a thoughtless good nature, and a sort of feeling for the moment which made him very sorry when others were in trouble. But he was not apt to put himself to any inconvenience, nor go a step out of his way, nor give up any pleasure to serve the best friend he had. He loved fun; and those who do should always see that it be harmless, and that they do not give up more for it than it is worth. I am not going to say a word against innocent merriment. I like it myself. But what the proverb says of gold, may be said of mirth; it may be bought too dear. If a young man finds that what he fancies is a good joke may possibly offend God, hurt his neighbor, afflict his parent, or make a modest girl blush, let him then be assured it is not fun, but wickedness, and he had better let it alone.

Jack Brown then, as good a heart as he had, did not know what it was to deny himself any thing. He was so good-natured indeed, that he never in his life refused to make one of a jolly set; but he was not good-natured enough to consider that those men whom he kept up all night roaring and laughing, had wives and children at home, who had little to eat, and less to wear, because they were keeping up the character of merry fellows, and good hearts at the public house.

THE MOUNTEBANK

One day he saw his father's plow-boy come galloping up to the door in great haste. This boy brought Brown word that his mother was dangerously ill, and that his father had sent his own best bay mare Smiler, that his son might lose no time, but set out directly to see his mother before she died. Jack burst into tears, lamented the danger of so fond a mother, and all the people in the shop extolled his good heart.

He sent back the boy directly, with a message that he would follow him in half an hour, as soon as the mare had baited: for he well knew that his father would not thank him for any haste he might make if Smiler was hurt.

Jack accordingly set off, and rode with such speed to the next town, that both himself and Smiler had a mind to another bait. They stopped at the Star; unluckily it was fair-day, and as he was walking about while Smiler was eating her oats, a bill was put in his hand setting forth, that on the stage opposite the Globe a mountebank was showing away, and his Andrew performing the finest tricks that ever were seen. He read—he stood still—he went on—"It will not hinder me," said he; "Smiler must rest; and I shall see my poor dear mother quite as soon if I just take a peep, as if I sit moping at the Star."

The tricks were so merry that the time seemed short, and when they were over he could not forbear going into the Globe and treating these choice spirits with a bowl of punch. Just as they were taking the last glass, Jack happened to say he was the best fives player in the country. "That is lucky," said the Andrew, "for there is a famous match now playing at the court, and you may never again have such an opportunity to show your skill." Brown declared "he could not stay, for that he had left his horse at the Star, and must set off on urgent business." They now all pretended to call his skill in question. This roused his pride, and he thought another half hour could break no squares. Smiler had now had a good feed of corn, and he would only have to push her on a little more; so to it he went.

He won the first game. This spurred him on; and he played till it was so dark they could not see a ball. Another bowl was called for from the winner. Wagers and bets now drained Brown not only of all the money he had won, but of all he had in his pocket, so that he was obliged to ask leave to go to the house where his horse was, to borrow enough to discharge his reckoning at the Globe.

All these losses brought his poor dear mother to his mind, and he marched off with rather a heavy heart to borrow the money, and to order Smiler out of the stable. The landlord expressed much surprise at seeing him, and the ostler declared there was no Smiler there; that he had been rode off above two hours ago by the merry Andrew, who said he come by order of the owner, Mr. Brown, to fetch him to the Globe, and to pay for his feed. It was indeed one of the neatest tricks the Andrew ever performed, for he made such a clean conveyance of Smiler, that neither Jack nor his father ever heard of her again.

It was night: no one could tell what road the Andrew took, and it was another hour or two before an advertisement could be drawn up for apprehending the horse-stealer. Jack had some doubts whether he should go on or return back. He knew that though his father might fear his wife most, yet he loved Smiler best. At length he took that courage from a glass of brandy which he ought to have taken from a hearty repentance, and he resolved to pursue his journey. He was obliged to leave his watch and silver buckles in pawn for a little old hack, which was nothing but skin and bone, and would hardly trot three miles an hour.

He knocked at his father's door about five in the morning. The family were all up. He asked the boy who opened the door how his mother was? "She is dead," said the boy; "she died yesterday afternoon." Here Jack's heart smote him, and he cried aloud, partly from grief, but more from the reproaches of his own conscience, for he found by computing the hours, that had he come straight on, he should have been in time to receive his mother's blessing.

The farmer now came from within, "I hear Smiler's step. Is Jack come?" "Yes, father," said Jack, in a low voice. "Then," cried the farmer, "run every man and boy of you and take care of the mare. Tom, do thou go and rub her down; Jem, run and get her a good feed of corn. Be sure walk her about that she may not catch cold." Young Brown came in. "Are you not an undutiful dog?" said the father; "you might have been here twelve hours ago. Your mother could not die in peace without seeing you. She said it was cruel return for all her fondness, that you could not make a little haste to see her; but it was always so, for she had wronged her other children to help you, and this was her reward." Brown sobbed out a few words, but his father replied, "Never cry, Jack, for the boy told me that it was out of regard for Smiler, that you were not here as soon as he was, and if 'twas your over care of her, why there's no great harm done. You could not have saved your poor mother, and you might have hurt the mare." Here Jack's double guilt flew into his face. He knew that his father was very covetous, and had lived on bad terms with his wife; and also that his own unkindness to her had been forgiven him out of love to the horse;

but to break to him how he had lost that horse through his own folly and want of feeling, was more than Jack had courage to do. The old man, however, soon got at the truth, and no words can describe his fury. Forgetting that his wife lay dead above stairs, he abused his son in a way not fit to be repeated; and though his covetousness had just before found an excuse for a favorite son neglecting to visit a dying parent, yet he now vented his rage against Jack as an unnatural brute, whom he would cut off with a shilling, and bade him never see his face again.

Jack was not allowed to attend his mother's funeral, which was a real grief to him; nor would his father advance even the little money, which was needful to redeem his things at the Star. He had now no fond mother to assist him, and he set out on his return home on his borrowed hack, full of grief. He had the added mortification of knowing that he had also lost by his folly a little hoard of money which his mother had saved up for him.

When Brown got back to his own town he found that the story of Smiler and the Andrew had got thither before him, and it was thought a very good joke at the Grayhound. He soon recovered his spirits as far as related to the horse, but as to his behavior to his dying mother it troubled him at times to the last day of his life, though he did all he could to forget it. He did not, however, go on at all better, nor did he engage in one frolic the less for what had passed at the Globe; his good heart continually betrayed him into acts of levity and vanity.

Jack began at length to feel the reverse of that proverb, Keep your shop and your shop will keep you. He had neglected his customers, and they forsook him. Quarter-day came round; there was much to pay and little to receive. He owed two years' rent. He was in arrears to his men for wages. He had a long account with his currier. It was in vain to apply to his father. He had now no mother. Stock was the only true friend he had in the world, and had helped him out of many petty scrapes, but he knew Stock would advance no money in so hopeless a case. Duns came fast about him. He named a speedy day for payment; but as soon as they were out of the house, and the danger put off to a little distance, he forgot every promise, was as merry as ever, and run the same round of thoughtless gayety. Whenever lie was in trouble, Stock did not shun him, because that was the moment to throw in a little good advice. He one day asked him if he always intended to go on in this course? "No," said he, "I am resolved by and by to reform, grow sober, and go to church. Why I am but five and twenty, man; I am stout and healthy, and likely to live long; I can repent, and grow melancholy and good at any time."

"Oh Jack!" said Stock, "don't cheat thyself with that false hope. What thou dost intend to do, do quickly. Didst thou never read about the heart growing hardened by long indulgence in sin? Some folks, who pretend to mean well, show that they mean nothing at all, by never beginning to put their good resolutions into practice; which made a wise man once say, that hell is paved with good intentions. We can not repent when we please. It is the goodness of God which leadeth us to repentance."

"I am sure," replied Jack, "I am no one's enemy but my own."

"It is as foolish," said Stock, "to say a bad man is no one's enemy but his own, as that a good man is no one's friend but his own. There is no such neutral character. A bad man corrupts or offends all within reach of his example, just as a good man benefits or instructs all within the sphere of his influence. And there is no time when we can say that this transmitted good and evil will end. A wicked man may be punished for sins he never committed himself, if he has been the cause of sin in others, as surely as a saint will be rewarded for more good deeds than he himself has done, even for the virtues and good actions of all those who are made better by his instruction, his example, or his writings."

Michaelmas-day was at hand. The landlord declared he would be put off no longer, but would seize for rent if it was not paid him on that day, as well as for a considerable sum due to him for leather. Brown at last began to be frightened. He applied to Stock to be bound for him. This, Stock flatly refused. Brown now began to dread the horrors of a jail, and really seemed so very contrite, and made so many vows and promises of amendment, that at length Stock was prevailed on, together with two or three of Brown's other friends, to advance each a small sum of money to quiet the landlord. Brown promising to make over to them every part of his stock, and to be guided in future by their advice, declaring that he would turn over a new leaf, and follow Mr. Stock's example, as well as his direction in every thing.

Stock's good nature was at length wrought upon, and he raised the money. The truth is, he did not know the worst, nor how deeply Brown was involved. Brown joyfully set out on the very quarter-day to a town at some distance, to carry his landlord this money, raised by the imprudent kindness of his friend. At his departure Stock put him in mind of the old story of Smiler and the Merry Andrew, and he promised to his own head that he would not even call at a public house till he had paid the money.

He was as good as his word. He very triumphantly passed by several. He stopped a little under the window of one where the sounds of merriment and loud laughter caught his ear. At another he heard the enticing notes of a fiddle and the light heels of the merry dancers. Here his heart had well-nigh failed him, but the dread of a jail on the one hand, and what he feared almost as much, Mr. Stock's anger on the other, spurred him on; and he valued himself not a little at having got the better of this temptation. He felt quite happy when he found he had reached the door of his landlord without having yielded to one idle inclination.

He knocked at the door. The maid who opened it said her master was not at home. "I am sorry for it," said he, strutting about; and with a boasting air he took out his money. "I want to pay him my rent: he needed not to have been afraid of me." The servant, who knew her master was very much afraid of him, desired him to walk in, for her master would be at home in half an hour. "I will call again," said he; "but no, let him call on me, and the sooner the better: I shall be at the Blue Posts." While he had been talking, he took care to open his black leather case, and to display the bank bills to the servant, and then, in a swaggering way, he put up his money and marched off to the Blue Posts.

He was by this time quite proud of his own resolution, and having tendered the money, and being clear in his own mind that it was the landlord's own fault and not his that it was not paid, he went to refresh himself at the Blue Posts. In a barn belonging to this public house a set of strollers were just going to perform some of that sing-song ribaldry, by which our villages are corrupted, the laws broken, and that money drawn from the poor for pleasure, which is wanted by their families for bread. The name of the last new song which made part of the entertainment, made him think himself in high luck, that he should have just that half hour to spare. He went into the barn, but was too much delighted with the actor, who sung his favorite song, to remain a quiet hearer. He leaped out of the pit, and got behind the two ragged blankets which served for a curtain. He sung so much better than the actors themselves, that they praised and admired him to a degree which awakened all his vanity. He was so intoxicated with their flattery, that he could do no less than invite them all to supper, an invitation which they were too hungry not to accept.

He did not, however, quite forget his appointment with his landlord; but the half hour was long since past by. "And so," says he, "as I know he is a mean curmudgeon, who goes to bed by daylight to save candles, it will be too late to speak with him to-night; besides, let him call upon me; it is his business and not mine. I left word where I was to be found; the money is ready, and if I don't pay him to-night, I can do it before breakfast."

By the time these firm resolutions were made, supper was ready. There never was a more jolly evening. Ale and punch were as plenty as water. The actors saw what a vain fellow was feasting them, and as they wanted victuals and he wanted flattery, the business was soon settled. They ate, and Brown sung. They pretended to be in raptures. Singing promoted drinking, and every fresh glass produced a new song or a story still more merry than the former. Before morning, the players, who were engaged to act in another barn a dozen miles off, stole away quietly. Brown having dropt asleep, they left him to finish his nap by himself. As to him his dreams were gay and pleasant, and the house being quite still, he slept comfortably till morning.

As soon as he had breakfasted, the business of the night before popped into his head. He set off once more to his landlord's in high spirits, gayly singing by the way, scraps of all the tunes he had picked up the night before from his new friends. The landlord opened the door himself, and reproached him with no small surliness for not having kept his word with him the evening before, adding, that he supposed he was come now with some more of his shallow excuses. Brown put on all that haughtiness which is common to people who, being generally apt to be in the wrong, happen to catch themselves doing a right action; he looked big, as some sort of people do when they have money to pay. "You need not have been so anxious about your money," said he, "I was not going to break or run away." The landlord well knew this was the common language of those who are ready to do both. Brown haughtily added, "You shall see I am a man of my word; give me a receipt." The landlord had it ready and gave it him.

Brown put his hand in his pocket for his black leathern case in which the bills were; he felt, he searched, he examined, first one pocket, then the other; then both waistcoat pockets, but no leather case could he find. He looked terrified. It was indeed the face of real terror, but the landlord conceived it to be that of guilt, and abused him heartily for putting his old tricks upon him; he swore he would not be imposed upon any longer; the money or a jail—there lay his choice.

Brown protested for once with great truth that he had no intention to deceive; declared that he had actually brought the money, and knew not what was become of it; but the thing was far too unlikely to gain credit. Brown now called to mind that he had fallen asleep on the settle in the room where they had supped. This raised his spirits; for he had no doubt but the case had fallen out of his pocket; he said he would step to the public house and search for it, and would be back directly. Not one word of this did the landlord believe, so inconvenient is it to have a bad character. He swore Brown should not stir out of his house without a constable, and made him wait while he sent for one. Brown, guarded by the constable, went back to the Blue Posts, the landlord charging the officer not to lose sight of the culprit. The caution was needless; Brown had not the least design of running away, so firmly persuaded was he that he should find his leather case.

But who can paint his dismay, when no tale or tidings of the leather case could be had! The master, the mistress, the boy, the maid of the public house, all protested they were innocent. His suspicions soon fell on the strollers with whom he had passed the night; and he now found out for the first time, that a merry evening did not always produce a happy morning. He obtained a warrant, and proper officers were sent in pursuit of the strollers. No one, however, believed he had really lost any thing; and as he had not a shilling left to defray the expensive treat he had given, the master of the inn agreed with the other landlord in thinking this story was a trick to defraud them both, and Brown remained in close custody. At length the officers returned, who said they had been obliged to let the strollers go, as they could not fix the charge on any one, and they had offered to swear before a justice that they had seen nothing of the leather case. It was at length agreed that as he had passed the evening in a crowded barn, he had probably been robbed there, if at all; and among so many, who could pretend to guess at the thief?

Brown raved like a madman; he cried, tore his hair, and said he was ruined for ever. The abusive language of his old landlord, and his new creditor at the Blue Posts, did not lighten his sorrow. His landlord would be put off no longer. Brown declared he could neither find bail nor raise another shilling; and as soon as the forms of law were made out, he was sent to the county jail.

Here it might have been expected that hard living and much leisure would have brought him to reflect a little on his past follies. But his heart was not truly touched. The chief thing which grieved him at first was his having abused the kindness of Stock, for to him he should appear guilty of a real fraud, where indeed he had been only vain, idle, and imprudent. And it is worth while here to remark, that vanity, idleness, and imprudence, often bring a man to utter ruin both of soul and body, though silly people do not put them in the catalogue of heavy sins, and those who indulge in them are often reckoned honest, merry fellows, with the best hearts in the world.

I wish I had room to tell my readers what befell Jack in his present doleful habitation, and what became of him afterward. I promise them, however, that they shall certainly know the first of next month, when I hope they will not forget to inquire for the fourth part of the Shoemakers, or Jack Brown in prison.

PART IV

JACK BROWN IN PRISON

Brown was no sooner lodged in his doleful habitation, and a little recovered from his first surprise, than he sat down and wrote his friend Stock the whole history of the transaction. Mr. Stock, who had long known the exceeding lightness and dissipation of his mind, did not so utterly disbelieve the story as all the other creditors did. To speak the truth, Stock was the only one among them who had good sense enough to know, that a man may be completely ruined, both in what relates to his property and his soul, without committing Old Bailey crimes. He well knew that idleness, vanity, and the love of pleasure, as it is falsely called, will bring a man to a morsel of bread, as surely as those things which are reckoned much greater sins, and that they undermine his principles as certainly, though not quite so fast.

Stock was too angry with what had happened to answer Brown's letter, or to seem to take the least notice of him. However, he kindly and secretly undertook a journey to the hard-hearted old farmer, Brown's father, to intercede with him, and to see if he would do any thing for his son. Stock did not pretend to excuse Jack, or even to lessen his offenses; for it was a rule of his never to disguise truth or to palliate wickedness. Sin was still sin in his eyes, though it were committed by his best friend; but though he would not soften the sin, he felt tenderly for the sinner. He pleaded with the old farmer on the ground that his son's idleness and other vices would gather fresh strength in a jail. He told him that the loose and worthless company which he would there keep, would harden him in vice, and if he was now wicked, he might there become irreclaimable.

But all his pleas were urged in vain. The farmer was not to be moved; indeed he argued, with some justice, that he ought not to make his industrious children beggars to save one rogue from the gallows.

Mr. Stock allowed the force of his reasoning, though he saw the father was less influenced by this principle of justice than by resentment on account of the old story of Smiler. People, indeed, should take care that what appears in their conduct to proceed from justice, does not really proceed from revenge. Wiser men than Farmer Brown often deceive themselves, and fancy they act on better principles than they really do, for want of looking a little more closely into their own hearts, and putting down every action to its true motive. When we are praying against deceit, we should not forget to take self-deceit into the account.

Mr. Stock at length wrote to poor Jack; not to offer him any help, that was quite out of the question, but to exhort him to repent of his evil ways; to lay before him the sins of his past life, and to advise him to convert the present punishment into a benefit, by humbling himself before God. He offered his interest to get his place of confinement exchanged for one of those improved prisons, where solitude and labor have been made the happy instruments of bringing many to a better way of thinking, and ended by saying, that if he ever gave any solid signs of real amendment he would still be his friend, in spite of all that was past.

If Mr. Stock had sent him a good sum of money to procure his liberty, or even to make merry with his wretched companions, Jack would have thought him a friend indeed. But to send him nothing but dry advice, and a few words of empty comfort, was, he thought, but a cheap, shabby way of showing his kindness. Unluckily the letter came just as he was going to sit down to one of those direful merry-makings which are often carried on with brutal riot within the doleful walls of a jail on the entrance of a new prisoner, who is often expected to give a feast to the rest.

When his companions were heated with gin; "Now," said Jack, "I'll treat you with a sermon, and a very pretty preachment it is." So saying, he took out Mr. Stock's kind and pious letter, and was delighted at the bursts of laughter it produced. "What a canting dog!" said one. "Repentance, indeed!" cried Tom Crew; "No, no, Jack, tell this hypocritical rogue that if we have lost our liberty, it is only for having been jolly, hearty fellows, and we have more spirit than to repent of that I hope: all the harm we have done is living a little too fast, like honest bucks as we are." "Ay, ay," said Jolly George, "had we been such sneaking miserly fellows as Stock, we need not have come hither. But if the ill nature of the laws has been so cruel as to clap up such fine hearty blades, we are no felons, however. We are afraid of no Jack Ketch; and I see no cause to repent of any sin that's not hanging matter. As to those who are thrust into the condemned hole indeed, and have but a few hours to live, they must see the parson, and hear a sermon, and such stuff. But I do not know what such stout young fellows as we are have to do with repentance. And so, Jack, let us have that rare new catch which you learnt of the strollers that merry night when you lost your pocket-book."

This thoughtless youth soon gave a fresh proof of the power of evil company, and of the quick progress of the heart of a sinner from bad to worse. Brown, who always wanted principle, soon grew to want feeling also. He joined in the laugh which was raised against Stock, and told many good stories, as they were called, in derision of the piety, sobriety, and self-denial of his old friend. He lost every day somewhat of those small remains of shame and decency which he had brought with him to the prison. He even grew reconciled to this wretched way of life, and the want of money seemed to him the heaviest evil in the life of a jail.

Mr. Stock finding from the jailor that his letter had been treated with ridicule, would not write to him any more. He did not come to see him nor send him any assistance, thinking it right to let him suffer that want which his vices had brought upon him. But as he still hoped that the time would come when he might be brought to a sense of his evil courses, he continued to have an eye upon him by means of the jailor, who was an honest, kind-hearted man.

Brown spent one part of his time in thoughtless riot, and the other in gloomy sadness. Company kept up his spirits; with his new friends he contrived to drown thought; but when he was alone he began to find that a merry fellow, when deprived of his companions and his liquor, is often a most forlorn wretch. Then it is that even a merry fellow says, Of laughter, what is it? and of mirth, it is madness.

As he contrived, however, to be as little alone as possible his gayety was commonly uppermost till that loathsome distemper, called the jail fever, broke out in the prison. Tom Crew, the ring-leader in all their evil practices, was first seized with it. Jack staid a little while with his comrade to assist and divert him, but of assistance he could give little, and the very thought of diversion was now turned into horror. He soon caught the distemper, and that in so dreadful a degree, that his life was in great danger. Of those who remained in health not a soul came near him, though he shared his last farthing with them. He had just sense enough left to feel this cruelty. Poor fellow! he did not know before, that the friendship of the worldly is at an end when there is no more drink or diversion to be had. He lay in the most deplorable condition; his body tormented with a dreadful disease, and his soul terrified and amazed at the approach of death: that death which he thought at so great a distance, and of which his comrades had so often assured him, that a young fellow of five and twenty was in no danger. Poor Jack! I can not help feeling for him. Without a shilling! without a friend! without one comfort respecting this world, and, what is far more terrible, without one hope respecting the next.

Let not the young reader fancy that Brown's misery arose entirely from his altered circumstances. It was not merely his being in want, and sick, and in prison, which made his condition so desperate. Many an honest man unjustly accused, many a persecuted saint, many a holy martyr has enjoyed sometimes more peace and content in a prison than wicked men have ever tasted in the height of their prosperity. But to any such comforts, to any comfort at all, poor Jack was an utter stranger.

A Christian friend generally comes forward at the very time when worldly friends forsake the wretched. The other prisoners would not come near Brown, though he had often entertained, and had never offended them; even his own father was not moved with his sad condition. When Mr. Stock informed him of it, he answered, "'Tis no more than he deserves. As he brews so he must bake. He has made his own bed, and let him lie in it." The hard old man had ever at his tongue's end some proverb of hardness, or frugality, which he contrived to turn in such a way as to excuse himself.

We shall now see how Mr. Stock behaved. He had his favorite sayings too; but they were chiefly on the side of kindness, mercy, or some other virtue. "I must not," said he, "pretend to call myself a Christian, if I do not requite evil with good." When he received the jailor's letter with the account of Brown's sad condition, Will Simpson and Tommy Williams began to compliment him on his own wisdom and prudence, by which he had escaped Brown's misfortunes. He only gravely said, "Blessed be God that I am not in the same misery. It is He who has made us to differ. But for his grace I might have been in no better condition. Now Brown is brought low by the hand of God, it is my time to go to him." "What, you!" said Will, "whom he cheated of your money?" "This is not a time to remember injuries," said Mr. Stock. "How can I ask forgiveness of my own sins, if I withhold forgiveness from him?" So saying, he ordered his horse, and set off to see poor Brown; thus proving that his was a religion not of words, but of deeds.

Stock's heart nearly failed him as he passed through the prison. The groans of the sick and dying, and, what to such a heart as his was still more moving, the brutal merriment of the healthy in such a place, pierced his very soul. Many a silent prayer did he put up as he passed along, that God would yet be pleased to touch their hearts, and that now (during this infectious sickness) might be the accepted time. The jailor observed him drop a tear, and asked the cause. "I can not forget," said he, "that the most dissolute of these men is still my fellow creature. The same God made them; the same Saviour died for them; how then can I hate the worst of them? With my advantages they might have been much better than I am; without the blessing of God on my good minister's instructions, I might have been worse than the worst of these. I have no cause for pride, much for thankfulness; 'Let us not be high-minded, but fear.'"

It would have moved a heart of stone to have seen poor miserable Jack Brown lying on his wretched bed, his face so changed by pain, poverty, dirt, and sorrow, that he could hardly be known for that merry soul of a jack-boot, as he used to be proud to hear himself called. His groans were so piteous that it made Mr. Stock's heart ache. He kindly took him by the hand, though he knew the distemper was catching. "How dost do, Jack?" said he, "dost know me?" Brown shook his head and said, "Know you? ay, that I do. I am sure I have but one friend in the world who would come to see me in this woeful condition. O, James! what have I brought myself to? What will become of my poor soul? I dare not look back, for that is all sin; nor forward, for that is all misery and woe."

Mr. Stock spoke kindly to him, but did not attempt to cheer him with false comfort, as is too often done. "I am ashamed to see you in this dirty place," says Brown. "As to the place, Jack," replied the other, "if it has helped to bring you to a sense of your past offenses, it will be no bad place for you. I am heartily sorry for your distress and your sickness; but if it should please God by them to open your eyes, and to show you that sin is a greater evil than the prison to which it has brought you, all may yet be well. I had rather see you in this humble penitent state, lying on this dirty bed, in this dismal prison, than roaring and rioting at the Grayhound, the king of the company, with handsome clothes on your back, and plenty of money in your pocket."

Brown wept bitterly, and squeezed his hand, but was too weak to say much. Mr. Stock then desired the jailor to let him have such things as were needful, and he would pay for them. He would not leave the poor fellow till he had given him, with his own hands, some broth which the jailor got ready for him, and some medicines which the doctor had sent. All this kindness cut Brown to the heart. He was just able to sob out, "My unnatural father leaves me to perish, and my injured friend is more than a father to me." Stock told him that one proof he must give of his repentance, was, that he must forgive his father, whose provocation had been very great. He then said he would leave him for the present to take some rest, and desired him to lift up his heart to God for mercy. "Dear James," replied Brown, "do you pray for me; God perhaps may hear you, but he will never hear the prayer of such a sinner as I have been." "Take care how you think so," said Stock. "To believe that God can not forgive you would be still a greater sin than any you have yet committed against him." He then explained to him in a few words, as well as he was able, the nature of repentance and forgiveness through a Saviour, and warned him earnestly against unbelief and hardness of heart.

Poor Jack grew much refreshed in body with the comfortable things he had taken; and a little cheered with Stock's kindness in coming so far to see and to forgive such a forlorn outcast, sick of an infectious distemper, and locked within the walls of a prison.

Surely, said he to himself, there must be some mighty power in a religion which can lead men to do such things! things so much against the grain as to forgive such an injury, and to risk catching such a distemper; but he was so weak he could not express this in words. He tried to pray, but he could not; at length overpowered with weariness, he fell asleep.

When Mr. Stock came back, he was surprised to find him so much better in body; but his agonies of mind were dreadful, and he had now got strength to express part of the horrors which he felt. "James," said he (looking wildly) "it is all over with me. I am a lost creature. Even your prayers can not save me." "Dear Jack," replied Mr. Stock, "I am no minister; it does not become me to talk much to thee: but I know I may adventure to say whatever is in the Bible. As ignorant as I am I shall be safe while I stick to that." "Ay," said the sick man, "you used to be ready enough to read to me, and I would not listen, or if I did it was only to make fun of what I heard, and now you will not so much as read a bit of a chapter to me."

This was the very point to which Stock longed to bring him. So he took a little Bible out of his pocket, which he always carried with him on a journey, and read slowly, verse by verse, the fifty-fifth chapter of Isaiah. When he came to the sixth and seventh verses, poor Jack cried so much that Stock was forced to stop. The words were, Let the wicked man forsake his way, and the unrighteous man his thoughts, and let him return unto the Lord. Here Brown stopped him, saying, "Oh, it is too late, too late for me." "Let me finish the verse," said Stock, "and you will see your error; you will see that it is never too late." So he read on—Let him return unto the Lord, and he will have mercy upon him, and to our God, and he will abundantly pardon. Here Brown started up, snatched the book out of his hand, and cried out, "Is that really there? No, no; that's of your own putting in, in order to comfort me; let me look at the words myself." "No, indeed," said Stock, "I would not for the world give you unfounded comfort, or put off any notion of my own for a Scripture doctrine." "But is it possible," cried the sick man, "that God may really pardon me? Dost think he can? Dost think he will?" "I dare not give thee false hopes, or indeed any hopes of my own. But these are God's own words, and the only difficulty is to know when we are really brought into such a state as that the words may be applied to us. For a text may be full of comfort, and yet may not belong to us."

Mr. Stock was afraid of saying more. He would not venture out of his depth; nor indeed was poor Brown able to bear more discourse just now. So he made him a present of the Bible, folding down such places as he thought might be best suited to his state, and took his leave, being obliged to return home that night. He left a little money with the jailor, to add a few comforts to the allowance of the prison, and promised to return in a short time.

When he got home, he described the sufferings and misery of Brown in a very moving manner; but Tommy Williams, instead of being properly affected by it, only said, "Indeed, master, I am not very sorry; he is rightly served." "How, Tommy," said Mr. Stock (rather sternly), "not sorry to see a fellow creature brought to the lowest state of misery; one too whom you have known so prosperous?" "No, master, I can't say I am; for Mr. Brown used to make fun of you, and laugh at you for being so godly, and reading your Bible."

"Let me say a few words to you, Tommy," said Mr. Stock. "In the first place you should never watch for the time of a man's being brought low by trouble to tell of his faults. Next, you should never rejoice at his trouble, but pity him, and pray for him. Lastly, as to his ridiculing me for my religion, if I can not stand an idle jest, I am not worthy the name of a Christian. He that is ashamed of me and my word—dost remember what follows, Tommy?" "Yes, master, it was last Sunday's text—of him shall the Son of Man be ashamed when he shall judge the world."

Mr. Stock soon went back to the prison. But he did not go alone. He took with him Mr. Thomas, the worthy minister who had been the guide and instructor of his youth, who was so kind as to go at his request and visit this forlorn prisoner. When they got to Brown's door, they found him sitting up in his bed with the Bible in his hand. This was a joyful sight to Mr. Stock, who secretly thanked God for it. Brown was reading aloud; they listened; it was the fifteenth of St. Luke. The circumstances of this beautiful parable of the prodigal son were so much like his own, that the story pierced him to the soul: and he stopped every minute to compare his own case with that of the prodigal. He was just got to the eighteenth verse, I will arise and go to my father—at that moment he spied his two friends; joy darted into his eyes. "Oh, dear Jem," said he, "it is not too late, I will arise and go to my Father, my heavenly Father, and you, sir, will show me the way, won't you?" said he to Mr. Thomas, whom he recollected. "I am very glad to see you in so hopeful a disposition," said the good minister. "Oh, sir," said Brown, "what a place is this to receive you in? Oh, see to what I have brought myself!"

"Your condition, as to this world, is indeed very low," replied the good divine. "But what are mines, dungeons, or galleys, to that eternal hopeless prison to which your unrepented sins must soon have consigned you? Even in the gloomy prison, on this bed of straw, worn down by pain, poverty, and want, forsaken by your worldly friends, an object of scorn to those with whom you used to carouse and riot; yet here, I say, brought thus low, if you have at last found out your own vileness, and your utterly undone state by sin, you may still be more an object of favor in the sight of God, than when you thought yourself prosperous and happy; when the world smiled upon you, and you passed your days and nights in envied gayety and unchristian riot. If you will but improve the present awful visitation; if you do but heartily renounce and abhor your present evil courses; if you even now turn to the Lord your Saviour with lively faith, deep repentance, and unfeigned obedience, I shall still have more hope of you than of many who are going on quite happy, because quite insensible. The heavy laden sinner, who has discovered the iniquity of his own heart, and his utter inability to help himself, may be restored to God's favor, and become happy, though in a dungeon. And be assured, that he who from deep and humble contrition dares not so much as lift up his eyes to heaven, when with a hearty faith he sighs out, Lord, be merciful to me a sinner, shall in no wise be cast out. These are the words of him who can not lie."

It is impossible to describe the self-abasement, the grief, the joy, the shame, the hope, and the fear which filled the mind of this poor man. A dawn of comfort at length shone on his benighted mind. His humility and fear of falling back into his former sins, if he should ever recover, Mr. Thomas thought were strong symptoms of a sound repentance. He improved and cherished every good disposition he saw arising in his heart, and particularly warned him against self-deceit, self-confidence, and hypocrisy.

After Brown had deeply expressed his sorrow for his offenses, Mr. Thomas thus addressed him. "There are two ways of being sorry for sin. Are you, Mr. Brown, afraid of the guilt of sin because of the punishment annexed to it, or are you afraid of sin itself? Do you wish to be delivered from the power of sin? Do you hate sin because you know it is offensive to a pure and holy God? Or are you only ashamed of it because it has brought you to a prison and exposed you to the contempt of the world? It is not said that the wages of this or that particular sin is death, but of sin in general; there is no exception made because it is a more creditable or a favorite sin, or because it is a little one. There are, I repeat, two ways of being sorry for sin. Cain was sorry—My punishment is greater than I can bear, said he; but here you see the punishment seemed to be the cause of concern, not the sin. David seems to have had a good notion of godly sorrow, when he says, Wash me from mine iniquity, cleanse me from my sin. And when

Job repented in dust and ashes, it is not said he excused himself, but he abhorred himself. And the prophet Isaiah called himself undone, because he was a man of unclean lips; for, said he 'I have seen the King, the Lord of hosts;' that is, he could not take the proper measure of his own iniquity till he had considered the perfect holiness of God."

One day, when Mr. Thomas and Mr. Stock came to see him, they found him more than commonly affected. His face was more ghastly pale than usual, and his eyes were red with crying. "Oh, sir," said he, "what a sight have I just seen! Jolly George, as we used to call him, the ring-leader of all our mirth, who was at the bottom of all the fun, and tricks, and wickedness that are carried on within these walls, Jolly George is just dead of the jail distemper! He taken, and I left! I would be carried into his room to speak to him, to beg him to take warning by me, and that I might take warning by him. But what did I see! what did I hear! not one sign of repentance; not one dawn of hope. Agony of body, blasphemies on his tongue, despair in his soul; while I am spared and comforted with hopes of mercy and acceptance. Oh, if all my old friends at the Grayhound could but then have seen Jolly George! A hundred sermons about death, sir, don't speak so home, and cut so deep, as the sight of one dying sinner."

Brown grew gradually better in his health, that is, the fever mended, but the distemper settled on his limbs, so that he seemed likely to be a poor, weakly cripple the rest of his life. But as he spent much of his time in prayer, and in reading such parts of the Bible as Mr. Thomas directed, he improved every day in knowledge and piety, and of course grew more resigned to pain and infirmity.

Some months after this, the hard-hearted father, who had never been prevailed upon to see him, or offer him the least relief, was taken off suddenly by a fit of apoplexy; and, after all his threatenings, he died without a will. He was one of those silly, superstitious men, who fancy they shall die the sooner for having made one; and who love the world and the things that are in the world so dearly, that they dread to set about any business which may put them in mind that they are not always to live in it. As, by this neglect, his father had not fulfilled his threat of cutting him off with a shilling, Jack, of course, went shares with his brothers in what their father left. What fell to him proved to be just enough to discharge him from prison, and to pay all his debts, but he had nothing left. His joy at being thus enabled to make restitution was so great that he thought little of his own wants. He did not desire to conceal the most trifling debt, nor to keep a shilling for himself.

Mr. Stock undertook to settle all his affairs. There did not remain money enough after every creditor was satisfied, even to pay for his removal home. Mr. Stock kindly sent his own cart for him with a bed in it, made as comfortable as possible, for he was too weak and lame to be removed any other way, and Mrs. Stock gave the driver particular charge to be tender and careful of him, and not to drive hard, nor to leave the cart a moment.

Mr. Stock would fain have taken him into his own house, at least for a time, so convinced was he of the sincere reformation both of heart and life; but Brown would not be prevailed on to be further burdensome to this generous friend. He insisted on being carried to the parish work-house, which he said was a far better place than he deserved. In this house Mr. Stock furnished a small room for him, and sent him every day a morsel of meat from his own dinner. Tommy Williams begged that he might always be allowed to carry it, as some atonement for his having for a moment so far forgotten his duty, as rather to rejoice than sympathize in Brown's misfortunes. He never thought of the fault without sorrow, and often thanked his master for the wholesome lesson he then gave him, and he was the better for it all his life.

Mrs. Stock often carried poor Brown a dish of tea, or a basin of good broth herself. He was quite a cripple, and never able to walk out as long as he lived. Mr. Stock, Will Simpson, and Tommy Williams laid their heads together, and contrived a sort of barrow on which he was often carried to church by some of his poor neighbors, of which Tommy was always one; and he requited their kindness, by reading a good book to them whenever they would call in; and he spent his time in teaching their children to sing psalms or say the catechism.

It was no small joy to him thus to be enabled to go to church. Whenever he was carried by the Grayhound, he was much moved, and used to put up a prayer full of repentance for the past, and praise for the present.

PART V

A DIALOGUE BETWEEN JAMES STOCK AND WILL SIMPSON, THE SHOEMAKERS, AS THEY SAT AT WORK, ON THE DUTY OF CARRYING RELIGION INTO OUR COMMON BUSINESS

James Stock, and his journeyman Will Simpson, as I informed my readers in the second part, had resolved to work together one hour every evening, in order to pay for Tommy Williams's schooling. This circumstance brought them to be a good deal together when the rest of the men were gone home. Now it happened that Mr. Stock had a pleasant way of endeavoring to turn all common events to some use; and he thought it right on the present occasion to make the only return in his power to Will Simpson for his great kindness. For, said he, if Will gives up so much of his time to help to provide for this poor boy, it is the least I can do to try to turn part of that time to the purpose of promoting Will's spiritual good. Now as the bent of Stock's own mind was religion, it was easy to him to lead their talk to something profitable. He always took especial care, however, that the subject should be introduced properly, cheerfully, and without constraint. As he well knew that great good may be sometimes done by a prudent attention in seizing proper opportunities, so he knew that the cause of piety had been sometimes hurt by forcing serious subjects where there was clearly no disposition to receive them. I say he had found out that two things were necessary to the promoting of religion among his friends; a warm zeal to be always on the watch for occasions, and a cool judgment to distinguish which was the right time and place to make use of them. To know how to do good is a great matter, but to know when to do it is no small one.

Simpson was an honest, good-natured, young man; he was now become sober, and rather religiously disposed. But he was ignorant; he did not know much of the grounds of religion, or of the corruption of his own nature. He was regular at church, but was first drawn thither rather by his skill in psalm-singing than by any great devotion. He had left off going to the Grayhound, and often read the Bible, or some other good book on the Sunday evening. This he thought was quite enough; he thought the Bible was the prettiest history book in the world, and that religion was a very good thing for Sundays. But he did not much understand what business people had with it on working days. He had left off drinking because it had brought Williams to the grave, and his wife to dirt and rags; but not because he himself had seen the evil of sin. He now considered swearing and Sabbath-breaking as scandalous and indecent, but he had not found out that both were to be left off because they are highly offensive to God, and grieve his Holy Spirit. As Simpson was less self-conceited than most ignorant people are, Stock had always a good hope that when he should come to be better acquainted with the word of God, and with the evil of his own heart, he would become one day a good Christian. The great hinderance to this was, that he fancied himself so already.

One evening Simpson had been calling to Stock's mind how disorderly the house and shop, where they were now sitting quietly at work, had formerly been, and he went on thus:

Will. How comfortably we live now, master, to what we used to do in Williams's time! I used then never to be happy but when we were keeping it up all night, but now I am as Merry as the day is long. I find I am twice as happy since I am grown good and sober.

Stock. I am glad you are happy, Will, and I rejoice that you are sober; but I would not have you take too much pride in your own goodness, for fear it should become a sin, almost as great as some of those you have left off. Besides, I would not have you make quite so sure that you are good.

Will. Not good, master! Why, don't you find me regular and orderly at work?

Stock. Very much so; and accordingly I have a great respect for you.

Will. I pay every one his own, seldom miss church, have not been drunk since Williams died, have handsome clothes for Sundays, and save a trifle every week.

Stock. Very true, and very laudable it is; and to all this you may add that you very generously work an hour for poor Tommy's education, every evening without fee or reward.

Will. Well, master, what can a man do more? If all this is not being good, I don't know what is.

Stock. All these things are very right, as far as they go, and you could not well be a Christian without doing them. But I shall make you stare, perhaps, when I tell you, you may do all these things, and many more, and yet be no Christian.

Will. No Christian! Surely, master, I do hope that after all I have done, you will not be so unkind as to say I am no Christian?

Stock. God forbid that I should say so, Will. I hope better things of you. But come now, what do you think it is to be a Christian?

Will. What! why to be christened when one is a child; to learn the catechism when one can read; to be confirmed when one is a youth; and to go to church when one is a man.

Stock. These are all very proper things, and quite necessary. They make part of a Christian's life. But for all that, a man may be exact in them all, and yet not be a Christian.

Will. Not be a Christian! ha! ha! ha! you are very comical, master.

Stock. No, indeed, I am very serious, Will. At this rate it would be a very easy thing to be a Christian, and every man who went through certain forms would be a good man; and one man who observed those forms would be as good as another. Whereas, if we come to examine ourselves by the word of God, I am afraid there are but few comparatively whom our Saviour would allow to be real Christians. What is your notion of a Christian's practice?

Will. Why, he must not rob, nor murder, nor get drunk. He must avoid scandalous things, and do as other decent orderly people do.

Stock. It is easy enough to be what the world calls a Christian, but not to be what the Bible calls so.

Will. Why, master, we working men are not expected to be saints, and martyrs, and apostles, and ministers.

Stock. We are not. And yet, Will, there are not two sorts of Christianity; we are called to practice the same religion which they practiced, and something of the same spirit is expected in us which we reverence in them. It was not saints and martyrs only to whom our Saviour said that they must crucify the world, with its affections and lusts. We are called to be holy in our measure and degree, as he who hath called us is holy. It was not only saints and martyrs who were told that they must be like-minded with Christ. That they must do all to the glory of God. That they must renounce the spirit of the world, and deny themselves. It was not to apostles only that Christ said, They must have their conversation in heaven. It was not to a few holy men, set apart for the altar, that he said, They must set their affections on things above. That they must not be conformed to the world. No, it was to fishermen, to publicans, to farmers, to day-laborers, to poor tradesmen, that he spoke when he told them, they must love not the world nor the things of the world. That they must renounce the hidden things of dishonesty, grow in grace, lay up for themselves treasures in Heaven.

Will. All this might be very proper for them to be taught, because they had not been bred up Christians, but heathens or Jews: and Christ wanted to make them his followers, that is, Christians. But thank God we do not want to be taught all this, for we are Christians, born in a Christian country, of Christian parents.

Stock. I suppose, then, you fancy that Christianity comes to people in a Christian country by nature?

Will. I think it comes by a good education, or a good example. When a fellow who has got any sense, sees a man cut off in his prime by drinking, like Williams, I think he will begin to leave it off. When he sees another man respected, like you, master, for honesty and sobriety, and going to church, why he will grow honest, and sober, and go to church: that is, he will see it his advantage to be a Christian.

Stock. Will, what you say is the truth, but 'tis not the whole truth. You are right as far as you go, but you do not go far enough. The worldly advantages of piety, are, as you suppose, in general great. Credit, prosperity, and health, almost naturally attend on a religious life, both because a religious life supposes a sober and industrious life, and because a man who lives in a course of duty puts himself in the way of God's blessing. But a true Christian has a still higher aim in view, and will follow religion even under circumstances when it may hurt his credit and ruin his prosperity, if it should ever happen to be the will of God that he should be brought into such a trying state.

Will. Well, master, to speak the truth, if I go to church on Sundays, and follow my work in the week, I must say I think that is being good.

Stock. I agree with you, that he who does both, gives the best outward signs that he is good, as you call it. But our going to church, and even reading the Bible, are no proofs that we are as good as we need be, but rather that we do both these in order to make us better than we are. We do both on Sundays, as means, by God's blessing, to make us better all the week. We are to bring the fruits of that chapter or of that sermon into our daily life, and try to get our inmost heart and secret thoughts, as well as our daily conduct, amended by them.

Will. Why, sure, master, you won't be so unreasonable as to want a body to be religious always? I can't do that, neither. I'm not such a hypocrite as to pretend to it.

Stock. Yes, you can be so in every action of your life.

Will. What, master! always to be thinking about religion?

Stock. No, far from it, Will; much less to be always talking about it. But you must be always under its power and spirit.

Will. But surely 'tis pretty well if I do this when I go to church; or while I am saying my prayers. Even you, master, as strict as you are, would not have me always on my knees, nor always at church, I suppose: for then how would your work be carried on? and how would our town be supplied with shoes?

Stock. Very true, Will. 'Twould be no proof of our religion to let our customers go barefoot; but 'twould be a proof of our laziness, and we should starve, as we ought to do. The business of the world must not only be carried on, but carried on with spirit and activity. We have the same authority for not being slothful in business, as we have for being fervent in spirit. Religion has put godliness and laziness as wide asunder as any two things in the world; and what God has separated let no man pretend to join. Indeed, the spirit of religion can have no fellowship with sloth, indolence, and self-indulgence. But still, a Christian does not carry on his common trade quite like another man, neither; for something of the spirit which he labors to attain at church, he carries with him into his worldly concerns. While there are some that set up for Sunday Christians, who have no notion that they are bound to be week-day Christians too.

Will. Why, master, I do think, if God Almighty is contented with one day in seven, he won't thank you for throwing him the other six into the bargain. I thought he gave us them for our own use; and I am sure nobody works harder all the week than you do.

Stock. God, it is true, sets apart one day in seven for actual rest from labor, and for more immediate devotion to his service. But show me that text wherein he says, Thou shalt love the Lord thy God on Sundays—Thou shalt keep my commandments on the Sabbath day—To be carnally minded on Sundays, is death—Cease to do evil, and learn to do well one day in seven—Grow in grace on the Lord's day—Is there any such text?

Will. No, to be sure there is not; for that would be encouraging sin on all the other days.

Stock. Yes, just as you do when you make religion a thing for the church, and not for the world. There is no one lawful calling, in pursuing which we may not serve God acceptably. You and I may serve him while we are stitching this pair of boots. Farmer Furrow, while he is plowing yonder field. Betsy West, over the way, while she is nursing her sick mother. Neighbor Incle, in measuring out his tapes and ribands. I say all these may serve God just as acceptably in those employments as at church; I had almost said more so.

Will. Ay, indeed; how can that be? Now you're too much on t'other side.

Stock. Because a man's trials in trade being often greater, they give him fresh means of glorifying God, and proving the sincerity of religion. A man who mixes in business, is naturally brought into continual temptations and difficulties. These will lead him, if he be a good man, to look more to God, than he perhaps would otherwise do; he sees temptations on the right hand and on the left; he knows that there are snares all around him: this makes him watchful; he feels that the enemy within is too ready to betray him: this makes him humble himself; while a sense of his own difficulties makes him tender to the failings of others.

Will. Then you would make one believe, after all, that trade or business must be sinful in itself, since it brings a man into all these snares and scrapes.

Stock. No, no, Will; trade and business don't create evil passions—they were in the heart before—only now and then they seem to lie snug a little—our concerns with the world bring them out into action a little more, and thus show both others and ourselves what we really are. But then as the world offers more trials on the one hand, so on the other it holds out more duties. If we are called to battle oftener, we have more opportunities of victory. Every temptation resisted, is an enemy subdued; and he that ruleth his own spirit, is better than he that taketh a city.

Will. I don't quite understand you, master.

Stock. I will try to explain myself. There is no passion more called out by the transactions of trade than covetousness. Now, 'tis impossible to withstand such a master sin as that, without carrying a good deal of the spirit of religion into one's trade.

Will. Well, I own I don't yet see how I am to be religious when I'm hard at work, or busy settling an account. I can't do two things at once; 'tis as if I were to pretend to make a shoe and cut out a boot at the same moment.

Stock. I tell you both must subsist together. Nay, the one must be the motive to the other. God commands us to be industrious, and if we love him, the desire of pleasing him should be the main spring of our industry.

Will. I don't see how I can always be thinking about pleasing God.

Stock. Suppose, now, a man had a wife and children whom he loved, and wished to serve; would he not be often thinking about them while he was at work? and though he would not be always thinking nor always talking about them, yet would not the very love he bore them be a constant spur to his industry? He would always be pursuing the same course from the same motive, though his words and even his thoughts must often be taken up in the common transactions of life.

Will. I say first one, then the other; now for labor, now for religion.

Stock. I will show that both must go together. I will suppose you were going to buy so many skins of our currier—that is quite a worldly transaction—you can't see what a spirit of religion has to do with buying a few calves' skins. Now, I tell you it has a great deal to do with it. Covetousness, a desire to make a good bargain, may rise up in your heart. Selfishness, a spirit of monopoly, a wish to get all, in order to distress others; these are evil desires, and must be subdued. Some opportunity of unfair gain offers, in which there may be much sin, and yet little scandal. Here a Christian will stop short; he will recollect, That he who maketh haste to be rich shall hardly be innocent. Perhaps the sin may be on the side of your dealer—he may want to overreach you—this is provoking—you are tempted to violent anger, perhaps to swear; here is a fresh demand on you for a spirit of patience and moderation, as there was before for a spirit of justice and self-denial. If, by God's grace, you get the victory over these temptations, you are the better man for having been called out to them; always provided, that the temptations be not of your own seeking. If you give way, and sink under these temptations, don't go and say trade and business have made you covetous, passionate and profane. No, no; depend upon it, you were so before; you would have had all these evil seeds lurking in your heart, if you had been loitering about at home and doing nothing, with the additional sin of idleness into the bargain. When you are busy, the devil often tempts you; when you are idle, you tempt the devil. If business and the world call these evil tempers into action, business and the world call that religion into action too which teaches us to resist them. And in this you see the week-day fruit of the Sunday's piety. 'Tis trade and business in the week which call us to put our Sunday readings, praying, and church-going into practice.

Will. Well, master, you have a comical way, somehow, of coming over one. I never should have thought there would have been any religion wanted in buying and selling a few calves' skins. But I begin to see there is a good deal in what you say. And, whenever I am doing a common action, I will try to remember that it must be done after a godly sort.

Stock. I hear the clock strike nine—let us leave off our work. I will only observe further, that one good end of our bringing religion into our business is, to put us in mind not to undertake more business than we can carry on consistently with our religion. I shall never commend that man's diligence, though it is often commended by the world, who is not diligent about the salvation of his soul. We are as much forbidden to be overcharged with the cares of life, as with its pleasures. I only wish to prove to you, that a discreet Christian may be wise for both worlds; that he may employ his hands without entangling his soul, and labor for the meat that perisheth, without neglecting that which endureth unto eternal life; that he may be prudent for time while he is wise for eternity.

PART VI

DIALOGUE THE SECOND. ON THE DUTY OF CARRYING RELIGION INTO OUR AMUSEMENTS

The next evening Will Simpson being got first to his work, Mr. Stock found him singing very cheerfully over his last. His master's entrance did not prevent his finishing his song, which concluded with these words:

"Since life is no more than a passage at best,
Let us strew the way over with flowers."

When Will had concluded his song, he turned to Mr. Stock, and said, "I thank you, master, for first putting it into my head how wicked it is to sing profane and indecent songs. I never sing any now which have any wicked words in them."

Stock. I am glad to hear it. So far you do well. But there are other things as bad as wicked words, nay worse perhaps, though they do not so much shock the ear of decency.

Will. What is that, master? What can be so bad as wicked words?

Stock. Wicked thoughts, Will. Which thoughts, when they are covered with smooth words, and dressed out in pleasing rhymes, so as not to shock modest young people by the sound, do more harm to their principles, than those songs of which the words are so gross and disgusting, that no person of common decency can for a moment listen to them.

Will. Well, master, I am sure that was a very pretty song I was singing when you came in, and a song which very sober, good people sing.

Stock. Do they? Then I will be bold to say that singing such songs is no part of their goodness. I heard indeed but two lines of it, but they were so heathenish that I desire to hear no more.

Will. Now you are really too hard. What harm could there be in it? There was not one indecent word.

Stock. I own, indeed, that indecent words are particularly offensive. But, as I said before, though immodest expressions offend the ear more, they do not corrupt the heart, perhaps, much more than songs of which the words are decent, and the principle vicious. In the latter case, because there is nothing that shocks his ear, a man listens till the sentiment has so corrupted his heart, that his ears grow hardened too; by long custom he loses all sense of the danger of profane diversions; and I must say I have often heard young women of character sing songs in company, which I should be ashamed to read by myself. But come, as we work, let us talk over this business a little; and first let us stick to this sober song of yours, that you boast so much about. (repeats)

"Since life is no more than a passage at best,
Let us strew the way over with flowers."

Now what do you learn by this?

Will. Why, master, I don't pretend to learn much by it. But 'tis a pretty tune and pretty words.

Stock. But what do these pretty words mean?

Will. That we must make ourselves merry because life is short.

Stock. Will! Of what religion are you?

Will. You are always asking one such odd questions, master; why a Christian, to be sure.

Stock. If I often ask you or others this question, it is only because I like to know what grounds I am to go upon when I am talking with you or them. I conceive that there are in this country two sorts of people, Christians and no Christians. Now, if people profess to be of this first description, I expect one kind of notions, opinions, and behavior from them; if they say they are of the latter, then I look for another set of notions and actions from them. I compel no man to think with me. I take every man at his word. I only expect him to think and believe according to the character he takes upon himself, and to act on the principles of that character which he professes to maintain.

Will. That's fair enough—I can't say but it is—to take a man at his own word, and on his own grounds.

Stock. Well then. Of whom does the Scripture speak when it says, Let us eat and drink, for to-morrow we die?

Will. Why of heathens, to be sure, not of Christians.

Stock. And of whom when it says, Let us crown ourselves with rosebuds before they are withered?

Will. O, that is Solomon's worldly fool.

Stock. You disapprove of both, then.

Will. To be sure I do. I should not be a Christian if I did not.

Stock. And yet, though a Christian, you are admiring the very same thought in the song you were singing. How do you reconcile this?

Will. O, there is no comparison between them. These several texts are designed to describe loose, wicked heathens. Now I learn texts as part of my religion. But religion, you know, has nothing to do with a song. I sing a song for my pleasure.

Stock. In our last night's talk, Will, I endeavored to prove to you that religion was to be brought into our business. I wish now to let you see that it is to be brought into our pleasure also. And that he who is really a Christian, must be a Christian in his very diversions.

Will. Now you are too strict again, master; as you last night declared, that in our business you would not have us always praying, so I hope that in our pleasure you would not have us always psalm-singing. I hope you would not have all one's singing to be about good things.

Stock. Not so, Will; but I would not have any part either of our business or our pleasure to be about evil things. It is one thing to be singing about religion, it is another thing to be singing against it. Saint Peter, I fancy, would not much have approved your favorite song. He, at least seemed to have another view of the matter, when he said, The end of all things is at hand. Now this text teaches much the same awful truth with the first line of your song. But let us see to what different purposes the apostle and the poet turn the very same thought. Your song says, because life is so short, let us make it merry. Let us divert ourselves so much on the road, that we may forget the end. Now what says the apostle, Because the end of all things is at hand be ye therefore sober and watch unto prayer.

Will. Why, master, I like to be sober too, and have left off drinking. But still I never thought that we were obliged to carry texts out of the Bible to try the soundness of a song; and to enable us to judge if we might be both merry and wise in singing it.

Stock. Providence has not so stinted our enjoyments, Will, but he has left us many subjects of harmless merriment; but, for my own part, I am never certain that any one is quite harmless till I have tried it by this rule that you seem to think so strict. There is another favorite catch which I heard you and some of the workmen humming yesterday.

Will. I will prove to you that there is not a word of harm in that; pray listen now. (sings.)

"Which is the best day to drink—Sunday, Monday,
Tuesday, Wednesday, Thursday, Friday, Saturday?"

Stock. Now, Will, do you really find you unwillingness to drink is so great that you stand in need of all these incentives to provoke you to it? Do you not find temptation strong enough without exciting your inclinations, and whetting your appetites in this manner? Can any thing be more unchristian than to persuade youth by pleasant words, set to the most alluring music, that the pleasures of drinking are so great, that every day in the week, naming them all successively, by way of fixing and enlarging the idea, is equally fit, equally proper, and equally delightful, for what?—for the low and sensual purpose of getting drunk. Tell me, Will, are you so very averse to pleasure? Are you naturally so cold and dead to all passion and temptation, that you really find it necessary to inflame your imagination, and disorder your senses, in order to excite a quicker relish for the pleasure of sin?

Will. All this is true enough, indeed; but I never saw it in this light before.

Stock. As I passed by the Grayhound last night, in my way to my evening's walk in the fields, I caught this one verse of a song which the club were singing:

"Bring the flask, the music bring,
Joy shall quickly find us;
Drink, and dance, and laugh, and sing,
And cast dull care behind us."

When I got into the fields, I could not forbear comparing this song with the second lesson last Sunday evening at church; these were the words: Take heed lest at any time your heart be overcharged with drunkenness, and so that day come upon you unawares, for as a snare shall it come upon all them that are on the face of the earth.

Will. Why, to be sure, if the second lesson was right, the song must be wrong.

Stock. I ran over in my mind also a comparison between such songs as that which begins with

"Drink, and drive care away,"

with those injunctions of holy writ, Watch and pray, therefore, that you enter not into temptation; and again, Watch and pray that you may escape all these things. I say I compared this with the song I allude to,

"Drink and drive care away,
Drink and be merry;
You'll ne'er go the faster
To the Stygian ferry."

I compared this with that awful admonition of Scripture how to pass the time. Not in rioting and drunkenness, not in chambering and wantonness, but put ye on the Lord Jesus Christ, and make not provision for the flesh to fulfill the lusts thereof.

Will. I am afraid then, master, you would not much approve of what I used to think a very pretty song, which begins with,

"A plague on those musty old lubbers
Who teach us to fast and to think."

Stock. Will, what would you think of any one who should sit down and write a book or a song to abuse the clergy?

Will. Why I should think he was a very wicked fellow, and I hope no one would look into such a book, or sing such a song.

Stock. And yet it must certainly be the clergy who are scoffed at in that verse, it being their professed business to teach us to think and be serious.

Will. Ay, master, and now you have opened my eyes, I think I can make some of those comparisons myself between the spirit of the Bible, and the spirit of these songs.

"Bring the flask, the goblet bring,"

won't stand very well in company with the threat of the prophet: Woe unto them that rise early, that they may mingle strong drink.

Stock. Ay, Will; and these thoughtless people who live up to their singing, seem to be the very people described in another place as glorying in their intemperance, and acting what their songs describe: They look at the wine and say it is red, it moveth itself aright in the cup.

Will. I do hope I shall for the future not only become more careful what songs I sing myself, but also not to keep company with those who sing nothing else but what in my sober judgment I now see to be wrong.

Stock. As we shall have no body in the world to come, it is a pity not only to make our pleasures here consist entirely in the delights of animal life, but to make our very songs consist in extolling and exalting those delights which are unworthy of the man as well as of the Christian. If, through temptation or weakness, we fall into errors, let us not establish and confirm them by picking up all the songs and scraps of verses which excuse, justify, and commend sin. That time is short, is a reason given by these song-mongers why we should give into greater indulgences. That time is short, is a reason given by the apostle why we should enjoy our dearest comforts as if we enjoyed them not.

Now, Will, I hope you will see the importance of so managing, that our diversions (for diversions of some kind we all require), may be as carefully chosen as our other employments. For to make them such as effectually drive out of our minds all that the Bible and the minister have been putting into them, seems to me as imprudent as it is unchristian. But this is not all. Such sentiments as these songs contain, set off by the prettiest music, heightened by liquor and all the noise and spirit of what is called jovial company, all this, I say, not only puts every thing that is right out of the mind, but puts every thing that is wrong into it. Such songs, therefore, as tend to promote levity, thoughtlessness, loose imaginations, false views of life, forgetfulness of death, contempt of whatever is serious, and neglect of whatever is sober, whether they be, love-songs, or drinking-songs, will not, can not be sung by any man or any woman who makes a serious profession of Christianity.[4]

[4] It is with regret I have lately observed that the fashionable author and singer of songs more loose, profane, and corrupt, than any of those here noticed, not only received a prize as the reward of his important services, but also received the public acknowledgments of an illustrious society for having contributed to the happiness of their country.

THE HISTORY OF TOM WHITE, THE POST BOY

PART I

Tom White was one of the best drivers of a post-chaise on the Bath road. Tom was the son of an honest laborer at a little village in Wiltshire; he was an active, industrious boy, and as soon as he was old enough he left his father, who was burdened with a numerous family, and went to live with Farmer Hodges, a sober, worthy man in the same village. He drove the wagon all the week; and on Sundays, though he was now grown up, the farmer required him to attend the Sunday School, carried on under the inspection of Dr. Shepherd, the worthy vicar, and always made him read his Bible in the evening after he had served his cattle; and would have turned him out of his service if he had ever gone to the ale-house for his own pleasure.

Tom, by carrying some wagon loads of faggots to the Bear inn, at Devizes, made many acquaintances in the stable-yard. He soon learned to compare his own carter's frock, and shoes thick set with nails, with the smart red jackets, and tight boots of the post-boys, and grew ashamed of his own homely dress; he was resolved to drive a chaise, to get money, and to see the world. Foolish fellow! he never considered that, though it is true, a wagoner works hard all day, yet he gets a quiet evening at home, and undisturbed rest at night. However, as there must be chaise-boys as well as plow-boys, there was no great harm in the change. The evil company to which it exposed him was the chief mischief. He left Farmer Hodges, though not without sorrow, at quitting so kind a master, and got himself hired at the Black Bear.

Notwithstanding the temptations to which he was now exposed, Tom's good education stood by him for some time. At first he was frightened to hear the oaths and wicked words which are too often uttered in a stable-yard. However, though he thought it very wrong, he had not the courage to reprove it, and the next step to being easy at seeing others sin is to sin ourselves. By degrees he began to think it manly, and a mark of spirit in others to swear; though the force of good habits was so strong that at first, when he ventured to swear himself, it was with fear, and in a low voice. But he was soon laughed out of his sheepishness, as they called it; and though he never became so profane and blasphemous as some of his companions (for he never swore in cool blood, or in mirth, as so many do), yet he would too often use a dreadful bad word when he was in a passion with his horses. And here I can not but drop a hint on the deep folly as well as wickedness, of being in a great rage with poor beasts, who, not having the gift of reason, can not be moved like human creatures, with all the wicked words that are said to them; though these dumb creatures, unhappily, having the gift of feeling, suffer as much as human creatures can do, at the cruel and unnecessary beatings given them. Tom had been bred up to think that drunkenness was a great sin, for he never saw Farmer Hodges drunk in his life, and where a farmer is sober himself, his men are less likely to drink, or if they do the master can reprove them with the better grace.

Tom was not naturally fond of drink, yet for the sake of being thought merry company, and a hearty fellow, he often drank more than he ought. As he had been used to go to church twice on Sunday, while he lived with the farmer (who seldom used his horses on that day, except to carry his wife to church behind him), Tom felt a little uneasy when he was sent the very first Sunday a long journey with a great family; for I can not conceal the truth, that too many gentlefolks will travel, when there is no necessity for it, on a Sunday, and when Monday would answer the end just as well. This is a great grief to all good and sober people, both rich and poor; and it is still more inexcusable in the great, who have every day at their command. However, he kept his thoughts to himself, though he could not now and then help thinking how quietly things were going on at the farmer's, whose wagoner on a Sunday led as easy a life as if he had been a gentleman. But he soon lost all thoughts of this kind, and in time did not know a Sunday from a Monday. Tom went on prosperously, as it is called, for three or four years, got plenty of money, but saved not a shilling. As soon as his horses were once in the stable, whoever would might see them fed for Tom. He had other fish to fry. Fives, cards, cudgel-playing, laying wagers, and keeping loose company, each of which he at first disliked, and each of which he soon learned to practice, ran away with all his money, and all his spare time; and though he was generally in the way as soon as the horses were ready (because if there was no driving there was no pay), yet he did not care whether the carriage was clean or dirty, if the horses looked well or ill, if the harness was whole, or the horses were shod. The certainty that the gains of to-morrow would make up for the extravagance of to-day, made him quite thoughtless and happy; for he was young, active, and healthy, and never foresaw that a rainy day might come, when he would want what he now squandered.

One day, being a little flustered with liquor as he was driving his return chaise through Brentford, he saw just before him another empty carriage, driven by one of his acquaintance; he whipped up his horses, resolving to outstrip the other, and swearing dreadfully that he would be at the Red Lion first—for a pint—"Done!" cried the other, "a wager." Both cut and spurred the poor beasts with the usual fury, as if their credit had been really at stake, or their lives had depended on that foolish contest. Tom's chaise had now got up to that of his rival, and they drove along side of each other with great fury and many imprecations. But in a narrow part Tom's chaise being in the middle, with his antagonist on one side, and a cart driving against him on the other, the horses reared, the carriages got entangled; Tom roared out a great oath to the other to stop, which he either could not, or would not do, but returned an horrid imprecation that he would win the wager if he was alive. Tom's horses took fright, and he himself was thrown to the ground with great violence. As soon as he could be got from under the wheels, he was taken up senseless, his leg was broken in two places, and his body was much bruised. Some people whom the noise had brought together, put him in the post-chaise in which the wagoner kindly assisted, but the other driver seemed careless and indifferent, and drove off, observing with a brutal coolness, "I am sorry I have lost my pint; I should have beat him hollow, had it not been for this little accident." Some gentlemen who came out of the inn, after reprimanding this savage, inquired who he was, wrote to inform his master, and got him discharged: resolving that neither they nor any of their friends would ever employ him, and he was long out of place, and nobody ever cared to be driven by him.

Tom was taken to one of those excellent hospitals with which London abounds. His agonies were dreadful, his leg was set, and a high fever came on. As soon as he was left alone to reflect on his condition; his first thought was that he should die, and his horror was inconceivable. Alas! said he, what will become of my poor soul? I am cut off in the very commission of three great sins: I was drunk, I was in a horrible passion, and I had oaths and blasphemies in my mouth. He tried to pray, but he could not; his mind was all distraction, and he thought he was so very wicked that God would not forgive him; because, said he, I have sinned against light and knowledge; I have had a sober education, and good examples; I was bred in the fear of God, and the knowledge of Christ, and I deserve nothing but punishment. At length he grew light-headed, and there was little hope of his life. Whenever he came to his senses for a few minutes, he cried out, O! that my old companions could now see me, surely they would take warning by my sad fate, and repent before it is too late.

By the blessing of God on the skill of the surgeon, and the care of the nurses, he however grew better in a few days. And here let me stop to remark, what a mercy it is that we live in a Christian country, where the poor, when sick, or lame, or wounded, are taken as much care of as any gentry: nay, in some respects more, because in hospitals and infirmaries there are more doctors and surgeons to attend, than most private gentlefolks can afford to have at their own houses, whereas there never was a hospital in the whole heathen world. Blessed be God for this, among the thousand other excellent fruits of the Christian religion! A religion which, like its Divine founder, while its grand object is the salvation of men's souls, teaches us also to relieve their bodily wants. It directs us never to forget that He who forgave sins, healed diseases, and while He preached the Gospel, fed the multitude.

It was eight weeks before Tom could be taken out of bed. This was a happy affliction; for by the grace of God, this long sickness and solitude gave him time to reflect on his past life. He began seriously to hate those darling sins which had brought him to the brink of ruin. He could now pray heartily; he confessed and lamented his iniquities, with many tears, and began to hope that the mercies of God, through the merits of a Redeemer, might yet be extended to him on his sincere repentance. He resolved never more to return to the same evil courses, but he did not trust in his own strength, but prayed that God would give him grace for the future, as well as pardon for the past. He remembered, and he was humbled at the thought, that he used to have short fits of repentance, and to form resolutions of amendment, in his wild and thoughtless days; and often when he had a bad head-ache after a drinking bout, or had lost his money at all-fours, he vowed never to drink or play again. But as soon as his head was well and his pockets recruited, he forgot all his resolutions. And how should it be otherwise? for he trusted in his own strength, he never prayed to God to strengthen him, nor ever avoided the next temptation. He thought that amendment was a thing to be set about at any time; he did not know that it is the grace of God which bringeth us to repentance.

The case was now different. Tom began to find that his strength was perfect weakness, and that he could do nothing without the Divine assistance, for which he prayed heartily and constantly. He sent home for his Bible and Prayer-book, which he had not opened for two years, and which had been given him when he left the Sunday School. He spent the chief part of his time in reading them, and derived great comfort, as well as great knowledge, from this employment of his time. The study of the Bible filled his heart with gratitude to God, who had not cut him off in the midst of his sins; but had given him space for repentance; and the agonies he had lately suffered with his broken leg increased the thankfulness that he had escaped the more dreadful pain of eternal misery. And here let me remark what encouragement this is for rich people to give away Bibles and good books, and not to lose all hope, though, for a time, they see little or no good effect from it. According to all appearance, Tom's books were never likely to do him any good, and yet his generous benefactor, who had cast his bread upon the waters, found it after many days; for this Bible, which had lain untouched for years, was at last made the instrument of his reformation. God will work in his own good time, and in his own way, but our zeal and our exertions are the means by which he commonly chooses to work.

As soon as he got well, and was discharged from the hospital, Tom began to think he must return to get his bread. At first he had some scruples about going back to his old employ: but, says he, sensibly enough, gentlefolks must travel, travelers must have chaises, and chaises must have drivers; 'tis a very honest calling, and I don't know that goodness belongs to one sort of business more than to another; and he who can be good in a state of great temptation, provided the calling be lawful, and the temptations are not of his own seeking, and he be diligent in prayer, maybe better than another man for aught I know: and all that belongs to us is, to do our duty in that state of life in which it shall please God to call us; and to leave events in God's hand. Tom had rubbed up his catechism at the hospital, and 'tis a pity that people don't look at their catechism sometimes when they are grown up; for it is full as good for men and women as it is for children; nay, better; for though the answers contained in it are intended for children to repeat, yet the duties enjoined in it are intended for men and woman to put in practice. It is, if I may so speak, the very grammar of Christianity and of our church, and they who understand every part of their catechism thoroughly, will not be ignorant of any thing which a plain Christian need know.

Tom now felt grieved that he was obliged to drive on Sundays. But people who are in earnest and have their hearts in a thing, can find helps in all cases. As soon as he had set down his company at their stage, and had seen his horses fed, says Tom, a man who takes care of his horses, will generally think it right to let them rest an hour or two at least. In every town it is a chance but there may be a church open during part of that time. If the prayers should be over, I'll try hard for the sermon; and if I dare not stay to the sermon it is a chance but I may catch the prayers; it is worth trying for, however; and as I used to think nothing of making a push, for the sake of getting an hour to gamble, I need not grudge to take a little pains extraordinary to serve God. By this watchfulness he soon got to know the hours of service at all the towns on the road he traveled; and while the horses fed, Tom went to church; and it became a favorite proverb with him, that prayers and provender hinder no man's journey; and I beg leave to recommend Tom's maxim to all travelers; whether master or servant, carrier or coachman.

At first his companions wanted to laugh and make sport of this—but when they saw that no lad on the road was up so early or worked so hard as Tom, when they saw no chaise so neat, no glasses so bright, no harness so tight, no driver so diligent, so clean, or so civil, they found he was no subject to make sport at. Tom indeed was very careful in looking after the linch-pins; in never giving his horses too much water when they were hot; nor, whatever was his haste, would he ever gallop them up hill, strike them across the head, or when tired, cut and slash them, or gallop them over the stones, as soon as he got into town, as some foolish fellows do. What helped to cure Tom of these bad practices, was the remark he met with in the Bible, that a good man is merciful to his beast. He was much moved one day on reading the Prophet Jonah, to observe what compassion the great God of heaven and earth had for poor beasts; for one of the reasons there given why the Almighty was unwilling to destroy the great city of Nineveh was, because there was much cattle in it. After this, Tom never could bear to see a wanton stroke inflicted. Doth God care for horses, said he, and shall man be cruel to them?

Tom soon grew rich for one in his station; for every gentleman on the road would be driven by no other lad if careful Tom was to be had. Being diligent, he got a great deal of money; being frugal, he spent but little; and having no vices, he wasted none, he soon found out that there was some meaning in that text which says, that godliness hath the promise of the life that now is, as well as that which is to come: for the same principles which make a man sober and honest, have also a natural tendency to make him healthy and rich; while a drunkard and spendthrift can hardly escape being sick and a beggar. Vice is the parent of misery in both worlds.

After a few years, Tom begged a holiday, and made a visit to his native village; his good character had got thither before him. He found his father was dead, but during his long illness Tom had supplied him with money, and by allowing him a trifle every week, had had the honest satisfaction of keeping him from the parish. Farmer Hodges was still living, but being grown old and infirm, he was desirous to retire from business. He retained a great regard for his old servant, Tom; and finding he was worth money, and knowing he knew something of country business, he offered to let him a small farm at an easy rate, and promised his assistance in the management for the first year, with the loan of a small sum of money, that he might set out with a pretty stock. Tom thanked him with tears in his eyes, went back and took a handsome leave of his master, who made him a present of a horse and cart, in acknowledgment of his long and faithful services; for, says he, I have saved many horses by Tom's care and attention, and I could well afford to do the same by every servant who did the same by me; and should be a richer man at the end of every year by the same generosity, provided I could meet with just and faithful servants who deserve the same rewards. Tom was soon settled in his new farm, and in less than a year had got every thing neat and decent about him. Farmer Hodges's long experience and friendly advice, joined to his own industry and hard labor, soon brought the farm to great perfection. The regularity, sobriety, peaceableness, and piety of his daily life, his constant attendance at church twice every Sunday, and his decent and devout behavior when there, soon recommended him to the notice of Dr. Shepherd, who was still living, a pattern of zeal, activity, and benevolence to all parish priests. The Doctor soon began to hold up Tom, or, as we must now more properly term him, Mr. Thomas White, to the imitation of the whole parish, and the frequent and condescending conversation of this worthy clergyman contributed no less than his preaching to the improvement of his new parishioner in piety.

Farmer White soon found out that a dairy could not well be carried on without a mistress, and began to think seriously of marrying; he prayed to God to direct him in so important a business. He knew that a tawdry, vain, dressy girl was not likely to make good cheese and butter, and that a worldly, ungodly woman would make a sad wife and mistress of a family. He soon heard of a young woman of excellent character, who had been bred up by the vicar's lady, and still lived in the family as upper maid. She was prudent, sober, industrious, and religious. Her neat, modest, and plain appearance at church (for she was seldom seen any where else out of her master's family), was an example to all persons in her station, and never failed to recommend her to strangers, even before they had an opportunity of knowing the goodness of her character. It was her character, however, which recommended her to Farmer White. He knew that favor is deceitful, and beauty is vain, but a woman that feareth the Lord, she shall be praised: ay, and not only praised, but chosen too, says Farmer White, as he took down his hat from the nail on which it hung, in order to go and wait on Dr. Shepherd, to break his mind, and ask his consent; for he thought it would be a very unhandsome return for all the favors he was receiving from his minister, to decoy away his faithful servant from her place, without his consent.

This worthy gentleman, though sorry to lose so valuable a member of his little family, did not scruple a moment about parting with her, when he found it would be so greatly to her advantage. Tom was agreeably surprised to hear she had saved fifty pounds by her frugality. The Doctor married them himself, farmer Hodges being present.

In the afternoon of the wedding-day, Dr. Shepherd condescended to call on Farmer and Mrs. White, to give a few words of advice on the new duties they had entered into; a common custom with him on these occasions. He often took an opportunity to drop, in the most kind and tender way, a hint upon the great indecency of making marriages, christenings, and above all, funerals, days of riot and excess, as is too often the case in country villages. The expectation that the vicar might possibly drop in, in his walks, on these festivals, often restrained excessive drinking, and improper conversation, even among those who were not restrained by higher motives, as Farmer and Mrs. White were.

What the Pastor said was always in such a cheerful, good-humored way that it was sure to increase the pleasure of the day, instead of damping it. "Well, farmer," said he, "and you, my faithful Sarah, any other friend might recommend peace and agreement to you on your marriage; but I, on the contrary, recommend cares and strifes."[5] The company stared—but Sarah, who knew that her old master was a facetious gentleman, and always had some meaning behind, looked serious. "Cares and strife, sir," said the farmer, "what do you mean?" "I mean," said he, "for the first, that your cares shall be who shall please God most, and your strifes, who shall serve him best, and do your duty most faithfully. Thus, all your cares and strifes being employed to the highest purposes, all petty cares and worldly strifes shall be at an end.

[5] See Dodd's Sayings.

"Always remember that you have both of you a better friend than each other." The company stared again, and thought no woman could have so good a friend as her husband. "As you have chosen each other from the best motives," continued the Doctor, "you have every reasonable ground to hope for happiness; but as this world is a soil in which troubles and misfortunes will spring up; troubles from which you can not save one another; misfortunes which no human prudence can avoid: then remember, 'tis the best wisdom to go to that friend who is always near, always willing, and always able to help you: and that friend is God."

"Sir," said Farmer White, "I humbly thank you for all your kind instructions, of which I shall now stand more in need than ever, as I shall have more duties to fulfill. I hope the remembrance of my past offenses will keep me humble, and that a sense of my remaining sin will keep me watchful. I set out in the world, sir, with what is called a good-natured disposition, but I soon found, to my cost, that without God's grace, that will carry a man but a little way. A good temper is a good thing, but nothing but the fear of God can enable one to bear up against temptation, evil company, and evil passions. The misfortune of breaking my leg, as I then thought it, has proved the greatest blessing of my life. It showed me my own weakness, the value of the Bible, and the goodness of God. How many of my brother drivers have I seen, since that time, cut off in the prime of life by drinking, or sudden accident, while I have not only been spared, but blessed and prospered. O, sir, it would be the joy of my heart, if some of my old comrades, good-natured, civil fellows (whom I can't help loving) could see as I have done, the danger of evil courses before it is too late. Though they may not hearken to you, sir, or any other minister, they may believe me because I have been one of them: and I can speak from experience, of the great difference there is, even as to worldly comfort, between a life of sobriety and a life of sin. I could tell them, sir, not as a thing I have read in a book, but as a truth I feel in my own heart, that to fear God and keep his commandments, will not only bring a man peace at last, but will make him happy now. And I will venture to say, sir, that all the stocks, pillories, prisons, and gibbets in the land, though so very needful to keep bad men in order, yet will never restrain a good man from committing evil half so much as that single text, How shall I do this great wickedness, and sin against God?" Dr. Shepherd condescended to approve of what the farmer had said, kindly shook him by the hand, and took leave.

PART II

THE WAY TO PLENTY; OR, THE SECOND PART OF TOM WHITE. WRITTEN IN 1795, THE YEAR OF SCARCITY

Tom White, as we have shown in the first part of this history, from an idle post boy was become a respectable farmer. God had blessed his industry, and he had prospered in the world. He was sober and temperate, and, as was the natural consequence, he was active and healthy. He was industrious and frugal, and he became prosperous in his circumstances. This is the ordinary course of Providence. But it is not a certain and necessary rule. God maketh his sun to shine on the just and on the unjust. A man who uses every honest means of thrift and industry, will, in most cases, find success attend his labors. But still, the race is not always to the swift nor the battle to the strong. God is sometimes pleased, for wise ends, to disappoint all the worldly hopes of the most upright man. His corn may be smitten by a blight; his barns may be consumed by fire; his cattle may be carried off by distemper. And to these, and other misfortunes, the good man is as liable as the spendthrift or the knave. Success is the common reward of industry, but if it were its constant reward, the industrious would be tempted to look no further than the present state. They would lose one strong ground of their faith. It would set aside the Scripture scheme. This world would then be looked on as a state of reward, instead of trial, and we should forget to look to a day of final retribution.

Farmer White never took it into his head, that, because he paid his debts, worked early and late, and ate the bread of carefulness, he was therefore to come into no misfortune like other folk, but was to be free from the common trials and troubles of life. He knew that prosperity was far from being a sure mark of God's favor, and had read in good books, and especially in the Bible, of the great poverty and afflictions of the best of men. Though he was no great scholar, he had sense enough to observe, that a time of public prosperity was not always a time of public virtue; and he thought that what was true of a whole nation might be true of one man. So the more he prospered the more he prayed that prosperity might not corrupt his heart. And when he saw lately signs of public distress coming on, he was not half so much frightened as some others were, because he thought it might do us good in the long run; and he was in hope that a little poverty might bring on a little penitence. The great grace he labored after was that of a cheerful submission. He used to say, that if the Lord's prayer had only contained those four little words. Thy will be done, it would be worth more than the biggest book in the world without them.

Dr. Shepherd, the worthy vicar (with whom the farmer's wife had formerly lived as housekeeper), was very fond of taking a walk with him about his grounds, and he used to say that he learned as much from the farmer as the farmer did from him. If the Doctor happened to observe, "I am afraid these long rains will spoil this fine piece of oats," the farmer would answer, "But then, sir, think how good it is for the grass." If the Doctor feared the wheat would be but indifferent, the farmer was sure the rye would turn out well. When grass failed, he did not doubt but turnips would be plenty. Even for floods and inundations he would find out some way to justify Providence. "'Tis better," said he, "to have our lands a little overflowed, than that the springs should be dried up, and our cattle faint for lack of water." When the drought came, he thanked God that the season would be healthy; and the high winds, which frightened others, he said, served to clear the air. Whoever, or whatever was wrong, he was always sure that Providence was in the right. And he used to say, that a man with ever so small an income, if he had but frugality and temperance, and would cut off all vain desires, and cast his care upon God, was richer than a lord who was tormented by vanity and covetousness. When he saw others in the wrong, he did not, however, abuse them for it, but took care to avoid the same fault. He had sense and spirit enough to break through many old, but very bad customs of his neighbors. "If a thing is wrong in itself," said he one day to Farmer Hodges, "a whole parish doing it can't make it right. And as to its being an old custom, why, if it be a good one, I like it the better for being old, because it has had the stamp of ages, and the sanction of experience on its worth. But if it be old as well as bad, that is another reason for my trying to put an end to it, that we may not mislead our children as our fathers have misled us."

THE ROOF-RAISING

Some years after he was settled, he built a large new barn. All the workmen were looking forward to the usual holiday of roof-raising. On this occasion it was a custom to give a dinner to the workmen, with so much liquor after it, that they got so drunk that they not only lost the remaining half-day's work, but they were not always able to work the following day.

Mrs. White provided a plentiful dinner for roof-raising, and gave each man his mug of beer. After a hearty meal they began to grow clamorous for more drink. The farmer, said, "My lads, I don't grudge you a few gallons of ale merely for the sake of saving my liquor, though that is some consideration, especially in these dear times; but I never will, knowingly, help any man to make a beast of himself. I am resolved to break through a bad custom. You are now well refreshed. If you will go cheerfully to your work, you will have half a day's pay to take on Saturday night more than you would have it this afternoon were wasted in drunkenness. For this your families will be better; whereas, were I to give you more liquor, when you have already had enough, I should help to rob them of their bread. But I wish to show you, that I have your good at heart full as much as your profit. If you will now go to work, I will give you all another mug at night when you leave off. Thus your time will be saved, your families helped, and my ale will not go to make reasonable creatures worse than brute beasts."

Here he stopped. "You are in right on't, master," said Tom, the thatcher; "you are a hearty man, farmer," said John Plane, the carpenter. "Come along, boys," said Tim Brick, the mason: so they all went merrily to work, fortified with a good dinner. There was only one drunken surly fellow that refused; this was Dick Guzzle, the smith. Dick never works above two or three days in the week, and spends the others at the Red Lion. He swore, that if the farmer did not give him as much liquor as he liked at roof-raising, he would not strike another stroke, but would leave the job unfinished, and he might get hands where he could. Farmer White took him at his word, and paid him off directly; glad enough to get rid of such a sot, whom he had only employed from pity to a large and almost starving family. When the men came for their mug in the evening, the farmer brought out the remains of the cold gammon; they made a hearty supper, and thanked him for having broken through a foolish custom, which was afterward much left off in that parish, though Dick would not come into it, and lost most of his work in consequence.

Farmer White's laborers were often complaining that things were so dear that they could not buy a bit of meat. He knew it was partly true, but not entirely; for it was before these very hard times that their complaints began. One morning he stepped out to see how an outhouse which he was thatching went on. He was surprised to find the work at a stand. He walked over to the thatcher's house. "Tom," said he, "I desire that piece of work may be finished directly. If a shower comes my grain will be spoiled." "Indeed, master, I sha'n't work to-day, nor to-morrow neither," said Tom. "You forget that 'tis Easter Monday, and to-morrow is Easter Tuesday. And so on Wednesday I shall thatch away, master. But it is hard if a poor man, who works all the seasons round, may not enjoy these few holidays, which come but once a year."

"Tom," said the farmer, "when these days were first put into our prayer-book, the good men who ordained them to be kept, little thought that the time would come when holiday should mean drunken-day, and that the seasons which they meant to distinguish by superior piety, should be converted into seasons of more than ordinary excess. How much dost think now I shall pay thee for this piece of thatch?" "Why, you know, master, you have let it to me by the great. I think between this and to-morrow night, as the weather is so fine, I could clear about four shillings, after I have paid my boy; but thatching does not come often, and other work is not so profitable." "Very well, Tom; and how much now do you think you may spend in these two holidays?" "Why, master, if the ale is pleasant, and the company merry, I do not expect to get off for less than three shillings." "Tom, can you do pounds, shillings, and pence?" "I can make a little score, master, behind the kitchen-door, with a bit of chalk, which is as much as I want." "Well, Tom, add the four shillings you would have earned to the three you intend to spend, what does that make?" "Let me see! three and four make seven. Seven shillings, master." "Tom, you often tell me the times are so bad that you can never buy a bit of meat. Now here is the cost of two joints at once: to say nothing of the sin of wasting time and getting drunk." "I never once thought of that," said Tom. "Now, Tom," said the farmer, "if I were you, I would step over to butcher Jobbins's, buy a shoulder of mutton, which being left from Saturday's market you will get a little cheaper. This I would make my wife bake in a deep dishful of potatoes. I would then go to work, and when the dinner was ready I would go and enjoy it with my wife and children; you need not give the mutton to the brats, the potatoes will have all the gravy, and be very savory for them." "Ay, but I have got no beer, master, the times are so hard that a poor man can't afford to brew a drop of drink now as we used to do."

"Times are bad, and malt is very dear, Tom, and yet both don't prevent you from spending seven shillings in keeping holiday. Now send for a quart of ale as it is to be a feast: and you will even then be four shillings richer than if you had gone to the public house. I would have you put by these four shillings, till you can add a couple to them; with this I would get a bushel of malt, and my wife should brew it, and you may take a pint of your own beer at home of a night, which will do you more good than a gallon at the Red Lion." "I have a great mind to take your advice, master, but I shall be made such fun of at the Lion! they will so laugh at me if I don't go!" "Let those laugh that win, Tom." "But master, I have got a friend to meet me there." "Then ask your friend to come and eat a bit of your cold mutton at night, and here is sixpence for another pot, if you will promise to brew a small cask of your own." "Thank you, master, and so I will; and I won't go to the Lion. Come boy, bring the helm, and fetch the ladder." And so Tom was upon the roof in a twinkling. The barn was thatched, the mutton bought, the beer brewed, the friend invited, and the holiday enjoyed.

THE SHEEP-SHEARING

Dr. Shepherd happened to say to Farmer White one day, that there was nothing that he disliked more than the manner in which sheep-shearing and harvest-home were kept by some in his parish. "What," said the good Doctor, "just when we are blessed with a prosperous gathering in of these natural riches of our land, the fleece of our flocks; when our barns are crowned with plenty, and we have, through the divine blessing on our honest labor, reaped the fruits of the earth in due season; is that very time to be set apart for ribaldry, and riot, and drunkenness? Do we thank God for his mercies, by making ourselves unworthy and unfit to enjoy them? When he crowns the year with his goodness, shall we affront him by our impiety? It is more than a common insult to his providence; it is a worse than brutal return to Him who openeth his hand and filleth all things living with plenteousness."

"I thank you for the hint, sir," said the farmer. "I am resolved to rejoice though, and others shall rejoice with me: and we will have a merry night on't."

So Mrs. White dressed a very plentiful supper of meat and pudding; and spread out two tables. The farmer sat at the head of one, consisting of some of his neighbors, and all his work-people. At the other sat his wife, with two long-benches on each side of her. On these benches sat all the old and infirm poor, especially those who lived in the work-house, and had no day of festivity to look forward to in the whole year but this. On the grass, in the little court, sat the children of his laborers, and of the other poor, whose employment it had been to gather flowers, and dress and adorn the horns of the ram; for the farmer did not wish to put an end to an old custom, if it was innocent. His own children stood by the table, and he gave them plenty of pudding, which they carried to the children of the poor, with a little draught of cider to every one. The farmer, who never sat down without begging a blessing on his meal, did it with suitable solemnity on the present joyful occasion.

Dr. Shepherd practiced one very useful method, which I dare say was not peculiar to himself; a method of which I doubt not other country clergymen have found the advantage. He was often on the watch to observe those seasons when a number of his parishioners were assembled together, not only at any season of festivity, but at their work. He has been known to turn a walk through a hay-field to good account, and has been found to do as much good by a few minutes' discourse with a little knot of reapers, as by a Sunday's sermon. He commonly introduced his religious observations by some questions relating to their employment; he first gained their affections by his kindness, and then converted his influence over them to their soul's good. The interest he took in their worldly affairs opened their hearts to the reception of those divine truths which he was always earnest to impress upon them. By these methods too he got acquainted with their several characters, their spiritual wants, their individual sins, dangers, and temptations, which enabled him to preach with more knowledge and successful application, than those ministers can do who are unacquainted with the state of their congregations. It was a remark of Dr. Shepherd, that a thorough acquaintance with human nature was one of the most important species of knowledge a clergyman could possess.

The sheep-shearing feast, though orderly and decent, was yet hearty and cheerful. Dr. Shepherd dropped in, with a good deal of company he had at his house, and they were much pleased. When the Doctor saw how the aged and infirm poor were enjoying themselves, he was much moved; he shook the farmer by the hand and said, "But thou, when thou makest a feast, call the blind, and the lame, and the halt; they can not recompense thee, but thou shalt be recompensed at the resurrection of the just."

"Sir," said the farmer, "'tis no great matter of expense; I kill a sheep of my own; potatoes are as plenty as blackberries, with people who have a little forethought. I save much more cider in the course of a year by never allowing any carousing in my kitchen, or drunkenness in my fields, than would supply many such feasts as these, so that I shall be never the poorer at Christmas. It is cheaper to make people happy, sir, than to make them drunk." The Doctor and the ladies condescended to walk from one table to the other, and heard many merry stories, but not one profane word, or one indecent song: so that he was not forced to the painful necessity either of reproving them, or leaving them in anger. When all was over, they sung the sixty-fifth Psalm, and the ladies all joined in it; and when they got home to the vicarage to tea, they declared they liked it better than any concert.

THE HARD WINTER

In the famous cold winter of the year 1795, it was edifying to see how patiently Farmer White bore that long and severe frost. Many of his sheep were frozen to death, but he thanked God that he had still many left. He continued to find in-door work that his men might not be out of employ. The season being so bad, which some others pleaded as an excuse for turning off their workmen, he thought a fresh reason for keeping them. Mrs. White was so considerate, that just at that time she lessened the number of her hogs, that she might have more whey and skim-milk to assist poor families. Nay, I have known her to live on boiled meat for a long while together, in a sickly season, because the pot liquor made such a supply of broth for the sick poor. As the spring came on, and things grew worse, she never had a cake, a pie, or a pudding in her house; notwithstanding she used to have plenty of these good things, and will again, I hope, when the present scarcity is over; though she says she will never use such white flour again, even if it should come down to five shillings a bushel.

All the parish now began to murmur. Farmer Jones was sure the frost had killed the wheat. Farmer Wilson said the rye would never come up. Brown, the malster, insisted the barley was dead at the root. Butcher Jobbins said beef would be a shilling a pound. All declared there would not be a hop to brew with. The orchards were all blighted; there would not be apples enough to make a pie; and as to hay there would be none to be had for love or money. "I'll tell you what," said Farmer White, "the season is dreadful; the crops unpromising just now; but 'tis too early to judge. Don't let us make things worse than they are. We ought to comfort the poor, and you are driving them to despair. Don't you know how much God was displeased with the murmurs of his chosen people? And yet, when they were tired of manna he sent them quails; but all did not do. Nothing satisfies grumblers. We have a promise on our side, that there shall be seed-time and harvest-time to the end. Let us then hope for a good day, but provide against an evil one. Let us rather prevent the evil before it is come upon us, than sink under it when it comes. Grumbling can not help us; activity can. Let us set about planting potatoes in every nook and corner, in case the corn should fail, which, however, I don't believe will be the case. Let us mend our management before we are driven to it by actual want. And if we allow our honest laborers to plant a few potatoes for their families in the headlands of our plowed fields, or other waste bits of ground, it will do us no harm, and be a great help to them. The way to lighten the load of any public calamity is not to murmur at it but put a hand to lessen it."

The farmer had many temptations to send his corn at an extravagant price to a certain seaport town, but as he knew that it was intended to export it against law, he would not be tempted to encourage unlawful gain; so he thrashed out a small mow at a time, and sold it to the neighboring poor far below the market-price. He served his own workmen first. This was the same to them as if he had raised their wages, and even better, as it was a benefit of which their families were sure to partake. If the poor in the next parish were more distressed than his own, he sold them at the same rate. For, said he, there is no distinction of parishes in heaven; and though charity begins at home, yet it ought not to end there.

He had been used in good times now and then to catch a hare or a partridge, as he was qualified; but he now resolved to give up that pleasure. So he parted from a couple of spaniels he had: for he said he could not bear that his dogs should be eating the meat, or the milk, which so many men, women, and children wanted.

THE WHITE LOAF

One day, it was about the middle of last July, when things seemed to be at the dearest, and the rulers of the land had agreed to set the example of eating nothing but coarse bread, Dr. Shepherd read, before sermon in the church, their public declaration, which, the magistrates of the county sent him, and which they had also signed themselves. Mrs. White, of course, was at church, and commended it mightily. Next morning the Doctor took a walk over to the farmer's, in order to settle further plans for the relief of the parish. He was much surprised to meet Mrs. White's little maid, Sally, with a very small white loaf, which she had been buying at a shop. He said nothing to the girl, as he never thought it right to expose the faults of a mistress to her servants; but walked on, resolving to give Mrs. White a severe lecture for the first time in his life. He soon changed his mind, for on going into the kitchen, the first person he saw was Tom the thatcher, who had had a sad fall from a ladder; his arm, which was slipped out of his sleeve, was swelled in a frightful manner. Mrs. White was standing at the dresser making the little white loaf into a poultice, which she laid upon the swelling in a large clean old linen cloth.

"I ask your pardon, my good Sarah," said the Doctor; "I ought not, however appearances were against you, to have suspected that so humble and prudent a woman as you are, would be led either to indulge any daintiness of your own, or to fly in the face of your betters, by eating white bread while they are eating brown. Whenever I come here, I see it is not needful to be rich in order to be charitable. A bountiful rich man would have sent Tom to a surgeon, who would have done no more for him than you have done; for in those inflammations the most skillful surgeon could only apply a poultice. Your kindness in dressing the wound yourself, will, I doubt not, perform the cure at the expense of that threepenny loaf and a little hog's lard. And I will take care that Tom shall have a good supply of rice from the subscription." "And he sha'n't want for skim-milk," said Mrs. White; "and was he the best lord in the land, in the state he is in, a dish of good rice milk would be better for him than the richest meat."

THE PARISH MEETING

On the tenth of August, the vestry held another meeting, to consult on the best method of further assisting the poor. The prospect of abundant crops now cheered every heart. Farmer White, who had a mind to be a little jocular with his desponding neighbors, said, "Well, neighbor Jones, all the wheat was killed, I suppose! the barley is all dead at the root!" Farmer Jones looked sheepish, and said, "To be sure the crops had turned out better than he thought." "Then," said Dr. Shepherd, "let us learn to trust Providence another time; let our experience of his past goodness strengthen our faith."

Among other things, they agreed to subscribe for a large quantity of rice, which was to be sold out to the poor at a very low price, and Mrs. White was so kind as to undertake the trouble of selling it. After their day's work was over, all who wished to buy at these reduced rates, were ordered to come to the farm on the Tuesday evening: Dr. Shepherd dropped in at the same time, and when Mrs. White had done weighing her rice, the Doctor spoke as follows:

"My honest friends, it has pleased God, for some wise end, to visit this land with a scarcity, to which we have been but little accustomed. There are some idle, evil-minded people, who are on the watch for the public distresses; not that they may humble themselves under the mighty hand of God (which is the true use to be made of all troubles) but that they may benefit themselves by disturbing the public peace. These people, by riot and drunkenness, double the evil which they pretend to cure. Riot will complete our misfortunes; while peace, industry, and good management, will go near to cure them. Bread, to be sure, is uncommonly dear. Among the various ways of making it cheaper, one is to reduce the quality of it, another to lessen the quantity we consume. If we can not get enough of coarse wheaten bread, let us make it of other grain. Or let us mix one half of potatoes, and one half of wheat. This last is what I eat in my own family; it is pleasant and wholesome. Our blessed Saviour ate barley-bread, you know, as we are told in the last month's Sunday reading of the Cheap Repository,[6] which I hope you have all heard, as I desired the master of the Sunday School to read it just after evening service, when I know many of the parents are apt to call in at the school. This is a good custom, and one of those little books shall be often read at that time.

[6] See Cheap Repository, Tract on the Scarcity, printed for T. Evans, Long-lane, West Smithfield, London.

"My good women, I truly feel for you at this time of scarcity; and I am going to show my good will, as much by my advice as my subscription. It is my duty, as your friend and minister, to tell you that one half of your present hardships is owing to bad management. I often meet your children without shoes and stockings, with great luncheons of the very whitest bread, and that three times a day. Half that quantity, and still less if it were coarse, put into a dish of good onion or leek porridge, would make them an excellent breakfast. Many too, of the very poorest of you, eat your bread hot from the oven; this makes the difference of one loaf in five; I assure you 'tis what I can not afford to do. Come, Mrs. White, you must assist me a little. I am not very knowing in these matters myself; but I know that the rich would be twice as charitable as they are, if the poor made a better use of their bounty. Mrs. White, do give these poor women a little advice how to make their pittance go further than it now does. When you lived with me you were famous for making us nice cheap dishes, and I dare say you are not less notable, now you manage for yourself."

"Indeed, neighbors," said Mrs. White, "what the good Doctor says is very true. A halfpenny worth of oatmeal, or groats, with a leek or onion, out of your own garden, which costs nothing, a bit of salt, and a little coarse bread, will breakfast your whole family. It is a great mistake at any time to think a bit of meat is so ruinous, and a great load of bread so cheap. A poor man gets seven or eight shillings a week; if he is careful he brings it home. I dare not say how much of this goes for tea in the afternoon, now sugar and butter are so dear, because I should have you all upon me; but I will say, that too much of this little goes even for bread, from a mistaken notion that it is the hardest fare. This, at all times, but particularly just now, is bad management. Dry peas, to be sure, have been very dear lately, but now they are plenty enough. I am certain then, that if a shilling or two of the seven or eight was laid out for a bit of coarse beef, a sheep's head, or any such thing, it would be well bestowed. I would throw a couple of pounds of this into the pot, with two or three handsful of gray peas, an onion, and a little pepper. Then I would throw in cabbage, or turnip, and carrot; or any garden stuff that was most plenty; let it stew two or three hours, and it will make a dish fit for his majesty. The working men should have the meat; the children don't want it: the soup will be thick and substantial, and requires no bread."

RICE MILK

"You who can get skim-milk, as all our workmen can, have a great advantage. A quart of this, and a quarter of a pound of rice you have just bought, a little bit of alspice, and brown sugar, will make a dainty and cheap dish."

"Bless your heart!" muttered Amy Grumble, who looked as dirty as a cinder-wench, with her face and fingers all daubed with snuff: "rice milk, indeed! it is very nice to be sure for those that can dress it, but we have not a bit of coal; rice is no use to us without firing;" "and yet," said the Doctor, "I see your tea-kettle boiling twice every day, as I pass by the poor-house, and fresh butter at thirteen-pence a pound on your shelf." "Oh, dear sir," cried Amy, "a few sticks serve to boil the tea-kettle." "And a few more," said the Doctor, "will boil the rice milk, and give twice the nourishment at a quarter of the expense."

RICE PUDDING

"Pray, Sarah," said the Doctor, "how did you use to make that pudding my children were so fond of? And I remember, when it was cold, we used to have it in the parlor for supper." "Nothing more easy," said Mrs. White: "I put half a pound of rice, two quarts of skim-milk, and two ounces of brown sugar."

"Well," said the Doctor, "and how many will this dine?" "Seven or eight, sir." "Very well, and what will it cost?" "Why, sir, it did not cost you so much, because we baked at home, and I used our own milk; but it will not cost above seven-pence to those who pay for both. Here, too, bread is saved."

"Pray, Sarah, let me put in a word," said Farmer White: "I advise my men to raise each a large bed of parsnips. They are very nourishing, and very profitable. Sixpenny worth of seed, well sowed and trod in, will produce more meals than four sacks of potatoes; and, what is material to you who have so little ground, it will not require more than an eighth part of the ground which the four sacks will take. Providence having contrived by the very formation of this root that it shall occupy but a very small space. Parsnips are very good the second day warmed in the frying pan, and a little rasher of pork, or bacon, will give them a nice flavor."

Dr. Shepherd now said, "As a proof of the nourishing quality of parsnips, I was reading in a history book this very day, that the American Indians make a great part of their bread of parsnips, though Indian corn is so famous; it will make a little variety too."

A CHEAP STEW

"I remember," said Mrs. White, "a cheap dish, so nice that it makes my mouth water. I peel some raw potatoes, slice them thin, put the slices into a deep frying-pan, or pot with a little water, an onion, and a bit of pepper. Then I get a bone or two of a breast of mutton, or a little strip of salt pork and put into it. Cover it down close, keep in the steam, and let it stew for an hour."

"You really give me an appetite, Mrs. White, by your dainty receipts," said the Doctor. "I am resolved to have this dish at my own table." "I could tell you another very good dish, and still cheaper," answered she. "Come, let us have it," cried the Doctor. "I shall write all down as soon as I get home, and I will favor any body with a copy of these receipts who will call at my house." "And I will do more, sir," said Mrs. White, "for I will put any of these women in the way how to dress it the first time, if they are at a loss. But this is my dish:

"Take two or three pickled herrings, put them into a stone jar, fill it up with potatoes, and a little water, and let it bake in the oven till it is done. I would give one hint more," added she; "I have taken to use nothing but potatoe starch; and though I say it, that should not say it, nobody's linen in a common way looks better than ours."

The Doctor now said, "I am sorry for one hardship which many poor people labor under: I mean the difficulty of getting a little milk. I wish all the farmers' wives were as considerate as you are, Mrs. White. A little milk is a great comfort to the poor, especially when their children are sick; and I have known it answer to the seller as well as to the buyer, to keep a cow or two on purpose to sell it by the quart, instead of making butter and cheese."

"Sir," said Farmer White, "I beg leave to say a word to the men, if you please, for all your advice goes to the women. If you will drink less gin, you may get more meat. If you abstain from the ale-house, you may, many of you, get a little one-way beer at home." "Ay, that we can, farmer," said poor Tom, the thatcher, who was now got well. "Easter Monday for that—I say no more. A word to the wise." The farmer smiled and went on: "The number of public houses in many a parish, brings on more hunger and rags than all the taxes in it, heavy as they are. All the other evils put together hardly make up the sum of that one. We are now making a fresh subscription for you. This will be our rule of giving: We will not give to sots, gamblers, and Sabbath-breakers. Those who do not set their young children to work on week-days, and send them to school and church on Sundays, deserve little favor. No man should keep a dog till he has more food than his family wants. If he feeds them at home, they rob his children; if he starves them, they rob his neighbors. We have heard in a neighboring city, that some people carried back the subscription loaves, because they were too coarse; but we hope better things of you." Here Betty Plane begged, with all humility, to put in a word. "Certainly," said the Doctor, "we will listen to all modest complaints, and try to redress them." "You are pleased to say, sir," said she, "that we might find much comfort from buying coarse bits of beef. And so we might; but you do not know, sir, that we could seldom get them, even when we had the money, and times were so bad." "How so, Betty?" "Sir, when we go to Butcher Jobbins for a bit of shin, or any other lean piece, his answer is, 'You can't have it to-day. The cook at the great house has bespoke it for gravy, or the Doctor's maid (begging your pardon, sir,) has just ordered it for soup.' Now, if such kind gentlefolk were aware that this gravy and soup not only consume a great deal of meat—which, to be sure, those have a right to do who can pay for it—but that it takes away those coarse pieces which the poor would buy, if they bought at all. For, indeed, the rich have been very kind, and I don't know what we should have done without them."

"I thank you for the hint, Betty," said the Doctor, "and I assure you I will have no more gravy soup. My garden will supply me with soups that are both wholesomer and better; and I will answer for my lady at the great house, that she will do the same. I hope this will become a general rule, and then we shall expect that butchers will favor you in the prices of the coarse pieces, if we who are rich, buy nothing but the prime. In our gifts we shall prefer, as the farmer has told you, those who keep steadily to their work. Such as come to the vestry for a loaf, and do not come to church for the sermon, we shall mark; and prefer those who come constantly, whether there are any gifts or not. But there is one rule from which we never will depart. Those who have been seen aiding or abetting any riot, any attack on butchers, bakers, wheat-mows, mills, or millers, we will not relieve; but with the quiet, contented, hard-working man, I will share my last morsel of bread. I shall only add, though it has pleased God to send us this visitation as a punishment, yet we may convert this short trial into a lasting blessing, if we all turn over a new leaf. Prosperity has made most of us careless. The thoughtless profusion of some of the rich could only be exceeded by the idleness and bad management of some of the poor. Let us now at last adopt that good old maxim, every one mend one. And may God add his blessing."

The people now cheerfully departed with their rice, resolving, as many of them as could get milk, to put one of Mrs. White's receipts in practice, and an excellent supper they had.

THE SUNDAY SCHOOL

I promised, in the Cure for Melancholy, to give some account of the manner in which Mrs. Jones set up her school. She did not much fear being able to raise the money; but money is of little use, unless some persons of sense and piety can be found to direct these institutions. Not that I would discourage those who set them up, even in the most ordinary manner, and from mere views of worldly policy. It is something gained to rescue children from idling away their Sabbaths in the fields or the streets. It is no small thing to keep them from those to which a day of leisure tempts the idle and the ignorant. It is something for them to be taught to read; it is much to be taught to read the Bible, and much, indeed, to be carried regularly to church. But, all this is not enough. To bring these institutions to answer their highest end, can only be effected by God's blessing on the best directed means, the choice of able teachers, and a diligent attention in some pious gentry to visit and inspect the schools.

ON RECOMMENDATIONS

Mrs. Jones had one talent that eminently qualified her to do good, namely, judgment; this, even in the gay part of her life, had kept her from many mistakes; but though she had sometimes been deceived herself, she was very careful not to deceive others, by recommending people to fill any office for which they were unfit, either through selfishness or false kindness. She used to say, there is always some one appropriate quality which every person must possess in order to fit them for any particular employment. "Even in this quality," said she to Mr. Simpson, the clergyman, "I do not expect perfection; but if they are destitute of this, whatever good qualities they may possess besides, though they may do for some other employment, they will not do for this. If I want a pair of shoes, I go to a shoemaker; I do not go to a man of another trade, however ingenious he may be, to ask him if he can not contrive to make me a pair of shoes. When I lived in London, I learned to be much on my guard as to recommendations. I found people often wanted to impose on me some one who was a burden to themselves. Once, I remember, when I undertook to get a matron for a hospital, half my acquaintance had some one to offer me. Mrs. Gibson sent me an old cook, whom she herself had discharged for wasting her own provisions; yet she had the conscience to recommend this woman to take care of the provisions of a large community. Mrs. Gray sent me a discarded housekeeper, whose constitution had been ruined by sitting up with Mrs. Gray's gouty husband, but who she yet thought might do well enough to undergo the fatigue of taking care of a hundred poor sick people. A third friend sent me a woman who had no merit but that of being very poor, and it would be charity to provide for her. The truth is, the lady was obliged to allow her a small pension till she could get her off her own hands, by turning her on those of others."

"It is very true, madam," said Mr. Simpson; "the right way is always to prefer the good of the many to the good of one; if, indeed, it can be called doing good to any one to place them in a station in which they must feel unhappy, by not knowing how to discharge the duties of it. I will tell you how I manage. If the persons recommended are objects of charity, I privately subscribe to their wants; I pity and help them, but, I never promote them to a station for which they are unfit, as I should by so doing hurt a whole community to help a distressed individual."

Thus Mrs. Jones resolved that the first step toward setting up her school should be to provide a suitable mistress. The vestry were so earnest in recommending one woman, that she thought it worth looking into. On inquiry, she found it was a scheme to take a large family off the parish; they never considered that a very ignorant woman, with a family of young children, was, of all others, the most unfit for a school, all they considered was, that the profits of the school might enable her to live without parish pay. Mrs. Jones refused another, though she could read well, and was decent in her conduct, because she used to send her children to the shop on Sundays. And she objected to a third, a very sensible woman, because she was suspected of making an outward profession of religion a cloak for immoral conduct. Mrs. Jones knew she must not be too nice, neither; she knew she must put up with many faults at last. "I know," said she to Mr. Simpson, "the imperfection of every thing that is human. As the mistress will have much to bear with from the children, so I expect to have something to bear with in the mistress; and she and I must submit to our respective trials, by thinking how much God has to bear with in us all. But there are certain qualities which are indispensable in certain situations. There are, in particular, three things which a good school-mistress must not be without: good sense, activity, and piety. Without the first, she will mislead others; without the second, she will neglect them; and without the third, though she may civilize, yet she will never christianize them."

Mr. Simpson said, "He really knew but of one person in the parish who was fully likely to answer her purpose: this," continued he, "is no other than my housekeeper, Mrs. Betty Crew. It will indeed be a great loss to me to part from her; and to her it will be a far more fatiguing life than that which she at present leads. But ought I to put my own personal comfort, or ought Betty to put her own ease and quiet, in competition with the good of above a hundred children? This will appear still more important, if we consider the good done by these institutions, not as fruit, but seed; if we take into the account how many yet unborn may become Christians, in consequence of our making these children Christians; for, how can we calculate the number which may be hereafter trained for heaven by those very children we are going to teach, when they themselves shall become parents, and you and I are dead and forgotten? To be sure, by parting from Betty, my peas-soup will not be quite so well-flavored, nor my linen so neatly got up; but the day is fast approaching, when all this will signify but little; but it will not signify little whether one hundred immortal souls were the better for my making this petty sacrifice. Mrs. Crew is a real Christian, has excellent sense, and had a good education from my mother. She has also had a little sort of preparatory training for the business; for, when the poor children come to the parsonage for broth on a Saturday evening, she is used to appoint them all to come at the same time; and, after she has filled their pitchers, she ranges them round her in the garden, and examines them in their catechism. She is just and fair in dealing out the broth and beef, not making my favor to the parents depend on the skill of their children; but her own old caps and ribands, and cast-off clothes, are bestowed as little rewards on the best scholars. So that, taking the time she spends in working for them, and the things she gives them, there is many a lady who does not exceed Mrs. Crew in acts of charity. This I mention to confirm your notion, that it is not necessary to be rich in order to do good; a religious upper servant has great opportunities of this sort, if the master is disposed to encourage her."

My readers, I trust, need not be informed, that this is that very Mrs. Betty Crew who assisted Mrs. Jones in teaching poor women to cut out linen and dress cheap dishes, as related in the Cure for Melancholy. Mrs. Jones, in the following week, got together as many of the mothers as she could, and spoke to them as follows:

MRS. JONES'S EXHORTATION

"My good women, on Sunday next I propose to open a school for the instruction of your children. Those among you who know what it is to be able to read your Bible, will, I doubt not, rejoice that the same blessing is held out to your children. You who are not able yourselves to read what your Saviour has done and suffered for you, ought to be doubly anxious that your children should reap a blessing which you have lost. Would not that mother be thought an unnatural monster who would stand by and snatch out of her child's mouth the bread which a kind friend had just put into it? But such a mother would be merciful, compared with her who should rob her children of the opportunity of learning to read the word of God when it is held out to them. Remember, that if you slight the present offer, or if, after having sent your children a few times you should afterward keep them at home under vain pretenses, you will have to answer for it at the day of judgment. Let not your poor children, then, have cause to say, 'My fond mother was my worst enemy. I might have been bred up in the fear of the Lord, and she opposed it for the sake of giving me a little paltry pleasure. For an idle holiday, I am now brought to the gates of hell!' My dear women, which of you could bear to see your darling child condemned to everlasting destruction? Which of you could bear to hear him accuse you as the cause of it? Is there any mother here present, who will venture to say, 'I will doom the children I bore to sin and hell, rather than put them or myself to a little present pain, by curtailing their evil inclinations! I will let them spend the Sabbath in ignorance and idleness, instead of rescuing them from vanity and sin, by sending them to school?' If there are any such here present, let that mother who values her child's pleasure more than his soul, now walk away, while I set down in my list the names of all those who wish to bring their young ones up in the way that leads to eternal life, instead of indulging them in the pleasures of sin, which are but for a moment."

When Mrs. Jones had done speaking, most of the women thanked her for her good advice, and hoped that God would give them grace to follow it; promising to send their children constantly. Others, who were not so well-disposed, were yet afraid to refuse, after the sin of so doing had been so plainly set before them. The worst of the women had kept away from this meeting, resolving to set their faces against the school. Most of those also who were present, as soon as they got home, set about providing their children with what little decent apparel they could raise. Many a willing mother lent her tall daughter her hat, best cap, and white handkerchief; and many a grateful father spared his linen waistcoat and bettermost hat, to induce his grown up son to attend; for it is a rule with which Mrs. Jones began, that she would not receive the younger children out of any family who did not send their elder ones. Too many made excuses that their shoes were old, or their hat worn out. But Mrs. Jones told them not to bring any excuse to her which they could not bring to the day of judgment; and among those excuses she would hardly admit any except accidents, sickness or attendance on sick parents or young children.

SUBSCRIPTIONS

Mrs. Jones, who had secured large subscriptions from the gentry, was desirous of getting the help and countenance of the farmers and trades-people, whose duty and interest she thought it was to support a plan calculated to improve the virtue and happiness of the parish. Most of them subscribed, and promised to see that their workmen sent their children. She met with little opposition till she called on farmer Hoskins. She told him, as he was the richest farmer in the parish, she came to him for a handsome subscription. "Subscription!" said he, "it is nothing but subscriptions, I think; a man, had need be made of money." "Farmer," said Mrs. Jones, "God has blessed you with abundant prosperity, and he expects you should be liberal in proportion to your great ability." "I do not know what you mean by blessing," said he: "I have been up early and late, lived hard while I had little, and now when I thought I had got forward in the world, what with tithes taxes, and subscriptions, it all goes, I think." "Mr. Hoskins," said Mrs. Jones, "as to tithes and taxes, you well know that the richer you are the more you pay; so that your murmurs are a proof of your wealth. This is but an ungrateful return for all your blessings." "You are again at your blessings," said the farmer; "but let every one work as hard as I have done, and I dare say he will do as well. It is to my own industry I owe what I have. My crops have been good, because I minded my plowing and sowing." "O farmer!" cried Mrs. Jones, "you forget whose suns and showers make your crops to grow, and who it is that giveth strength to get riches. But I do not come to preach, but to beg."

"Well, madam, what is the subscription now? Flannel or French? or weavers, or Swiss, or a new church, or large bread, or cheap rice? or what other new whim-wham for getting the money out of one's pocket?" "I am going to establish a Sunday School, farmer; and I come to you as one of the principal inhabitants of the parish, hoping your example will spur on the rest to give." "Why, then," said the farmer, "as one of the principal inhabitants of the parish, I will give nothing; hoping it will spur on the rest to refuse. Of all the foolish inventions, and new fangled devices to ruin the country, that of teaching the poor to read is the very worst." "And I, farmer, think that to teach good principles to the lower classes, is the most likely way to save the country. Now, in order to this, we must teach them to read." "Not with my consent, nor my money," said the farmer; "for I know it always does more harm than good." "So it may," said Mrs. Jones, "if you only teach them to read, and then turn them adrift to find out books for themselves.[7] There is a proneness in the heart to evil, which it is our duty to oppose, and which I see you are promoting. Only look round your own kitchen; I am ashamed to see it hung round with loose songs and ballads. I grant, indeed, it would be better for young men and maids, and even your daughters, not to be able to read at all, than to read such stuff as this. But if, when they ask for bread, you will give them a stone, nay worse, a serpent, yours is the blame." Then taking up a penny-book which had a very loose title, she went on: "I do not wonder, if you, who read such books as these, think it safer that people should not read at all." The farmer grinned, and said, "It is hard if a man of my substance may not divert himself; when a bit of fun costs only a penny, and a man can spare that penny, there is no harm done. When it is very hot, or very wet, and I come in to rest, and have drunk my mug of cider, I like to take up a bit of a jest-book, or a comical story, to make me laugh."

[7] *It was this consideration chiefly, which stimulated the conductors of the Cheap Repository to send forth that variety of little books so peculiarly suited to the young. They considered that by means of Sunday Schools, multitudes were now taught to read, who would be exposed to be corrupted by all the ribaldry and profaneness of loose songs, vicious stories, and especially by the new influx of corruption arising from jacobinial and atheistical pamphlets, and that it was a bounden duty to counteract such temptations.*

"O, Mr. Hoskins!" replied Mrs. Jones, "when you come in to rest from a burning sun or shower, do you never think of Him whose sun it is that is ripening your corn? or whose shower is filling the ear, or causing the grass to grow? I could tell you of some books which would strengthen such thoughts, whereas such as you read only serve to put them out of your head."

Mrs. Jones having taken pains to let Mr. Hoskins know that all the genteel and wealthy people had subscribed, he at last said, "Why, as to the matter of that, I do not value a crown; only I think it may be better bestowed; and I am afraid my own workmen will fly in my face if once they are made scholars; and that they will think themselves too good to work." "Now you talk soberly, and give your reasons," said Mrs. Jones; "weak as they are, they deserve an answer. Do you think that either man, woman, or child, ever did his duty the worse, only because he knew it the better?" "No, perhaps not." "Now, the whole extent of learning which we intend to give the poor, is only to enable them to read the Bible; a book which brings to us the glad tidings of salvation, in which every duty is explained, every doctrine brought into practice, and the highest truths made level to the meanest understanding. The knowledge of that book, and its practical influence on the heart, is the best security you can have, both for the industry and obedience of your servants. Now, can you think any man will be the worse servant for being a good Christian?" "Perhaps not." "Are not the duties of children, of servants, and the poor, individually and expressly set forth in the Bible?" "Yes." "Do you think any duties are likely to be as well performed from any human motives, such as fear or prudence, as from those religious motives which are backed with the sanction of rewards and punishments, of heaven or hell? Even upon your own principles of worldly policy, do you think a poor man is not less likely to steal a sheep or a horse, who was taught when a boy that it was a sin, that it was breaking a commandment, to rob a hen-roost, or an orchard, than one who has been bred in ignorance of God's law? Will your property be secured so effectually by the stocks on the green, as by teaching the boys in the school, that for all these things God will bring them in to judgment? Is a poor fellow who can read his Bible, so likely to sleep or to drink away his few hours of leisure, as one who can not read? He may, and he often does, make a bad use of his reading; but I doubt he would have been as bad without it; and the hours spent in learning to read will always have been among the most harmless ones of his life."

"Well, madam," said the farmer, "if you do not think that religion will spoil my young servants, I do not care if you do put me down for half a guinea. What has farmer Dobson given?" "Half a guinea," said Mrs. Jones. "Well," cried the farmer, "it shall never be said I do not give more than he, who is only a renter. Dobson half a guinea! Why, he wears his coat as threadbare as a laborer." "Perhaps," replied Mrs. Jones, "that is one reason why he gives so much." "Well, put me down a guinea," cried the farmer; "as scarce as guineas are just now, I'll never be put upon the same footing with Dobson, neither." "Yes, and you must exert yourself beside, in insisting that your workmen send their children, and often look into the school yourself, to see if they are there, and reward or discourage them accordingly," added Mrs. Jones. "The most zealous teachers will flag in their exertions, if they are not animated and supported by the wealthy; and your poor youth will soon despise religious instruction as a thing forced upon them, as a hardship added to their other hardships, if it be not made pleasant by the encouraging presence, kind words, and little gratuities, from their betters."

Here Mrs. Jones took her leave; the farmer insisted on waiting on her to the door. When they got into the yard, they spied Mr. Simpson, who was standing near a group of females, consisting of the farmer's two young daughters, and a couple of rosy dairy-maids, an old blind fiddler, and a woman who led him. The woman had laid a basket on the ground, out of which she was dealing some songs to the girls, who were kneeling round it, and eagerly picking out such whose title suited their tastes. On seeing the clergyman come up, the fiddler's companion (for I am sorry to say she was not his wife) pushed some of the songs to the bottom of the basket, turned round to the company, and, in a whining tone, asked if they would please to buy a godly book. Mr. Simpson saw through the hypocrisy at once, and instead of making any answer, took out of one of the girls' hands a song which the woman had not been able to snatch away. He was shocked and grieved to see that these young girls were about to read, to sing, and to learn by heart such ribaldry as he was ashamed even to cast his eyes on. He turned about to the girl, and gravely, but mildly said, "Young woman, what do you think should be done to a person who should be found carrying a box of poison round the country, and leaving a little at every house?" The girls agreed that such a person ought to be hanged. "That he should," said the farmer, "if I was upon the jury, and quartered too." The fiddler and his woman were of the same opinion, declaring, they would do no such a wicked thing for the world, for if they were poor they were honest. Mr. Simpson, turning to the other girl, said, "Which is of most value, the soul or the body?" "The soul, sir," said the girl. "Why so?" said he. "Because, sir, I have heard you say in the pulpit, the soul is to last forever." "Then," cried Mr. Simpson, in a stern voice, turning to the fiddler's woman, "are you not ashamed to sell poison for that part which is to last forever? poison for the soul?" "Poison?" said the terrified girl, throwing down the book, and shuddering as people do who are afraid they have touched something infectious. "Poison!" echoed the farmer's daughters, recollecting with horror the ratsbane which Lion, the old house-dog, had got at the day before, and after eating which she had seen him drop down dead in convulsions. "Yes," said Mr. Simpson to the woman, "I do again repeat, the souls of these innocent girls will be poisoned, and may be eternally ruined by this vile trash which you carry about."

"I now see," said Mrs. Jones to the farmer, "the reason why you think learning to read does more harm than good. It is indeed far better that they should never know how to tell a letter, unless you keep such trash as this out of their way, and provide them with what is good, or at least what is harmless. Still, this is not the fault of reading, but the abuse of it. Wine is still a good cordial, though it is too often abused to the purpose of drunkenness."

The farmer said that neither of his maids could read their horn-book, though he owned he often heard them singing that song which the parson thought so bad, but for his part it made them as merry as a nightingale.

"Yes," said Mrs. Jones, "as a proof that it is not merely being able to read which does the mischief, I have often heard, as I have been crossing a hay-field, young girls singing such indecent ribaldry as has driven me out of the field, though I well knew they could not read a line of what they were singing, but had caught it from others. So you see you may as well say the memory is a wicked talent because some people misapply it, as to say that reading is dangerous because some folks abuse it."

While they were talking, the fiddler and his woman were trying to steal away unobserved, but Mr. Simpson stopped them, and sternly said, "Woman, I shall have some further talk with you. I am a magistrate as well as a minister, and if I know it, I will no more allow a wicked book to be sold in my parish than a dose of poison." The girls threw away all their songs, thanked Mr. Simpson, begged Mrs. Jones would take them into her school after they had done milking in the evenings, that they might learn to read only what was proper. They promised they would never more deal with any but sober, honest hawkers, such as sell good little books, Christmas carols, and harmless songs, and desired the fiddler's woman never to call there again.

This little incident afterward confirmed Mrs. Jones in a plan she had before some thoughts of putting in practice. This was, after her school had been established a few months, to invite all the well-disposed grown-up youth of the parish to meet her at the school an hour or two on a Sunday evening, after the necessary business of the dairy, and of serving the cattle was over. Both Mrs. Jones and her agent had the talent of making this time pass so agreeably, by their manner of explaining Scripture, and of impressing the heart by serious and affectionate discourse, that in a short time the evening-school was nearly filled with a second company, after the younger ones were dismissed. In time, not only the servants, but the sons and daughters of the most substantial people in the parish attended. At length many of the parents, pleased with the improvement so visible in the young people, got a habit of dropping in, that they might learn how to instruct their own families; and it was observed that as the school filled, not only the fives-court and public houses were thinned, but even Sunday gossiping and tea-visiting declined. Even farmer Hoskins, who was at first very angry with his maids for leaving off those merry songs (as he called them) was so pleased by the manner in which the psalms were sung at the school, that he promised Mrs. Jones to make her a present of half a sheep toward her first May-day feast. Of this feast some account shall be given hereafter; and the reader may expect some further account of the Sunday School in the history of Hester Wilmot.

THE HISTORY OF HESTER WILMOT

BEING THE SECOND PART OF THE SUNDAY SCHOOL

Hester Wilmot was born in the parish of Weston, of parents who maintained themselves by their labor; they were both of them ungodly: it is no wonder therefore they were unhappy. They lived badly together, and how could they do otherwise? for their tempers were very different, and they had no religion to smooth down this difference, or to teach them that they ought to bear with each other's faults. Rebecca Wilmot was a proof that people may have some right qualities, and yet be but bad characters, and utterly destitute of religion. She was clean, notable, and industrious. Now I know some folks fancy that the poor who have these qualities need have no other, but this is a sad mistake, as I am sure every page in the Bible would show; and it is a pity people do not consult it oftener. They direct their plowing and sowing by the information of the Almanac: why will they not consult the Bible for the direction of their hearts and lives? Rebecca was of a violent, ungovernable temper; and that very neatness which is in itself so pleasing, in her became a sin, for her affection to her husband and children was quite lost in an over anxious desire to have her house reckoned the nicest in the parish. Rebecca was also a proof that a poor woman may be as vain as a rich one, for it was not so much the comfort of neatness, as the praise of neatness, which she coveted. A spot on her hearth, or a bit of rust on a brass candlestick, would throw her into a violent passion. Now it is very right to keep the hearth clean and the candlestick bright, but it is very wrong so to set one's affections on a hearth or a candlestick, as to make one's self unhappy if any trifling accident happens to them; and if Rebecca had been as careful to keep her heart without spot, or her life without blemish, as she was to keep her fire-irons free from either, she would have been held up in this history, not as a warning, but as a pattern, and in that case her nicety would have come in for a part of the praise. It was no fault in Rebecca, but a merit, that her oak table was so bright you could almost see to put your cap on in it; but it was no merit but a fault, that when John, her husband, laid down his cup of beer upon it so as to leave a mark, she would fly out into so terrible a passion that all the children were forced to run to corners; now poor John having no corner to run to, ran to the ale-house, till that which was first a refuge too soon became a pleasure.

Rebecca never wished her children to learn to read, because she said it would make them lazy, and she herself had done very well without it. She would keep poor Hester from church to stone the space under the stairs in fine patterns and flowers. I don't pretend to say there was any harm in this little decoration, it looks pretty enough, and it is better to let the children do that than nothing. But still these are not things to set one's heart upon; and besides Rebecca only did it as a trap for praise; for she was sulky and disappointed if any ladies happened to call in and did not seem delighted with the flowers which she used to draw with a burnt stick on the whitewash of the chimney corners. Besides, all this finery was often done on a Sunday, and there is a great deal of harm in doing right things at a wrong time, or in wasting much time on things which are of no real use, or in doing any thing at all out of vanity. Now I beg that no lazy slattern of a wife will go and take any comfort in her dirt from what is here said against Rebecca's nicety; for I believe, that for one who makes her husband unhappy through neatness, twenty do so by dirt and laziness. All excuses are wrong, but the excess of a good quality is not so uncommon as the excess of a bad one; and not being so obvious, perhaps, for that very reason requires more animadversion.

John Wilmot was not an ill-natured man, but he had no fixed principle. Instead of setting himself to cure his wife's faults by mild reproof and good example, he was driven by them into still greater faults himself. It is a common case with people who have no religion, when any cross accident befalls them, instead of trying to make the best of a bad matter, instead of considering their trouble as a trial sent from God to purify them, or instead of considering the faults of others as a punishment for their own sins, instead of this I say, what do they do, but either sink down at once into despair, or else run for comfort into evil courses. Drinking is the common remedy for sorrow, if that can be called a remedy, the end of which is to destroy soul and body. John now began to spend all his leisure hours at the Bell. He used to be fond of his children: but when he could not come home in quiet, and play with the little ones, while his wife dressed him a bit of hot supper, he grew in time not to come home at all. He who has once taken to drink can seldom be said to be guilty of one sin only; John's heart became hardened. His affection for his family was lost in self-indulgence. Patience and submission on the part of the wife, might have won much upon a man of John's temper; but instead of trying to reclaim him, his wife seemed rather to delight in putting him as much in the wrong as she could, that she might be justified in her constant abuse of him. I doubt whether she would have been as much pleased with his reformation as she was with always talking of his faults, though I know it was the opinion of the neighbors, that if she had taken as much pains to reform her husband by reforming her own temper, as she did to abuse him and expose him, her endeavors might have been blessed with success. Good Christians, who are trying to subdue their own faults, can hardly believe that the ungodly have a sort of savage satisfaction in trying, by indulgence of their own evil tempers, to lessen the happiness of those with whom they have to do. Need we look any further for a proof of our own corrupt nature, when we see mankind delight in sins which have neither the temptations of profit or the allurement of pleasure, such as plaguing, vexing, or abusing each other.

Hester was the eldest of their five children; she was a sharp sensible girl, but at fourteen years old she could not tell a letter, nor had she ever been taught to bow her knee to Him who made her, for John's or rather Rebecca's house, had seldom the name of God pronounced in it, except to be blasphemed.

It was just about this time, if I mistake not, that Mrs. Jones set up her Sunday School, of which Mrs. Betty Crew was appointed mistress, as has been before related. Mrs. Jones finding that none of the Wilmots were sent to school, took a walk to Rebecca's house, and civilly told her, she called to let her know that a school was opened to which she desired her to send her children on Sunday following, especially her oldest daughter Hester. "Well," said Rebecca, "and what will you give her if I do?" "Give her!" replied Mrs. Jones, "that is rather a rude question, and asked in a rude manner: however, as a soft answer turneth away wrath, I assure you that I will give her the best of learning; I will teach her to fear God and keep his commandments." "I would rather you would teach her to fear me, and keep my house clean," said this wicked woman. "She sha'n't come, however, unless you will pay her for it." "Pay her for it!" said the lady; "will it not be reward enough that she will be taught to read the word of God without any expense to you? For though many gifts both of books and clothing will be given the children, yet you are not to consider these gifts so much in the light of payment as an expression of good will in your benefactors." "I say," interrupted Rebecca, "that Hester sha'n't go to school. Religion is of no use that I know of, but to make people hate their own flesh and blood; and I see no good in learning but to make folks proud, and lazy, and dirty. I can not tell a letter myself, and, though I say it, that should not say it, there is not a notabler woman in the parish." "Pray," said Mrs. Jones mildly, "do you think that young people will disobey their parents the more for being taught to fear God?" "I don't think any thing about it," said Rebecca; "I sha'n't let her come, and there's the long and short of the matter. Hester has other fish to fry; but you may have some of these little ones if you will." "No," said Mrs. Jones, "I will not; I have not set up a nursery, but a school. I am not at all this expense to take crying babes out of the mother's way, but to instruct reasonable beings in the road to eternal life: and it ought to be a rule in all schools not to take the troublesome young children unless the mother will try to spare the elder ones, who are capable of learning." "But," said Rebecca, "I have a young child which Hester must nurse while I dress dinner. And she must iron the rags, and scour the irons, and dig the potatoes, and fetch the water to boil them." "As to nursing the child, that is indeed a necessary duty, and Hester ought to stay at home part of the day to enable you to go to church; and families should relieve each other in this way, but as to all the rest, they are no reasons at all, for the irons need not be scoured so often, and the rags should be ironed, and the potatoes dug, and the water fetched on the Saturday; and I can tell you that neither your minister here, nor your Judge hereafter, will accept of any such excuse."

All this while Hester staid behind pale and trembling lest her unkind mother should carry her point. She looked up at Mrs. Jones with so much love and gratitude as to win her affection, and this good lady went on trying to soften this harsh mother. At last Rebecca condescended to say, "Well I don't know but I may let her come now and then when I can spare her, provided I find you make it worth her while." All this time she had never asked Mrs. Jones to sit down, nor had once bid her young children be quiet, though they were crying and squalling the whole time. Rebecca fancied this rudeness was the only way she had of showing she thought herself to be as good as her guest, but Mrs. Jones never lost her temper. The moment she went out of the house, Rebecca called out loud enough for her to hear, and ordered Hester to get the stone and a bit of sand to scrub out the prints of that dirty woman's shoes. Hester in high spirits cheerfully obeyed, and rubbed out the stains so neatly, that her mother could not help lamenting that so handy a girl was going to be spoiled, by being taught godliness, and learning any such nonsense.

Mrs. Jones, who knew the world, told her agent, Mrs. Crew, that her grand difficulty would arise not so much from the children as the parents. These, said she, are apt to fall into that sad mistake, that because their children are poor, and have little of this world's goods, the mothers must make it up to them in false indulgence. The children of the gentry are much more reproved and corrected for their faults, and bred up in far stricter discipline. He was a king who said, Chasten thy son, and let not thy rod spare for his crying. But do not lose your patience; the more vicious the children are, you must remember the more they stand in need of your instruction. When they are bad, comfort yourself with thinking how much worse they would have been but for you; and what a burden they would become to society if these evil tempers were to receive no check. The great thing which enabled Mrs. Crew to teach well, was the deep insight she had got into the corruption of human nature. And I doubt if any one can make a thoroughly good teacher of religion and morals, who wants the master-key to the heart. Others, indeed, may teach knowledge, decency, and good manners; but those, however valuable, are not Christianity. Mrs. Crew, who knew that out of the heart proceed lying, theft, and all that train of evils which begin to break out even in young children, applied her labors to correct this root of evil. But though a diligent, she was a humble teacher, well knowing that unless the grace of God blessed her labors, she should but labor in vain.

Hester Wilmot never failed to attend the school, whenever her perverse mother would give her leave, and her delight in learning was so great, that she would work early and late to gain a little time for her book. As she had a quick capacity, she learned soon to spell and read, and Mrs. Crew observing her diligence, used to lend her a book to carry home, that she might pick up a little at odd times. It would be well if teachers would make this distinction. To give, or lend books to those who take no delight in them is a useless expense; while it is kind and right to assist well-disposed young people with every help of this sort. Those who love books seldom hurt them, while the slothful who hate learning, will wear out a book more in a week, than the diligent will do in a year. Hester's way was to read over a question in her catechism, or one verse in her hymn book, by fire-light before she went to bed; this she thought over in the night: and when she was dressing herself in the morning, she was glad to find she always knew a little more than she had done the morning before. It is not to be believed how much those people will be found to have gained at the end of the year, who are accustomed to work up all the little odd ends and remnants of leisure; who value time even more than money; and who are convinced that minutes are no more to be wasted than pence. Nay, he who finds he has wasted a shilling may by diligence hope to fetch it up again: but no repentance or industry can ever bring back one wasted hour. My good young reader, if ever you are tempted to waste an hour, go and ask a dying man what he would give for that hour which you are throwing away, and according as he answers so do you act.

As her mother hated the sight of a book, Hester was forced to learn out of sight: it was no disobedience to do this, as long as she wasted no part of that time which it was her duty to spend in useful labor. She would have thought it a sin to have left her work for her book; but she did not think it wrong to steal time from her sleep, and to be learning an hour before the rest of the family were awake. Hester would not neglect the washing-tub, or the spinning-wheel, even to get on with her catechism; but she thought it fair to think over her questions while she was washing and spinning. In a few months she was able to read fluently in St. John's Gospel, which is the easiest. But Mrs. Crew did not think it enough that her children could read a chapter, she would make them understand it also. It is in a good degree owing to the want of religious knowledge in teachers, that there is so little religion in the world. Unless the Bible is laid open to the understanding, children may read from Genesis to the Revelation, without any other improvement than barely learning how to pronounce the words. Mrs. Crew found there was but one way to compel their attention; this was by obliging them to return back again to her the sense of what she had read to them, and this they might do in their own words, if they could not remember the words of Scripture. Those who had weak capacities, would, to be sure, do this but very imperfectly; but even the weakest, if they were willing would retain something. She so managed, that saying the catechism was not merely an act of the memory, but of the understanding; for she had observed formerly that those who had learned the catechism in the common formal way, when they were children, had never understood it when they became men and women, and it remained in the memory without having made any impression on the mind. Thus this fine summary of the Christian religion is considered as little more than a form of words, the being able to repeat which, is a qualification for being confirmed by the bishop, instead of being considered as really containing those grounds of Christian faith and practice, by which they are to be confirmed Christians.

Mrs. Crew used to say to Mrs. Jones, those who teach the poor must indeed give line upon line, precept upon precept, here a little and there a little, as they can receive it. So that teaching must be a great grievance to those who do not really make it a labor of love. I see so much levity, obstinacy, and ignorance, that it keeps my own forbearance in continual exercise, insomuch that I trust I am getting good myself, while I am doing good to others. No one, madam, can know till they try, that after they have asked a poor untaught child the same question nineteen times, they must not lose their temper, but go on and ask it the twentieth. Now and then, when I am tempted to be impatient, I correct myself by thinking over that active proof which our blessed Saviour requires of our love to him when he says, Feed my lambs.

Hester Wilmot had never been bred to go to church, for her father and mother had never thought of going themselves, unless at a christening in their own family, or at a funeral of their neighbors, both of which they considered merely as opportunities for good eating and drinking, and not as offices of religion.

As poor Hester had no comfort at home, it was the less wonder she delighted in her school, her Bible, and her church; for so great is God's goodness, that he is pleased to make religion a peculiar comfort to those who have no other comfort. The God whose name she had seldom heard but when it was taken in vain, was now revealed to her as a God of infinite power, justice, and holiness. What she read in her Bible, and what she felt in her own heart, convinced her she was a sinner, and her catechism said the same. She was much distressed one day on thinking over this promise which she had just made (in answer to the question which fell to her lot), To renounce the devil and all his works, the pomps and vanities of this wicked world, and all the sinful lusts of the flesh. I say she was distressed on finding that these were not merely certain words which she was bound to repeat, but certain conditions which she was bound to perform. She was sadly puzzled to know how this was to be done, till she met with these words in her Bible: My grace is sufficient for thee. But still she was at a loss to know how this grace was to be obtained. Happily Mr. Simpson preached on the next Sunday from this text, Ask and ye shall receive, etc. In this sermon was explained to her the nature, the duty, and the efficacy of prayer. After this she opened her heart to Mrs. Crew, who taught her the great doctrines of Scripture, in a serious but plain way. Hester's own heart led her to assent to that humbling doctrine of the catechism, that We are by nature born in sin; and truly glad was she to be relieved by hearing of That spiritual grace by which we have a new birth unto righteousness. Thus her mind was no sooner humbled by one part than it gained comfort from another. On the other hand, while she was rejoicing in a lively hope in God's mercy through Christ, her mistress put her in mind that that was only the true repentance by which we forsake sin. Thus the catechism, explained by a pious teacher, was found to contain all the articles of the Christian faith.

Mrs. Jones greatly disapproved the practice of turning away the scholars, because they were grown up. Young people, said she, want to be warned at sixteen more than they did at six, and they are commonly turned adrift at the very age when they want most instruction; when dangers and temptations most beset them. They are exposed to more evil by the leisure of a Sunday evening, than by the business of a whole week; but then religion must be made pleasant, and instruction must be carried on in a kind, and agreeable, and familiar way. If they once dislike the teacher, they will soon get to dislike what is taught, so that a master or mistress is in some measure answerable for the future piety of young persons, inasmuch as that piety depends on their manner of making religion pleasant as well as profitable.

To attend Mrs. Jones's evening instructions was soon thought not a task but a holiday. In a few months it was reckoned a disadvantage to the character of any young person in the parish to know that they did not attend the evening school. At first, indeed, many of them came only with a view to learn amusement; but, by the blessing of God, they grew fond of instruction, and some of them became truly pious. Mrs. Jones spoke to them on Sunday evening as follows: "My dear young women, I rejoice at your improvement; but I rejoice with trembling. I have known young people set out well, who afterward fell off. The heart is deceitful. Many like religious knowledge, who do not like the strictness of a religious life. I must therefore watch whether those who are diligent at church and school, are diligent in their daily walk. Whether those who say they believe in God, really obey him. Whether they who profess to love Christ keep His commandments. Those who hear themselves commended for early piety, may learn to rest satisfied with the praise of man. People may get a knack at religious phrases without being religious; they may even get to frequent places of worship as an amusement, in order to meet their friends, and may learn to delight in a sort of spiritual gossip, while religion has no power in their hearts. But I hope better things of you, and things that accompany salvation, though I thus speak."

What became of Hester Wilmot, with some account of Mrs. Jones's May-day feast for her school, my readers shall be told next month.

THE NEW GOWN

Hester Wilmot, I am sorry to observe, had been by nature peevish and lazy; she would, when a child, now and then slight her work, and when her mother was unreasonable she was too apt to return a saucy answer; but when she became acquainted with her own heart, and with the Scriptures, these evil tempers were, in a good measure, subdued, for she now learned to imitate, not her violent mother, but Him who was meek and lowly. When she was scolded for doing ill, she prayed for grace to do better; and the only answer she made to her mother's charge, "that religion only served to make people lazy," was to strive to do twice as much work, in order to prove that it really made them diligent. The only thing in which she ventured to disobey her mother was, that when she ordered her to do week-day's work on a Sunday, Hester cried, and said, she did not dare to disobey God; but to show that she did not wish to save her own labor, she would do a double portion of work on the Saturday night, and rise two hours earlier on Monday morning.

Once, when she had worked very hard, her mother told her that she would treat her with a holiday the following Sabbath, and take her a fine walk to eat cakes and drink ale at Weston fair, which, though it was professed to be kept on the Monday, yet, to the disgrace of the village, always began on the Sunday evening.[8] Rebecca, who would on no account have wasted the Monday, which was a working day, in idleness and pleasure, thought she had a very good right to enjoy herself at the fair on the Sunday evening, as well as to take her children. Hester earnestly begged to be left at home, and her mother, in a rage, went without her. A wet walk, and more ale than she was used to drink, gave Rebecca a dangerous fever. During this illness Hester, who would not follow her to a scene of dissolute mirth, attended her night and day, and denied herself necessaries that her sick mother might have comforts; and though she secretly prayed to God that this sickness might change her mother's heart, yet she never once reproached her, or put her in mind that it was caught by indulging in a sinful pleasure.

[8] This practice is too common. Those fairs which profess to be kept on Monday, commonly begin on the Sunday. It is much to be wished that magistrates would put a stop to it, as Mr. Simpson did at Weston, at the request of Mrs. Jones. There is another great evil worth the notice of justices. In many villages, during the fair, ale is sold at private houses, which have no license, to the great injury of sobriety and good morals.

Another Sunday night her father told Hester he thought she had now been at school long enough for him to have a little good of her learning, so he desired she would stay at home and read to him. Hester cheerfully ran and fetched her Testament. But John fell a laughing, calling her a fool, and said, it would be time enough to read the Testament to him when he was going to die, but at present he must have something merry. So saying, he gave her a songbook which he had picked up at the Bell. Hester, having cast her eyes over it, refused to read it, saying, she did not dare offend God by reading what would hurt her own soul. John called her a canting hypocrite, and said he would put the Testament into the fire, for that there was not a more merry girl than she was before she became religious. Her mother, for once, took her part; not because she thought her daughter in the right, but because she was glad of any pretense to show her husband was in the wrong; though she herself would have abused Hester for the same thing if John had taken her part. John, with a shocking oath, abused them both, and went off in a violent passion. Hester, instead of saying one undutiful word against her father, took up a Psalter in order to teach her little sisters; but Rebecca was so provoked at her for not joining her in her abuse of her husband, that she changed her humor, said John was in the right, and Hester a perverse hypocrite, who only made religion a pretense for being undutiful to her parents. Hester bore all in silence, and committed her cause to Him who judgeth righteously. It would have been a great comfort to her if she had dared to go to Mrs. Crew, and to have joined in the religious exercises of the evening at school. But her mother refused to let her, saying it would only harden her heart in mischief. Hester said not a word, but after having put the little ones to bed, and heard them say their prayers out of sight, she went and sat down in her own little loft, and said to herself, "It would be pleasant to me to have taught my little sisters to read; I thought it was my duty, for David has said, Come ye children, hearken unto me, and I will teach you the fear of the Lord. It would have been still more pleasant to have passed the evening at school, because I am still ignorant, and fitter to learn than to teach; but I can not do either without flying in the face of my mother; God sees fit to-night to change my pleasant duties into a painful trial. I give up my will, and I submit to the will of my father; but when he orders me to commit a known sin, then I dare not do it, because, in so doing, I must disobey my Father which is in heaven."

Now, it so fell out, that this dispute happened on the very Sunday next before Mrs. Jones's yearly feast. On May-day all the school attended her to church, each in a stuff gown of their own earning, and a cap and white apron of her giving. After church there was an examination made into the learning and behavior of the scholars; those who were most perfect in their chapters, and who brought the best character for industry, humility, and sobriety, received a Bible or some other good book.

Now Hester had been a whole year hoarding up her little savings, in order to be ready with a new gown on the May-day feast. She had never got less than two shillings a week by her spinning, beside working for the family, and earning a trifle by odd jobs. This money she faithfully carried to her mother every Saturday night, keeping back by consent only twopence a week toward the gown. The sum was complete, the pattern had long been settled, and Hester had only on the Monday morning to go to the shop, pay her money, and bring home her gown to be made. Her mother happened to go out early that morning to iron in a gentleman's family, where she usually staid a day or two, and Hester was busy putting the house in order before she went to the shop.

On that very Monday there was to be a meeting at the Bell of all the idle fellows in the parish. John Wilmot, of course, was to be there. Indeed he had accepted a challenge of the blacksmith to match at all-fours. The blacksmith was flush of money, John thought himself the best player; and, that he might make sure of winning, he resolved to keep himself sober, which he knew was more than the other would do. John was so used to go upon tick for ale, that he got to the door of the Bell before he recollected that he could not keep his word with the gambler without money, and he had not a penny in his pocket, so he sullenly turned homeward. He dared not apply to his wife, as he knew he should be more likely to get a scratched face than a sixpence from her; but he knew that Hester had received two shillings for her last week's spinning on Saturday, and, perhaps, she might not yet have given it to her mother. Of the hoarded sum he knew nothing. He asked her if she could lend him half a crown, and he would pay her next day. Hester, pleased to see him in a good humor after what had passed the night before, ran up and fetched down her little box, and, in the joy of her heart that he now desired something she could comply with without wounding her conscience, cheerfully poured out her whole little stock on the table. John was in raptures at the sight of three half crowns and a sixpence, and eagerly seized it, box and all, together with a few hoarded halfpence at the bottom, though he had only asked to borrow half a crown. None but one whose heart was hardened by a long course of drunkenness could have taken away the whole, and for such a purpose. He told her she should certainly have it again next morning, and, indeed, intended to pay it, not doubting but he should double the sum. But John overrated his own skill, or luck, for he lost every farthing to the blacksmith, and sneaked home before midnight, and quietly walked up to bed. He was quite sober, which Hester thought a good sign. Next morning she asked him, in a very humble way, for the money, which she said she would not have done, but that if the gown was not bought directly it would not be ready in time for the feast. John's conscience had troubled him a little for what he had done—for when he was not drunk he was not ill-natured—and he stammered out a broken excuse, but owned he had lost the money, and had not a farthing left. The moment Hester saw him mild and kind her heart was softened, and she begged him not to vex, adding, that she would be contented never to have a new gown as long as she lived, if she could have the comfort of always seeing him come home sober as he was last night. For Hester did not know that he had refrained from getting drunk, only that he might gamble with a better chance of success, and that when a gamester keeps himself sober, it is not that he may practice a virtue, but that he may commit a worse crime.

"I am indeed sorry for what I have done," said he; "you can not go to the feast, and what will Madam Jones say?" "Yes, but I can," said Hester; "for God looks not at the gown, but at the heart, and I am sure he sees mine full of gratitude at hearing you talk so kindly; and if I thought my dear father would change his present evil courses, I should be the happiest girl at the feast to-morrow." John walked away mournfully, and said to himself, "Surely there must be something in religion, since it can thus change the heart. Hester was once a pert girl, and now she is as mild as a lamb. She was once an indolent girl, and now she is up with the lark. She was a vain girl, and would do any thing for a new ribbon; and now she is contented to go in rags to a feast at which every one else is to have a new gown. She deprived herself of the gown to give me the money; and yet this very girl, so dutiful in some respects, would submit to be turned out of doors rather than read a loose book at my command, or break the Sabbath. I do not understand this; there must be some mystery in it." All this he said as he was going to work. In the evening he did not go to the Bell; whether it was owing to his new thoughts, or to his not having a penny in his pocket, I will not take upon me positively to say; but I believe it was a little of one and a little of the other.

As the pattern of the intended gown had long been settled in the family, and as Hester had the money by her, it was looked on as good as bought, so that she was trusted to get it brought home and made in her mother's absence. Indeed, so little did Rebecca care about the school, that she would not have cared any thing about the gown, if her vanity had not made her wish that her daughter should be the best dressed of any girl at the feast. Being from home, as was said before, she knew nothing of the disappointment. On May-day morning, Hester, instead of keeping from the feast because she had not a new gown, or meanly inventing any excuse for wearing an old one, dressed herself out as neatly as she could in her poor old things, and went to join the school in order to go to church. Whether Hester had formerly indulged a little pride of heart, and talked of this gown rather too much, I am not quite sure; certain it is, there was a great hue and cry made at seeing Hester Wilmot, the neatest girl, the most industrious girl in the school, come to the May-day feast in an old stuff gown, when every other girl was so creditably dressed. Indeed, I am sorry to say, there were two or three much too smart for their station, and who had dizened themselves out in very improper finery, which Mrs. Jones made them take off before her. "I mean this feast," said she, "as a reward of industry and piety, and not as a trial of skill who can be finest and outvie the rest in show. If I do not take care, my feast will become an encouragement, not to virtue, but to vanity. I am so great a friend to decency of apparel, that I even like to see you deny your appetites that you may be able to come decently dressed to the house of God. To encourage you to do this, I like to set apart this one day of innocent pleasure, against which you may be preparing all the year, by laying aside something every week toward buying a gown out of all your savings. But, let me tell you, that meekness and an humble spirit is of more value in the sight of God and good men, than the gayest cotton gown, or the brightest pink ribbon in the parish."

Mrs. Jones for all this, was as much surprised as the rest at Hester's mean garb; but such is the power of a good character, that she gave her credit for a right intention, especially as she knew the unhappy state of her family. For it was Mrs. Jones's way, (and it is not a bad way,) always to wait, and inquire into the truth before she condemned any person of good character, though appearances were against them. As we can not judge of people's motives, said she, we may, from ignorance, often condemn their best actions, and approve of their worst. It will be always time enough to judge unfavorably, and let us give others credit as long as we can, and then we in our turn, may expect a favorable judgment from others, and remember who has said, Judge not, that ye be not judged.

Hester was no more proud of what she had done for her father, than she was humbled by the meanness of her garb: and notwithstanding Betty Stiles, one of the girls whose finery had been taken away, sneered at her, Hester never offered to clear herself, by exposing her father, though she thought it right, secretly to inform Mrs. Jones of what had passed. When the examination of the girls began, Betty Stiles was asked some questions on the fourth and fifth commandments, which she answered very well. Hester was asked nearly the same questions, and though she answered them no better than Betty had done, they were all surprised to see Mrs. Jones rise up, and give a handsome Bible to Hester, while she gave nothing to Betty. This girl cried out rather pertly, "Madam, it is very hard that I have no book: I was as perfect as Hester." "I have often told you," said Mrs. Jones, "that religion is not a thing of the tongue but of the heart. That girl gives me the best proof that she has learned the fourth commandment to good purpose, who persists in keeping holy the Sabbath day, though commanded to break it, by a parent whom she loves. And that girl best proves that she keeps the fifth, who gives up her own comfort, and clothing, and credit, to honor and obey her father and mother, even though they are not such as she could wish. Betty Stiles, though she could answer the questions so readily, went abroad last Sunday when she should have been at school, and refused to nurse her sick mother, when she could not help herself. Is this having learned those two commandments to any good purpose?"

Farmer Hoskins, who stood by, whispered Mrs. Jones, "Well, madam, now you have convinced even me of the benefit of a religious instruction; now I see there is a meaning to it. I thought it was in at one ear and out at the other, and that a song was as well as a psalm, but now I have found the proof of the pudding is in the eating. I see your scholars must do what they hear, and obey what they learn. Why at this rate, they will all be better servants for being really godly, and so I will add a pudding to next year's feast."

The pleasure Hester felt in receiving a new Bible, made her forget that she had on an old gown. She walked to church in a thankful frame: but how great was her joy, when she saw, among a number of working men, her own father going into church. As she passed by him she cast on him a look of so much joy and affection that it brought tears into his eyes, especially when he compared her mean dress with that of the other girls, and thought who had been the cause of it. John, who had not been at church for some years, was deeply struck with the service. The confession with which it opens went to his heart. He felt, for the first time, that he was a miserable sinner, and that there was no health in him. He now felt compunction for sin in general, though it was only his ill-behavior to his daughter which had brought him to church. The sermon was such as to strengthen the impression which the prayers had made; and when it was over, instead of joining the ringers (for the belfry was the only part of the church John liked, because it usually led to the ale-house), he quietly walked back to his work. It was, indeed, the best day's work he ever made. He could not get out of his head the whole day, the first words he heard at church: When the wicked man turneth away from his wickedness, and doeth that which is lawful and right, he shall save his soul alive. At night, instead of going to the Bell, he went home, intending to ask Hester to forgive him; but as soon as he got to the door, he heard Rebecca scolding his daughter for having brought such a disgrace on the family as to be seen in that old rag of a gown, and insisted on knowing what she had done with her money. Hester tried to keep the secret, but her mother declared she would turn her out of doors if she did not tell the truth. Hester was at last forced to confess she had given it to her father. Unfortunately for poor John, it was at this very moment that he opened the door. The mother now divided her fury between her guilty husband and her innocent child, till from words she fell to blows. John defended his daughter and received some of the strokes intended for the poor girl. This turbulent scene partly put John's good resolution to flight, though the patience of Hester did him almost as much good as the sermon he had heard. At length the poor girl escaped up stairs, not a little bruised, and a scene of much violence passed between John and Rebecca. She declared she would not sit down to supper with such a brute, and set off to a neighbor's house, that she might have the pleasure of abusing him the longer. John, whose mind was much disturbed, went up stairs without his supper. As he was passing by Hester's little room he heard her voice, and as he concluded she was venting bitter complaints against her unnatural parents, he stopped to listen, resolved to go in and comfort her. He stopped at the door, for, by the light of the moon, he saw her kneeling by her bedside, and praying so earnestly that she did not hear him. As he made sure she could be praying for nothing but his death, what was his surprise to hear these words: "O Lord have mercy upon my dear father and mother, teach me to love them, to pray for them, and do them good; make me more dutiful and more patient, that, adorning the doctrine of God, my Saviour, I may recommend his holy religion, and my dear parents may be brought to love and fear thee, through Jesus Christ."

Poor John, who would never have been hard-hearted if he had not been a drunkard, could not stand this; he fell down on his knees, embraced his child, and begged her to teach him how to pray. He prayed himself as well as he could, and though he did not know what words to use, yet his heart was melted; he owned he was a sinner, and begged Hester to fetch the prayer-book, and read over the confession with which he had been so struck at church. This was the pleasantest order she had ever obeyed. Seeing him deeply affected with a sense of sin, she pointed out to him the Saviour of sinners; and in this manner she passed some hours with her father, which were the happiest of her life; such a night was worth a hundred cotton or even silk gowns. In the course of the week Hester read over the confession, and some other prayers to her father so often that he got them by heart, and repeated them while he was at work. She next taught him the fifty-first psalm. At length he took courage to kneel down and pray before he went to bed. From that time he bore his wife's ill-humor much better than he had ever done, and, as he knew her to be neat, and notable, and saving, he began to think, that if her temper was not quite so bad, his home might still become as pleasant a place to him as ever the Bell had been; but unless she became more tractable he did not know what to do with his long evenings after the little ones were in bed, for he began, once more, to delight in playing with them. Hester proposed that she herself should teach him to read an hour every night, and he consented. Rebecca began to storm, from the mere trick she had got of storming; but finding that he now brought home all his earnings, and that she got both his money and his company (for she had once loved him), she began to reconcile herself to this new way of life. In a few months John could read a psalm. In learning to read it he also got it by heart, and this proved a little store for private devotion, and while he was mowing or reaping, he could call to mind a text to cheer his labor. He now went constantly to church, and often dropped in at the school on a Sunday evening to hear their prayers. He expressed so much pleasure at this, that one day Hester ventured to ask him if they should set up family prayer at home? John said he should like it mightily, but as he could not yet read quite well enough, he desired Hester to try to get a proper book and begin next Sunday night. Hester had bought of a pious hawker, for three half pence,[9] the Book of Prayers, printed for the Cheap Repository, and knew she should there find something suitable.

[9] These prayers may be had also divided into two parts, one fit for private persons, the other for families, price one half-penny.

When Hester read the exhortation at the beginning of this little book, her mother who sat in the corner, and pretended to be asleep, was so much struck that she could not find a word to say against it. For a few nights, indeed, she continued to sit still, or pretended to rock the young child while her husband and daughter were kneeling at their prayers. She expected John would have scolded her for this, and so perverse was her temper, that she was disappointed at his finding no fault with her. Seeing at last that he was very patient, and that though he prayed fervently himself he suffered her to do as she liked, she lost the spirit of opposition for want of something to provoke it. As her pride began to be subdued, some little disposition to piety was awakened in her heart. By degrees she slid down on her knees, though at first it was behind the cradle, or the clock, or in some corner where she thought they would not see her. Hester rejoiced even in this outward change in her mother, and prayed that God would at last be pleased to touch her heart as he had done that of her father.

As John now spent no idle money, he had saved up a trifle by working over-hours; this he kindly offered to Hester to make up for the loss of her gown. Instead of accepting it, Hester told him, that as she herself was young and healthy, she could soon be able to clothe herself out of her own savings, and begged him to make her mother a present of this gown, which he did. It had been a maxim of Rebecca, that it was better not to go to church at all, than go in an old gown. She had, however, so far conquered this evil notion, that she had lately gone pretty often. This kindness of the gown touched her not a little, and the first Sunday she put it on, Mr. Simpson happened to preach from this text, God resisteth the proud but giveth grace to the humble. This sermon so affected Rebecca that she never once thought she had her new gown on, till she came to take it off when she went to bed, and that very night instead of skulking behind, she knelt down by her husband, and joined in prayer with much fervor.

There, was one thing sunk deep in Rebecca's mind; she had observed that since her husband had grown religious he had been so careful not to give her any offense, that he was become scrupulously clean; took off his dirty shoes before he sat down, and was very cautious not to spill a drop of beer on her shining table. Now it was rather remarkable, that as John grew more neat, Rebecca grew more indifferent to neatness. But both these changes arose from the same cause, the growth of religion in their hearts. John grew cleanly from the fear of giving pain to his wife, while Rebecca grew indifferent from having discovered the sin and folly of an over-anxious care about trifles. When the heart is once given up to God, such vanities in a good degree die of themselves.

Hester continues to grow in grace, and in knowledge. Last Christmas-day she was appointed under teacher in the school, and many people think that some years hence, if any thing should happen to Mrs. Crew, Hester may be promoted to be head mistress.

BETTY BROWN,

THE ST. GILES'S ORANGE GIRL; WITH SOME ACCOUNT OF MRS. SPONGE, THE MONEY-LENDER

Betty Brown, the orange girl, was born nobody knows where, and bred nobody knows how. No girl in all the streets of London could drive a barrow more nimbly, avoid pushing against passengers more dexterously, or cry her "fine China oranges" in a shriller voice. But then she could neither sew, nor spin, nor knit, nor wash, nor iron, nor read, nor spell. Betty had not been always in so good a situation as that in which we now describe her. She came into the world before so many good gentlemen and ladies began to concern themselves so kindly, that the poor girl might have a little learning. There was no charitable society then as there is now, to pick up poor friendless children in the streets,[10] and put them into a good house, and give them meat, and drink, and lodging, and learning, and teach them to get their bread in an honest way, into the bargain. Whereas, this now is often the case in London; blessed be God, who has ordered the bounds of our habitation, and cast our lot in such a country!

[10] The Philanthropic.

The longest thing that Betty can remember is, that she used to crawl up out of a night cellar, stroll about the streets, and pick cinders from the scavengers' carts. Among the ashes she sometimes found some ragged gauze and dirty ribands; with these she used to dizen herself out, and join the merry bands on the first of May. This was not, however, quite fair, as she did not lawfully belong either to the female dancers, who foot it gayly round the garland, or to the sooty tribe, who, on this happy holiday, forget their year's toil in Portman square, cheered by the tender bounty of her whose wit has long enlivened the most learned, and whose tastes and talents long adorned the most polished societies. Betty, however, often got a few scraps, by appearing to belong to both parties. But as she grew bigger and was not an idle girl, she always put herself in the way of doing something. She would run of errands for the footmen, or sweep the door for the maid of any house where she was known; she would run and fetch some porter, and never was once known either to sip a drop by the way, or steal the pot. Her quickness and fidelity in doing little jobs, got her into favor with a lazy cook-maid, who was too apt to give away her master's cold meat and beer, not to those who were most in want, but to those who waited upon her, and did the little things for her which she ought to have done herself.

The cook, who found Betty a dexterous girl, soon employed her to sell ends of candles, pieces of meat and cheese, the lumps of butter, or any thing else she could crib from the house. These were all carried to her friend, Mrs. Sponge, who kept a little shop, and a kind of eating-house for poor working people, not far from the Seven Dials. She also bought as well as sold, many kinds of second-hand things, and was not scrupulous to know whether what she bought was honestly come by, provided she could get it for a sixth part of what it was worth. But if the owner presumed to ask for its real value, then she had sudden qualms of conscience, instantly suspected the things were stolen, and gave herself airs of honesty, which often took in poor silly people, and gave her a sort of half reputation among the needy and ignorant, whose friend she hypocritically pretended to be.

To this artful woman Betty carried the cook's pilferings; and as Mrs. Sponge would give no great price for these in money, the cook was willing to receive payment for her eatables in Mrs. Sponge's drinkables; for she dealt in all kinds of spirits. I shall only just remark here, that one receiver, like Mrs. Sponge, makes many pilferers, who are tempted to commit these petty thieveries, by knowing how easy it is to dispose of them at such iniquitous houses.

Betty was faithful to both her employers, which is extraordinary, considering the greatness of the temptation and her utter ignorance of good and evil. One day she ventured to ask Mrs. Sponge, if she could not assist her to get into a more settled way of life. She told her that when she rose in the morning she never knew where she should lie at night, nor was she ever sure of a meal beforehand. Mrs. Sponge asked her what she thought herself fit for. Betty, with fear and trembling, said there was one trade for which she thought herself qualified, but she had not the ambition to look so high—it was far above her humble views—that was, to have a barrow, and sell fruit, as several other of Mrs. Sponge's customers did, whom she had often looked up to with envy, little expecting herself ever to attain so independent a station.

Mrs. Sponge was an artful woman. Bad as she was, she was always aiming at something of a character; this was a great help to her trade. While she watched keenly to make every thing turn to her own profit, she had a false fawning way of seeming to do all she did out of pity and kindness to the distressed; and she seldom committed an extortion, but she tried to make the persons she cheated believe themselves highly obliged to her kindness. By thus pretending to be their friend, she gained their confidence; and she grew rich herself, while they thought she was only showing favor to them. Various were the arts she had of getting rich; and the money she got by grinding the poor, she spent in the most luxurious living;

while she would haggle with her hungry customers for a farthing, she would spend pounds on the most costly delicacies for herself.

Mrs. Sponge, laying aside that haughty look and voice, well known to such as had the misfortune to be in her debt, put on the hypocritical smile and soft canting tone, which she always assumed, when she meant to flatter her superiors, or take in her dependents. "Betty," said she, "I am resolved to stand your friend. These are sad times to be sure. Money is money now. Yet I am resolved to put you in a handsome way of living. You shall have a barrow, and well furnished too." Betty could not have felt more joy or gratitude, if she had been told that she should have a coach. "O, madam," said Betty, "it is impossible. I have not a penny in the world toward helping me to set up." "I will take care of that," said Mrs. Sponge; "only you must do as I bid you. You must pay me interest for my money; and you will, of course, be glad also to pay so much every night for a nice hot supper which I get ready quite out of kindness, for a number of poor working people. This will be a great comfort for such a friendless girl as you, for my victuals and drink are the best, and my company the merriest of any in all St. Giles's." Betty thought all this only so many more favors, and curtseying to the ground, said, "To be sure, ma'am, and thank you a thousand times into the bargain. I never could hope for such a rise in life."

Mrs. Sponge knew what she was about. Betty was a lively girl, who had a knack at learning any thing; and so well looking through all her dirt and rags, that there was little doubt she would get custom. A barrow was soon provided, and five shillings put into Betty's hands. Mrs. Sponge kindly condescended to go to show her how to buy the fruit; for it was a rule with this prudent gentlewoman, and one from which she never departed, that no one should cheat but herself; and suspecting from her own heart the fraud of all other dealers, she was seldom guilty of the weakness of being imposed upon.

Betty had never possessed such a sum before. She grudged to lay it out all at once, and was ready to fancy she could live upon the capital. The crown, however, was laid out to the best advantage. Betty was carefully taught in what manner to cry her oranges; and received many useful lessons how to get off the bad with the good, and the stale with the fresh. Mrs. Sponge also lent her a few bad sixpences, for which she ordered her to bring home good ones at night. Betty stared. Mrs. Sponge said, "Betty, those who would get money, must not be too nice about trifles. Keep one of these sixpences in your hand, and if an ignorant young customer gives you a good sixpence, do you immediately slip it into your other hand, and give him the bad one, declaring that it is the very one you have just received, and be ready to swear that you have not another sixpence in the world. You must also learn how to treat different sorts of customers. To some you may put off, with safety, goods which would be quite unsaleable to others. Never offer bad fruit, Betty, to those who know better; never waste the good on those who may be put off with worse; put good oranges at top to attract the eye, and the mouldy ones under for sale."

Poor Betty had not a nice conscience, for she had never learned that grand, but simple rule of all moral obligation, Never do that to another which you would not have another do to you. She set off with her barrow, as proud and as happy as if she had been set up in the first shop in Covent Garden. Betty had a sort of natural good temper, which made her unwilling to impose, but she had no principle which told her it was sin to do so. She had such good success, that when night came, she had not an orange left. With a light heart she drove her empty barrow to Mrs. Sponge's door. She went in with a merry face, and threw down on the counter every farthing she had taken. "Betty," said Mrs. Sponge, "I have a right to it all, as it was got by my money. But I am too generous to take it. I will therefore only take a sixpence for this day's use of my five shillings. This is a most reasonable interest, and I will lend you the same sum to trade with to-morrow, and so on; you only paying me sixpence for the use of it every night, which will be a great bargain to you. You must also pay me my price every night for your supper, and you shall have an excellent lodging above stairs; so you see every thing will now be provided for you in a genteel manner, through my generosity."[11]

[11] For an authentic account of numberless frauds of this kind, see that very useful work of Mr. Colquhoun on the "Police of the Metropolis of London."

Poor Betty's gratitude blinded her so completely, that she had forgot to calculate the vast proportion which this generous benefactress was to receive out of her little gains. She thought herself a happy creature, and went in to supper with a number of others of her own class. For this supper, and for more porter and gin than she ought to have drunk, Betty was forced to pay so high that it ate up all the profits of the day, which, added to the daily interest, made Mrs. Sponge a rich return for her five shillings.

Betty was reminded again of the gentility of her new situation, as she crept up to bed in one of Mrs. Sponge's garrets, five stories high. This loft, to be sure, was small and had no window, but what it wanted in light was made up in company, as it had three beds and thrice as many lodgers. Those gentry had one night, in a drunken frolic, broken down the door, which happily had never been replaced; for since that time, the lodgers had died much seldomer of infectious distempers, than when they were close shut in. For this lodging Betty paid twice as much to her good friend as she would have done to a stranger. Thus she continued with great industry and a thriving trade, as poor as on the first day, and not a bit nearer to saving money enough to buy her even a pair of shoes, though her feet were nearly on the ground.

One day, as Betty was driving her barrow through a street near Holborn, a lady from a window called out to her that she wanted some oranges. While the servant went to fetch a plate, the lady entered into some talk with Betty, having been struck with her honest countenance and civil manner. She questioned her as to her way of life, and the profits of her trade; and Betty, who had never been so kindly treated before by so genteel a person, was very communicative. She told her little history as far as she knew it, and dwelt much on the generosity of Mrs. Sponge, in keeping her in her house, and trusting her with so large a capital as five shillings. At first it sounded like a very good-natured thing; but the lady, whose husband was one of the justices of the new police, happened to know more of Mrs. Sponge than was good, which led her to inquire still further. Betty owned, that to be sure it was not all clear profit, for that besides that the high price of the supper and bed ran away with all she got, she paid sixpence a-day for the use of the five shillings. "And how long have you done this?" said the lady. "About a year, madam."

The lady's eyes were at once opened. "My poor girl," said she, "do you know that you have already paid for that single five shillings the enormous sum of £7 10s.? I believe it is the most profitable five shillings Mrs. Sponge ever laid out." "O no, madam," said the girl, "that good gentlewoman does the same kindness to ten or twelve other poor friendless creatures like me." "Does she so?" said the lady; "then I never heard of a more lucrative trade than this woman carries on, under the mask of charity, at the expense of her poor deluded fellow-creatures."

"But, madam," said Betty, who did not comprehend this lady's arithmetic, "what can I do? I now contrive to pick up a morsel of bread without begging or stealing. Mrs. Sponge has been very good to me; and I don't see how I can help myself."

"I will tell you," said the lady; "if you will follow my advice, you may not only maintain yourself honestly but independently. Only oblige yourself to live hard for a little time, till you have saved five shillings out of your own earnings. Give up that expensive supper at night, drink only one pint of porter, and no gin at all. As soon as you have scraped together the five shillings, carry it back to your false friend; and if you are industrious, you will, at the end of the year, have saved £7 10s. If you can make a shift to live now, when you have this heavy interest to pay, judge how things will mend when your capital becomes your own. You will put some clothes on your back; and, by leaving the use of spirits, and the company in which you drink them, your health, your morals, and your condition will mend."

The lady did not talk thus to save her money. She would willingly have given the girl the five shillings; but she thought it was beginning at the wrong end. She wanted to try her. Beside, she knew there was more pleasure, as well as honor, in possessing five shillings of one's own saving, than of another's giving. Betty promised to obey. She owned she had got no good by the company or the liquor at Mrs. Sponge's. She promised that very night to begin saving the expense of the supper; and that she would not taste a drop of gin till she had the five shillings beforehand. The lady, who knew the power of good habits, was contented with this, thinking, that if the girl could abstain for a certain time, it would become easy to her. She therefore, at present, said little about the sin of drinking, and only insisted on the expense of it.

In a very few weeks Betty had saved up the five shillings. She went to carry back this money with great gratitude to Mrs. Sponge. This kind friend began to abuse her most unmercifully. She called her many hard names, not fit to repeat, for having forsaken the supper, by which she swore she herself got nothing at all; but as she had the charity to dress it for such beggarly wretches, she insisted they should pay for it, whether they eat it or not. She also brought in a heavy score for lodging, though Betty had paid for it every night, and had given notice of her intending to quit her. By all these false pretenses, she got from her, not only her own five shillings, but all the little capital with which Betty was going to set up for herself. All was not sufficient to answer her demands—she declared she would send her to prison; but while she went to call a constable, Betty contrived to make off.

With a light pocket and a heavy heart she went back to the lady; and with many tears told her sad story. The lady's husband, the justice, condescended to listen to Betty's tale. He said Mrs. Sponge had long been upon his books as a receiver of stolen goods. Betty's evidence strengthened his bad opinion of her. "This petty system of usury," said the magistrate, "may be thought trifling; but it will no longer appear so, when you reflect that if one of these female sharpers possesses a capital of seventy shillings, or £3 10s., with fourteen steady regular customers, she can realize a fixed income of one hundred guineas a year. Add to this the influence such a loan gives her over these friendless creatures, by compelling them to eat at her house, or lodge, or buy liquors, or by taking their pawns, and you will see the extent of the evil. I pity these poor victims: you, Betty, shall point out some of them to me. I will endeavor to open their eyes on their own bad management. It is not by giving to the importunate shillings and half-crowns, and turning them adrift to wait for the next accidental relief, that much good is done. It saves trouble, indeed, but that trouble being the most valuable part of charity, ought not to be spared; at least by those who have leisure as well as affluence. It is one of the greatest acts of kindness to the poor to mend their economy, and to give them right views of laying out their little money to advantage. These poor blinded creatures look no further than to be able to pay this heavy interest every night, and to obtain the same loan on the same hard terms the next day. Thus they are kept in poverty and bondage all their lives; but I hope as many as hear of this will go on a better plan, and I shall be ready to help any who are willing to help themselves." This worthy magistrate went directly to Mrs. Sponge's with proper officers; and he soon got to the bottom of many iniquities. He not only made her refund poor Betty's money, but committed her to prison for receiving stolen goods, and various other offenses, which may, perhaps, make the subject of another history.

Betty was now set up in trade to her heart's content. She had found the benefit of leaving off spirits, and she resolved to drink them no more. The first fruits of this resolution was, that in a fortnight she bought her a pair of new shoes; and as there was now no deduction for interest, or for gin, her earnings became considerable. The lady made her a present of a gown and a hat, on the easy condition that she should go to church. She accepted the terms, at first rather as an act of obedience to the lady than from a sense of higher duty. But she soon began to go from a better motive. This constant attendance at church, joined to the instructions of the lady, opened a new world to Betty. She now heard, for the first time, that she was a sinner; that God had given a law which was holy, just, and good; that she had broken this law, had been a swearer, a Sabbath-breaker, and had lived without God in the world. All this was sad news to Betty; she knew, indeed, before, that there were sinners, but she thought they were only to be found in the prisons, or at Botany Bay, or in those mournful carts which she had sometimes followed with her barrow, with the unthinking crowd, to Tyburn. She was deeply struck with the great truths revealed in the Scripture, which were quite new to her; her heart smote her, and she became anxious to flee from the wrath to come. She was desirous of improvement, and said, "she would give up all the profits of her barrow, and go into the hardest service, rather than live in sin and ignorance."

"Betty," said the lady, "I am glad to see you so well disposed, and will do what I can for you. Your present way of life, to be sure, exposes you to much danger; but the trade is not unlawful in itself, and we may please God in any calling, provided it be not a dishonest one. In this great town there must be barrow-women to sell fruit. Do you, then, instead of forsaking your business, set a good example to those in it, and show them, that though a dangerous trade, it need not be a wicked one. Till Providence points out some safer way of getting your bread, let your companions see that it is possible to be good even in this. Your trade being carried on in the open street, and your fruit bought in an open shop, you are not so much obliged to keep sinful company as may be thought. Take a garret in an honest house, to which you may go home in safety at night. I will give you a bed, and a few necessaries to furnish your room; and I will also give you a constant Sunday's dinner. A barrow-woman, blessed be God and our good laws, is as much her own mistress on Sundays as a duchess; and the church and the Bible are as much open to her. You may soon learn as much of religion as you are expected to know. A barrow-woman may pray as heartily morning and night, and serve God as acceptably all day, while she is carrying on her little trade, as if she had her whole time to spare.

"To do this well, you must mind the following

RULES FOR RETAIL DEALERS.

"Resist every temptation to cheat.
"Never impose bad goods on false pretenses.
"Never put off bad money for good.
"Never use profane or uncivil language.

"Never swear your goods cost so much, when you know it is false. By so doing you are guilty of two sins in one breath, a lie and an oath.

"To break these rules will be your chief temptation. God will mark how you behave under them, and will reward or punish you accordingly. These temptations will be as great to you, as higher trials are to higher people; but you have the same God to look to for strength to resist them as they have. You must pray to him to give you this strength. You shall attend a Sunday School, where you will be taught these good things; and I will promote you as you shall be found to deserve."

Poor Betty here burst into tears of joy and gratitude, crying out, "What! shall such a poor friendless creature as I be treated so kindly, and learn to read the word of God too? Oh, madam, what a lucky chance brought me to your door." "Betty," said the lady, "what you have just said shows the need you have of being better taught; there is no such thing as chance; and we offend God when we call that luck or chance which is brought about by his will or pleasure. None of the events of your life have happened by chance; but all have been under the direction of a good and kind Providence. He has permitted you to experience want and distress, that you might acknowledge his hand in your present comfort and prosperity. Above all, you must bless his goodness in sending you to me, not only because I have been of use to you in your worldly affairs, but because he has enabled me to show you the danger of your state from sin and ignorance, and to put you in a way to know his will and to keep his commandments, which is eternal life."

How Betty, by industry and piety, rose in the world, till at length she came to keep that handsome sausage shop near the Seven Dials, and was married to that very hackney-coachman, whose history and honest character may be learned from that ballad of the Cheap Repository which bears his name, may be shown hereafter.

BLACK GILES THE POACHER

CONTAINING SOME ACCOUNT OF A FAMILY WHO HAD RATHER LIVE BY THEIR WITS THAN THEIR WORK

PART I

Poaching Giles lives on the borders of those great moors in Somersetshire. Giles, to be sure, has been a sad fellow in his time; and it is none of his fault if his whole family do not end their career, either at the gallows or Botany Bay. He lives at that mud cottage with the broken windows, stuffed with dirty rags, just beyond the gate which divides the upper from the lower moor. You may know the house at a good distance by the ragged tiles on the roof, and the loose stones which are ready to drop out from the chimney; though a short ladder, a hod of mortar, and half an hour's leisure time, would have prevented all this, and made the little dwelling tight enough. But as Giles had never learned any thing that was good, so he did not know the value of such useful sayings, as, that "a tile in time saves nine."

Besides this, Giles fell into that common mistake, that a beggarly looking cottage, and filthy ragged children, raised most compassion, and of course drew most charity. But as cunning as he was in other things, he was out in his reckoning here; for it is neatness, housewifery, and a decent appearance, which draw the kindness of the rich and charitable while they turn away disgusted from filth and laziness; not out of pride, but because they see that it is next to impossible to mend the condition of those who degrade themselves by dirt and sloth; and few people care to help those who will not help themselves.

The common on which Giles's hovel stands, is quite a deep marsh in a wet winter: but in summer it looks green and pretty enough. To be sure it would be rather convenient when one passes that way in a carriage, if one of the children would run out and open the gate; but instead of any one of them running out as soon as they heard the wheels, which would be quite time enough, what does Giles do, but set all his ragged brats, with dirty faces, matted locks, and naked feet and legs, to lie all day upon a sand bank hard by the gate, waiting for the slender chance of what may be picked up from travelers. At the sound of a carriage, a whole covey of these little scare-crows start up, rush to the gate, and all at once thrust out their hats and aprons; and for fear this, together with the noise of their clamorous begging, should not sufficiently frighten the horses, they are very apt to let the gate slap full against you, before you are half way through, in their eager scuffle to snatch from each other the halfpence which you have thrown out to them. I know two ladies who were one day very near being killed by these abominable tricks.

Thus five or six little idle creatures, who might be earning a trifle by knitting at home, who might be useful to the public by working in the field, and who might assist their families by learning to get their bread twenty honest ways, are suffered to lie about all day, in the hope of a few chance halfpence, which, after all, they are by no means sure of getting. Indeed, when the neighboring gentlemen found out that opening the gate was a family trade, they soon left off giving any thing. And I myself, though I used to take out a penny ready to give, had there been only one to receive it, when I see a whole family established in so beggarly a trade, quietly put it back again in my pocket, and give nothing at all. And so few travelers pass that way, that sometimes after the whole family have lost a day, their gains do not amount to two-pence.

As Giles had a far greater taste for living by his wits than his work, he was at one time in hopes that his children might have got a pretty penny by tumbling for the diversion of travelers, and he set about training them in that indecent practice; but unluckily the moors being level, the carriage traveled faster than the children tumbled. He envied those parents who lived on the London road, over the Wiltshire downs, which downs being very hilly, it enables the tumbler to keep pace with the traveler, till he sometimes extorts from the light and unthinking, a reward instead of a reproof. I beg leave, however, to put all gentlemen and ladies in mind, that such tricks are a kind of apprenticeship to the trades of begging and thieving; and that nothing is more injurious to good morals than to encourage the poor in any habits which may lead them to live upon chance.

Giles, to be sure, as his children grew older, began to train them to such other employments as the idle habits they had learned at the gate very properly qualified them for. The right of common, which some of the poor cottagers have in that part of the country, and which is doubtless a considerable advantage to many, was converted by Giles into the means of corrupting his whole family; for his children, as soon as they grew too big for the trade of begging at the gate, were promoted to the dignity of thieves on the moor. Here he kept two or three asses, miserable beings, which if they had the good fortune to escape an untimely death by starving, did not fail to meet with it by beating. Some of the biggest boys were sent out with these lean and galled animals to carry sand or coals about the neighboring towns. Both sand and coals were often stolen before they got them to sell; or if not, they always took care to cheat in selling them. By long practice in this art, they grew so dexterous, that they could give a pretty good guess how large a coal they could crib out of every bag before the buyer would be likely to miss it.

All their odd time was taken up under the pretense of watching their asses on the moor, or running after five or six half-starved geese: but the truth is these boys were only watching for an opportunity to steal an old goose of their neighbor's, while they pretended to look after their own. They used also to pluck the quills or the down from these live creatures, or half milk a cow before the farmer's maid came with her pail. They all knew how to calculate to a minute what time to be down in a morning to let out their lank hungry beasts, which they had turned over night into the farmer's field to steal a little good pasture. They contrived to get there just time enough to escape being caught replacing the stakes they had pulled out for the cattle to get over. For Giles was a prudent long-headed fellow; and whenever he stole food for his colts, took care never to steal stakes from the hedges at the same place. He had sense enough to know that the gain did not make up for the danger; he knew that a loose fagot, pulled from a neighbor's pile of wood after the family were gone to bed, answered the end better, and was not half the trouble.

Among the many trades which Giles professed, he sometimes practiced that of a rat-catcher; but he was addicted to so many tricks, that he never followed the same trade long; for detection will, sooner or later, follow the best concerted villany. Whenever he was sent for to a farm house, his custom was to kill a few of the old rats, always taking care to leave a little stock of young ones alive, sufficient to keep up the breed; "for," said he, "if I were to be such a fool as to clear a house or a barn at once, how would my trade be carried on?" And where any barn was overstocked, he used to borrow a few rats from thence, just to people a neighboring granary which had none; and he might have gone on till now, had he not unluckily been caught one evening emptying his cage of rats under parson Wilson's barn door.

This worthy minister, Mr. Wilson, used to pity the neglected children of Giles, as much as he blamed the wicked parents. He one day picked up Dick, who was far the best of Giles's bad boys. Dick was loitering about in a field behind the parson's garden in search of a hen's nest, his mother having ordered him to bring home a few eggs that night, by hook or by crook, as Giles was resolved to have some pan-cakes for supper, though he knew that eggs were a penny a-piece. Mr. Wilson had long been desirous of snatching some of this vagrant family from ruin; and his chief hopes were bent on Dick, as the least hackneyed in knavery. He had once given him a new pair of shoes, on his promising to go to school next Sunday; but no sooner had Rachel, the boy's mother, got the shoes into her clutches, than she pawned them for a bottle of gin; and ordered the boy to keep out of the parson's sight, and to be sure to play his marbles on Sunday for the future, at the other end of the parish, and not near the churchyard. Mr. Wilson, however, picked up the boy once more, for it was not his way to despair of any body. Dick was just going to take to his heels, as usual, for fear the old story of the shoes should be brought forward; but finding he could not get off, what does he do but run into a little puddle of muddy water which lay between him and the parson, that the sight of his naked feet might not bring on the dreaded subject. Now it happened that Mr. Wilson was planting a little field of beans, so he thought this a good opportunity to employ Dick, and he told him he had got some pretty easy work for him. Dick did as he was bid; he willingly went to work, and readily began to plant his beans with dispatch and regularity according to the directions given him.

While the boy was busily at work by himself, Giles happened to come by, having been skulking round the back way to look over the parson's garden wall, to see if there was any thing worth climbing over for on the ensuing night. He spied Dick, and began to scold him for working for the stingy old parson, for Giles had a natural antipathy to whatever belonged to the church. "What has he promised thee a day?" said he; "little enough, I dare say." "He is not to pay me by the day," said Dick, "but says he will give me so much when I have planted this peck, and so much for the next." "Oh, oh! that alters the case," said Giles. "One may, indeed, get a trifle by this sort of work. I hate your regular day-jobs, where one can't well avoid doing one's work for one's money. Come, give me a handful of beans, I will teach thee how to plant when thou art paid for planting by the peck. All we have to do in that case is to dispatch the work as fast as we can, and get rid of the beans with all speed; and as to the seed coming up or not, that is no business of ours; we are paid for planting, not for growing. At the rate thou goest on thou wouldst not get six-pence to night. Come along, bury away." So saying he took his hatful of the seed, and where Dick had been ordered to set one bean, Giles buried a dozen; of course the beans were soon out. But though the peck was emptied, the ground was unplanted. But cunning Giles knew this could not be found out till the time when the beans might be expected to come up, "and then, Dick," says he "the snails and the mice may go shares in the blame, or we can lay the fault on the rooks or the black-birds." So saying, he sent the boy into the parsonage to receive his pay, taking care to secure about a quarter of the peck of beans for his own colt. He put both bag and beans into his own pocket to carry home, bidding Dick tell Mr. Wilson that he had planted the beans and lost the bag.

In the meantime Giles's other boys were busy in emptying the ponds and trout-streams in the neighboring manor. They would steal away the carp and tench when they were no bigger than gudgeons. By this untimely depredation they plundered the owner of his property, without enriching themselves. But the pleasure of mischief was reward enough. These, and a hundred other little thieveries, they committed with such dexterity, that old Tim Crib, whose son was transported last assizes for sheep stealing, used to be often reproaching his boys that Giles's sons were worth a hundred of such blockheads as he had; for scarce a night passed but Giles had some little comfortable thing for supper which his boys had pilfered in the day, while his undutiful dogs never stole any thing worth having. Giles, in the meantime, was busy in his way, but as busy as he was in laying his nets, starting coveys, and training dogs, he always took care that his depredations should not be confined merely to game.

Giles's boys had never seen the inside of a church since they were christened, and the father thought he knew his own interest better than to force them to it; for church-time was the season of their harvest. Then the hen's nests were searched, a stray duck was clapped under the smock-frock, the tools which might have been left by chance in a farm-yard were picked up, and all the neighboring pigeon-houses were thinned, so that Giles used to boast to tawny Rachel, his wife, that Sunday was to them the most profitable day in the week. With her it was certainly the most laborious day, as she always did her washing and ironing on the Sunday morning, it being, as she said, the only leisure day she had, for on the other days she went about the country telling fortunes, and selling dream-books and wicked songs. Neither her husband's nor her children's clothes were ever mended, and if Sunday, her idle day, had not come about once in every week, it is likely they would never have been washed neither. You might however see her as you were going to church smoothing her own rags on her best red cloak, which she always used for her ironing-cloth on Sundays, for her cloak when she traveled, and for her blanket at night; such a wretched manager was Rachel! Among her other articles of trade, one was to make and sell peppermint, and other distilled waters. These she had the cheap art of making without trouble and without expense, for she made them without herbs and without a still. Her way was, to fill so many quart bottles with plain water, putting a spoonful of mint water in the mouth of each; these she corked down with rosin, carrying to each customer a phial of real distilled water to taste by way of sample. This was so good that her bottles were commonly bought up without being opened; but if any suspicion arose, and she was forced to uncork a bottle, by the few drops of distilled water lying at top she even then escaped detection, and took care to get out of reach before the bottle was opened a second time. She was too prudent ever to go twice to the same house.

THE UPRIGHT MAGISTRATE

There is hardly any petty mischief that is not connected with the life of a poacher. Mr. Wilson was aware of this; he was not only a pious clergyman, but an upright justice. He used to say, that people who were really conscientious, must be so in small things as well as in great ones, or they would destroy the effect of their own precept, and their example would not be of general use. For this reason he never would accept of a hare or a partridge from any unqualified person in the parish: he did not content himself with shuffling the thing off by asking questions, and pretending to take it for granted in a general way that the game was fairly come at; but he used to say, that by receiving the booty he connived at a crime, made himself a sharer in it; and if he gave a present to the man who brought it, he even tempted him to repeat the fault.

One day poor Jack Weston, an honest fellow in the neighborhood, whom Mr. Wilson had kindly visited and relieved in a long sickness, from which he was but just recovered, was brought before him as he was sitting on the justice's bench; Jack was accused of having knocked down a hare; and of all the birds in the air, who should the informer be but black Giles the poacher? Mr. Wilson was grieved at the charge; he had a great regard for Jack, but he had still a greater regard for the law. The poor fellow pleaded guilty. He did not deny the fact, but said he did not consider it as a crime, for he did not think game was private property, and he owned he had a strong temptation for doing what he had done, which he hoped would plead his excuse. The justice desired to know what this temptation was. "Sir," said the poor fellow, "you know I was given over this spring in a bad fever. I had no friend in the world but you, sir. Under God you saved my life by your charitable relief; and I trust also you may have helped to save my soul by your prayers and your good advice; for, by the grace of God, I have turned over a new leaf since that sickness.

"I know I can never make you amends for all your goodness, but I thought it would be some comfort to my full heart if I could but once give you some little token of my gratitude. So I had trained a pair of nice turtle doves for Madam Wilson, but they were stolen from me, sir, and I do suspect black Giles stole them. Yesterday morning, sir, as I was crawling out to my work, for I am still but very weak, a fine hare ran across my path. I did not stay to consider whether it was wrong to kill a hare, but I felt it was right to show my gratitude; so, sir, without a moment's thought I did knock down the hare, which I was going to carry to your worship, because I knew madam was fond of hare. I am truly sorry for my fault, and will submit to whatever punishment your worship may please to inflict."

Mr. Wilson was much moved with this honest confession, and touched with the poor fellow's gratitude. What added to the effect of the story, was the weak condition, and pale sickly looks of the offender. But this worthy magistrate never suffered his feelings to bias his integrity; he knew that he did not sit on that bench to indulge pity, but to administer justice; and while he was sorry for the offender, he would never justify the offense. "John," said he, "I am surprised that you could for a moment forget that I never accept any gift which causes the giver to break a law. On Sunday I teach you from the pulpit the laws of God, whose minister I am. At present I fill the chair of a magistrate, to enforce and execute the laws of the land. Between those and the other there is more connection than you are aware. I thank you, John, for your affection to me, and I admire your gratitude; but I must not allow either affection or gratitude to be brought as a plea for a wrong action. It is not your business nor mine, John, to settle whether the game laws are good or bad. Till they are repealed we must obey them. Many, I doubt not, break these laws through ignorance, and many, I am certain, who would not dare to steal a goose or a turkey, make no scruple of knocking down a hare or a partridge. You will hereafter think yourself happy that this your first attempt has proved unsuccessful, as I trust you are too honest a fellow ever to intend to turn poacher. With poaching much moral evil is connected; a habit of nightly depredation; a custom of prowling in the dark for prey produces in time a disrelish for honest labor. He whose first offense was committed without much thought or evil intention, if he happens to succeed a few times in carrying off his booty undiscovered, grows bolder and bolder: and when he fancies there is no shame attending it, he very soon gets to persuade himself that there is also no sin. While some people pretend a scruple about stealing a sheep, they partly live by plundering of warrens. But remember that the warrener pays a high rent, and that therefore his rabbits are as much his property as his sheep. Do not then deceive yourselves with these false distinctions. All property is sacred, and as the laws of the land are intended to fence in that property, he who brings up his children to break down any of these fences, brings them up to certain sin and ruin. He who begins with robbing orchards, rabbit-warrens, and fish-ponds, will probably end with horse-stealing or highway robbery. Poaching is a regular apprenticeship to bolder crimes. He whom I may commit as a boy to sit in the stocks for killing a partridge, may be likely to end at the galleys for killing a man.

"Observe, you who now hear me, the strictness and impartiality of justice. I know Giles to be a worthless fellow, yet it is my duty to take his information; I know Jack Weston to be an honest youth, yet I must be obliged to make him pay the penalty. Giles is a bad man, but he can prove this fact; Jack is a worthy lad, but he has committed this fault. I am sorry for you, Jack; but do not let it grieve you that Giles has played worse tricks a hundred times, and yet got off, while you were detected in the very first offense, for that would be grieving because you are not as great a rogue as Giles. At this moment you think your good luck is very unequal; but all this will one day turn out in your favor. Giles it not the more a favorite of heaven because he has hitherto escaped Botany Bay, or the hulks; nor is it any mark of God's displeasure against you, John, that you were found out in your very first attempt."

Here the good justice left off speaking, and no one could contradict the truth of what he had said. Weston humbly submitted to his sentence, but he was very poor, and knew not where to raise the money to pay his fine. His character had always been so fair, that several farmers present kindly agreed to advance a trifle each to prevent his being sent to prison, and he thankfully promised to work out the debt. The justice himself, though he could not soften the law, yet showed Weston so much kindness that he was enabled before the year was out, to get out of this difficulty. He began to think more seriously than he had ever yet done, and grew to abhor poaching, not merely from fear, but from principle.

We shall soon see whether poaching Giles always got off so successfully. Here we have seen that worldly prosperity is no sure sign of goodness. Next month we may, perhaps, see that the "triumph of the wicked is short;" for I then promise to give the second part of the Poacher, together with the entertaining story of the Widow Brown's Apple-tree.

PART II

HISTORY OF WIDOW BROWN'S APPLE-TREE

I think my readers got so well acquainted last month with black Giles the poacher, that they will not expect this month to hear any great good, either of Giles himself, his wife Rachel, or any of their family. I am sorry to expose their tricks, but it is their fault, not mine. If I pretend to speak about people at all, I must tell the truth. I am sure, if folks would but turn about and mend, it would be a thousand times pleasanter to me to write their histories; for it is no comfort to tell of any body's faults. If the world would but grow good, I should be glad enough to publish it: but till it really becomes so, I must go on describing it as it is; otherwise, I should only mislead my readers, instead of instructing them. It is the duty of a faithful historian to relate the evil with the good.

As to Giles and his boys, I am sure old Widow Brown has good reason to remember their dexterity. Poor woman! she had a fine little bed of onions in her neat and well-kept garden; she was very fond of her onions, and many a rheumatism has she caught by kneeling down to weed them in a damp day, notwithstanding the little flannel cloak and the bit of an old mat which Madam Wilson gave her, because the old woman would needs weed in wet weather. Her onions she always carefully treasured up for her winter's store; for an onion makes a little broth very relishing, and is indeed the only savory thing poor people are used to get. She had also a small orchard, containing about a dozen apple-trees, with which in a good year she had been known to make a couple of barrels of cider, which she sold to her landlord toward paying her rent, besides having a little keg which she was able to keep back for her own drinking. Well! would you believe it, Giles and his boys marked both onions and apples for their own; indeed, a man who stole so many rabbits from the warrener, was likely enough to steal onions for sauce. One day, when the widow was abroad on a little business, Giles and his boys made a clear riddance of the onion bed; and when they had pulled up every single onion, they then turned a couple of pigs into the garden, who, allured by the smell, tore up the bed in such a manner, that the widow, when she came home, had not the least doubt but the pigs had been the thieves. To confirm this opinion, they took care to leave the latch half open at one end of the garden, and to break down a slight fence at the other end.

I wonder how any body can find in his heart not to pity and respect poor old widows. There is something so forlorn and helpless in their condition, that methinks it is a call on every body, men, women, and children, to do them all the kind services that fall in their way. Surely their having no one to take their part, is an additional reason for kind-hearted people not to hurt and oppress them. But it was this very reason which led Giles to do this woman an injury. With what a touching simplicity is it recorded in Scripture, of the youth whom our blessed Saviour raised from the dead, that he was the only son of his mother, and she was a widow!

It happened unluckily for poor Widow Brown that her cottage stood quite alone. On several mornings together (for roguery gets up much earlier than industry) Giles and his boys stole regularly into her orchard, followed by their jack-asses. She was so deaf that she could not hear the asses if they had brayed ever so loud, and to this Giles trusted; for he was very cautious in his rogueries, since he could not otherwise have contrived so long to keep out of prison; for, though he was almost always suspected, he had seldom been taken up, and never convicted. The boys used to fill their bags, load their asses, and then march off; and if, in their way to the town where the apples were to be sold, they chanced to pass by one of their neighbors who might be likely to suspect them, they then all at once began to scream out, "Buy my coal! Buy my sand!"

Besides the trees in her orchard, poor Widow Brown had in her small garden one apple-tree particularly fine; it was a red streak, so tempting and so lovely, that Giles's family had watched it with longing eyes, till at last they resolved on a plan for carrying off all this fine fruit in their bags. But it was a nice point to manage. The tree stood directly under her chamber window, so that there was some danger that she might spy them at the work. They, therefore, determined to wait till the next Sunday morning when they knew she would not fail to be at church. Sunday came, and during service Giles attended. It was a lone house, as I said before, and the rest of the parish were safe at church. In a trice the tree was cleared, the bags were filled, the asses were whipped, the thieves were off, the coast was clear, and all was safe and quiet by the time the sermon was over.

Unluckily, however, it happened that this tree was so beautiful, and the fruit so fine, that the people, as they used to pass to and from the church, were very apt to stop and admire Widow Brown's red-streaks; and some of the farmers rather envied her that in that scarce season, when they hardly expected to make a pie out of a large orchard, she was likely to make a cask of cider from a single tree. I am afraid, indeed, if I must speak out, she herself rather set her heart too much upon this fruit, and had felt as much pride in her tree as gratitude to a good Providence for it; but this failing of hers was no excuse for Giles. The covetousness of this thief had for once got the better of his caution; the tree was too completely stripped, though the youngest boy, Dick, did beg hard that his father would leave the poor old woman enough for a few dumplings; and when Giles ordered Dick, in his turn, to shake the tree, the boy did it so gently that hardly any apples fell, for which he got a good stroke of the stick with which the old man was beating down the apples.

The neighbors, on their return from church, stopped as usual, but it was not, alas! to admire the apples, for apples there were none left, but to lament the robbery, and console the widow. Mean time the red-streaks were safely lodged in Giles's hovel under a few bundles of new hay which he had contrived to pull from a farmer's mow the night before for the use of his jack-asses. Such a stir, however, began to be made about the widow's apple-tree, that Giles, who knew how much his character had laid him open to suspicion, as soon as he saw the people safe in church again in the afternoon, ordered his boys to carry each a hatful of the apples and thrust them in a little casement window which happened to be open in the house of Samuel Price, a very honest carpenter in that parish, who was at church with his whole family. Giles's plan, by this contrivance, was to lay the theft on Price's sons in case the thing should come to be further inquired into. Here Dick put in a word, and begged and prayed his father not to force them to carry the apples to Price's. But all he got by his begging was such a knock as had nearly laid him on the earth. "What, you cowardly rascal," said Giles, "you will go and 'peach, I suppose, and get your father sent to jail."

Poor Widow Brown, though her trouble had made her still weaker than she was, went to church again in the afternoon; indeed she rightly thought that her being in trouble was a new reason why she ought to go. During the service she tried with all her might not to think of her red-streaks, and whenever they would come into her head, she took up her prayer-book directly, and so she forgot them a little; and, indeed, she found herself much easier when she came out of the church than when she went in; an effect so commonly produced by prayer, that methinks it is a pity people do not try it oftener. Now it happened, oddly enough, that on that Sunday, of all the Sundays in the year, the widow should call in to rest a little at Samuel Price's, to tell over again the lamentable story of the apples, and to consult with him how the thief might be brought to justice. But oh, reader! guess, if you can, for I am sure I can not tell you, what was her surprise, when, on going into Samuel Price's kitchen, she saw her own red-streaks lying on the window! The apples were of a sort too remarkable, for color, shape, and size, to be mistaken. There was not such another tree in the parish. Widow Brown immediately screamed out, "Alas-a-day! as sure as can be, here are my red-streaks; I could swear to them in any court." Samuel Price, who believed his sons to be as honest as himself, was shocked and troubled at the sight. He knew he had no red-streaks of his own, he knew there were no apples in the window when he went to church; he did verily believe these apples to be the widow's. But how came they there he could not possibly guess. He called for Tom, the only one of his sons who now lived at home. Tom was at the Sunday School, which he had never once missed since Mr. Wilson, the minister, had set up one in the parish. Was such a boy likely to do such a deed?

A crowd was by this time got about Price's door, among which were Giles and his boys, who had already taken care to spread the news that Tom Price was the thief. Most people were unwilling to believe it. His character was very good, but appearances were strongly against him. Mr. Wilson, who had staid to christen a child, now came in. He was much concerned that Tom Price, the best boy in his school, should stand accused of such a crime. He sent for the boy, examined, and cross-examined him. No marks of guilt appeared. But still, though he pleaded not guilty, there lay the red-streaks in his father's window. All the idle fellows in the place, who were most likely to have committed such a theft themselves, were the very people who fell with vengeance on poor Tom. The wicked seldom give any quarter. "This is one of your sanctified ones!" cried they. "This was all the good that Sunday School did!" For their parts they never saw any good come by religion. Sunday was the only day for a little pastime, and if poor boys must be shut up with their godly books, when they ought to be out taking a little pleasure, it was no wonder they made themselves amends by such tricks. Another said he would like to see Parson Wilson's righteous one well whipped. A third hoped he would be clapped in the stocks for a young hypocrite as he was; while old Giles, who thought the only way to avoid suspicion was by being more violent than the rest, declared, "that he hoped the young dog would be transported for life."

Mr. Wilson was too wise and too just to proceed against Tom without full proof. He declared the crime was a very heavy one, and he feared that heavy must be the punishment. Tom, who knew his own innocence, earnestly prayed to God that it might be made to appear as clear as the noon-day; and very fervent were his secret devotions on that night.

Black Giles passed his night in a very different manner. He set off, as soon as it was dark, with his sons and their jack-asses, laden with their stolen goods. As such a cry was raised about the apples, he did not think it safe to keep them longer at home, but resolved to go and sell them at the next town, borrowing, without leave, a lame colt out of the moor to assist in carrying off his booty.

Giles and his eldest sons had rare sport all the way in, thinking that, while they were enjoying the profit of their plunder, Tom Price would be whipped round the marketplace at least, if not sent beyond sea. But the younger boy, Dick, who had naturally a tender heart, though hardened by his long familiarity with sin, could not help crying when he thought that Tom Price might, perhaps, be transported for a crime which he himself had helped to commit. He had had no compunction about the robbery, for he had not been instructed in the great principles of truth and justice; nor would he therefore, perhaps, have had much remorse about accusing an innocent boy. But though utterly devoid of principle, he had some remains of natural feeling and of gratitude. Tom Price had often given him a bit of his own bread and cheese; and once, when Dick was like to be drowned, Tom had jumped into the pond with his clothes on, and saved his life when he was just sinking; the remembrance of all this made his heart heavy. He said nothing; but as he trotted barefoot after the asses, he heard his father and brothers laugh at having outwitted the godly ones; and he grieved to think how poor Tom would suffer for his wickedness, yet fear kept him silent; they called him a sulky dog, and lashed the asses till they bled.

In the mean time Tom Price kept up his spirits as well as he could. He worked hard all day, and prayed heartily night and morning. "It is true," said he to himself, "I am not guilty of this sin; but let this accusation set me on examining myself, and truly repenting of all my other sins; for I find enough to repent of, though, I thank God, I did not steal the widow's apples."

At length Sunday came, and Tom went to school as usual. As soon as he walked in there was a great deal of whispering and laughing among the worst of the boys; and he overheard them say, "Who would have thought it! This is master's favorite! This is Parson Wilson's sober Tommy! We sha'n't have Tommy thrown in our teeth again if we go to get a bird's nest, or gather a few nuts on a Sunday." "Your demure ones are always hypocrites," says another. "The still sow sucks all the milk," says a third.

Giles's family had always kept clear of the school. Dick, indeed, had sometimes wished to go; not that he had much sense of sin, or desire after goodness, but he thought if he could once read, he might rise in the world, and not be forced to drive asses all his life. Through this whole Saturday night he could not sleep. He longed to know what would be done to Tom. He began to wish to go to school, but he had not courage—sin is very cowardly. So on the Sunday morning he went and sat himself down under the church wall. Mr. Wilson passed by. It was not his way to reject the most wicked, till he had tried every means to bring them over, and even then he pitied and prayed for them. He had, indeed, long left off talking to Giles's sons; but seeing Dick sitting by himself, he once more spoke to him, desired him to leave off his vagabond life, and go with him into the school. The boy hung down his head, but made no answer. He did not, however, either rise up and run away, or look sulky, as he used to do. The minister desired him once more to go. "Sir," said the boy, "I can't go; I am so big I am ashamed." "The bigger you are the less time you have to lose." "But, sir, I can't read." "Then it is high time you should learn." "I should be ashamed to begin to learn my letters." "The shame is not in beginning to learn them, but in being content never to know them." "But, sir, I am so ragged!" "God looks at the heart, and not at the coat." "But, sir, I have no shoes and stockings." "So much the worse. I remember who gave you both. (Here Dick colored.) It is bad to want shoes and stockings, but still if you can drive your asses a dozen miles without them, you may certainly walk a hundred yards to school without them." "But, sir, the good boys will hate me, and won't speak to me." "Good boys hate nobody, and as to not speaking to you, to be sure they will not keep your company while you go on in your present evil courses; but as soon as they see you wish to reform, they will help you, and pity you, and teach you; and so come along." Here Mr. Wilson took this dirty boy by the hand, and gently pulled him forward, kindly talking to him all the way, in the most condescending manner.

How the whole school stared to see Dick Giles come in! No one, however, dared to say what he thought. The business went on, and Dick slunk into a corner, partly to hide his rags, and partly to hide his sin; for last Sunday's transaction sat heavy on his heart, not because he had stolen the apples, but because Tom Price had been accused. This, I say, made him slink behind. Poor boy! he little thought there was One saw him who sees all things, and from whose eye no hole nor corner can hide the sinner: "For he is about our bed, and about our path, and spieth out all our ways."

It was the custom in that school, and an excellent custom it is, for the master, who was a good and wise man, to mark down in his pocket-book all the events of the week, that he might turn them to some account in his Sunday evening instructions; such as any useful story in the newspaper, any account of boys being drowned as they were out in a pleasure boat on Sundays, any sudden death in the parish, or any other remarkable visitation of Providence; insomuch, that many young people in the place, who did not belong to the school, and many parents also, used to drop in for an hour on a Sunday evening, when they were sure to hear something profitable. The minister greatly approved this practice, and often called in himself, which was a great support to the master, and encouragement to the people who attended.

The master had taken a deep concern in the story of Widow Brown's apple-tree. He could not believe Tom Price was guilty, nor dared he pronounce him innocent; but he resolved to turn the instructions of the present evening to this subject. He began thus: "My dear boys, however light some of you may make of robbing an orchard, yet I have often told you there is no such thing as a little sin, if it be wilful or habitual. I wish now to explain to you, also, that there is hardly such a thing as a single solitary sin. You know I teach you not merely to repeat the commandments as an exercise for your memory, but as a rule for your conduct. If you were to come here only to learn to read and spell on a Sunday, I should think that was not employing God's day for God's work; but I teach you to read that you may, by this means, come so to understand the Bible and the Catechism, as to make every text in the one, and every question and answer in the other, to be so fixed in your hearts, that they may bring forth in you the fruits of good living."

Master. How many commandments are there?

Boy. Ten.

Master. How many commandments did that boy break who stole Widow Brown's apples?

Boy. Only one, master; the eighth.

Master. What is the eighth?

Boy. Thou shalt not steal.

Master. And you are very sure that this was the only one he broke? Now suppose I could prove to you that he probably broke not less than six out of those ten commandments, which the great Lord of heaven himself stooped down from his eternal glory to deliver to men, would you not, then, think it a terrible thing to steal, whether apples or guineas?

Boy. Yes, master.

Master. I will put the case. Some wicked boy has robbed Widow Brown's orchard. (Here the eyes of every one were turned on poor Tom Price, except those of Dick Giles, who fixed his on the ground.) I accuse no one, continued the master; Tom Price is a good boy, and was not missing at the time of the robbery; these are two reasons why I presume that he is innocent; but whoever it was, you allow that by stealing these apples he broke the eighth commandment?

Boy. Yes, master.

Master. On what day were these apples stolen?

Boy. On Sunday.

Master. What is the fourth commandment?

Boy. Thou shalt keep holy the Sabbath-day.

Master. Does that person keep holy the Sabbath-day who loiters in an orchard on Sunday, when he should be at church, and steals apples when he ought to be saying his prayers?

Boy. No, master.

Master. What command does he break?

Boy. The fourth.

Master. Suppose this boy had parents who had sent him to church, and that he had disobeyed them by not going, would that be keeping the fifth commandment?

Boy. No, master; for the fifth commandment says, Thou shalt honor thy father and thy mother.

This was the only part of the case in which poor Dick Giles's heart did not smite him; he knew he had disobeyed no father; for his father, alas! was still wickeder than himself, and had brought him up to commit the sin. But what a wretched comfort was this! The master went on.

Master. Suppose this boy earnestly coveted this fruit, though it belonged to another person, would that be right?

Boy. No, master; for the tenth commandment says, thou shalt not covet.

Master. Very well. Here are four of God's positive commands already broken. Now do you think thieves ever scruple to use wicked words?

Boy. I am afraid, not, master.

Here Dick Giles was not so hardened but that he remembered how many curses had passed between him and his father while they were filling the bags, and he was afraid to look up. The master went on.

I will now go one step further. If the thief, to all his other sins, has added that of accusing the innocent to save himself, if he should break the ninth commandment, by bearing false witness against a harmless neighbor, then six commandments are broken for an apple. But if it be otherwise, if Tom Price should be found guilty, it is not his good character shall save him. I shall shed tears over him, but punish him I must, and that severely. "No, that you sha'n't," roared out Dick Giles, who sprung from his hiding place, fell on his knees, and burst out a crying; "Tom Price is as good a boy as ever lived; it was father and I who stole the apples!"

It would have done your heart good to have seen the joy of the master, the modest blushes of Tom Price, and the satisfaction of every honest boy in the school. All shook hands with Tom, and even Dick got some portion of pity. I wish I had room to give my readers the moving exhortation which the master gave. But while Mr. Wilson left the guilty boy to the management of the master, he thought it became him, as a minister and a magistrate, to go to the extent of the law in punishing the father. Early on the Monday morning he sent to apprehend Giles. In the meantime Mr. Wilson was sent for to a gardener's house two miles distant, to attend a man who was dying. This was a duty to which all others gave way in his mind. He set out directly; but what was his surprise, on his arrival, to see, on a little bed on the floor, poaching Giles lying in all the agonies of death! Jack Weston, the same poor young man against whom Giles had informed for killing a hare, was kneeling by him, offering him some broth, and talking to him in the kindest manner. Mr. Wilson begged to know the meaning of all this; and Jack Weston spoke as follows:

"At four in the morning, as I was going out to mow, passing under the high wall of this garden, I heard a most dismal moaning. The nearer I came, the more dismal it grew. At last, who should I see but poor Giles groaning, and struggling under a quantity of bricks and stones, but not able to stir. The day before he had marked a fine large net on this old wall, and resolved to steal it, for he thought it might do as well to catch partridges as to preserve cherries; so, sir, standing on the very top of this wall, and tugging with all his might to loosen the net from the hooks which fastened it, down came Giles, net, wall, and all; for the wall was gone to decay. It was very high, indeed, and poor Giles not only broke his thigh, but has got a terrible blow on his head, and is bruised all over like a mummy. On seeing me, sir, poor Giles cried out, 'Oh, Jack! I did try to ruin thee by lodging that information, and now thou wilt be revenged by letting me lie here and perish.' 'God forbid, Giles!' cried I; 'thou shalt see what sort of revenge a

Christian takes.' So, sir, I sent off the gardener's boy to fetch a surgeon, while I scampered home and brought on my back this bit of a hammock, which is, indeed, my own bed, and put Giles upon it: we then lifted him up, bed and all, as tenderly as if he had been a gentleman, and brought him in here. My wife has just brought him a drop of nice broth; and now, sir, as I have done what I could for this poor perishing body, it was I who took the liberty to send to you to come to try to help his poor soul, for the doctor says he can't live."

Mr. Wilson could not help saying to himself, "Such an action as this is worth a whole volume of comments on that precept of our blessed Master, Love your enemies; do good to them that hate you." Giles's dying groans confirmed the sad account Weston had just given. The poor wretch could neither pray himself nor attend to the minister. He could only cry out, "Oh! sir, what will become of me? I don't know how to repent. O, my poor wicked children! Sir, I have bred them all up in sin and ignorance. Have mercy on them, sir; let me not meet them in the place of torment to which I am going. Lord grant them that time for repentance which I have thrown away!" He languished a few days, and died in great misery:—a fresh and sad instance that people who abuse the grace of God, and resist his Spirit, find it difficult to repent when they will.

Except the minister and Jack Weston, no one came to see poor Giles, besides Tommy Price, who had been so sadly wronged by him. Tom often brought him his own rice-milk or apple-dumpling; and Giles, ignorant and depraved as he was, often cried out, "That he thought now there must be some truth in religion, since it taught even a boy to deny himself, and to forgive an injury." Mr. Wilson, the next Sunday, made a moving discourse on the danger of what are called petty offenses. This, together with the awful death of Giles, produced such an effect that no poacher has been able to show his head in that parish ever since.

TAWNEY RACHEL;

OR, THE FORTUNE TELLER; WITH SOME ACCOUNT OF DREAMS, OMENS, AND CONJURORS

Tawney Rachel was the wife of poaching Giles. There seemed to be a conspiracy in Giles's whole family to maintain themselves by tricks and pilfering. Regular labor and honest industry did not suit their idle habits. They had a sort of genius at finding out every unlawful means to support a vagabond life. Rachel traveled the country with a basket on her arm. She pretended to get her bread by selling laces, cabbage-nets, ballads, and history books, and used to buy old rags and rabbit-skins. Many honest people trade in these things, and I am sure I do not mean to say a word against honest people, let them trade in what they will. But Rachel only made this traffic a pretense for getting admittance into farmers' kitchens in order to tell fortunes.

She was continually practicing on the credulity of silly girls; and took advantage of their ignorance to cheat and deceive them. Many an innocent servant has she caused to be suspected of a robbery, while she herself, perhaps, was in league with the thief. Many a harmless maid has she brought to ruin by first contriving plots and events herself, and then pretending to foretell them. She had not, to be sure, the power of really foretelling things, because she had no power of seeing into futurity; but she had the art sometimes to bring them about according as she foretold them. So she got that credit for her wisdom which really belonged to her wickedness.

Rachel was also a famous interpreter of dreams, and could distinguish exactly between the fate of any two persons who happened to have a mole on the right or the left cheek. She had a cunning way of getting herself off when any of her prophecies failed. When she explained a dream according to the natural appearance of things, and it did not come to pass; then she would get out of the scrape by saying, that this sort of dreams went by contraries. Now of two very opposite things, the chance always is that one of them may turn out to be true; so in either case she kept up the cheat.

Rachel, in one of her rambles, stopped at the house of Farmer Jenkins. She contrived to call when she knew the master of the house was from home, which indeed was her usual way. She knocked at the door; the maids being in the field haymaking, Mrs. Jenkins went to open it herself. Rachel asked her if she would please to let her light her pipe? This was a common pretense, when she could find no other way of getting into a house. While she was filling her pipe, she looked at Mrs. Jenkins, and said, she could tell her some good fortune. The farmer's wife, who was a very inoffensive, but a weak and superstitious woman, was curious to know what she meant. Rachel then looked about carefully, and shutting the door with a mysterious air, asked her if she was sure nobody would hear them. This appearance of mystery was at once delightful and terrifying to Mrs. Jenkins, who, with trembling agitation, bid the cunning woman speak out. "Then," said Rachel in a solemn whisper, "there is to my certain knowledge a pot of money hid under one of the stones in your cellar." "Indeed!" said Mrs. Jenkins, "it is impossible, for now I think of it, I dreamed last night I was in prison for debt." "Did you really?" said Rachel; "that is quite surprising. Did you dream this before twelve o'clock or after?" "O it was this morning, just before I awoke." "Then I am sure it is true, for morning dreams always go by contraries," cried Rachel. "How lucky it was you dreamed it so late." Mrs. Jenkins could hardly contain her joy, and asked how the money was to be come at. "There is but one way," said Rachel: "I must go into the cellar. I know by my art under which stone it lies, but I must not tell." Then they both went down into the cellar, but Rachel refused to point out the stone unless Mrs. Jenkins would put five pieces of gold into a basin and do as she directed. The simple woman, instead of turning her out of doors for a cheat, did as she was bid. She put the guineas into a basin which she gave into Rachel's hand. Rachel strewed some white powder over the gold, muttered some barbarous words, and pretended to perform the black art. She then told Mrs. Jenkins to put the basin quietly down within the cellar; telling her that if she offered to look into it, or even to speak a word, the charm would be broken. She also directed her to lock the cellar door, and on no pretense to open it in less than forty-eight hours. "If," added she, "you closely follow these directions, then, by the power of my art, you will find the basin conveyed to the very stone under which the money lies hid, and a fine treasure it be!" Mrs. Jenkins, who firmly believed every word the woman said, did exactly as she was told, and Rachel took her leave with a handsome reward.

When Farmer Jenkins came home he desired his wife to draw him a cup of cider; this she put off so long that he began to be displeased. At last she begged he would be so good as to drink a little beer instead. He insisted on knowing the reason, and when at last he grew angry, she told him all that had passed; and owned that as the pot of gold had happened to be in the cider cellar, she did not dare open the door, as she was sure it would break the charm. "And it would be a pity you know," said she, "to lose a good fortune for the sake of a draught of cider." The farmer, who was not so easily imposed upon, suspected a trick. He demanded the key, and went and opened the cellar door; there he found the basin, and in it five round pieces of tin covered with powder. Mrs. Jenkins burst out a-crying; but the farmer thought of nothing but of getting a warrant to apprehend the cunning woman. Indeed she well proved her claim to that name, when she insisted that the cellar door might be kept locked till she had time to get out of the reach of all pursuit.

Poor Sally Evans! I am sure she rued the day that ever she listened to a fortune teller. Sally was as harmless a girl as ever churned a pound of butter; but Sally was credulous, ignorant, and superstitious. She delighted in dream books, and had consulted all the cunning women in the country to tell her whether the two moles on her cheek denoted that she was to have two husbands, or two children. If she picked up an old horse-shoe going to church, she was sure that would be a lucky week. She never made a black pudding without borrowing one of the parson's old wigs to hang in the chimney, firmly believing there was no other means to preserve them from burning. She would never go to bed on Midsummer eve without sticking up in her room the well-known plant called Midsummer-men, as the bending of the leaves to the right or to the left would not fail to tell her whether Jacob, of whom we shall speak presently, was true or false. She would rather go five miles about than pass near a church-yard at night. Every seventh year she would not eat beans because they grew downward in the pod, instead of upward; and, though a very neat girl, she would rather have gone with her gown open than to have taken a pin from an old woman, for fear of being bewitched. Poor Sally had so many unlucky days in her calendar, that a large portion of her time became of little use, because on these days she did not dare set about any new work. And she would have refused the best offer in the country if made to her on a Friday, which she thought so unlucky a day that she often said what a pity it was that there were any Friday in the week. Sally had twenty pounds left her by her grandmother. She had long been courted by Jacob, a sober lad, with whom she lived fellow servant at a creditable farmer's. Honest Jacob, like his namesake of old, thought it little to wait seven years to get this damsel to wife, because of the love he bore her, for Sally had promised to marry him when he could match her twenty pounds with another of his own.

Now there was one Robert, a rambling idle young gardener, who instead of sitting down steadily in one place, used to roam about the country, and do odd jobs where he could get them. No one understood any thing about him, except that he was a down-looking fellow, who came nobody knew whence, and got his bread nobody knew how, and never had a penny in his pocket. Robert, who was now in the neighborhood, happened to hear of Sally Evans and her twenty pounds. He immediately conceived a longing desire for the latter. So he went to his old friend Rachel the fortune teller, told her all he had heard of Sally, and promised if she could bring about a marriage between them, she should go shares in the money.

Rachel undertook the business. She set off to the farmhouse, and fell to singing one of her most enticing songs just under the dairy window. Sally was so struck with the pretty tune, which was unhappily used, as is too often the case, to set off some very loose words, that she jumped up, dropped the skimming dish into the cream and ran out to buy the song. While she stooped down to rummage the basket for those songs which had the most tragical pictures (for Sally had a tender heart, and delighted in whatever was mournful) Rachel looked stedfastly in her face, and told her she knew by art that she was born to good fortune, but advised her not to throw herself away. "These two moles on your cheek," added she, "show you are in some danger." "Do they denote husbands or children?" cried Sally, starting up, and letting fall the song of the Children in the Wood. "Husbands," muttered Rachel. "Alas! poor Jacob!" said Sally, mournfully, "then he will die first, won't he?" "Mum for that," quoth the fortune teller, "I will say no more." Sally was impatient, but the more curiosity she discovered, the more mystery Rachel affected. At last, she said, "If you will cross my hand with a piece of silver, I will tell your fortune. By the power of my art I can do this three ways; first by cards, next by the lines on your hand, or by turning a cup of tea grounds; which will you have?" "O, all! all!" cried Sally, looking up with reverence to this sun-burnt oracle of wisdom, who was possessed of no less than three different ways of diving into the secrets of futurity. Alas! persons of better sense than Sally have been so taken in; the more is the pity. The poor girl said she would run up stairs to her little box where she kept her money tied up in a bit of an old glove, and would bring down a bright queen Anne's sixpence very crooked. "I am sure," added she, "it is a lucky one, for it cured me of a very bad ague last spring, by only laying it nine nights under my pillow without speaking a word. But then you must know what gave the virtue to this sixpence was, that it had belonged to three young men of the name of John; I am sure I had work enough to get it. But true it is, it certainly cured me. It must be the sixpence you know, for I am sure I did nothing else for my ague, except by taking some bitter stuff every three hours which the doctor called bark. To be sure I had no ague soon after I took it, but I am certain it was owing to the crooked sixpence, and not to the bark. And so, good woman, you may come in if you will, for there is not a soul in the house but me." This was the very thing Rachel wanted to know, and very glad she was to learn it.

While Sally was above stairs untying her glove, Rachel slipped into the parlor, took a small silver cup from the beaufet, and clapped it into her pocket. Sally ran down lamenting that she had lost her sixpence, which she verily believed was owing to her having put it into a left glove, instead of a right one. Rachel comforted her by saying, that if she gave her two plain ones instead, the charm would work just as well. Simple Sally thought herself happy to be let off so easily, never calculating that a smooth shilling was worth two crooked sixpences. But this skill was a part of the black art in which Rachel excelled. She took the money and began to examine the lines of Sally's left hand. She bit her withered lip, shook her head, and bade her poor dupe beware of a young man who had black hair. "No, indeed," cried Sally, all in a fright, "you mean black eyes, for our Jacob has got brown hair; 'tis his eyes that are black." "That is the very thing I was going to say," muttered Rachel; "I meant eyes, though I said hair, for I know his hair is as brown as a chestnut, and his eyes as black as a sloe." "So they are, sure enough," cried Sally; "how in the world could you have known that?" forgetting that she herself had just told her so. And it is thus that these hags pick out of the credulous all which they afterwards pretend to reveal to them. "O, I know a pretty deal more than that," said Rachel, "but you must beware of this man." "Why, so," cried Sally, with great quickness. "Because," answered Rachel, "you are fated to marry a man worth a hundred of him, who has blue eyes, light hair, and a stoop in the shoulders." "No, indeed, I can't," said Sally; "I have promised Jacob, and Jacob I will marry." "You can not, child," returned Rachel in a solemn tone; "it is out of your power, you are fated to marry the blue eyes and light hair." "Nay, indeed," said Sally, sighing deeply, "if I am fated, I must; I know there's no resisting one's fate." This is a common cant with poor deluded girls, who are not aware that they themselves make their fate by their folly, and then complain there is no resisting it. "What can I do?" said Sally. "I will tell you that, too," said Rachel. "You must take a walk next Sunday afternoon to the church-yard, and the first man you meet in a blue coat, with a large posey of pinks and southern-wood in his bosom, sitting on the church-yard wall, about seven o'clock, he will be the man." "Provided," said Sally, much disturbed, "that he has blue eyes and stoops." "It to be sure," said Rachel, "otherwise it is not the right man." "But if I should mistake," said Sally, "for two men may happen to have a coat and eyes of the same color?" "To prevent that," replied Rachel, "if it is the right man, the two first letters of his name will be R. P. This man has got money beyond sea." "O, I do not value money," said Sally, with tears in her eyes, "for I love Jacob better than house or land; but if I am fated to marry another, I can't help it; you know there is no struggling against my fate."

Poor Sally thought of nothing, and dreamed of nothing, all the week but the blue coat and the blue eyes. She made a hundred blunders at her work. She put her rennet into the butterpan, and her skimming-dish into the cheese-tub. She gave the curds to the hogs, and put the whey into the vats. She put her little knife out of her pocket for fear it should cut love, and would not stay in the kitchen if there was not an even number of people, lest it should break the charm. She grew cold and mysterious in her behavior to faithful Jacob, whom she truly loved. But the more she thought of the fortune teller, the more she was convinced that brown hair and black eyes were not what she was fated to marry, and therefore though she trembled to think it, Jacob could not be the man.

On Sunday she was too uneasy to go to church; for poor Sally had never been taught that her being uneasy was only a fresh reason why she ought to go thither. She spent the whole afternoon in her little garret, dressing in all her best. First she put on her red riband, which she had bought at last Lammas fair; then she recollected that red was an unlucky color, and changed it for a blue riband, tied in a true lover's knot; but suddenly calling to mind that poor Jacob had bought this knot for her of a pedlar at the door, and that she had promised to wear it for his sake, her heart smote her, and she laid it by, sighing to think she was not fated to marry the man who had given it to her. When she had looked at herself twenty times in the glass (for one vain action always brings on another) she set off trembling and shaking every step she went. She walked eagerly toward the church-yard, not daring to look to the right or left, for fear she would spy Jacob, who would have offered to walk with her, and so have spoilt it all. As soon as she came within sight of the wall, she spied a man sitting upon it: her heart beat violently. She looked again; but alas! the stranger not only had on a black coat, but neither hair nor eyes answered the description. She now happened to cast her eyes on the church-clock, and found she was two hours before her time. This was some comfort. She walked away and got rid of the two hours as well as she could, paying great attention not to walk over any straws which lay across, and carefully looking to see if there were never an old horse-shoe in the way, that infallible symptom of good-fortune. While the clock was striking seven, she returned to the church-yard, and O! the wonderful power of fortune tellers! there she saw him! there sat the very man! his hair as light as flax, his eyes as blue as butter-milk, and his shoulders as round as a tub. Every tittle agreed, to the very nosegay in his waistcoat button-hole. At first, indeed, she thought it had been sweet-briar, and glad to catch at a straw, whispered to herself, It is not he, and I shall marry Jacob still; but on looking again, she saw it was southern-wood plain enough, and that of course all was over. The man accosted her with some very nonsensical, but too acceptable, compliments. She was naturally a modest girl, and but for Rachel's wicked arts, would not have had courage to talk with a strange man; but how could she resist her fate you know? After a little discourse, she asked him with a trembling heart, what might be his name? Robert Price, at your service, was the answer. "Robert Price, that is R. P. as sure as I am alive, and the fortune teller was a witch! It is all out! O the wonderful art of fortune tellers!"

The little sleep she had that night was disturbed with dreams of graves, and ghosts, and funerals, but as they were morning dreams, she knew those always went by contraries, and that a funeral denoted a wedding. Still a sigh would now and then heave, to think that in that wedding Jacob would have no part. Such of my readers as know the power which superstition has over the weak and credulous mind, scarcely need be told, that poor Sally's happiness was soon completed. She forgot all her vows to Jacob; she at once forsook an honest man whom she loved, and consented to marry a stranger, of whom she knew nothing, from a ridiculous notion that she was compelled to do so by a decree which she had it not in her power to resist. She married this Robert Price, the strange gardener, whom she soon found to be very worthless, and very much in debt. He had no such thing as "money beyond sea," as the fortune teller had told her; but alas! he had another wife there. He got immediate possession of Sally's twenty pounds. Rachel put in for her share, but he refused to give her a farthing and bid her get away or he would have her taken up on the vagrant act. He soon ran away from Sally, leaving her to bewail her own weakness; for it was that indeed, and not any irresistible fate, which had been the cause of her ruin. To complete her misery, she herself was suspected of having stole the silver cup which Rachel had pocketed. Her master, however, would not prosecute her, as she was falling into a deep decline, and she died in a few months of a broken heart, a sad warning to all credulous girls.

Rachel, whenever she got near home, used to drop her trade of fortune telling, and only dealt in the wares of her basket. Mr. Wilson, the clergyman, found her one day dealing out some very wicked ballads to some children. He went up with a view to give her a reprimand; but had no sooner begun his exhortation than up came a constable, followed by several people. "There she is, that is the old witch who tricked my wife out of the five guineas," said one of them; "do your office, constable, seize that old hag. She may tell fortunes and find pots of gold in Taunton jail, for there she will have nothing else to do!" This was that very Farmer Jenkins, whose wife had been cheated by Rachel of the five guineas. He had taken pains to trace her to her own parish: he did not so much value the loss of the money, as he thought it was a duty he owed the public to clear the country of such vermin. Mr. Wilson immediately committed her. She took her trial at the next assizes, when she was sentenced to a year's imprisonment. In the mean time, the pawnbroker to whom she had sold the silver cup, which she had stolen from poor Sally's master, impeached her; and as the robbery was fully proved upon Rachel, she was sentenced for this crime to Botany Bay; and a happy day it was for the county of Somerset, when such a nuisance was sent out of it. She was transported much about the same time that her husband Giles lost his life in stealing the net from the garden wall, as related in the second part of poaching Giles.

I have thought it my duty to print this little history, as a kind of warning to all young men and maidens not to have any thing to say to cheats, impostors, cunning women, fortune tellers, conjurors, and interpreters of dreams. Listen to me, your true friend, when I assure you that God never reveals to weak and wicked women those secret designs of his providence, which no human wisdom is able to foresee. To consult these false oracles is not only foolish, but sinful. It is foolish, because they are themselves as ignorant as those whom they pretend to teach; and is sinful, because it is prying into that futurity which God, in mercy as well as wisdom, hides from men. God indeed orders all things; but when you have a mind to do a foolish thing, do not fancy you are fated to do it. This is tempting Providence, and not trusting him. It is indeed charging God with folly. Providence is his gift, and you obey him better when you make use of prudence, under the direction of prayer, than when you madly run into ruin, and think you are only submitting to your fate. Never fancy that you are compelled to undo yourself, or to rush upon your own destruction, in compliance with any supposed fatality. Never believe that God conceals his will from a sober Christian who obeys his laws, and reveals it to a vagabond gypsy who runs up and down breaking the laws both of God and man. King Saul never consulted the witch till he left off serving God. The Bible will direct us what to do better than any conjuror, and there are no days unlucky but those which we make so by our own vanity, sin, and folly.

STORIES FOR PERSONS OF THE MIDDLE RANKS

THE HISTORY OF MR. FANTOM,

(THE NEW FASHIONED PHILOSOPHER,)

AND HIS MAN WILLIAM

Mr. Fantom was a retail trader in the city of London. As he had no turn to any expensive vices, he was reckoned a sober decent man, but he was covetous and proud, selfish and conceited. As soon as he got forward in the world, his vanity began to display itself, though not in the ordinary method, that of making a figure and living away; but still he was tormented with a longing desire to draw public notice, and to distinguish himself. He felt a general discontent at what he was with a general ambition to be something which he was not; but this desire had not yet turned itself to any particular object. It was not by his money he could hope to be distinguished, for half his acquaintance had more, and a man must be rich indeed to be noted for his riches in London. Mr. Fantom's mind was a prey to his vain imaginations. He despised all those little acts of kindness and charity which every man is called to perform every day; and while he was contriving grand schemes, which lay quite out of his reach, he neglected the ordinary duties of life, which lay directly before him. Selfishness was his governing principle. He fancied he was lost in the mass of general society; and the usual means of attaching importance to insignificance occurred to him; that of getting into clubs and societies. To be connected with a party would at least make him known to that party, be it ever so low and contemptible; and this local importance it is which draws off vain minds from those scenes of general usefulness, in which, though they are of more value, they are of less distinction.

About this time he got hold of a famous little book, written by the NEW PHILOSOPHER, whose pestilent doctrines have gone about seeking whom they may destroy; these doctrines found a ready entrance into Mr. Fantom's mind; a mind at once shallow and inquisitive, speculative and vain, ambitious and dissatisfied. As almost every book was new to him, he fell into the common error of those who begin to read late in life—that of thinking that what he did not know himself, was equally new to others; and he was apt to fancy that he and the author he was reading were the only two people in the world who knew any thing. This book led to the grand discovery; he had now found what his heart panted after—a way to distinguish himself. To start out a full grown philosopher at once, to be wise without education, to dispute without learning, and to make proselytes without argument, was a short cut to fame, which well suited his vanity and his ignorance. He rejoiced that he had been so clever as to examine for himself, pitied his friends who took things upon trust, and was resolved to assert the freedom of his own mind. To a man fond of bold novelties and daring paradoxes, solid argument would be flat, and truth would be dull, merely because it is not new. Mr. Fantom believed, not in proportion to the strength of the evidence, but to the impudence of the assertion. The trampling on holy ground with dirty shoes, the smearing the sanctuary with filth and mire, the calling prophets and apostles by the most scurrilous names was new, and dashing, and dazzling. Mr. Fantom, now being set free from the chains of slavery and superstition, was resolved to show his zeal in the usual way, by trying to free others; but it would have hurt his vanity had he known that he was the convert of a man who had written only for the vulgar, who had invented nothing, no, not even one idea of original wickedness; but who had stooped to rake up out of the kennel of infidelity, all the loathsome dregs and offal dirt, which politer unbelievers had thrown away as too gross and offensive for the better bred readers.

Mr. Fantom, who considered that a philosopher must set up with a little sort of stock in trade, now picked up all the common-place notions against Christianity, which have been answered a hundred times over: these he kept by him ready cut and dried, and brought out in all companies with a zeal which would have done honor to a better cause, but which the friends to a better cause are not so apt to discover. He soon got all the cant of the new school. He prated about narrowness, and ignorance, and bigotry, and prejudice, and priestcraft on the one hand; and on the other, of public good, the love of mankind, and liberality, and candor, and toleration, and above all, benevolence. Benevolence, he said, made up the whole of religion, and all the other parts of it were nothing but cant, and jargon, and hypocrisy. By benevolence he understood a gloomy and indefinite anxiety about the happiness of people with whom he was utterly disconnected, and whom Providence had put it out of his reach either to serve or injure. And by the happiness this benevolence was so anxious to promote, he meant an exemption from the power of the laws, and an emancipation from the restraints of religion, conscience, and moral obligation.

Finding, however, that he made but little impression on his old club at the Cat and Bagpipes, he grew tired of their company. This club consisted of a few sober citizens, who met of an evening for a little harmless recreation after business; their object was, not to reform parliament, but their own shops; not to correct the abuses of government, but of parish officers; not to cure the excesses of administration, but of their own porters and apprentices; to talk over the news of the day without aspiring to direct the events of it. They read the papers with that anxiety which every honest man feels in the daily history of his country. But as trade, which they did understand, flourished, they were careful not to reprobate those public measures by which it was protected, and which they did not understand. In such turbulent times it was a comfort to each to feel he was a tradesman, and not a statesman; that he was not called to responsibility for a trust for which he found he had no talents, while he was at full liberty to employ the talents he really possessed, in fairly amassing a fortune, of which the laws would be the best guardian, and government the best security. Thus a legitimate self-love, regulated by prudence, and restrained by principle, produced peaceable subjects and good citizens; while in Fantom, a boundless selfishness and inordinate vanity converted a discontented trader into a turbulent politician.

There was, however, one member of the Cat and Bagpipes whose society he could not resolve to give up, though they seldom agreed, as indeed no two men in the same class and habits of life could less resemble each other. Mr. Trueman was an honest, plain, simple-hearted tradesman of the good old cut, who feared God and followed his business; he went to church twice on Sundays, and minded his shop all the week, spent frugally, gave liberally, and saved moderately. He lost, however, some ground in Mr. Fantom's esteem, because he paid his taxes without disputing, and read his Bible without doubting.

Mr. Fantom now began to be tired of every thing in trade except the profits of it; for the more the word benevolence was in his mouth, the more did selfishness gain dominion in his heart. He, however, resolved to retire for a while into the country, and devote his time to his new plans, schemes, theories, and projects for the public good. A life of talking, and reading, and writing, and disputing, and teaching, and proselyting, now struck him as the only life; so he soon set out for the country with his family; for unhappily Mr. Fantom had been the husband of a very worthy woman many years before the new philosophy had discovered that marriage was a shameful infringement on human liberty, and an abridgement of the rights of man. To this family was now added his new footman, William Wilson, whom he had taken with a good character out of a sober family. Mr. Fantom was no sooner settled than he wrote to invite Mr. Trueman to come and pay him a visit, for he would have burst if he could not have got some one to whom he might display his new knowledge; he knew that if on the one hand Trueman was no scholar, yet on the other he was no fool; and though he despised his prejudices, yet he thought he might be made a good decoy duck; for if he could once bring Trueman over, the whole club at the Cat and Bagpipes might be brought to follow his example; and thus he might see himself at the head of a society of his own proselytes; the supreme object of a philosopher's ambition. Trueman came accordingly. He soon found that however he might be shocked at the impious doctrines his friend maintained, yet that an important lesson might be learned even from the worst enemies of truth; namely, an ever wakeful attention to their grand object. If they set out with talking of trade or politics, of private news or public affairs, still Mr. Fantom was ever on the watch to hitch in his darling doctrines; whatever he began with, he was sure to end with a pert squib at the Bible, a vapid jest on the clergy, the miseries of superstition, and the blessings of philosophy. "Oh!" said Trueman to himself, "when shall I see Christians half so much in earnest? Why is it that almost all zeal is on the wrong side?"

"Well, Mr. Fantom," said Trueman one day at breakfast, "I am afraid you are leading but an idle sort of life here." "Idle, sir!" said Fantom, "I now first begin to live to some purpose; I have indeed lost too much time, and wasted my talents on a little retail trade, in which one is of no note; one can't distinguish one's self." "So much the better," said Trueman; "I had rather not distinguish myself, unless it was by leading a better life than my neighbors. There is nothing I should dread more than being talked about. I dare say now heaven is in a good measure filled with people whose names were never heard out of their own street and village. So I beg leave not to distinguish myself!" "Yes, but one may, if it is only by signing one's name to an essay or paragraph in a newspaper," said Fantom. "Heaven keep John Trueman's name out of a newspaper," interrupted he in a fright, "for if it be there, it must either be found in the Old Bailey or the bankrupt list, unless, indeed, I were to remove shop, or sell off my old stock. Well, but Mr. Fantom, you, I suppose, are now as happy as the day is long?" "Oh yes," replied Fantom, with a gloomy sigh, which gave the lie to his words, "perfectly happy! I wonder you do not give up all your sordid employments, and turn philosopher!" "Sordid indeed!" said Trueman, "do not call names, Mr. Fantom; I shall never be ashamed of my trade. What is it has made this country so great? a country whose merchants are princes? It is trade, Mr. Fantom, trade. I can not say indeed, as well as I love business, but now and then, when I am overworked, I wish I had a little more time to look after my soul; but the fear that I should not devote the time, if I had it, to the best purpose, makes me work on, though often, when I am balancing my accounts, I tremble, lest I should neglect to balance the great account. But still, since, like you, I am a man of no education, I am more afraid of the temptations of leisure, than of those of business; I never was bred to read more than a chapter in the Bible, or some other good book, or the magazine and newspaper; and all that I can do now, after shop is shut, is to take a walk with my children in the field besides. But if I had nothing to do from morning to night, I might be in danger of turning politician or philosopher. No, neighbor Fantom, depend upon it, that where there is no learning, next to God's grace, the best preservative of human virtue is business. As to our political societies, like the armies in the cave of Adullam, 'every man that is in distress, and every man that is in debt, and every man that is discontented, will always join themselves unto them.'"

Fantom. You have narrow views, Trueman. What can be more delightful than to see a paper of one's own in print against tyranny and superstition, contrived with so much ingenuity, that, though the law is on the look-out for treason and blasphemy, a little change of name defeats its scrutiny. For instance; you may stigmatize England under the name of Rome, and Christianity under the name of Popery. The true way is to attack whatever you have a mind to injure, under another name, and the best means to destroy the use of a thing, is to produce a few incontrovertible facts against the abuses it. Our late travelers have inconceivably helped on the cause of the new philosophy, in their ludicrous narratives of credulity, miracles, indulgences, and processions, in popish countries, all which they ridicule under the broad and general name of Religion, Christianity, and the Church. "And are not you ashamed to defend such knavery?" said Mr. Trueman. "Those who have a great object to accomplish," replied Mr. Fantom, "must not be nice about the means. But to return to yourself, Trueman; in your little confined situation you can be of no use." "That I deny," interrupted Trueman; "I have filled all the parish offices with some credit. I never took a bribe at an election, no not so much as a treat; I take care of my apprentices, and do not set them a bad example by running to plays and Saddler's Wells, in the week or jaunting about in a gig all day on Sundays; for I look upon it that the country jaunt of the master on Sundays exposes his servants to more danger than their whole week's temptation in trade put together."

Fantom. I once had the same vulgar prejudices about the church and the Sabbath, and all that antiquated stuff. But even on your own narrow principles, how can a thinking being spend his Sunday better (if he must lose one day in seven by having any Sunday at all) than by going into the country to admire the works of nature.

Trueman. I suppose you mean the works of God: for I never read in the Bible that Nature made any thing. I should rather think that she herself was made by Him, who, when He said, "thou shalt not murder," said also, "thou shalt keep holy the Sabbath day." But now do you really think that all the multitude of coaches, chariots, chaises, vis-a-vis, booby-hutches, sulkies, sociables, phaetons, gigs, curricles, cabrioles, chairs, stages, pleasure-carts, and horses, which crowd our roads; all those country-houses within reach, to which the London friends pour in to the gorgeous Sunday feast, which the servants are kept from church to dress; all those public houses under the signs of which you read these alluring words, an ordinary on Sundays; I say, do you really believe that all those houses and carriages are crammed with philosophers, who go on Sunday into the country to admire the works of nature, as you call it! Indeed, from the reeling gait of some of them, when they go back at night, one might take them for a certain sect called the tippling philosophers. Then in answer to your charge, that a little tradesman can do no good, it is not true; I must tell you that I belong to the Sick Man's Friend, and to the Society for relieving prisoners for small debts.

Fantom. I have no attention to spare for that business, though I would pledge myself to produce a plan by which the national debt might be paid off in six months; but all yours are petty occupations.

Trueman. Then they are better suited to petty men of petty fortune. I had rather have an ounce of real good done with my own hands, and seen with my own eyes, than speculate about doing a ton in a wild way, which I know can never be brought about.

Fantom. I despise a narrow field. Oh, for the reign of universal benevolence! I want to make all mankind good and happy.

Trueman. Dear me! sure that must be a wholesale sort of a job; had you not better try your hand at a town or a parish first!

Fantom. Sir, I have a plan in my head for relieving the miseries of the whole world. Every thing is bad as it now stands. I would alter all the laws; and do away all the religions, and put an end to all the wars in the world. I would every where redress the injustice of fortune, or what the vulgar call Providence. I would put an end to all punishments; I would not leave a single prisoner on the face of the globe. This is what I call doing things on a grand scale. "A scale with a vengeance," said Trueman. "As to releasing the prisoners, however, I do not so much like that, as it would be liberating a few rogues at the expense of all honest men; but as to the rest of your plans, if all Christian countries would be so good as to turn Christians, it might be helped on a good deal. There would be still misery enough left indeed; because God intended this world should be earth and not heaven. But, sir, among all your oblations, you must abolish human corruption before you can make the world quite as perfect as you pretend. You philosophers seem to me to be ignorant of the very first seed and principle of misery—sin, sir, sin: your system of reform is radically defective; for it does not comprehend that sinful nature from which all misery proceeds. You accuse government of defects which belong to man, to individual man, and of course to man collectively. Among all your reforms you must reform the human heart; you are only hacking at the branches, without striking at the root. Banishing impiety out of the world, would be like striking off all the pounds from an overcharged bill; and all the troubles which would be left, would be reduced to mere shillings, pence, and farthings, as one may say."

Fantom. Your project would rivet the chains which mine is designed to break.

Trueman. Sir, I have no projects. Projects are in general the offspring of restlessness, vanity, and idleness. I am too busy for projects, too contented for theories, and, I hope, have too much honesty and humility for a philosopher. The utmost extent of my ambition at present is, to redress the wrongs of a parish apprentice who has been cruelly used by his master; indeed I have another little scheme, which is to prosecute a fellow in our street who has suffered a poor wretch in a workhouse, of which he had the care, to perish through neglect, and you must assist me.

Fantom. The parish must do that. You must not apply to me for the redress of such petty grievances. I own that the wrongs of the Poles and South Americans so fill my mind as to leave me no time to attend to the petty sorrows of workhouses and parish apprentices. It is provinces, empires, continents, that the benevolence of the philosopher embraces; every one can do a little paltry good to his next neighbor.

Trueman. Every one can, but I do not see that every one does. If they would, indeed, your business would be ready done at your hands, and your grand ocean of benevolence would be filled with the drops which private charity would throw into it. I am glad, however, you are such a friend to the prisoners, because I am just now getting a little subscription from our club, to set free our poor old friend, Tom Saunders, a very honest brother tradesman, who got first into debt, and then into jail, through no fault of his own, but merely through the pressure of the times. We have each of us allowed a trifle every week toward maintaining Tom's young family since he has been in prison; but we think we shall do much more service to Saunders, and, indeed, in the end, lighten our expense, by paying down at once a little sum to restore him to the comforts of life, and put him in the way of maintaining his family again. We have made up the money all except five guineas; I am already promised four, and you have nothing to do but give me the fifth. And so for a single guinea, without any of the trouble, the meetings, and the looking into his affairs, which we have had; which, let me tell you, is the best, and to a man of business, the dearest part of charity, you will at once have the pleasure (and it is no small one) of helping to save a worthy family from starving, of redeeming an old friend from jail, and of putting a little of your boasted benevolence into action. Realize! Master Fantom—there is nothing like realizing. "Why, hark ye, Mr. Trueman," said Fantom, stammering, and looking very black; "do not think I value a guinea; no, sir, I despise money; it is trash; it is dirt, and beneath the regard of a wise man. It is one of the unfeeling inventions of artificial society. Sir, I could talk to you for half a day on the abuse of riches, and on my own contempt for money."

Trueman. O, pray do not give yourself the trouble; it will be an easier way by half of vindicating yourself from one, and of proving the other, just to put your hand in your pocket and give me a guinea, without saying a word about it; and then to you, who value time so much, and money so little, it will cut the matter short. But come now (for I see you will give nothing), I should be mighty glad to know what is the sort of good you do yourself, since you always object to what is done by others? "Sir," said Mr. Fantom; "the object of a true philosopher is to diffuse light and knowledge. I wish to see the whole world enlightened."

Trueman. Amen! if you mean with the light of the gospel. But if you mean that one religion is as good as another, and that no religion is best of all; and that we shall become wiser and better by setting aside the very means which Providence bestowed to make us wise and good; in short, if you want to make the whole world philosophers, why they had better stay as they are. But as to the true light, I wish to reach the very lowest, and I therefore bless God for charity-schools, as instruments of diffusing it among the poor.

Fantom, who had no reason to suspect that his friend was going to call upon him for a subscription on this account, ventured to praise them, saying, "I am no enemy to these institutions. I would, indeed, change the object of instruction, but I would have the whole world instructed."

Here Mrs. Fantom, who, with her daughter, had quietly sat by at their work, ventured to put in a word, a liberty she seldom took with her husband, who, in his zeal to make the whole world free and happy, was too prudent to include his wife among the objects on whom he wished to confer freedom and happiness. "Then, my dear," said she, "I wonder you do not let your own servants be taught a little. The maids can scarcely tell a letter, or say the Lord's Prayer, and you know you will not allow them time to learn. William, too, has never been at church since we came out of town. He was at first very orderly and obedient, but now he is seldom sober of an evening; and in the morning, when he should be rubbing the tables in the parlor, he is generally lolling upon them, and reading your little manual of the new philosophy." "Mrs. Fantom," said her husband, angrily, "you know that my labors for the public good leave me little time to think of my own family. I must have a great field; I like to do good to hundreds at once."

"I am very glad of that, papa," said Miss Polly; "for then I hope you will not refuse to subscribe to all those pretty children at the Sunday School, as you did yesterday, when the gentlemen came a begging, because that is the very thing you were wishing for; there are two or three hundred to be done good at once."

Trueman. Well, Mr. Fantom, you are a wonderful man to keep up such a stock of benevolence at so small an expense. To love mankind so dearly, and yet avoid all opportunities of doing them good; to have such a noble zeal for the millions, and to feel so little compassion for the units; to long to free empires and enlighten kingdoms; and yet deny instruction to your own village, and comfort to your own family. Surely none but a philosopher could indulge so much philanthropy and so much frugality at the same time. But come, do assist me in a partition I am making in our poor-house; between the old, whom I want to have better fed, and the young, whom I want to have more worked.

Fantom. Sir, my mind is so engrossed with the partition of Poland, that I can not bring it down to an object of such insignificance. I despise the man whose benevolence is swallowed up in the narrow concerns of his own family, or parish, or country.

Trueman. Well, now I have a notion that it is as well to do one's own duty as the duty of another man; and that to do good at home is as well as to do good abroad. For my part, I had as lieve help Tom Saunders to freedom as a Pole or a South American, though I should be very glad to help them too. But one must begin to love somewhere; and to do good somewhere; and I think it is as natural to love one's own family, and to do good in one's own neighborhood, as to any body else. And if every man in every family, parish, and country, did the same, why then all the schemes would meet, and the end of one parish, where I was doing good, would be the beginning of another parish where somebody else was doing good; so my schemes would jut into my neighbor's; his projects would unite with those of some other local reformer; and all would fit with a sort of dove-tail exactness. And what is better, all would join in forming a living comment on that practical precept; "Thou shalt love the Lord thy God with all thy heart, and thy neighbor as thyself."

Fantom. Sir, a man of large views will be on the watch for great occasions to prove his benevolence.

Trueman. Yes, sir; but if they are so distant that he can not reach them, or so vast that he can not grasp them, he may let a thousand little, snug, kind, good actions slip through his fingers in the meanwhile; and so between the great things that he can not do, and the little ones that he will not do, life passes and nothing will be done.

Just at this moment Miss Polly Fantom (whose mother had gone out some time before) started up, let fall her work, and cried out, "O, papa, do but look what a monstrous great fire there is yonder on the common! If it were the fifth of November I should think it were a bonfire. Look how it blazes." "I see plain enough what it is," said Mr. Fantom, sitting down again without the least emotion. "It is Jenkins's cottage on fire." "What, poor John Jenkins, who works in our garden, papa?" said the poor girl, in great terror. "Do not be frightened, child," answered Fantom; "we are safe enough; the wind blows the other way. Why did you disturb us for such a trifle, as it was so distant? Come, Mr. Trueman, sit down." "Sit down!" said Mr. Trueman; "I am not a stock, nor a stone, but a man, made of the same common nature with Jenkins, whose house is burning. Come along—let us fly and help him," continued he, running to the door in such haste that he forgot to take his hat, though it hung just before him. "Come, Mr. Fantom—come, my little dear; I wish your mamma was here; I am sorry she went out just now; we may all do some good; every body may be of some use at a fire. Even you, Miss Polly, may save some of these poor people's things in your apron, while your papa and I hand the buckets." All this he said as he ran along with the young lady in his hand, not doubting but Fantom and his whole family were following close behind him. But the present distress was neither grand enough nor far enough from home to satisfy the wide-stretched benevolence of the philosopher, who sat down within sight of the flames to work at a new pamphlet, which now swallowed up his whole soul, on Universal Benevolence.

His daughter, indeed, who happily was not yet a philosopher, with Mr. Trueman, followed by the maids, reached the scene of distress. William Wilson, the footman, refused to assist, glad of such an opportunity of being revenged on Jenkins, whom he called a surly fellow, for presuming to complain because William always purloined the best fruit for himself before he set it on his master's table. Jenkins, also, whose duty it was to be out of doors, had refused to leave his own work in the garden to do Will's work in the house while he got drunk, or read the Rights of Man.

The little dwelling of Jenkins burned very furiously. Mr. Trueman's exertions were of the greatest service. He directed the willing, and gave an example to the slothful. By living in London, he had been more used to the calamity of fire than the country people, and knew better what was to be done. In the midst of the bustle he saw one woman only who never attempted to be of the least use. She ran backward and forward, wringing her hands, and crying out in a tone of piercing agony, "Oh, my child! my little Tommy! will no one save my Tommy?" Any woman might have uttered the same words, but the look which explained them could only come from a mother. Trueman did not stay to ask if she were owner of the house, and mother of the child. It was his way to do all the good that could be done first, and then to ask questions. All he said was, "Tell me which is the room?" The poor woman, now speechless through terror, could only point up to a little window in the thatch, and then sunk on the ground.

Mr. Trueman made his way through a thick smoke, and ran up the narrow staircase which the fire had not reached. He got safely to the loft, snatched up the little creature, who was sweetly sleeping in its poor hammock, and brought him down naked in his arms: and as he gave him to the half-distracted mother, he felt that her joy and gratitude would have been no bad pay for the danger he had run, even if no higher motive had set him to work. Poor Jenkins, half stupefied by his misfortune, had never thought of his child; and his wife, who expected every hour to make him father to a second, had not been able to do any thing toward saving little Tommy.

Mr. Trueman now put the child into Miss Fantom's apron, saying, "Did not I tell you, my dear, that every body could be of use at a fire?" He then desired her to carry the child home, and ordered the poor woman to follow her; saying, he would return himself as soon as he had seen all safe in the cottage.

When the fire was quite out, and Mr. Trueman could be of no further use, he went back to Mr. Fantom's. The instant he opened the parlor door he eagerly cried out, "Where is the poor woman, Mr. Fantom?" "Not in my house, I assure you," answered the philosopher. "Give me leave to tell you, it was a very romantic thing to send her and her child to me; you should have provided for them at once, like a prudent man." "I thought I had done so," replied Trueman, "by sending them to the nearest and best house in the parish, as the poor woman seemed to stand in need of immediate assistance." "So immediate," said Fantom, "that I would not let her come into my house, for fear of what might happen. So I packed her off, with her child in her arms, to the workhouse; with orders to the overseers not to let her want for any thing."

"And what right have you, Mr. Fantom," cried Trueman in a high tone, "to expect that the overseers will be more humane than yourself! But is it possible you can have sent that helpless creature, not only to walk, but to carry a naked child at such a time of night, to a place so distant, so ill provided, and in such a condition? I hope at least you have furnished them with clothes; for all their own little stores were burnt." "Not I, indeed;" said Fantom. "What is the use of parish officers, but to look after these petty things?"

It was Mr. Trueman's way, when he began to feel very angry, not to allow himself to speak, "because," he used to say, "if I give vent to my feelings, I am sure, by some hasty word, to cut myself out work for repentance." So without making any answer, or even changing his clothes, which were very wet and dirty from having worked so hard at the fire, he walked out again, having first inquired the road the woman had taken. At the door he met Mrs. Fantom returning from her visit. He told her his tale; which she had no sooner heard, than she kindly resolved to accompany him in search of Jenkins's wife. She had a wide common to walk over before she could reach either the workhouse or the nearest cottage. She had crawled along with her baby as far as she was able; but having met with no refreshment at Mr. Fantom's, and her strength quite failing her, she had sunk down on the middle of the common. Happily, Mr. Trueman and Mrs. Fantom came up at this very time. The former had had the precaution to bring a cordial, and the latter had gone back and stuffed her pockets with old baby linen. Mr. Trueman soon procured the assistance of a laborer, who happened to pass by, to help him to carry the mother, and Mrs. Fantom carried the little shivering baby.

As soon as they were safely lodged, Mr. Trueman set off in search of poor Jenkins, who was distressed to know what was become of his wife and child; for having heard that they were seen going toward Mr. Fantom's, he despaired of any assistance from that quarter. Mr. Trueman felt no small satisfaction in uniting this poor man to his little family. There was something very moving in this meeting, and in the pious gratitude they expressed for their deliverance. They seemed to forget they had lost their all, in the joy they felt that they had not lost each other. And some disdainful great ones might have smiled to see so much rapture expressed at the safety of a child born to no inheritance but poverty. These are among the feelings with which Providence sometimes overpays the want of wealth. The good people also poured out prayers and blessings on their deliverer, who, not being a philosopher, was no more ashamed of praying with them than he had been of working for them. Mr. Trueman, while assisting at the fire, had heard that Jenkins and his wife were both very honest, and very pious people; so he told them he would not only pay for their new lodgings, but undertook to raise a little subscription among his friends at the Cat and Bagpipes toward rebuilding their cottage; and further engaged that if they would promise to bring up the child in the fear of God, he would stand godfather.

This exercise of Christian charity had given such a cheerful flow to Mr. Trueman's spirits, that long before he got home he had lost every trace of ill-humor. "Well, Mr. Fantom," said he gayly, as he opened the door, "now do tell me how you could possibly refuse going to help me to put out the fire at poor Jenkins's?" "Because," said Fantom, "I was engaged, sir, in a far nobler project than putting out a fire in a little thatched cottage. Sir, I was contriving to put out a fire too; a conflagration of a far more dreadful kind—a fire, sir, in the extinction of which universal man is concerned—I was contriving a scheme to extinguish the fires of the Inquisition." "Why, man, they don't blaze that I know of," retorted Trueman. "I own, that of all the abominable engines which the devil ever invented to disgrace religion and plague mankind, that Inquisition was the very worst. But I do not believe popery has ventured at these diabolical tricks since the earthquake at Lisbon, so that a bucket of real water, carried to the real fire at Jenkins's cottage, would have done more good than a wild plan to put out an imaginary flame which no longer burns. And let me tell you, sir, dreadful as that evil was, God can send his judgments on other sins besides superstition; so it behoves us to take heed of the other extreme or we may have our earthquakes too." "The hand of God is not shortened, sir, that it can not destroy, any more than it can not save. In the meantime, I must repeat it; you and I are rather called upon to serve a neighbor from perishing in the flames of his house, just under our own window, than to write about the fires of the Inquisition; which, if fear, or shame, or the restoration of common sense had not already put out, would have hardly received a check from such poor hands as you and I."

"Sir," said Fantom, "Jenkins is an impertinent fellow; and I owe him a grudge, because he says he had rather forfeit the favor of the best master in England than work in my garden on a Sunday. And when I ordered him to read the Age of Reason, instead of going to church, he refused to work for me at all, with some impertinent hint about God and Mammon."

"Oh, did he so?" said Mr. Trueman. "Now I will stand godfather to his child, and made him a handsome present into the bargain. Indeed, Mr. Fantom, a man must be a philosopher with a vengeance, if when he sees a house on fire, he stays to consider whether the owner has offended him. Oh, Mr. Fantom, I will forgive you still, if you will produce me, out of all your philosophy, such a sentence as 'Love your enemy—do good to them that hate you—if thine enemy hunger, feed him; if he thirst, give him drink;' I will give up the blessed gospel for the Age of Reason, if you will only bring me one sentiment equivalent to this."

Next day Mr. Trueman was obliged to go to London on business, but returned soon, as the time he had allotted to spend with Mr. Fantom was not yet elapsed. He came down the sooner indeed, that he might bring a small sum of money which the gentlemen at the Cat and Bagpipes had cheerfully subscribed for Jenkins. Trueman did not forget to desire his wife to make up also a quantity of clothing for this poor family, to which he did not neglect to add a parcel of good books, which, indeed, always made a part of his charities; as he used to say, there was something cruel in the kindness which was anxious to relieve the bodies of men, but was negligent of their souls. He stood in person to the new-born child, and observed with much pleasure, that Jenkins and his wife thought a christening, not a season for merry-making, but a solemn act of religion. And they dedicated their infant to his Maker with becoming seriousness.

Trueman left the cottage and got back to Mr. Fantom's, just as the family were going to sit down to dinner, as he had promised.

When they sat down, Mr. Fantom was not a little out of humor to see his table in some disorder. William was also rather more negligent than usual. If the company called for bread, he gave them beer, and he took away the clean plates, and gave them dirty ones. Mr. Fantom soon discovered that his servant was very drunk; he flew into a violent passion, and ordered him out of the room, charging that he should not appear in his presence in that condition. William obeyed; but having slept an hour or two, and got about half sober, he again made his appearance. His master gave him a most severe reprimand, and called him an idle, drunken, vicious fellow. "Sir," said William, very pertly, "if I do get drunk now and then, I only do it for the good of my country, and in obedience to your wishes." Mr. Fantom, thoroughly provoked, now began to scold him in words not fit to be repeated; and asked him what he meant. "Why, sir," said William, "you are a philosopher you know; and I have often overheard you say to your company, that private vices are public benefits; and so I thought that getting drunk was as pleasant a way of doing good to the public as any, especially when I could oblige my master at the same time."

"Get out of my house," said Mr. Fantom, in a great rage. "I do not desire to stay a moment longer," said William, "so pay me my wages." "Not I, indeed," replied the master; "nor will I give you a character; so never let me see your face again." William took his master at his word, and not only got out of the house, but went out of the country too as fast as possible. When they found he was really gone, they made a hue-and-cry, in order to detain him till they examined if he had left every thing in the house as he had found it. But William had got out of reach, knowing he could not stand such a scrutiny. On examination, Mr. Fantom found that all his old port was gone, and Mrs. Fantom missed three of her best new spoons. William was pursued, but without success; and Mr. Fantom was so much discomposed that he could not for the rest of the day talk on any subject but his wine and his spoons, nor harangue on any project but that of recovering both by bringing William to justice.

Some days passed away, in which Mr. Fantom, having had time to cool, began to be ashamed that he had been betrayed into such ungoverned passion. He made the best excuse he could; said no man was perfect, and though he owned he had been too violent, yet still he hoped William would be brought to the punishment he deserved. "In the meantime," said Trueman, "seeing how ill philosophy has agreed with your man, suppose you were to set about teaching your maids a little religion?" Mr. Fantom coolly replied, "that the impertinent retort of a drunken footman could not spoil a system." "Your system, however, and your own behavior," said Trueman, "have made that footman a scoundrel, and you are answerable for his offenses." "Not I, truly," said Fantom; "he has seen me do no harm; he has neither seen me cheat, gamble, nor get drunk; and I defy you to say I corrupt my servants. I am a moral man, sir."

"Mr. Fantom," said Trueman, "if you were to get drunk every day, and game every night, you would, indeed, endanger your own soul, and give a dreadful example to your family; but great as those sins are, and God forbid that I should attempt to lessen them! still they are not worse, nay, they are not so bad, as the pestilent doctrines with which you infect your house and your neighborhood. A bad action is like a single murder. The consequence may end with the crime, to all but the perpetrator; but a wicked principle is throwing lighted gunpowder into a town; it is poisoning a river; there are no bounds, no certainty, no ends to its mischief. The ill effects of the worst action may cease in time, and the consequences of your bad example may end with your life; but souls may be brought to perdition by a wicked principle after the author of it has been dead for ages."

Fantom. You talk like an ignoramus who has never read the new philosophy. All this nonsense of future punishment is now done away. It is our benevolence which makes us reject your creed; we can no more believe in a Deity who permits so much evil in the present world, than one who threatens eternal punishment in the next.

Trueman. What! shall mortal man be more merciful than God? Do you pretend to be more compassionate than that gracious Father who sent his own Son into the world to die for sinners?

Fantom. You take all your notions of the Deity from the vulgar views your Bible gives you of him. "To be sure I do," said Trueman. "Can you tell me any way of getting a better notion of him? I do not want any of your farthing-candle philosophy in the broad sunshine of the gospel, Mr. Fantom. My Bible tells me that 'God is love;' not merely loving, but LOVE. Now, do you think a Being, whose very essence is love, would permit any misery among his children here, if it was not to be, some way or other, or some where or other, for their good? You forget, too, that in a world where there is sin, there must be misery. Then, too, I suppose, God permits this very misery, partly to exercise the sufferers, and partly to try the prosperous; for by trouble God corrects some and tries others. Suppose, now, Tom Saunders had not been put in prison, you and I—no, I beg pardon, you saved your guinea; well, then, our club and I could not have shown our kindness in getting him out; nor would poor Saunders himself have had an opportunity of exercising his own patience and submission under want and imprisonment. So you see one reason why God permits misery is, that good men may have an opportunity of lessening it." Mr. Fantom replied, "There is no object which I have more at heart; I have, as I told you, a plan in my head of such universal benevolence as to include the happiness of all mankind." "Mr. Fantom," said Trueman, "I feel that I have a general good will to all my brethren of mankind; and if I had as much money in my purse as love in my heart, I trust I should prove it. All I say is, that, in a station of life where I can not do much, I am more called upon to procure the happiness of a poor neighbor, who has no one else to look to, than to form wild plans for the good of mankind, too extensive to be accomplished, and too chimerical to be put in practice. It is the height of folly for a little ignorant tradesman to distract himself with projecting schemes which require the wisdom of scholars, the experience of statesmen, and the power of kings to accomplish. I can not free whole countries, nor reform the evils of society at large, but I can free an aggrieved wretch in a workhouse; I can relieve the distresses of one of my journeymen; and I can labor to reform myself and my own family."

Some weeks after this a letter was brought to Mr. Fantom from his late servant, William, who had been turned away for drunkenness, as related above, and who had also robbed his master of some wine and some spoons. Mr. Fantom, glancing his eye over the letter, said, "It is dated from Chelmsford jail; that rascal has got into prison. I am glad of it with all my heart; it is the fittest place for such scoundrels. I hope he will be sent to Botany Bay, if not hanged." "O, ho! my good friend," said Trueman; "then I find that in abolishing all prisons you would just let one stand for the accommodation of those who would happen to rob you. General benevolence, I see, is compatible with particular resentments, though individual kindness is not consistent with universal philanthropy." Mr. Fantom drily observed that he was not fond of jokes, and proceeded to read the letter. It expressed an earnest wish that his late master would condescend to pay him one visit in his dark and doleful abode, as he wished to say a few words to him before the dreadful sentence of the law, which had already been pronounced, should be executed.

"Let us go and see the poor fellow," said Trueman; "it is but a morning's ride. If he is really so near his end it would be cruel to refuse him." "Not I, truly," said Fantom; "he deserves nothing at my hands but the halter he is likely to meet with. Such port is not to be had for money! and the spoons—part of my new dozen!" "As to the wine," said Trueman, "I am afraid you must give that up, but the only way to get any tidings of the spoons is to go and hear what he has to say; I have no doubt but he will make such a confession as may be very useful to others, which, you know, is one grand advantage of punishments; and, besides, we may afford him some little comfort." "As to comfort, he deserves none from me," said Fantom; "and as to his confessions, they can be of no use to me, but as they give me a chance of getting my spoons; so I do not much care if I do take a ride with you."

When they came to the prison, Mr. Trueman's tender heart sunk within him. He deplored the corrupt nature of man, which makes such rigorous confinement indispensably needful, not merely for the punishment of the offender, but for the safety of society. Fantom, from mere trick and habit, was just preparing a speech on benevolence, and the cruelty of imprisonment; for he had a set of sentiments collected from the new philosophy which he always kept by him. The naming a man in power brought out the ready cut and dried phrase against oppression. The idea of rank included every vice, that of poverty every virtue; and he was furnished with all the invectives against the cruelty of laws, punishments, and prisons, which the new lexicon has produced. But his mechanical benevolence was suddenly checked; the recollection of his old port and his new spoons cooled his ardor, and he went on without saying a word.

When they reached the cell where the unhappy William was confined, they stopped at the door. The poor wretch had thrown himself on the ground, as well as his chains would permit. He groaned piteously, and was so swallowed up with a sense of his own miseries, that he neither heard the door open nor saw the gentlemen. He was attempting to pray, but in an agony which made his words hardly intelligible. Thus much they could make out—"God be merciful to me a sinner, the chief of sinners!" then, suddenly attempting to start up, but prevented by his irons, he roared out, "O, God! thou canst not be merciful to me, for I have denied thee; I have ridiculed my Saviour who died for me; I have broken his laws; I have derided his word; I have resisted his Spirit; I have laughed at that heaven which is shut against me; I have denied the truth of those torments which await me. To-morrow! to-morrow! O for a longer space for repentance! O for a short reprieve from hell!"

Mr. Trueman wept so loud that it drew the attention of the criminal, who now lifted up his eyes, and cast on his late master a look so dreadful that Fantom wished for a moment that he had given up all hope of the spoons, rather than have exposed himself to such a scene. At length the poor wretch said, in a low voice that would have melted a heart of stone, "O, sir, are you there? I did indeed wish to see you before my dreadful sentence is put in execution. O, sir, to-morrow! to-morrow! But I have a confession to make to you." This revived Mr. Fantom, who again ventured to glance a hope at the spoons. "Sir," said William, "I could not die without making my confession." "Ay, and restitution, too, I hope," replied Fantom. "Where are my spoons?" "Sir, they are gone with the rest of my wretched booty. But oh, sir! those spoons make so petty an article in my black account, that I hardly think of them. Murder! sir—murder is the crime for which I am justly doomed to die. O, sir, who can abide the anger of an offended God? Who can dwell with everlasting burnings?" As this was a question which even a philosopher could not answer, Mr. Fantom was going to steal off, especially as he now gave up all hope of the spoons; but William called him back: "Stay, sir, I conjure you, as you will answer it at the bar of God. You must hear the sins of which you have been the occasion. You are the cause of my being about to suffer a shameful death. Yes, sir, you made me a drunkard, a thief, and a murderer." "How dare you, William," cried Mr. Fantom, with great emotion, "accuse me of being the cause of such horrid crimes?" "Sir," answered the criminal, "from you I learned the principles which lead to those crimes. By the grace of God I should never have fallen into sins deserving of the gallows, if I had not overheard you say there was no hereafter, no judgment, no future reckoning. O, sir, there is a hell, dreadful, inconceivable, eternal!"

Here, through the excess of anguish, the poor fellow fainted away. Mr. Fantom, who did not at all relish this scene, said to his friend, "Well, sir, we will go, if you please, for you see there is nothing to be done."

"Sir," replied Mr. Trueman, mournfully, "you may go if you please, but I shall stay, for I see there is a great deal to be done." "What!" rejoined the other, "do you think it possible his life can be saved?" "No, indeed," said Trueman, "but I hope it possible his soul may be saved!" "I do not understand these things," said Fantom, making toward the door. "Nor I, neither," said Trueman, "but as a fellow-sinner, I am bound to do what I can for this poor man. Do you go home, Mr. Fantom, and finish your treatise on universal benevolence, and the blessed effects of philosophy; and, hark ye, be sure you let the frontispiece of your book represent William on the gibbet; that will be what our minister calls a PRACTICAL ILLUSTRATION. You know I hate theories; this is realizing; this is PHILOSOPHY made easy to the meanest capacity. This is the precious fruit which grows on that darling tree, so many slips of which have been transplanted from that land of liberty of which it is the native, but which, with all your digging, planting, watering, dunging, and dressing, will, I trust, never thrive in this blessed land of ours."

Mr. Fantom sneaked off to finish his work at home, and Mr. Trueman staid to finish his in the prison. He passed the night with the wretched convict; he prayed with him and for him, and read to him the penitential psalms, and some portions of the gospel. But he was too humble and too prudent a man to venture out of his depth by arguments and consolations which he was not warranted to use; this he left for the clergyman—but he pressed on William the great duty of making the only amends now in his power to those whom he had led astray. They then drew up the following paper, which Mr. Trueman got printed, and gave away at the place of execution:

THE LAST WORDS, CONFESSION, AND DYING SPEECH OF WILLIAM WILSON, WHO WAS EXECUTED AT CHELMSFORD, FOR MURDER

"I was bred up in the fear of God, and lived with credit in many sober families, in which I was a faithful servant; but being tempted by a little higher wages, I left a good place to go and live with Mr. Fantom, who, however, made good none of his fine promises, but proved a hard master. Full of fine words and charitable speeches in favor of the poor; but apt to oppress, overwork, and underpay them. In his service I was not allowed time to go to church. This troubled me at first, till I overheard my master say, that going to church was a superstitious prejudice, and only meant for the vulgar. Upon this I resolved to go no more, for I thought there could not be two religions, one for the master and one for the servant. Finding my master never prayed, I, too, left off praying; this gave Satan great power over me, so that I from that time fell into almost every sin. I was very uneasy at first, and my conscience gave me no rest; but I was soon reconciled by overhearing my master and another gentleman say, that death was only an eternal sleep, and hell and judgment were but an invention of priests to keep the poor in order. I mention this as a warning to all masters and mistresses to take care what they converse about while servants are waiting at table. They can not tell how many souls they have sent to perdition with such loose talk. The crime for which I die is the natural consequence of the principles I learned of my master. A rich man, indeed, who throws off religion, may escape the gallows, because want does not drive him to commit those crimes which lead to it; but what shall restrain a needy man, who has been taught that there is no dreadful reckoning? Honesty is but a dream without the awful sanctions of heaven and hell. Virtue is but a shadow, if it be stripped of the terrors and promises of the gospel. Morality is but an empty name, if it be destitute of the principle and power of Christianity. O, my dear fellow servants! take warning by my sad fate; never be tempted away from a sober service for the sake of a little more wages; never venture your immortal souls to houses where God is not feared. And now hear me, O my

God! though I have blasphemed thee! Forgive me, O my Saviour! though I have denied thee! O Lord, most holy! O God, most mighty! deliver me from the bitter pains of eternal death, and receive my soul, for His sake who died for sinners.

"WILLIAM WILSON."

Mr. Trueman would never leave this poor penitent till he was launched into eternity, but he attended him with the minister in the cart. This pious clergyman never cared to say what he thought of William's state. When Mr. Trueman ventured to mention his hope, that though his penitence was late, yet it was sincere, and spoke of the dying thief on the cross as a ground of encouragement, the minister with a very serious look, made this answer: "Sir, that instance is too often brought forward on occasions to which it does not apply: I do not choose to say any thing to your application of it in the present case, but I will answer you in the words of a good man speaking of the penitent thief: 'There is one such instance given that nobody might despair, and there is but one, that nobody might presume.'"

Poor William was turned off just a quarter before eleven; and may the Lord have mercy on his soul!

THE TWO WEALTHY FARMERS, OR, THE HISTORY OF MR. BRAGWELL

PART I—THE VISIT

Mr. Bragwell and Mr. Worthy happened to meet last year at Weyhill fair. They were glad to see each other, as they had but seldom met of late; Mr. Bragwell having removed some years before from Mr. Worthy's neighborhood, to a distant village where he had bought an estate.

Mr. Bragwell was a substantial farmer and grazier. He had risen in the world by what worldly men call a run of good fortune. He had also been a man of great industry; that is, he had paid a diligent and constant attention to his own interest. He understood business, and had a knack of turning almost every thing to his own advantage. He had that sort of sense which good men call cunning, and knaves call wisdom. He was too prudent ever to do any thing so wrong that the law could take hold of him; yet he was not over scrupulous about the morality of an action, when the prospect of enriching himself by it was very great, and the chance of hurting his character was small. The corn he sent home to his customers was not always quite so good as the samples he had produced at market; and he now and then forgot to name some capital blemish in the horses he sold at fair. He scorned to be guilty of the petty fraud of cheating in weights and measures, for he thought that was a beggarly sin; but he valued himself on his skill in making a bargain, and fancied it showed his superior knowledge of the world to take advantage of the ignorance of a dealer.

It was his constant rule to undervalue every thing he was about to buy, and to overvalue every thing he was about to sell; but as he seldom lost sight of his discretion, he avoided every thing that was very shameful; so that he was considered merely as a hard dealer, and a keen hand at a bargain. Now and then when he had been caught in pushing his own advantage too far, he contrived to get out of the scrape by turning the whole into a jest, saying it was a good take in, a rare joke, and he had only a mind to divert himself with the folly of his neighbor, who could be so easily imposed on.

Mr. Bragwell, however, in his way, set a high value on his character: not indeed that he had a right sense of its worth; he did not consider reputation as desirable because it increases influence, and for that reason strengthens the hands of a good man, and enlarges his sphere of usefulness: but he made the advantage of reputation, as well as of every other good, center in himself. Had he observed a strict attention to principle, he feared he should not have got on so fast in the world as those do who consult expediency rather than probity, while, without a certain degree of character, he knew also, that he should forfeit that confidence which put other men in his power, and would set them as much on their guard against him, as he, who thought all mankind pretty much alike, was on his guard against them.

Mr. Bragwell had one favorite maxim; namely, that a man's success in life was a sure proof of his wisdom: and that all failure and misfortune was the consequence of a man's own folly. As this opinion was first taken up by him from vanity and ignorance, so it was more and more confirmed by his own prosperity. He saw that he himself had succeeded greatly without either money or education to begin with, and he therefore now despised every man, however excellent his character or talents might be, who had not the same success in life. His natural disposition was not particularly bad, but prosperity had hardened his heart. He made his own progress in life the rule by which the conduct of all other men was to be judged, without any allowance for their peculiar disadvantages, or the visitations of Providence. He thought, for his part, that every man of sense could command success on his undertakings, and control and dispose the events of his own life.

But though he considered those who had had less success than himself as no better than fools, yet he did not extend this opinion to Mr. Worthy, whom he looked upon not only as a good but a wise man. They had been bred up when children in the same house; but with this difference, that Worthy was the nephew of the master, and Bragwell the son of the servant.

Bragwell's father had been plowman in the family of Mr. Worthy's uncle, a sensible man who farmed a small estate of his own, and who, having no children, bred up young Worthy as his son, instructed him in the business of husbandry, and at his death left him his estate. The father of Worthy was a pious clergyman, who lived with his brother the farmer, in order to help out a narrow income. He had bestowed much pains on the instruction of his son, and used frequently to repeat to him a saying, which he had picked up in a book written by one of the greatest men this country ever produced—That there were two things with which every man ought to be acquainted, RELIGION, AND HIS OWN BUSINESS. While he therefore took care that his son should be made an excellent farmer, he filled up his leisure hours in improving his mind: so that young Worthy had read more good books, and understood them better, than most men in his station. His reading, however, had been chiefly confined to husbandry and divinity, the two subjects which were of the most immediate importance to him.

The reader will see by this time that Mr. Bragwell and Mr. Worthy were as likely to be as opposite to each other as two men could well be, who were nearly of the same age and condition, and who were neither of them without credit in the world. Bragwell indeed made far the greater figure; for he liked to cut a dash, as he called it. It was his delight to make the ancient gentry of the neighborhood stare, at seeing a grazier vie with them in show, and exceed them in expense. And while it was the study of Worthy to conform to his station, and to set a good example to those about him, it was the delight of Bragwell to eclipse, in his way of life, men of larger fortune. He did not see how much his vanity raised the envy of his inferiors, the ill-will of his equals, and the contempt of his betters.

His wife was a notable stirring woman, but vain, violent, and ambitious; very ignorant, and very high-minded. She had married Bragwell before he was worth a shilling, and as she had brought him a good deal of money, she thought herself the grand cause of his rising in the world; and thence took occasion to govern him most completely. Whenever he ventured to oppose her, she took care to put him in mind that he owed every thing to her; that had it not been for her, he might still have been stumping after a plow-tail, or serving hogs in old Worthy's farm-yard; but that it was she who made a gentleman of him. In order to set about making him a gentleman, she had begun by teasing him till he had turned away all his poor relations who worked on the farm; she next drew him off from keeping company with his old acquaintances, and at last persuaded him to remove from the place where he had got his money. Poor woman! she had not sense and virtue enough to see how honorable it is for a man to raise himself in the world by fair means, and then to help forward his poor relations and friends; engaging their services by his kindness, and endeavoring to turn his own advancement in life to the best account, and of making it the instrument of assisting those who had a natural claim to his protection.

Mrs. Bragwell was an excellent mistress, according to her own notions of excellence; for no one could say she ever lost an opportunity of scolding a servant, or was ever guilty of the weakness of overlooking a fault. Toward her two daughters her behavior was far otherwise. In them she could see nothing but perfections, but her extravagant fondness for these girls was full as much owing to pride as to affection. She was bent on making a family, and having found out that she was too ignorant, and too much trained to the habits of getting money, ever to hope to make a figure herself, she looked to her daughters as the persons who were to raise the family of the Bragwells; and to this hope she foolishly submitted to any drudgery for their sakes and bore every kind of impertinence from them.

The first wish of her heart was to set them above their neighbors; for she used to say, what was the use of having substance, if her daughters might not carry themselves above girls who had nothing? To do her justice, she herself would be about early and late to see that the business of the house was not neglected. She had been bred to great industry, and continued to work when it was no longer necessary, both from early habit, and the desire of heaping up money for her daughters. Yet her whole notion of gentility was, that it consisted in being rich and idle; and, though she was willing to be a drudge herself, she resolved to make her daughters gentlewomen on this principle. To be well dressed, to eat elegantly, and to do nothing, or nothing which is of any use, was what she fancied distinguished people in genteel life. And this is too common a notion of a fine education among a certain class; they do not esteem things by their use, but by their show. They estimate the value of their children's education by the money it costs, and not by the knowledge and goodness it bestows. People of this stamp often take a pride in the expense of learning, instead of taking pleasure in the advantage of it. And the silly vanity of letting others see that they can afford any thing, often sets parents on letting their daughters learn not only things of no use, but things which may be really hurtful in their situation; either by setting them above their proper duties, or by taking up their time in a way inconsistent with them.

Mrs. Bragwell sent her daughters to a boarding-school, where she instructed them to hold up their heads as high as any body; to have more spirit than to be put upon by any one; never to be pitiful about money, but rather to show that they could afford to spend with the best; to keep company with the richest and most fashionable girls in the school, and to make no acquaintance with the farmers' daughters.

They came home at the usual age of leaving school, with a large portion of vanity grafted on their native ignorance. The vanity was added, but the ignorance was not taken away. Of religion they could not possibly learn any thing, since none was taught, for at that place Christianity was considered as a part of education which belonged only to charity schools. They went to church indeed once a Sunday, yet effectually to counteract any benefit such an attendance might produce, it was the rule of the school that they should use only French prayer-books; of course, such superficial scholars as the Miss Bragwells would always be literally praying in an unknown tongue; while girls of better capacity and more industry would infallibly be picking out the nominative case, the verb, and a participle of a foreign language, in the solemn act of kneeling before the Father of Spirits, "who searcheth the heart and trieth the reins." During the remainder of the Sunday they learned their worldly tasks, all except actual needle-work, which omission alone marked the distinction of Sunday from other days; and the governess being a French Roman Catholic, it became a doubtful point with some people, whether her zeal or her negligence in the article of religion would be most to the advantage of her pupils. Of knowledge the Miss Bragwells had got just enough to laugh at their fond parents' rustic manners and vulgar language, and just enough taste to despise and ridicule every girl who was not as vainly dressed as themselves.

The mother had been comforting herself for the heavy expense of their bringing up, by looking forward to the pleasure of seeing them become fine ladies, and the pride of marrying them above their station; and to this hope she constantly referred in all her conversations with them; assuring them that all her happiness depended on their future elevation.

Their father hoped, with far more judgment, that they would be a comfort to him both in sickness and in health. He had no learning himself, and could write but poorly, and owed what skill he had in figures to his natural turn of business. He reasonably hoped that his daughters, after all the money he had spent on them, would now write his letters and keep his accounts. And as he was now and then laid up with a fit of the gout, he was enjoying the prospect of having two affectionate children to nurse him, as well as two skillful assistants to relieve him.

When they came home, however, he had the mortification to find, that though he had two smart showy ladies to visit him, he had neither dutiful daughters to nurse him, nor faithful stewards to keep his books, nor prudent children to manage his house. They neither soothed him by their kindness when he was sick, nor helped him by their industry when he was busy. They thought the maid might take care of him in the gout as she did before; for they fancied that nursing was a coarse and servile employment; and as to their skill in ciphering he soon found, to his cost, that though they knew how to spend both pounds, shillings, and pence, yet they did not know how so well to cast them up. Indeed it is to be regretted that women in general, especially in the middle class, are so little grounded in so indispensable, solid, and valuable an acquirement as arithmetic.

Mrs. Bragwell being one day very busy in preparing a great dinner for the neighbors, ventured to request her daughters to assist in making the pastry. They asked her with a scornful smile, whether she had sent them to a boarding school to learn to cook; and added, that they supposed she would expect them next to make hasty-puddings for the hay-makers. So saying, they coolly marched off to their music. When the mother found her girls too polite to be of any use, she would take comfort in observing how her parlor was set out with their filagree and flowers, their embroidery and cut paper. They spent the morning in bed, the noon in dressing, the evening at the harpsichord, and the night in reading novels.

With all these fine qualifications it is easy to suppose, that as they despised their sober duties, they no less despised their plain neighbors. When they could not get to a horse-race, a petty-ball, or a strolling play, with some company as idle and as smart as themselves, they were driven for amusement to the circulating library. Jack, the plow-boy, on whom they had now put a livery jacket, was employed half his time in trotting backward and forward with the most wretched trash the little neighboring bookshop could furnish. The choice was often left to Jack, who could not read, but who had general orders to bring all the new things, and a great many of them.

It was a misfortune, that at the school at which they had been bred, and at some others, there was no system of education which had any immediate reference to the station of life to which the girls chiefly belonged. As persons in the middle line, for want of that acquaintance with books, and with life and manners, which the great possess, do not always see the connection between remote consequences and their causes, the evils of a corrupt and inappropriate system of education do not strike them so forcibly; and provided they can pay for it, which is made the grand criterion between the fit and the unfit, they are too little disposed to consider the value, or rather the worthlessness, of the thing which is paid for: but literally go on to give their money for that which is not bread.

Their subsequent course of reading serves to establish all the errors of their education. Instead of such books as might help to confirm and strengthen them in all the virtues of their station, in humility, economy, meekness, contentment, self-denial, and industry; the studies now adopted are, by a graft on the old stock, made to grow on the habits acquired at school. Of those novels and plays which are so eagerly devoured by persons of this description, there is perhaps scarce one which is not founded upon principles which would lead young women of the middle ranks to be discontented with their station. It is rank—it is elegance—it is beauty—it is sentimental feelings—it is sensibility—it is some needless, or some superficial, or some hurtful quality, even in that fashionable person to whom the author ascribes it, which is the ruling principle. This quality transferred into the heart and the conduct of an illiterate woman in an inferior station, becomes absurdity, becomes sinfulness.

Things were in this state in the family we are describing, or rather growing worse; for idleness and vanity are never at a stand; when these two wealthy farmers, Bragwell and Worthy, met at Weyhill fair, as was said before. After many hearty salutations had passed between them, it was agreed that Mr. Bragwell should spend the next day with his old friend whose house was not many miles distant. Bragwell invited himself in the following manner: "We have not had a comfortable day's chat for years," said he; "and as I am to look at a drove of lean beasts in your neighborhood, I will take a bed at your house, and we will pass the evening debating as we used to do. You know I always loved a bit of an argument, and am not reckoned to make the worst figure at our club. I had not, to be sure, such good learning as you had, because your father was a parson, and you got it for nothing; but I can bear my part pretty well for all that. When any man talks to me about his learning, I ask if it has helped him to get a good estate; if he says no, then I would not give him a rush for it; for of what use is all the learning in the world, if it does not make a man rich? But as I was saying, I will come and see you to-morrow; but now don't let your wife put herself in a fuss for me: don't alter your own plain way; for I am not proud, I assure you, nor above my old friends; though I thank God, I am pretty well in the world."

To all this flourishing speech Mr. Worthy coolly answered, that certainly worldly prosperity ought never make any man proud, since it is God who giveth strength to get riches, and without his blessing, 'tis in vain to rise up early, and to eat the bread of carefulness.

About the middle of the next day Mr. Bragwell reached Mr. Worthy's neat and pleasant dwelling. He found every thing in the reverse of his own. It had not so many ornaments, but it had more comforts. And when he saw his friend's good old-fashioned arm-chair in a warm corner, he gave a sigh to think how his own had been banished to make room for his daughter's piano-forte. Instead of made flowers in glass cases, and tea-chests and screens too fine to be used, which he saw at home, and about which he was cautioned, and scolded as often as he came near them; his daughters watching his motions with the same anxiety as they would have watched the motions of a cat in a china shop. Instead of this, I say, he saw some neat shelves of good books for the service of the family, and a small medicine chest for the benefit of the poor.

Mrs. Worthy and her daughters had prepared a plain but neat and good dinner. The tarts were so excellent that Bragwell felt a secret kind of regret that his own daughters were too genteel to do any thing so very useful. Indeed he had been always unwilling to believe that any thing which was very proper and very necessary, could be so extremely vulgar and unbecoming as his daughters were always declaring it to be. And his late experience of the little comfort he found at home, inclined him now still more strongly to suspect that things were not so right there as he had been made to suppose. But it was in vain to speak; for his daughters constantly stopped his mouth by a favorite saying of theirs, which equally indicated affectation and vulgarity, that it was better to be out of the world than out of the fashion.

Soon after dinner the women went out to their several employments; and Mr. Worthy being left alone with his guest, the following discourse took place:

Bragwell. You have a couple of sober, pretty looking girls, Worthy; but I wonder they don't tiff off a little more. Why, my girls have as much, fat and flour on their heads as would half maintain my reapers in suet pudding.

Worthy. Mr. Bragwell, in the management of my family, I don't consider what I might afford only, though that is one great point; but I consider also what is needful and becoming in a man of my station; for there are so many useful ways of laying out money, that I feel as if it were a sin to spend one unnecessary shilling. Having had the blessing of a good education myself I have been able to give the like advantage to my daughters. One of the best lessons I have taught them is, to know themselves; and one proof that they have learned this lesson is, that they are not above any of the duties of their station. They read and write well, and when my eyes are bad, they keep my accounts in a very pretty manner. If I had put them to learn what you call genteel things, these might have been of no use to them, and so both time and money thrown away; or they might have proved worse than nothing to them by leading them into wrong notions, and wrong company. Though we do not wish them to do the laborious parts of the dairy work, yet they always assist their mother in the management of it. As to their appearance, they are every day nearly as you see them now, and on Sunday they are very neatly dressed, but it is always in a decent and modest way. There are no lappets, fringes, furbelows, and tawdry ornaments; no trains, turbans, and flounces, fluttering about my cheese and butter. And I should feel no vanity, but much mortification, if a stranger, seeing Farmer Worthy's daughters at church, should ask who those fine ladies were.

Bragwell. Now I own I should like to have such a question asked concerning my daughters; I like to make people stare and envy. It makes one feel one-self somebody. I never feel the pleasure of having handsome things so much as when I see they raise curiosity; and enjoy the envy of others as a fresh evidence of my own prosperity. But as to yourself, to be sure, you best know what you can afford; and indeed that there is some difference between your daughters and the Miss Bragwells.

Worthy. For my part, before I engage in any expense, I always ask myself these two short questions; First, can I afford it? Secondly, is it proper for me?

Bragwell. Do you so? Now I own I ask myself but one; for if I find I can afford it, I take care to make it proper for me. If I can pay for a thing, no one has a right to hinder me from having it.

Worthy. Certainly. But a man's own prudence, his love of propriety and sense of duty, ought to prevent him from doing an improper thing, as effectually as if there were somebody to hinder him.

Bragwell. Now, I think a man is a fool who is hindered from having any thing he has a mind to; unless indeed, he is in want of money to pay for it. I am no friend to debt. A poor man must want on.

Worthy. But I hope my children have not learned to want any thing which is not proper for them. They are very industrious; they attend to business all day, and in the evening they sit down to their work and a good book. I take care that neither their reading nor conversation shall excite any desires or tastes unsuitable to their condition. They have little vanity, because the kind of knowledge they have is of too sober a sort to raise admiration; and from that vanity which attends a little smattering of frivolous accomplishments, I have secured them, by keeping them in total ignorance of all such. I think they live in the fear of God. I trust they are humble and pious, and I am sure they seem cheerful and happy. If I am sick, it is pleasant to see them dispute which shall wait upon me; for they say the maid can not do it so tenderly as themselves.

This part of the discourse staggered Bragwell. An involuntary tear rushed into his eye. Vain as he was, he could not help feeling what a difference a religious and a worldly education made on the heart, and how much the former regulated even the natural temper. Another thing which surprised him was, that these girls living a life of domestic piety, without any public diversions, should be so very cheerful and happy; while his own daughters, who were never contradicted, and were indulged with continual amusements, were always sullen and ill tempered. That they who were more humored, should be less grateful, and they who were more amused less happy, disturbed him much. He envied Worthy the tenderness of his children, though he would not own it, but turned it off thus:

Bragwell. But my girls are too smart to make mops of, that is the truth. Though ours is a lonely village, it is wonderful to see how soon they get the fashions. What with the descriptions in the magazines, and the pictures in the pocket-books, they have them in a twinkling and out-do their patterns all to nothing. I used to take in the Country Journal, because it was useful enough to see how oats went, the time of high water, and the price of stocks. But when my ladies came home, forsooth, I was soon wheedled out of that, and forced to take a London paper, that tells a deal about the caps and feathers, and all the trumpery of the quality, and the French dress, and the French undress. When I want to know what hops are a bag, they are snatching the paper to see what violet soap is a pound. And as to the dairy, they never care how cow's milk goes, as long as they can get some stuff which they call milk of roses. Seeing them disputing violently the other day about cream and butter, I thought it a sign they were beginning to care for the farm, till I found it was cold cream for the hands, and jessamine butter for the hair.

Worthy. But do your daughters never read?

Bragwell. Read! I believe they do too. Why our Jack, the plow-boy, spends half his time in going to a shop in our market town, where they let out books to read, with marble covers. And they sell paper with all manner of colors on the edges, and gim-cracks, and powder-puffs, and wash-balls, and cards without any pips, and every thing in the world that's genteel and of no use. 'Twas but the other day I met Jack with a basket full of these books; so having some time to spare, I sat down to see a little what they were about.

Worthy. Well, I hope you there found what was likely to improve your daughters, and teach them the true use of time.

Bragwell. O, as to that, you are pretty much out. I could make neither head nor tail of it; it was neither fish, flesh, nor good red-herring; it was all about my lord, and Sir Harry, and the captain. But I never met with such nonsensical fellows in my life. Their talk was no more like that of my old landlord, who was a lord you know, nor the captain of our fencibles, than chalk is like cheese. I was fairly taken in at first, and began to think I had got hold of a godly book; for there was a deal about hope and despair, and death, and heaven, and angels, and torments, and everlasting happiness. But when I got a little on, I found there was no meaning in all these words, or if any, it was a bad meaning. Eternal misery, perhaps, only meant a moment's disappointment about a bit of a letter; and everlasting happiness meant two people talking nonsense together for five minutes. In short, I never met with such a pack of lies. The people talk such wild gibberish as no folks in their sober senses ever did talk; and the things that happen to them are not like the things that ever happen to me or any of my acquaintance. They are at home one minute, and beyond sea the next; beggars to-day, and lords to-morrow; waiting-maids in the morning, and duchesses at night. Nothing happens in a natural gradual way, as it does at home; they grow rich by the stroke of a wand, and poor by the magic of a word; the disinherited orphan of this hour is the overgrown heir of the next; now a bride and bridegroom turn out to be brother and sister, and the brother and sister prove to be no relations at all. You and I, master Worthy, have worked hard many years, and think it very well to have scraped a trifle of money together; you, a few hundreds, I suppose, and I a few thousands. But one would think every man in these books had the bank of England in his 'scrutoire. Then there is another thing which I never met with in true life. We think it pretty well, you know, if one has got one thing, and another has got another. I will tell you how I mean. You are reckoned sensible, our parson is learned, the squire is rich, I am rather generous, one of your daughters is pretty, and both mine are genteel. But in these books (except here and there one, whom they make worse than Satan himself), every man and woman's child of them, are all wise, and witty, and generous, and rich, and handsome, and genteel; and all to the last degree. Nobody is middling, or good in one thing, and bad in another, like my live acquaintance; but it is all up to the skies, or down to the dirt. I had rather read Tom Hickathrift, or Jack the Giant Killer, a thousand times.

Worthy. You have found out, Mr. Bragwell, that many of these books are ridiculous; I will go further, and say, that to me they appear wicked also; and I should account the reading of them a great mischief, especially to people in middling and low life, if I only took into the account the great loss of time such reading causes, and the aversion it leaves behind for what is more serious and solid. But this, though a bad part, is not the worst. These books give false views of human life. They teach a contempt for humble and domestic duties; for industry, frugality, and retirement. Want of youth and beauty is considered in them as ridiculous. Plain people, like you and me, are objects of contempt. Parental authority is set at naught. Nay, plots and contrivances against parents and guardians fill half the volumes. They consider love as the great business of human life, and even teach that it is impossible for this love to be regulated or restrained; and to the indulgence of this passion every duty is therefore sacrificed. A country life, with a kind mother or a sober aunt, is described as a state of intolerable misery; and one would be apt to fancy from their painting, that a good country-house is a prison, and a worthy father the jailor. Vice is set off with every ornament which can make it pleasing and amiable; while virtue and piety are made ridiculous, by tacking to them something that is silly or absurd. Crimes which would be considered as hanging matter at our county assizes—at least if I were a juryman, I should bring in the whole train of heroes, Guilty—Death—are here made to the appearance of virtue, by being mixed with some wild flight of unnatural generosity. Those crying sins, ADULTERY, GAMING, DUELS, and SELF-MURDER, are made so familiar, and the wickedness of them is so disguised by fine words and soft descriptions, that even innocent girls get loose to their abhorrence, and talk with complacency of things which should not be so much as named by them.

I should not have said so much on this mischief, continued Mr. Worthy, from which I dare say, great folks fancy people in our station are safe enough, if I did not know and lament that this corrupt reading is now got down even among some of the lowest class. And it is an evil which is spreading every day. Poor industrious girls, who get their bread by the needle or the loom, spend half the night in listening to these books. Thus the labor of one girl is lost, and the minds of the rest are corrupted; for though their hands are employed in honest industry, which might help to preserve them from a life of sin, yet their hearts are at the very time polluted by scenes and descriptions which are too likely to plunge them into it; and when their vain weak heads compare the soft and delicious lives of the heroines in the book, with their own mean garb and hard labor, the effect is obvious; and I think I do not go too far when I say, that the vain and showy manner in which young women, who have to work for their bread, have taken to dress themselves, added to the poison they draw from these books, contribute together to bring them to destruction, more than almost any other cause. Now tell me, do not you think these wild books will hurt your daughters?

Bragwell. Why I do think they are grown full of schemes, and contrivances and whispers, that's the truth on't. Every think is a secret. They always seem to be on the look-out for something, and when nothing comes on't, then they are sulky and disappointed. They will keep company with their equals; they despise trade and farming; and I own I'm for the stuff. I should not like them to marry any but a man of substance, if he was ever so smart. Now they will hardly sit down with a substantial country dealer. But if they hear of a recruiting party in our market-town, on goes the finery—off they are. Some flimsy excuse is patched up. They want something at the book-shop or the milliner's; because, I suppose, there is a chance that some Jack-a-napes of an ensign may be there buying sticking plaster. In short, I do grow a little uneasy; for I should not like to see all I have saved thrown away on a knapsack.

So saying, they both rose and walked out to view the farm. Mr. Bragwell affected greatly to admire the good order of every thing he saw; but never forgot to compare it with something larger, and handsomer, or better of his own. It was easy to see that self was his standard of perfection in every thing. All he himself possessed gained some increased value in his eyes from being his; and in surveying the property of his friend, he derived food for his vanity, from things which seemed least likely to raise it. Every appearance of comfort, of success, of merit, in any thing which belonged to Mr. Worthy led him to speak of some superior advantage of his own of the same kind; and it was clear that the chief part of the satisfaction he felt in walking over the farm of his friend, was caused by thinking how much larger his own was.

Mr. Worthy, who felt a kindness for him, which all his vanity could not cure, was always on the watch how to turn their talk on some useful point. And whenever people resolve to go into company with this view, it is commonly their own fault, if some opportunity of turning it to account does not offer.

He saw Bragwell was intoxicated with pride, and undone by success; and that his family was in the high road to ruin through mere prosperity. He thought that if some means could be found to open his eyes on his own character, to which he was now totally blind, it might be of the utmost service to him. The more Mr. Worthy reflected, the more he wished to undertake the kind office. He was not sure that Mr. Bragwell would bear it, but he was very sure it was his duty to attempt it. As Mr. Worthy was very humble himself, he had great patience and forbearance with the fault's of others. He felt no pride at having escaped the errors into which they had fallen, for he knew who it was had made him to differ. He remembered that God had given him many advantages; a pious father and a religious education: this made him humble under a sense of his own sins, and charitable toward the sins of others, who had not the same privileges.

Just as he was going to try to enter into a very serious conversation with his guest, he was stopped by the appearance of his daughter, who told them supper was ready. This interruption obliges me to break off also, and I shall reserve what follows to the next month, when I promise to give my readers the second part of this history.

PART II

A CONVERSATION

Soon after supper Mrs. Worthy left the room with her daughters, at her husband's desire; for it was his intention to speak more plainly to Bragwell than was likely to be agreeable to him to hear before others. The two farmers being seated at their little table, each in a handsome old-fashioned great chair, Bragwell began:

"It is a great comfort, neighbor Worthy, at a certain time of life to be got above the world: my notion is, that a man should labor hard the first part of his days, that he may then sit down and enjoy himself the remainder. Now, though I hate boasting, yet as you are my oldest friend, I am about to open my heart to you. Let me tell you then I reckon I have worked as hard as any man in my time, and that I now begin to think I have a right to indulge a little. I have got my money with character, and I mean to spend it with credit. I pay every one his own, I set a good example, I keep to my church, I serve God, I honor the king, and I obey the laws of the land."

"This is doing a great deal indeed," replied Mr. Worthy; "but," added he, "I doubt that more goes to the making up all these duties than men are commonly aware of. Suppose then that you and I talk the matter over coolly; we have the evening before us. What if we sit down together as two friends and examine one another."

Bragwell, who loved argument, and who was not a little vain both of his sense and his morality, accepted the challenge, and gave his word that he would take in good part any thing that should be said to him. Worthy was about to proceed, when Bragwell interrupted him for a moment, by saying, "But stop, friend, before we begin I wish you would remember that we have had a long walk, and I want a little refreshment; have you no liquor that is stronger than this cider? I am afraid it will give me a fit of the gout."

Mr. Worthy immediately produced a bottle of wine, and another of spirits; saying, that though he drank neither spirits nor even wine himself, yet his wife always kept a little of each as a provision in case of sickness or accidents.

Farmer Bragwell preferred the brandy, and began to taste it. "Why," said he, "this is no better than English; I always use foreign myself." "I bought this for foreign," said Mr. Worthy. "No, no, it is English spirits, I assure you; but I can put you into a way to get foreign nearly as cheap as English." Mr. Worthy replied that he thought that was impossible.

Bragwell. Oh no; there are ways and means—a word to the wise—there is an acquaintance of mine that lives upon the south coast—you are a particular friend and I will get you half-a-dozen gallons for a trifle.

Worthy. Not if it be smuggled, Mr. Bragwell, though I should get it for sixpence a bottle. "Ask no questions," said the other, "I never say any thing to any one, and who is the wiser?" "And so this is your way of obeying the laws of the land," said Mr. Worthy, "here is a fine specimen of your morality."

Bragwell. Come, come, don't make a fuss about trifles. If every one did it indeed it would be another thing; but as to my getting a little good brandy cheap, why that can't hurt the revenue much.

Worthy. Pray Mr. Bragwell, what should you think of a man who would dip his hand into a bag and take out a few guineas?

Bragwell. Think? why I think that he should be hanged, to be sure.

Worthy. But suppose that bag stood in the king's treasury?

Bragwell. In the king's treasury! worse and worse! What! rob the king's treasury! Well, I hope if any one has done it, the robber will be taken up and executed; for I suppose we shall be taxed to pay the damage.

Worthy. Very true. If one man takes money out of the treasury, others must be obliged to pay the more into it. But what think you if the fellow should be found to have stopped some money in its way to the treasury, instead of taking it out of the bag after it got there?

Bragwell. Guilty, Mr. Worthy; it is all the same in my opinion. If I were judge I would hang him without benefit of clergy.

Worthy. Hark ye, Mr. Bragwell, he that deals in smuggled brandy is the man who takes to himself the king's money in its way to the treasury, and he as much robs the government as if he dipped his hand into a bag of guineas in the treasury chamber. It comes to the same thing exactly. Here Bragwell seemed a little offended, and exclaimed, "What, Mr. Worthy! do you pretend to say I am not an honest man because I like to get my brandy as cheap as I can? and because I like to save a shilling to my family? Sir, I repeat it; I do my duty to God and my neighbor. I say the Lord's prayer most days, I go to church on Sundays, I repeat my creed, and keep the ten commandments; and though I now and then get a little brandy cheap, yet upon the whole, I will venture to say, I do as much as can be expected of any man, and more than the generality."

Worthy. Come then, since you say you keep the commandments, you can not be offended if I ask you whether you understand them.

Bragwell. To be sure I do. I dare say I do: look ye, Mr. Worthy, I don't pretend to much reading, I was not bred to it as you were. If my father had been a parson, I fancy I should have made as good a figure as some other folks, but I hope good sense and a good heart may teach a man his duty without much scholarship.

Worthy. To come to the point; let us now go through the ten commandments, and let us take along with us those explanations of them which our Saviour gave us in his sermon on the mount.

Bragwell. Sermon on the mount! why the ten commandments are in the 20th chapter of Exodus. Come, come, Mr. Worthy, I know where to find the commandments as well as you do; for it happens that I am churchwarden, and I can see from the altar-piece where the ten commandments are, without your telling me, for my pew directly faces it.

Worthy. But I advise you to read the sermon on the mount, that you may see the full meaning of them.

Bragwell. What! do you want to make me believe there are two ways of keeping the commandments?

Worthy. No; but there may be two ways of understanding them.

Bragwell. Well, I am not afraid to be put to the proof; I defy any man to say I do not keep at least all the four first that are on the left side of the altar-piece.

Worthy. If you can prove that, I shall be more ready to believe you observe those of the other table; for he who does his duty to God, will be likely to do his duty to his neighbor also.

Bragwell. What! do you think that I serve two Gods? Do you think then that I make graven images, and worship stocks or stones? Do you take me for a papist or an idolater?

Worthy. Don't triumph quite so soon, Master Bragwell. Pray is there nothing in the world you prefer to God, and thus make an idol of? Do you not love your money, or your lands, or your crops, or your cattle, or your own will, or your own way, rather better than you love God? Do you never think of these with more pleasure than you think of him, and follow them more eagerly than your religious duty?

Bragwell. Oh! there's nothing about that in the 20th chapter of Exodus.

Worthy. But Jesus Christ has said, "He that loveth father or mother more than me is not worthy of me." Now it is certainly a man's duty to love his father and his mother; nay, it would be wicked not to love them, and yet we must not love even these more than our Creator and our Saviour. Well, I think on this principle, your heart pleads guilty to the breach of the first and second commandments; let us proceed to the third.

Bragwell. That is about swearing, is it not?

Mr. Worthy, who had observed Bragwell guilty of much profaneness in using the name of his Maker (though all such offensive words have been avoided in writing this history), now told him that he had been waiting the whole day for an opportunity to reprove him for his frequent breach of the third commandment.

"Good L—d! I break the third commandment!" said Bragwell; "no indeed, hardly ever; I once used to swear a little, to be sure, but I vow I never do it now, except now and then when I happen to be in a passion: and in such a case, why, good G—d, you know the sin is with those who provoke me, and not with me; but upon my soul, I don't think I have sworn an oath these three months; no, not I, faith, as I hope to be saved."

Worthy. And yet you have broken this holy law not less than five or six times in the last speech you have made.

Bragwell. Lord bless me! Sure you mistake. Good heavens, Mr. Worthy, I call G—d to witness, I have neither cursed nor swore since I have been in the house.

Worthy. Mr. Bragwell, this is the way in which many who call themselves very good sort of people deceive themselves. What! is it no profanation of the name of your Maker to use it lightly, irreverently and familiarly as you have done? Our Saviour has not only told us not to swear by the immediate name of God, but he has said, "swear not at all, neither by heaven nor by the earth," and in order to hinder our inventing any other irreligious exclamations or expressions, he has even added, "but let your communications be yea, yea, and nay, nay; for whatsoever is more than this simple affirmation and denial cometh of evil." Nay, more, so greatly do I reverence that high and holy name, that I think even some good people have it too frequently in their mouths; and that they might convey the idea without the word.

Bragwell. Well, well, I must take a little more care, I believe. I vow to heaven I did not know there had been so much harm in it; but my daughters seldom speak without using some of these words, and yet they wanted to make me believe the other day that it was monstrous vulgar to swear.

Worthy. Women, even gentlewomen, who ought to correct this evil habit in their fathers, and husbands, and children, are too apt to encourage it by their own practice. And indeed they betray the profaneness of their own minds also by it; for none who venerate the holy name of God, can either profane in this manner themselves, or hear others do so without being exceedingly pained at it.

Bragwell. Well, since you are so hard upon me, I believe I must e'en give up this point—so let us pass on to the next, and here I tread upon sure ground; for as sharp as you are upon me, you can't accuse me of being a Sabbath breaker, since I go to church every Sunday of my life, unless on some very extraordinary occasion.

Worthy. For those occasions the gospel allows, by saying, "the Sabbath was made for man, and not man for the Sabbath." Our own sickness, or attending on the sickness of others, are lawful impediments.

Bragwell. Yes, and I am now and then obliged to look at a drove of beasts, or to go a journey, or take some medicine, or perhaps some friend may call upon me, or it may be very cold, or very hot, or very rainy.

Worthy. Poor excuse! Mr. Bragwell. Do you call these lawful impediments? I am afraid they will not pass for such on the day of judgment. But how is the rest of your Sunday spent?

Bragwell. O, why, I assure you I often go to church in the afternoon also, and even if I am ever so sleepy.

Worthy. And so you finish your nap at church, I suppose.

Bragwell. Why, as to that, to be sure we do contrive to have something a little nicer than common for dinner on a Sunday: in consequence of which one eats, you know, a little more than ordinary; and having nothing to do on that day, has more leisure to take a cheerful glass; and all these things will make one a little heavy, you know.

Worthy. And don't you take a little ride in the morning, and look at your sheep when the weather is good; and so fill your mind just before you go to church with thoughts of them; and when the weather is bad, don't you settle an account? or write a few letters of business after church.

Bragwell. I can't say but I do; but that is nothing to any body, as long as I set a good example by keeping to my church.

Worthy. And how do you pass your Sunday evenings?

Bragwell. My wife and daughters go a visiting Sunday afternoons. My daughters are glad to get out, at any rate; and as to my wife, she says that being ready dressed, it is a pity to lose the opportunity; besides, it saves her time on a week day; so then you see I have it all my own way, and when I have got rid of the ladies, who are ready to faint at the smell of tobacco, I can venture to smoke a pipe, and drink a sober glass of punch with half a dozen friends.

Worthy. Which punch, being made of smuggled brandy, and drank on the Lord's day, and very vain, as well as profane and worldly company, you are enabled to break both the law of God, and that of your country at a stroke: and I suppose when you are got together, you speak of your cattle, or of your crops, after which perhaps you talk over a few of your neighbors' faults, and then you brag a little of your own wealth or your own achievements.

Bragwell. Why, you seem to know us so well, that any one would think you had been sitting behind the curtain; and yet you are a little mistaken too; for I think we have hardly said a word for several of our last Sundays on any thing but politics.

Worthy. And do you find that you much improve your Christian charity by that subject?

Bragwell. Why to be sure we do quarrel till we are very near fighting, that is the worst on't.

Worthy. And then you call names, and swear a little, I suppose.

Bragwell. Why when one is contradicted and put in a passion, you know, and when people especially if they are one's inferiors, won't adopt one's opinions, flesh and blood won't bear it.

Worthy. And when all your friends are gone home, what becomes of the rest of the evening?

Bragwell. That is just as it happens; sometimes I read the newspaper; and as one is generally most tired on the days one does nothing, I go to bed earlier on Sundays than on other days, that I may be more fit to get up to my business the next morning.

Worthy. So you shorten Sunday as much as you can, by cutting off a bit at both ends, I suppose; for I take it for granted you lie a little later in the morning.

Bragwell. Come, come, we sha'n't get through the whole ten to-night, if you stand snubbing one at this rate. You may pass over the fifth; for my father and mother have been dead ever since I was a boy, so I am clear of that scrape.

Worthy. There are, however, many relative duties included in that commandment; unkindness to all kindred is forbidden.

Bragwell. O, if you mean my turning off my nephew Tom, the plowboy, you must not blame me for that, it was all my wife's fault. He was as good a lad as ever lived to be sure, and my own brother's son; but my wife could not bear that a boy in a carter's frock should be about the house, calling her aunt. We quarreled like dog and cat about it; and when he was turned away she and I did not speak for a week.

Worthy. Which was a fresh breach of the commandment; a worthy nephew turned out of doors, and a wife not spoken to for a week, are no very convincing proofs of your observance of the fifth commandment.

Bragwell. Well, I long to come to the sixth, for you don't think I commit murder, I hope.

Worthy. I am not sure of that.

Bragwell. Murder! what, I kill any body?

Worthy. Why, the laws of the land, indeed, and the disgrace attending it, are almost enough to keep any man from actual murder; let me ask, however, do you never give way to unjust anger, and passion, and revenge? as for instance, do you never feel your resentment kindle against some of the politicians who contradict you on a Sunday night? and do you never push your animosity against somebody that has affronted you, further than the occasion can justify?

Bragwell. Hark'ee, Mr. Worthy, I am a man of substance, and no man shall offend me without my being even with him. So as to injuring a man, if he affronts me first, there's nothing but good reason in that.

Worthy. Very well! only bear in mind, that you willfully break this commandment, whether you abuse your servant, are angry at your wife, watch for a moment to revenge an injury on your neighbor, or even wreak your passion on a harmless beast; for you have then the seeds of murder working in your breast; and if there were no law, no gibbet, to check you, and no fear of disgrace neither, I am not sure where you would stop.

Bragwell. Why, Mr. Worthy, you have a strange way of explaining the commandments; so you set me down for a murderer, merely because I bear hatred to a man who has done me a hurt, and am glad to do him a like injury in my turn. I am sure I should want spirit if I did not.

Worthy. I go by the Scripture rule, which says, "he that hateth his brother is a murderer," and again, "pray for them that despitefully use you and persecute you." Besides, Mr. Bragwell, you made it a part of your boast that you said the Lord's prayer every day, wherein you pray to God to forgive you your trespasses as you forgive them that trespass against you. If therefore you do not forgive them that trespass against you, in that case you daily pray that your own trespasses may never be forgiven. Now own the truth; did you last night lie down in a spirit of forgiveness and charity with the whole world?

Bragwell. Yes, I am in charity with the whole world in general; because the greater part of it has never done me any harm. But I won't forgive old Giles, who broke down my new hedge yesterday for firing— Giles, who used to be so honest.

Worthy. And yet you expect that God will forgive you who have broken down his sacred laws, and have so often robbed him of his right—you have robbed him of the honor due unto his name—you have robbed him of his holy day by doing your own work, and finding your own pleasure in it—you have robbed his poor, particularly in the instance of Giles, by withholding from them, as overseer, such assistance as should prevent their being driven to the sin of stealing.

Bragwell. Why, you are now charging me with other men's sins as well as my own.

Worthy. Perhaps the sins which we cause other men to commit, through injustice, inconsideration, and evil example, may dreadfully swell the sum of our responsibility in the great day of account.

Bragwell. Well, come, let us make haste and get through these commandments. The next is, "Thou shalt not commit adultery." Thank God, neither I nor my family can be said to break the seventh commandment.

Worthy. Here again, remember how Christ himself hath said, "whoso looketh on a woman to lust after her, hath already committed adultery with her in his heart." These are no far-fetched expressions of mine, Mr. Bragwell, they are the words of Jesus Christ. I hope you will not charge him with having carried this too far; for if you do, you charge him with being mistaken in the religion he taught; and this can only be accounted for, by supposing him an impostor.

Bragwell. Why, upon my word, Mr. Worthy, I don't like these sayings of his which you quote upon me so often, and that is the truth of it, and I can't say I feel much disposed to believe them.

Worthy. I hope you believe in Jesus Christ. I hope you believe that creed of yours, which you also boasted of repeating so regularly.

Bragwell. Well, well, I'll believe any thing you say, rather than stand quarreling with you.

Worthy. I hope then, you will allow, that since it is adultery to look at a woman with even an irregular thought, it follows from the same rule, that all immodest dress in your daughters, or indecent jests and double meanings in yourself; all loose songs or novels; and all diversions also which have a like dangerous tendency, are forbidden by the seventh commandment; for it is most plain from what Christ has said, that it takes in not only the act, but the inclination, the desire, the indulged imagination; the act is only the last and highest degree of any sin; the topmost round, as it were, of a ladder, to which all the lower rounds are only as so many steps and stages.

Bragwell. Strict indeed! Mr. Worthy; but let us go on to the next; you won't pretend to say I steal; Mr. Bragwell, I trust, was never known to rob on the highway, to break open his neighbor's house, or to use false weights or measures.

Worthy. No, nor have you ever been under any temptation to do it, and yet there are a thousand ways of breaking the eighth commandment besides actual stealing. For instance do you never hide the faults of the goods you sell, and heighten the faults of those you buy? Do you never take advantage of an ignorant dealer, and ask more for a thing than it is worth? Do you never turn the distressed circumstances of a man who has something to sell, to your unfair benefit; and thus act as unjustly by him as if you had stolen? Do you never cut off a shilling from a workman's wages, under the pretense which your conscience can't justify? Do you never pass off an unsound horse for a sound one? Do you never conceal the real rent of your estate from the overseers, and thereby rob the poor-rates of their legal due?

Bragwell. Pooh! these things are done every day. I sha'n't go to set up for being better than my neighbors in these sort of things; these little matters will pass muster—I don't set up for a reformer—if I am as good as the rest of my neighbors, no man can call me to account: I am not worse, I trust, and don't pretend to be better.

Worthy. You must be tried hereafter at the bar of God, and not by a jury of your fellow-creatures; and the Scriptures are given us, in order to show by what rule we shall be judged. How many or how few do as you do, is quite aside from the question; Jesus Christ has even told us to strive to enter in at the strait gate; so we ought rather to take fright, from our being like the common run of people, than to take comfort from our being so.

Bragwell. Come, I don't like all this close work—it makes a man feel I don't know how—I don't find myself so happy as I did—I don't like this fishing in troubled waters; I'm as merry as the day is long when I let these things alone. I'm glad we are got to the ninth. But I suppose I shall be lugged in there too, head and shoulders. Any one now who did not know me, would really think I was a great sinner, by your way of putting things; I don't bear false witness, however.

Worthy. You mean, I suppose, you would not swear away any man's life falsely before a magistrate, but do you take equal care not to slander or backbite him? Do you never represent a good action of a man you have quarreled with, as if it were a bad one? or do you never make a bad one worse than it is, by your manner of telling it? Even when you invent no false circumstances, do you never give such a color to those you relate, as to leave a false impression on the mind of the hearers? Do you never twist a story so as to make it tell a little better for yourself, and a little worse for your neighbor, than truth and justice warrant?

Bragwell. Why, as to that matter, all this is only natural.

Worthy. Ay, much too natural to be right, I doubt. Well, now we have got to the last of the commandments.

Bragwell. Yes, I have run the gauntlet finely through them all; you will bring me in guilty here, I suppose, for the pleasure of going through with it; for you condemn without judge or jury, Master Worthy.

Worthy. The culprit, I think, has hitherto pleaded guilty to the evidence brought against him. The tenth commandment, however, goes to the root and principle of evil, it dives to the bottom of things; this command checks the first rising of sin in the heart; teaches us to strangle it in the birth, as it were, before it breaks out in those acts which are forbidden: as, for instance, every man covets before he proceeds to steal; nay, many covet, knowing they can do it with impunity, who dare not steal, lest they should suffer for it.

Bragwell. Why, look'ee, Mr. Worthy, I don't understand these new fashioned explanations; one should not have a grain of sheer goodness left, if every thing one does is to be fritted away at this rate. I am not, I own, quite so good as I thought, but if what you say were true, I should be so miserable, I should not know what to do with myself. Why, I tell you all the world may be said to break the commandments at this rate.

Worthy. Very true. All the world, and I myself also, are but too apt to break them, if not in the letter, at least in the spirit of them. Why, then, all the world are (as the Scripture expresses it) "guilty before God." And if guilty, they should own they are guilty, and not stand up and justify themselves, as you do, Mr. Bragwell.

Bragwell. Well, according to my notion, I am a very honest man, and honesty is the sum and substance of all religion, say I.

Worthy. All truth, honesty, justice, order, and obedience grow out of the Christian religion. The true Christian acts at all times, and on all occasions, from the pure and spiritual principle of love to God and Christ. On this principle he is upright in his dealings, true to his word, kind to the poor, helpful to the oppressed. In short, if he truly loves God, he must do justice, and can't help loving mercy. Christianity is a uniform consistent thing. It does not allow us to make up for the breach of one part of God's law, by our strictness in observing another. There is no sponge in one duty, that can wipe out the spot of another sin.

Bragwell. Well, but at this rate, I should be always puzzling and blundering, and should never know for certain whether I was right or not; whereas I am now quite satisfied with myself, and have no doubts to torment me.

Worthy. One way of knowing whether we really desire to obey the whole law of God is this; when we find we have as great a regard to that part of it, the breach of which does not touch our own interest, as to that part which does. For instance, a man robs me; I am in a violent passion with him, and when it is said to me, doest thou well to be angry? I answer, I do well. Thou shalt not steal is a law of God, and this fellow has broken that law. Ay, but says conscience, 'tis thy own property which is in question. He has broken thy hedge, he has stolen thy sheep, he has taken thy purse. Art thou therefore sure whether it is his violation of thy property, or of God's law which provokes thee? I will put a second case: I hear another swear most grievously; or I meet him coming drunk out of an ale-house; or I find him singing a loose, profane song. If I am not as much grieved for this blasphemer, or this drunkard, as I was for this robber; if I do not take the same pains to bring him to a sense of his sin, which I did to bring the robber to justice, "how dwelleth the love of God in me?" Is it not clear that I value my own sheep more than God's commandments? That I prize my purse more than I love my Maker? In short, whenever I find out that I am more jealous for my own property than for God's law; more careful about my own reputation than his honor, I always suspect I have got upon wrong ground, and that even my right actions are not proceeding from a right principle.

Bragwell. Why, what in the world would you have me do? It would distract me, if I must run up every little action to its spring, in this manner.

Worthy. You must confess that your sins are sins. You must not merely call them sins, while you see no guilt in them; but you must confess them so as to hate and detest them; so as to be habitually humbled under the sense of them; so as to trust for salvation not in your freedom from them, but in the mercy of a Saviour; and so as to make it the chief business of your life to contend against them, and in the main to forsake them. And remember, that if you seek for a deceitful gayety, rather than a well-grounded cheerfulness; if you prefer a false security to final safety, and now go away to your cattle and your farm, and dismiss the subject from your thoughts, lest it should make you uneasy, I am not sure that this simple discourse may not appear against you at the day of account, as a fresh proof that you "loved darkness rather than light," and so increase your condemnation.

Mr. Bragwell was more affected than he cared to own. He went to bed with less spirits and more humility than usual. He did not, however, care to let Mr. Worthy see the impression which it had made upon him; but at parting next morning, he shook him by the hand more cordially than usual, and made him promise to return his visit in a short time.

What befell Mr. Bragwell and his family on his going home may, perhaps, make the subject of a future part of this history.

PART III

THE VISIT RETURNED

Mr. Bragwell, when he returned home from his visit to Mr. Worthy, as recorded in the second part of this history, found that he was not quite so happy as he had formerly been. The discourses of Mr. Worthy had broken in not a little on his comfort. And he began to suspect that he was not so completely in the right as his vanity had led him to believe. He seemed also to feel less satisfaction in the idle gentility of his own daughters, since he had been witness to the simplicity, modesty, and usefulness of those of Mr. Worthy. And he could not help seeing that the vulgar violence of his wife did not produce so much family happiness at home, as the humble piety and quiet diligence of Mrs. Worthy produced in the house of his friend.

Happy would it have been for Mr. Bragwell, if he had followed up those new convictions of his own mind, which would have led him to struggle against the power of evil principles in himself, and to have controlled the force of evil habits in his family. But his convictions were just strong enough to make him uneasy under his errors, without driving him to reform them. The slight impression soon wore off, and he fell back into his old practices. Still his esteem for Mr. Worthy was not at all abated by the plain-dealing of that honest friend. It is true, he dreaded his piercing eye: he felt that his example held out a constant reproof to himself. Yet such is the force of early affection and rooted reverence, that he longed to see him at his house. This desire, indeed, as is commonly the case, was made up of mixed motives. He wished for the pleasure of his friend's company; he longed for that favorite triumph of a vulgar mind, an opportunity of showing him his riches; and he thought it would raise his credit in the world to have a man of Mr. Worthy's character at his house.

Mr. Bragwell, it is true, still went on with the same eagerness in gaining money, and the same ostentation in spending it. But though he was as covetous as ever, he was not quite so sure that it was right to be so. While he was actually engaged abroad indeed, in transactions with his dealers, he was not very scrupulous about the means by which he got his money; and while he was indulging in festivity with his friends at home, he was easy enough as to the manner in which he spent it. But a man can neither be making bargains, nor making feasts always; there must be some intervals between these two great objects for which worldly men may be said to live; and in some of these intervals the most worldly form, perhaps, some random plans of amendment. And though many a one may say in the fullness of enjoyment, "Soul take thine ease, eat, drink, and be merry;" yet hardly any man, perhaps, allows himself to say, even in the most secret moments, I will never retire from business—I will never repent—I will never think of death—eternity shall never come into my thoughts. The most that such a one probably ventures to say is, I need not repent yet; I will continue such a sin a little longer; it will be time enough to think on the next world when I am no longer fit for the business or the pleasures of this.

Such was the case with Bragwell. He set up in his mind a general distant sort of resolution, that some years hence, when he should be a few years older, a few thousands richer; when a few more of his present schemes should be completed, he would then think of altering his course of life. He would then certainly set about spending a religious old age; he would reform some practices in his dealings, or perhaps, quit business entirely; he would think about reading good books, and when he had completed such a purchase, he would even begin to give something to the poor; but at present he really had little to spare for charity. The very reason why he should have given more was just the cause he assigned for not giving at all, namely the hardness of the times. The true grand source of charity, self-denial, never came into his head. Spend less that you may save more, he would have thought a shrewd maxim enough. But spend less that you may spare more, never entered into his book of proverbs.

At length the time came when Mr. Worthy had promised to return his visit. It was indeed a little hastened by notice that Mr. Bragwell would have in the course of the week a piece of land to sell by auction; and though Mr. Worthy believed the price was likely to be above his pocket, yet he knew it was an occasion which would be likely to bring the principal farmers of that neighborhood together, some of whom he wanted to meet. And it was on this occasion that Mr. Bragwell prided himself, that he should show his neighbors so sensible a man as his dear friend Mr. Worthy.

Worthy arrived at his friend's house on the Saturday, time enough to see the house, and garden, and grounds of Mr. Bragwell by daylight. He saw with pleasure (for he had a warm and generous heart) those evident signs of his friend's prosperity; but as he was a man of sober mind, and was a most exact dealer in truth, he never allowed his tongue the license of immodest commendation, which he used to say either savored of flattery or envy. Indeed he never rated mere worldly things so highly as to bestow upon them undue praise. His calm approbation somewhat disappointed the vanity of Mr. Bragwell, who could not help secretly suspecting that his friend, as good a man as he was, was not quite free from envy. He felt, however, very much inclined to forgive this jealousy, which he feared the sight of his ample property, and handsome habitation must naturally awaken in the mind of a man whose own possessions were so inferior. He practiced the usual trick of ordinary and vulgar minds, that of pretending himself to find some fault with those things which were particularly deserving praise, when he found Worthy disposed to pass them over in silence.

When they came in to supper, he affected to talk of the comforts of Mr. Worthy's little parlor, by way of calling his attention to his own large one. He repeated the word snug, as applied to every thing at Mr. Worthy's, with the plain design to make comparisons favorable to his own more ample domains. He contrived, as he passed by his chair, by a seeming accident, to push open the door of a large beaufet in the parlor, in which all the finery was most ostentatiously set out to view. He protested with a look of satisfaction which belied his words, that for his part he did not care a farthing for all this trumpery; and then smiling and rubbing his hands, added, with an air of no small importance, what a good thing it is though, for people of substance, that the tax on plate is taken off. "You are a happy man, Mr. Worthy; you do not feel these things; tax or no tax, it is all the same to you." He took care during this speech, by a cast of his eye, to direct Mr. Worthy's attention to a great profusion of the brightest cups, salvers, and tankards, and other shining ornaments, which crowded the beaufet. Mr. Worthy gravely answered Mr. Bragwell, "It was indeed a tax which could not affect so plain a man as myself; but as it fell on a mere luxury, and therefore could not hurt the poor, I was always sorry that it could not be made productive enough to be continued. A man in my middling situation, who is contented with a good glass of beer, poured from a handsome earthen mug, the glass, the mug, and the beer, all of English manufacture, will be but little disturbed at taxes on plate or on wine; but he will regret, as I do, that many of these taxes are so much evaded, that new taxes are continually brought on to make up the deficiencies of the old."

During supper the young ladies sat in disdainful silence, not deigning to bestow the smallest civility on so plain a man as Mr. Worthy. They left the room with their mamma as soon as possible, being impatient to get away to ridicule their father's old-fashioned friend at full liberty.

THE DANCE; OR, THE CHRISTMAS MERRY-MAKING; EXEMPLIFYING THE EFFECTS OF MODERN EDUCATION IN A FARMHOUSE.

As soon as they were gone, Mr. Worthy asked Bragwell how his family comforts stood, and how his daughters, who, he said, were really fine young women, went on. "O, as to that," replied Bragwell, "pretty much like other men's handsome daughters, I suppose, that is, worse and worse. I really begin to apprehend that their fantastical notions have gained such a head, that after all the money I have scraped together, I shall never get them well married.

"Betsy has just lost as good an offer as any girl could desire: young Wilson, an honest substantial grazier as any in the country. He not only knows every thing proper for his station, but is pleasing in his behavior, and a pretty scholar into the bargain; he reads history-books and voyages of a winter's evening, to his infirm father, instead of going to the card-assembly in our town; he neither likes drinking nor sporting, and is a sort of a favorite with our parson, because he takes in the weekly numbers of a fine Bible with cuts, and subscribes to the Sunday School, and makes a fuss about helping the poor; and sets up soup-shops, and sells bacon at an under price, and gives odd bits of ground to his laborers to help them in these dear times, as they call them; but I think they are good times for us, Mr. Worthy.

"Well, for all this, Betsy only despised him, and laughed at him; but as he is both handsome and rich, I thought she might come round at last; and so I invited him to come and stay a day or two at Christmas, when we have always a little sort of merry-making here. But it would not do. He scorned to talk that palavering stuff which she has been used to in the marble-covered books I told you of. He told her, indeed, that it would be the happiness of his heart to live with her; which I own I thought was as much as could be expected of any man. But miss had no notion of marrying any one who was only desirous of living with her. No, and forsooth, her lover must declare himself ready to die for her, which honest Wilson was not such a fool as to offer to do. In the afternoon, however, he got a little into her favor by making out a rebus or two in the Lady's Diary, and she condescended to say, she did not think Mr. Wilson had been so good a scholar; but he soon spoiled all again. We had a little dance in the evening. The young man, though he had not much taste for those sort of gambols, yet thought he could foot it a little in the old fashioned way. So he asked Betsy to be his partner. But when he asked what dance they should call, miss drew up her head, and in a strange gibberish, said she should dance nothing but a Menuet de la Cour, and ordered him to call it. Wilson stared, and honestly told her she must call it herself; for he could neither spell nor pronounce such outlandish words, nor assist in such an outlandish performance. I burst out a laughing, and told him, I supposed it something like questions and commands; and if so, that was much merrier than dancing. Seeing her partner standing stock still, and not knowing how to get out of the scrape, the girl began by herself, and fell to swimming, and sinking, and capering, and flourishing, and posturing, for all the world just like the man on the slack rope at our fair. But seeing Wilson standing like a stuck pig, and we all laughing at her, she resolved to wreak her malice upon him; so, with a look of rage and disdain, she advised him to go down country bumpkin, with the dairy maid, who would make a much fitter partner, as well as wife, for him, than she could do.

"'I am quite of your mind, miss,' said he, with more spirit than I thought was in him; 'you may make a good partner for a dance, but you would make a sad one to go through life with. I will take my leave of you, miss, with this short story. I had lately a pretty large concern in hay-jobbing, which took me to London. I waited a good while in the Hay-market for my dealer, and, to pass away the time, I stepped into a sort of foreign singing play-house there, where I was grieved to the heart to see young women painted and dizened out, and capering away just as you have been doing. I thought it bad enough in them, and wondered the quality could be entertained with such indecent mummery. But little did I think to meet with the same paint, finery, and posturing tricks in a farm-house. I will never marry a woman who despises me, nor the station in which I should place her, and so I take my leave.' Poor girl, how she was provoked! to be publicly refused, and turned off, as it were, by a grazier! But it was of use to some of the other girls, who have not held up their heads quite so high since, nor painted quite so red, but have condescended to speak to their equals.

"But how I run on! I forget it is Saturday night, and that I ought to be paying my workmen, who are all waiting for me without."

SATURDAY NIGHT, OR THE WORKMEN'S WAGES

As soon as Mr. Bragwell had done paying his men, Mr. Worthy, who was always ready to extract something useful from accidental circumstances, said to him, "I have made it a habit, and I hope not an unprofitable one, of trying to turn to some moral use, not only all the events of daily life, but all the employments of it, too. And though it occurs so often, I hardly know one that sets me thinking more seriously than the ordinary business you have been discharging." "Ay," said Bragwell, "it sets me thinking too, and seriously, as you say, when I observe how much the price of wages is increased." "Yes, yes, you are ready enough to think of that," said Worthy, "but you say not a word of how much the value of your land is increased, and that the more you pay, the more you can afford to pay. But the thoughts I spoke of are quite of another cast.

"When I call in my laborers, on a Saturday night, to pay them, it often brings to my mind the great and general day of account, when I, and you, and all of us, shall be called to our grand and awful reckoning, when we shall go to receive our wages, master and servants, farmer and laborer. When I see that one of my men has failed of the wages he should have received, because he has been idling at a fair; another has lost a day by a drinking-bout, a third confesses that, though he had task-work, and might have earned still more, yet he has been careless, and has not his full pay to receive; this, I say, sometimes sets me on thinking whether I also have made the most of my time. And when I come to pay even the more diligent, who have worked all the week, when I reflect that even these have done no more than it was their duty to do, I can not help saying to myself, Night is come, Saturday night is come. No repentance, or diligence on the part of these poor men can now make a bad week's work good. This week has gone into eternity. To-morrow is the season of rest; working-time is over. 'There is no knowledge nor device in the grave.' My life also will soon be swallowed up in eternity; soon the space allotted me for diligence, for labor, will be over. Soon will the grand question be asked, 'What hast thou done? Give an account of thy stewardship. Didst thou use thy working days to the end for which they were given? With some such thoughts I commonly go to bed, and they help to quicken me to a keener diligence for the next week."

SOME ACCOUNT OF A SUNDAY IN MR. BRAGWELL'S FAMILY

Mr. Worthy had been for so many years used to the sober ways of his own well-ordered family, that he greatly disliked to pass a Sunday in any house of which religion was not the governing principle. Indeed, he commonly ordered his affairs, and regulated his journeys with an eye to this object. "To pass a Sunday in an irreligious family," said he, "is always unpleasant, often unsafe. I seldom find I can do them any good, and they may perhaps do me some harm. At least, I am giving a sanction to their manner of passing it, if I pass it in the same manner. If I reprove them, I subject myself to the charge of singularity, and of being righteous over-much; if I do not reprove them, I confirm and strengthen them in evil. And whether I reprove them or not, I certainly partake of their guilt, if I spend it as they do."

He had, however, so strong a desire to be useful to Mr. Bragwell, that he at length determined to break through his common practice, and pass the Sunday at his house. Mr. Worthy was surprised to find that though the church bell was going, the breakfast was not ready, and expressed his wonder how this could be the case in so industrious a family. Bragwell made some awkward excuses. He said his wife worked her servants so hard all the week, that even she, as notable as she was, a little relaxed from the strictness of her demands on Sunday mornings; and he owned that in a general way no one was up early enough for church. He confessed that his wife commonly spent the morning in making puddings, pies, syllabubs, and cakes, to last through the week; as Sunday was the only leisure time she and her maids had. Mr. Worthy soon saw an uncommon bustle in the house. All hands were busy. It was nothing but baking, and boiling, and stewing, and frying, and roasting, and running, and scolding, and eating. The boy was kept from church to clean the plate, the man to gather the fruit, the mistress to make the cheese-cakes, the maids to dress the dinner, and the young ladies to dress themselves.

The truth was, Mrs. Bragwell, who had heard much of the order and good management of Mr. Worthy's family, but who looked down with disdain upon them as far less rich than herself, was resolved to indulge her vanity on the present occasion. She was determined to be even with Mrs. Worthy, in whose praises Bragwell had been so loud, and felt no small pleasure in the hope of making her guest uneasy, in comparing her with his own wife, when he should be struck dumb with the display both of her skill and her wealth. Mr. Worthy was indeed struck to behold as large a dinner as he had been used to see at a justice's meeting. He, whose frugal and pious wife had accustomed him only to such a plain Sunday's dinner as could be dressed without keeping any one from church, when he surveyed the loaded table of his friend, instead of feeling that envy which the grand preparations were meant to raise, felt nothing but disgust at the vanity of his friend's wife, mixed with much thankfulness for the piety and simplicity of his own.

After having made the dinner wait a long time, the Misses Bragwell marched in, dressed as if they were going to the assize-ball; they looked very scornfully at having been so hurried, though they had been dressing ever since they got up, and their fond father, when he saw them so fine, forgave all their impertinence, and cast an eye of triumph on Mr. Worthy, who felt he had never loved his own humble daughters so well as at that moment.

In the afternoon the whole party went to church. To do them justice, it was indeed their common practice once a day, when the weather was good, and the road was neither dusty nor dirty, when the minister did not begin too early, when the young ladies had not been disappointed of their bonnets on the Saturday night, and when they had no smart company in the house, who rather wished to stay at home. When this last was the case, which, to say the truth, happened pretty often, it was thought a piece of good manners to conform to the humor of the guests. Mr. Bragwell had this day forborne to ask any of his usual company, well knowing that their vain and worldly conversation would only serve to draw on him some new reprimand from his friend.

Mrs. Bragwell and her daughters picked up, as usual, a good deal of acquaintance at church. Many compliments passed, and much of the news of the week was retailed before the service began. They waited with impatience for the reading of the lessons as a licensed season for whispering, and the subject begun during the lessons, was finished while they were singing the psalms. The young ladies made an appointment for the afternoon with a friend in the next pew, while their mamma took the opportunity of inquiring aloud, the character of a dairy maid, which she observed, with a compliment to her own good management, would save time on a week-day.

Mr. Worthy, who found himself quite in a new world, returned home with his friend alone. In the evening he ventured to ask Bragwell, if he did not, on a Sunday night at least, make it a custom to read and pray with his family. Bragwell told him he was sorry to say he had no family at home, else he should like to do it for the sake of example. But as his servants worked hard all the week, his wife was of opinion that they should then have a little holiday. Mr. Worthy pressed it home upon him, whether the utter neglect of his servants' principles was not likely to make a heavy article in his final account; and asked him if he did not believe that the too general liberty of meeting together, jaunting, and diverting themselves on Sunday evenings, was not often found to produce the worst effects on the morals of servants and the good order of families? "I put it to your conscience," said he, "Mr. Bragwell, whether Sunday, which was meant as a blessing and a benefit, is not, as it is commonly kept, turned into the most mischievous part of the week, by the selfish kindness of masters, who, not daring to set their servants about any public work, allot them that day to follow their own devices, that they themselves may, with more rigor, refuse them a little indulgence, and a reasonable holiday, in the working part of the week, which a good servant has now and then a fair right to expect. Those masters who will give them half, or all of the Lord's day, will not spare them a single hour of a working day. Their work must be done; God's work may be let alone."

Mr. Bragwell owned that Sunday had produced many mischiefs in his own family. That the young men and maids, having no eye upon them, frequently went to improper places with other servants turned adrift like themselves. That in these parties the poor girls were too frequently led astray, and the men got to public houses and fives-playing. But it was none of his business to watch them. His family only did as others do; indeed it was his wife's concern; and as she was so good a manager on other days, that she would not spare them an hour to visit a sick father or mother, it would be hard, she said, if they might not have Sunday afternoon to themselves, and she could not blame them for making the most of it. Indeed, she was so indulgent in this particular, that she often excused the men from going to church, that they might serve the beasts, and the maids, that they might get the milking done before the holiday part of the evening came on. She would not, indeed, hear of any competition between doing her work and taking their pleasure; but when the difference lay between their going to church and taking their pleasure, he must say that for his wife, she always inclined to the good-natured side of the question. She is strict enough in keeping them sober, because drunkenness is a costly sin; and to do her justice, she does not care how little they sin at her expense.

"Well," said Mr. Worthy, "I always like to examine both sides fairly, and to see the different effects of opposite practices; now, which plan produces the greater share of comfort to the master, and of profit to the servants in the long run? Your servants, 'tis likely, are very much attached to you, and very fond of living where they get their own way in so great a point."

"O, as to that," replied Bragwell, "you are quite out. My house is a scene of discord, mutiny, and discontent. And though there is not a better manager in England than my wife, yet she is always changing her servants, so that every quarter-day is a sort of jail delivery at my house; and when they go off, as they often do, at a moment's warning, to own the truth, I often give them money privately, that they may not carry my wife before the justice to get their wages."

"I see," said Mr. Worthy, "that all your worldly compliances do not procure you even worldly happiness. As to my own family, I take care to let them see that their pleasure is bound up with their duty, and that what they may call my strictness, has nothing in view but their safety and happiness. By this means I commonly gain their love, as well as secure their obedience. I know that, with all my care, I am liable to be disappointed, 'from the corruption that is in the world through sin.' But whenever this happens, so far from encouraging me in remissness, it only serves to quicken my zeal. If, by God's blessing, my servant turns out a good Christian, I have been an humble instrument in his hand of saving a soul committed to my charge."

Mrs. Bragwell came home, but brought only one of her daughters with her; the other, she said, had given them the slip, and was gone with a young friend, and would not return for a day or two. Mr. Bragwell was greatly displeased, as he knew that young friend had but a slight character, and kept bad acquaintances. Mrs. Bragwell came in, all hurry and bustle, saying, if her family did not go to bed with the lamb on Sundays, when they had nothing to do, how could they rise with the lark on Mondays, when so much was to be done.

Mr. Worthy had this night much matter for reflection. "We need not," said he, "go into the great world to look for dissipation and vanity. We can find both in a farmhouse. 'As for me and my house,' continued he, 'we will serve the Lord' every day, but especially on Sunday. 'It is the day which the Lord hath made; hath made for himself; we will rejoice in it,' and consider the religious use of it, not only as a duty, but as a privilege."

The next morning Mr. Bragwell and his friend set out early for the Golden Lion. What passed on this little journey, my readers shall hear soon.

PART IV

THE SUBJECT OF PRAYER DISCUSSED IN A MORNING'S RIDE

It was mentioned in the last part of this history, that the chief reason which had drawn Mr. Worthy to visit his friend just at the present time was, that Mr. Bragwell had a small estate to sell by auction. Mr. Worthy, though he did not think he should be a bidder, wished to be present, as he had business to settle with one or two persons who were expected at the Golden Lion on that day, and he had put off his visit till he had seen the sale advertised in the county paper.

Mr. Bragwell and Mr. Worthy set out early on the Monday morning, on their way to the Golden Lion, a small inn in a neighboring market-town. As they had time before them, they had agreed to ride slowly that they might converse on some useful subject, but here, as usual, they had two opinions about the same thing. Mr. Bragwell's notion of a useful subject was, something by which money was to be got, and a good bargain struck. Mr. Worthy was no less a man of business than his friend. His schemes were wise, and his calculations just; his reputation for integrity and good sense made him the common judge and umpire in his neighbors' affairs, while no one paid a more exact attention to every transaction of his own. But the business of getting money was not with him the first, much less was it the whole concern of the day. He sought, in the first place, 'the kingdom of God and his righteousness.' Every morning when he rose, he remembered that he had a Maker to worship as well as a family to maintain. Religion, however, never made him neglect business, though it sometimes made him postpone it. He used to say, no man had any reason to expect God's blessing through the day who did not ask it in the morning; nor was he likely to spend the day in the fear of God who did not begin it with his worship. But he had not the less sense, spirit, and activity, when he was among men abroad, because he had first served God at home.

As these two farmers rode along, Mr. Worthy took occasion, from the fineness of the day, and the beauty of the country through which they passed, to turn the discourse to the goodness of God, and our infinite obligations to him. He knew that the transition from thanksgiving to prayer would be natural and easy; and he, therefore, sliding by degrees into that important subject, observed that secret prayer was a duty of universal obligation, which every man has it in his power to fulfill, and which he seriously believed was the ground-work of all religious practice, and of all devout affections.

Mr. Bragwell felt conscious that he was very negligent and irregular in the performance of this duty; indeed, he considered it as a mere ceremony, or at least, as a duty which might give way to the slightest temptation of drowsiness at night, or business in the morning. As he knew he did not live in the conscientious performance of this practice, he tried to ward off the subject, knowing what a home way his friend had of putting things. After some evasion, he at last said, he certainly thought private prayer a good custom, especially for people who had time; and that those who were sick, or old, or out of business, could not do better; but that for his part, he believed much of these sort of things was not expected from men in active life.

Worthy. I should think, Mr. Bragwell, that those who are most exposed to temptations stand most in need of prayer; now there are few, methinks, who are more exposed to temptation than men in business; for those must be in most danger, at least from the world, who have most to do with it. And if this be true, ought we not to prepare ourselves in the closet for the trials of the market, the field, and the shop? It is but putting on our armor before we go out to battle.

Bragwell. For my part, I think example is the whole of religion, and if the master of a family is orderly, and regular, and goes to church, he does every thing which can be required of him, and no one has a right to call him to an account for any thing more.

Worthy. Give me leave to say, Mr. Bragwell, that highly as I rate a good example, still I must set a good principle above it. I know I must keep good order, indeed, for the sake of others; but I must keep a good conscience for my own sake. To God I owe secret piety, I must, therefore, pray to him in private; to my family I owe a Christian example, and for that, among other reasons, I must not fail to go to church.

Bragwell. You are talking, Mr. Worthy, as if I were an enemy to religion. Sir, I am no heathen—Sir, I am a Christian; I belong to the church; I go to church; I always drink prosperity to the church. You yourself, as strict as you are, in never missing it twice a day, are not a warmer friend to the church than I am.

Worthy. That is to say, you know its inestimable value as a political institution; but you do not seem to know that a man may be very irreligious under the best religious institutions; and that even the most excellent only furnishes the means of being religious, and is no more religion itself than brick and mortar are prayers and thanksgivings. I shall never think, however high their profession, and even however regular their attendance, that those men truly respect the church, who bring home little of that religion which is taught in it into their own families or their own hearts; or, who make the whole of Christianity to consist in a mere formal attendance there. Excuse me, Mr. Bragwell.

Bragwell. Mr. Worthy, I am persuaded that religion is quite a proper thing for the poor; and I don't think that the multitude can ever be kept in order without it; and I am a sort of a politician, you know. We must have bits, and bridles, and restraints for the vulgar.

Worthy. Your opinion is very just, as far as it goes; but it does not go far enough, since it does not go to the root of the evil; for while you value yourself on the soundness of this principle as a politician, I wish you also to see the reason of it as a Christian; depend upon it, if religion be good for the community at large, it is equally good for every family; and what is right for a family is equally right for each individual in it. You have therefore yourself brought the most unanswerable argument why you ought to be religious yourself, by asking how we shall keep others in order without religion. For, believe me, Mr. Bragwell, there is no particular clause to except you in the gospel. There are no exceptions there in favor of any one class of men. The same restraints which are necessary for the people at large, are equally necessary for men of every order, high and low, rich and poor, bond and free, learned and ignorant. If Jesus Christ died for no one particular rank, class, or community, then there is no one rank, class, or community, exempt from the obedience to his laws enjoined by the gospel. May I ask you, Mr. Bragwell, what is your reason for going to church?

Bragwell. Sir, I am shocked at your question. How can I avoid doing a thing so customary and so creditable? Not go to church, indeed! What do you take me for, Mr. Worthy? I am afraid you suspect me to be a papist, or a heathen, or of some religion or other that is not Christian.

Worthy. If a foreigner were to hear how violently one set of Christians in this country often speak against another, how earnest would he suppose us all to be in religious matters: and how astonished to discover that many a man has perhaps little other proof to give of the sincerity of his own religion, except the violence with which he hates the religion of another party. It is not irreligion which such men hate; but the religion of the man, or the party, whom we are set against; now hatred is certainly no part of the religion of the gospel. Well, you have told me why you go to church; now pray tell me, why do you confess there on your bended knees, every Sunday, that "you have erred and strayed from God's ways?" "that there is no health in you? that you have done what you ought not to do? and that you are a miserable sinner?"

Bragwell. Because it is in the Common Prayer Book, to be sure; a book which I have heard you yourself say was written by wise and good men; the glory of Christianity, the pillars of the Protestant church.

Worthy. But have you no other reason?

Bragwell. No, I can't say I have.

Worthy. When you repeat that excellent form of confession, do you really feel that you are a miserable sinner?

Bragwell. No, I can't say I do. But that is no objection to my repeating it: because it may suit the case of many who are so. I suppose the good doctors who drew it up, intended that part for wicked people only, such as drunkards, and thieves, and murderers; for I imagine they could not well contrive to make the same prayer quite suit an honest man and a rogue; and so I suppose they thought it better to make a good man repeat a prayer which suited a rogue, than to make a rogue repeat a prayer which suited a good man; and you know it is so customary for every body to repeat the general confession, that it can't hurt the credit of the most respectable persons, though every respectable person must know they have no particular concern in it; as they are not sinners.

Worthy. Depend upon it, Mr. Bragwell, those good doctors you speak of, were not quite of your opinion; they really thought that what you call honest men were grievous sinners in a certain sense, and that the best of us stand in need of making that humble confession. Mr. Bragwell, do you believe in the fall of Adam?

Bragwell. To be sure I do, and a sad thing for Adam it was; why, it is in the Bible, is it not? It is one of the prettiest chapters in Genesis. Don't you believe it, Mr. Worthy?

Worthy. Yes, truly I do. But I don't believe it merely because I read it in Genesis; though I know, indeed, that I am bound to believe every part of the word of God. But I have still an additional reason for believing in the fall of the first man.

Bragwell. Have you, indeed? Now, I can't guess what that can be.

Worthy. Why, my own observation of what is within myself teaches me to believe it. It is not only the third chapter of Genesis which convinces me of the truth of the fall, but also the sinful inclinations which I find in my own heart corresponding with it. This is one of those leading truths of Christianity of which I can never doubt a moment: first because it is abundantly expressed or implied in Scripture; and next, because the consciousness of the evil nature, I carry about me confirms the doctrine beyond all doubt. Besides, is it not said in Scripture, that by one man sin entered into the world, and that "all we, like lost sheep, have gone astray?" "that by one man's disobedience many were made sinners?" and so again in twenty more places that I could tell you of?

Bragwell. Well; I never thought of this. But is not this a very melancholy sort of doctrine, Mr. Worthy?

Worthy. It is melancholy, indeed, if we stop here. But while we are deploring this sad truth, let us take comfort from another, that "as in Adam all die, so in Christ shall all be made alive."

Bragwell. Yes; I remember I thought those very fine words, when I heard them said over my poor father's grave. But as it was in the burial of the dead, I did not think of taking it to myself; for I was then young and hearty, and in little danger of dying, and I have been so busy ever since, that I have hardly had time to think of it.

Worthy. And yet the service pronounced at the burial of all who die, is a solemn admonition to all who live. It is there said, as indeed the Scripture says also, "I am the resurrection and the life; whosoever believeth in me shall never die, but I will raise him up at the last day." Now do you think you believe in Christ, Mr. Bragwell?

Bragwell. To be sure I do; why you are always fancying me an atheist.

Worthy. In order to believe in Christ, we must believe first in our own guilt and our own unworthiness; and when we do this we shall see the use of a Saviour, and not till then.

Bragwell. Why, all this is a new way of talking. I can't say I ever meddled with such subjects before in my life. But now, what do you advise a man to do upon your plan of religion?

Worthy. Why, all this leads me back to the ground from which we set out, I mean the duty of prayer; for if we believe that we have an evil nature within us, and that we stand in need of God's grace to help us, and a Saviour to redeem us, we shall be led of course to pray for what we so much need; and without this conviction we shall not be led to pray.

Bragwell. Well, but don't you think, Mr. Worthy, that you good folks who make so much of prayer, have lower notions than we have of the wisdom of the Almighty? You think he wants to be informed of the thing you tell him; whereas, I take it for granted that he knows them already, and that, being so good as he is, he will give me every thing he sees fit to give me, without my asking it.

Worthy. God, indeed, who knows all things, knows what we want before we ask him; but still has he not said that, "with prayer and supplication we must make known our requests unto him?" Prayer is the way in which God has said that his favor must be sought. It is the channel through which he has declared it his sovereign will and pleasure that his blessings should be conveyed to us. What ascends up in prayer, descends to us again in blessings. It is like the rain which just now fell, and which had been drawn up from the ground in vapors to the clouds before it descended from them to the earth in that refreshing shower. Besides prayer has a good effect on our minds; it tends to excite a right disposition toward God in us, and to keep up a constant sense of our dependence. But above all, it is the way to get the good things we want. "Ask," says the Scripture, "and ye shall receive."

Bragwell. Now, that is the very thing which I was going to deny: for the truth is, men do not always get what they ask; I believe if I could get a good crop for asking it, I would pray oftener than I do.

Worthy. Sometimes, Mr. Bragwell, men "ask and receive not, because they ask amiss;" "they ask that they may consume it on their lusts." They ask worldly blessings, perhaps, when they should ask spiritual ones. Now, the latter, which are the good things I spoke of, are always granted to those who pray to God for them, though the former are not. I have observed in the case of some worldly things I have sought for, that the grant of my prayer would have caused the misery of my life; so that God equally consults our good in what he withholds, and in what he bestows.

Bragwell. And yet you continue to pray on, I suppose?

Worthy. Certainly; but then I try to mend as to the object of my prayers. I pray for God's blessing and favor, which is better than riches.

Bragwell. You seem very earnest on this subject.

Worthy. To cut the matter short; I ask then, whether prayer is not positively commanded in the gospel? When this is the case, we can never dispute about the necessity or the duty of a thing, as we may when there is no such command. Here, however, let me just add also, that a man's prayers may be turned into no small use in the way of discovering to him whatever is amiss in his life.

Bragwell. How so, Mr. Worthy?

Worthy. Why, suppose now, you were to try yourself by turning into the shape of a prayer every practice in which you allow yourself. For instance, let the prayer in the morning be a sort of preparation for the deeds of the day, and the prayer at night a sort of retrospection of those deeds. You, Mr. Bragwell, I suspect, are a little inclined to covetousness; excuse me, sir. Now, suppose after you have been during a whole day a little too eager to get rich; suppose, I say, you were to try how it would sound to beg of God at night on your knees, to give you still more money, though you have already so much that you know not what to do with it. Suppose you were to pray in the morning, "O Lord, give me more riches, though those I have are a snare and a temptation to me;" and ask him in the same solemn manner to bless all the grasping means you intend to make use of in the day, to add to your substance?

Bragwell. Mr. Worthy, I have no patience with you for thinking I could be so wicked.

Worthy. Yet to make such a covetous prayer as this is hardly more wicked, or more absurd, than to lead the life of the covetous, by sinning up to the spirit of that very prayer which you would not have the courage to put into words. Still further observe how it would sound to confess your sins, and pray against them all, except one favorite sin. "Lord, do thou enable me to forsake all my sins, except the love of money;" "in this one thing pardon thy servant." Or, "Do thou enable me to forgive all who have injured me, except old Giles." This you will object against as a wicked prayer, it must be wicked in practice. It is even the more shocking to make it the language of the heart, or of the life, than of the lips. And yet, because you have been used to see people act thus, and have not been used to hear them pray thus, you are shocked at the one, and not shocked at the other.

Bragwell. Shocked, indeed! Why, at this rate, you would teach one to hate one's self.

Worthy. Hear me out, Mr. Bragwell; you turned your good nephew, Tom Broad, out of doors, you know; you owned to me it was an act of injustice. Now, suppose on the morning of your doing so you had begged of God, in a solemn act of prayer, to prosper the deed of cruelty and oppression, which you intended to commit that day. I see you are shocked at the thought of such a prayer. Well, then, would not hearty prayer have kept you from committing that wicked action? In short, what a life must that be, no act of which you dare beg God to prosper and bless? If once you can bring yourself to believe that it is your bounden duty to pray for God's blessing on your day's work, you will certainly grow careful about passing such a day as you may safely ask his blessing upon. The remark may be carried to sports, diversions, company. A man, who once takes up the serious use of prayer, will soon find himself obliged to abstain from such diversions, occupations, and societies, as he can not reasonably desire that God will bless to him; and thus he will see himself compelled to leave off either the practice or the prayer. Now, Mr. Bragwell, I need not ask you which of the two he that is a real Christian will give up, sinning or praying.

Mr. Bragwell began to feel that he had not the best of the argument, and was afraid he was making no great figure in the eyes of his friend. Luckily, however, he was relieved from the difficulty into which the necessity of making some answer must have brought him, by finding they were come to the end of their little journey: and he never beheld the bunch of grapes, which decorated the sign of the Golden Lion, with more real satisfaction.

I refer my readers for the transactions at the Golden Lion, and for the sad adventures which afterward befell Mr. Bragwell's family, to the fifth part of the History of the Two Wealthy Farmers.

THE GOLDEN LION

Mr. Bragwell and Mr. Worthy alighted at the Golden Lion. It was market-day: the inn, the yard, the town was all alive. Bragwell was quite in his element. Money, company, and good cheer always set his spirits afloat. He felt himself the principal man in the scene. He had three great objects in view; the sale of his land; the letting Mr. Worthy see how much he was looked up to by so many substantial people, and the showing these people what a wise man his most intimate friend, Mr. Worthy was. It was his way to try to borrow a little credit from every person, and every thing he was connected with, and by the credit to advance his interest and increase his wealth.

The farmers met in a large room; and while they were transacting their various concerns, those whose pursuits were the same naturally herded together. The tanners were drawn to one corner, by the common interest which they took in bark and hides. A useful debate was carrying on at another little table, whether the practice of sowing wheat or of planting it were most profitable. Another set were disputing whether horses or oxen were best for plowing. Those who were concerned in canals, sought the company of other canalers; while some, who were interested in the new bill for inclosures, wisely looked out for such as knew most about waste lands.

Mr. Worthy was pleased with all these subjects, and picked up something useful on each. It was a saying of his, that most men understood some one thing, and that he who was wise would try to learn from every man something on the subject he best knew; but Mr. Worthy made a further use of the whole. What a pity is it, said he, that Christians are not so desirous to turn their time to good account as men of business are! When shall we see religious persons as anxious to derive profit from the experience of others as these farmers? When shall we see them as eager to turn their time to good account? While I approve these men for not being slothful in business, let me improve the hint, by being also fervent in spirit.

SHOWING HOW MUCH WISER THE CHILDREN OF THIS GENERATION ARE THAN THE CHILDREN OF LIGHT

When the hurry was a little over, Mr. Bragwell took a turn on the bowling-green. Mr. Worthy followed him, to ask why the sale of the estate was not brought forward. "Let the auctioneer proceed to business," said he; "the company will be glad to get home by daylight. I speak mostly with a view to others; for I do not think of being a purchaser myself." "I know it," said Bragwell, "or I would not be such a fool as to let the cat out of the bag. But is it really possible," proceeded he, with a smile of contempt, "that you should think I will sell my estate before dinner? Mr. Worthy, you are a clever man at books, and such things; and perhaps can make out an account on paper in a handsomer manner than I can. But I never found much was to be got by fine writing. As to figures, I can carry enough of them in my head to add, divide, and multiply more money than your learning will ever give you the fingering of. You may beat me at a book, but you are a very child at a bargain. Sell my land before dinner, indeed!"

Mr. Worthy was puzzled to guess how a man was to show more wisdom by selling a piece of ground at one hour than another, and desired an explanation. Bragwell felt rather more contempt for his understanding than he had ever done before. "Look'ee, Mr. Worthy," said he, "I do not think that knowledge is of any use to a man, unless he has sense enough to turn it to account. Men are my books, Mr. Worthy; and it is by reading, spelling, and putting them together to good purpose, that I have got up in the world. I shall give you a proof of this to-day. These farmers are most of them come to the Lion with a view of purchasing this bit of land of mine, if they should like the bargain. Now, as you know a thing can't be any great bargain both to the buyer and the seller too, to them and to me, it becomes me as a man of sense, who has the good of his family at heart, to secure the bargain to myself. I would not cheat any man, sir, but I think it fair enough to turn his weakness to my own advantage; there is no law against that, you know; and this is the use of one man's having more sense than another. So, whenever I have a piece of land to sell, I always give a handsome dinner, with plenty of punch and strong beer. We fill up the morning with other business; and I carefully keep back my talk about the purchase till we have dined. At dinner we have, of course a slice of politics. This puts most of us into a passion, and you know anger is thirsty. Besides 'Church and King' naturally brings on a good many other toasts. Now, as I am master of the feast, you know it would be shabby in me to save my liquor; so I push about the glass one way, and the tankard the other, till all my company are as merry as kings. Every man is delighted to see what a fine hearty fellow he has to deal with, and Mr. Bragwell receives a thousand compliments. By this time they have gained as much in good humor as they have lost in sober judgment, and this is the proper moment for setting the auctioneer to work, and this I commonly do to such good purpose, that I go home with my purse a score or two pounds heavier than if they had not been warmed by their dinner. In the morning men are cool and suspicious, and have all their wits about them; but a cheerful glass cures all distrust. And what is lucky, I add to my credit as well as my pocket, and get more praise for my dinner than blame for my bargain."

Mr. Worthy was struck with the absurd vanity which could tempt a man to own himself guilty of an unfair action for the sake of showing his wisdom. He was beginning to express his disapprobation, when they were told dinner was on the table. They went in, and were soon seated. All was mirth and good cheer. Every body agreed that no one gave such hearty dinners as Mr. Bragwell. Nothing was pitiful where he was master of the feast. Bragwell, who looked with pleasure on the excellent dinner before him, and enjoyed the good account to which he should turn it, heard their praises with delight, and cast an eye on Worthy, as much as to say Who is the wise man now? Having a mind, for his own credit, to make his friend talk, he turned to him saying, "Mr. Worthy, I believe no people in the world enjoy life more than men of our class. We have money and power, we live on the fat of the land, and have as good right to gentility as the best."

"As to gentility, Mr. Bragwell," replied Worthy, "I am not sure that this is among the wisest of our pretensions. But I will say, that ours is a creditable and respectable business. In ancient times, farming was the employment of princes and patriarchs; and, now-a-days, an honest, humane, sensible, English yeoman, I will be bold to say, is not only a very useful, but an honorable character. But then, he must not merely think of enjoying life as you call it, but he must think of living up to the great ends for which he was sent into the world. A wealthy farmer not only has it in his power to live well, but to do much good. He is not only the father of his own family, but his workmen, his dependants, and the poor at large, especially in these hard times. He has in his power to raise into credit all the parish offices which have fallen into disrepute by getting into bad hands; and he can convert, what have been falsely thought mean offices, into very important ones, by his just and Christian-like manner of filling them. An upright juryman, a conscientious constable, a humane overseer, an independent elector, an active superintendent of a work-house, a just arbitrator in public disputes, a kind counselor in private troubles;

such a one, I say, fills up a station in society no less necessary, and, as far as it reaches, scarcely less important than that of a magistrate, a sheriff of a county, or even a member of parliament. That can never be a slight or degrading office, on which the happiness of a whole parish may depend."

Bragwell, who thought the good sense of his friend reflected credit on himself, encouraged Worthy to go on, but he did it in his own vain way. "Ay, very true, Mr. Worthy," said he, "you are right; a leading man in our class ought to be looked up to as an example, as you say; in order to which, he should do things handsomely and liberally, and not grudge himself, or his friends, any thing;" casting an eye of complacency on the good dinner he had provided. "True," replied Mr. Worthy, "he should be an example of simplicity, sobriety, and plainness of manners. But he will do well," added he, "not to affect a frothy gentility, which will sit but clumsily upon him. If he has money, let him spend prudently, lay up moderately for his children, and give liberally to the poor. But let him rather seek to dignify his own station by his virtues, than to get above it by his vanity. If he acts thus, then, as long as his country lasts, a farmer of England will be looked upon as one of its most valuable members; nay more, by this conduct, he may contribute to make England last the longer. The riches of the farmer, corn and cattle, are the true riches of a nation; but let him remember, that though corn and cattle enrich a country, nothing but justice, integrity, and religion, can preserve it."

Here one of the company, who was known to be a man of loose principles, and who seldom went to public worship, said he had no objection to religion, and was always ready to testify his regard to it by drinking church and king. On this Mr. Worthy remarked, that he was afraid that too many contented themselves with making this toast include the whole of their religion, if not of their loyalty. "It is with real sorrow," continued he, "that I am compelled to observe, that though there are numberless honorable instances to the contrary, yet I have seen more contempt and neglect of Christianity in men of our calling, than in almost any other. They too frequently hate the rector on account of his tithes, to which he has as good a right as they have to their farms, and the curate on account of his poverty; but the truth is, religion itself is often the concealed object of their dislike. I know too many, who, while they affect a violent outward zeal for the church, merely because they conceive its security to be somehow connected with their own political advantages, yet prove the hollowness of their attachment, by showing little regard to its ministers, and less to its ordinance."

Young Wilson, the worthy grazier, whom Miss Bragwell turned off because he did not understand French dances, thanked Mr. Worthy for what he had said, and hoped he should be the better for it as long as he lived, and desired his leave to be better acquainted. Most of the others declared they had never heard a finer speech, and then, as is usual, proceeded to show the good effect it had on them, by loose conversation, hard drinking, and whatever could counteract all that Worthy had been saying.

Mr. Worthy was much concerned to hear Mr. Bragwell, after dinner, whisper to the waiter, to put less and less water into every fresh bowl of punch. This was his old way; if the time they had to sit was long, then the punch was to be weaker, as he saw no good in wasting money to make it stronger than the time required. But if time pressed, then the strength was to be increased in due proportion, as a small quantity must then intoxicate them as much in a short time as would be required of a greater quantity had the time been longer. This was one of Mr. Bragwell's nice calculations; and this was the sort of skill on which he so much valued himself.

At length the guests were properly primed for business; just in that convenient stage of intoxication which makes men warm and rash, yet keeps short of that absolute drunkenness which disqualifies for business, the auctioneer set to work. All were bidders, and, if possible, all would have been purchasers;

so happily had the feast and the punch operated. They bid on with a still increasing spirit, till they got so much above the value of the land, that Bragwell with a wink and a whisper, said: "Who would sell his land fasting? Eh! Worthy?" At length the estate was knocked down, at a price very far above its worth.

As soon as it was sold, Bragwell again said softly to Worthy, "Five from fifty and there remain forty-five. The dinner and drink won't cost me five pounds, and I have got fifty more than the land was worth. Spend a shilling to gain a pound! This is what I call practical arithmetic, Mr. Worthy."

Mr. Worthy was glad to get out of this scene; and seeing that his friend was quite sober, he resolved as they rode home, to deal plainly with him. Bragwell had found out, among his calculations, that there were some sins which could only be committed, by a prudent man, one at a time. For instance, he knew that a man could not well get rich and get drunk at the same moment; so that he used to practice one first, and the other after; but he had found out that some vices made very good company together; thus, while he had watched himself in drinking, lest he should become as unfit to sell as his guests were to buy, he had indulged, without measure, in the good dinner he had provided. Mr. Worthy, I say, seeing him able to bear reason, rebuked him for this day's proceedings with some severity. Bragwell bore his reproofs with that sort of patience which arises from an opinion of one's own wisdom, accompanied by a recent flush of prosperity. He behaved with that gay good humor, which grows out of united vanity and good fortune. "You are too squeamish, Mr. Worthy," said he, "I have done nothing discreditable. These men came with their open eyes. There is no compulsion used. They are free to bid or to let it alone. I make them welcome, and I shall not be thought a bit the worse of by them to-morrow, when they are sober. Others do it besides me, and I shall never be ashamed of any thing as long as I have custom on my side."

Worthy. I am sorry, Mr. Bragwell, to hear you support such practices by such arguments. There is not, perhaps, a more dangerous snare to the souls of men than is to be found in that word CUSTOM. It is a word invented to reconcile corruption with credit, and sin with safety. But no custom, no fashion, no combination of men, to set up a false standard can ever make a wrong action right. That a thing is often done, is so far from a proof of its being right, that it is the very reason which will set a thinking man to inquire if it be not really wrong, lest he should be following "a multitude to do evil." Right is right, though only one man in a thousand pursues it; and wrong will be forever wrong, though it be the allowed practice of the other nine hundred and ninety-nine. If this shameful custom be really common, which I can hardly believe, that is a fresh reason why a conscientious man should set his face against it. And I must go so far as to say (you will excuse me, Mr. Bragwell) that I see no great difference, in the eye of conscience, whatever there may be in the eye of the law, between your making a man first lose his reason, and then getting fifty guineas out of his pocket, because he has lost it, and your picking the fifty guineas out of his pocket, if you had met him dead drunk in his way home to-night. Nay, he who meets a man already drunk and robs him, commits but one sin; while he who makes him drunk first that he may rob him afterward, commits two.

Bragwell gravely replied: "Mr. Worthy, while I have the practice of people of credit to support me, and the law of the land to protect me, I see no reason to be ashamed of any thing I do." "Mr. Bragwell," answered Worthy, "a truly honest man is not always looking sharp about him, to see how far custom and the law will bear him out; if he be honest on principle, he will consult the law of his conscience, and if he be a Christian, he will consult the written law of God. We never deceive ourselves more than when we overreach others. You would not allow that you had robbed your neighbor for the world, yet you are not ashamed to own you have outwitted him. I have read this great truth in the works of a heathen, Mr. Bragwell, that the chief misery of man arises from his not knowing how to make right calculations."

Bragwell. Sir, the remark does not belong to me. I have not made an error of a farthing. Look at the account, sir—right to the smallest fraction.

Worthy. Sir, I am talking of final accounts; spiritual calculations; arithmetic in the long run. Now, in this, your real Christian is the only true calculator; he has found out that we shall be richer in the end, by denying, than by indulging ourselves. He knows that when the balance comes to be struck, when profit and loss shall be summed up, and the final account adjusted, that whatever ease, prosperity, and delight we had in this world, yet if we have lost our souls in the end, we can not reckon that we have made a good bargain. We can not pretend that a few items of present pleasure make any great figure, set over against the sum total of eternal misery. So you see it is only for want of a good head at calculation that men prefer time to eternity, pleasure to holiness, earth to heaven. You see if we get our neighbor's money at the price of our own integrity; hurt his good name, but destroy our own souls; raise our outward character, but wound our inward conscience; when we come to the last reckoning, we shall find that we were only knaves in the second instance, but fools in the first. In short, we shall find that whatever other wisdom we possessed, we were utterly ignorant of the skill of true calculation.

Notwithstanding this rebuff, Mr. Bragwell got home in high spirits, for no arguments could hinder him from feeling that he had the fifty guineas in his purse.

There is to a worldly man something so irresistible in the actual possession of present, and visible, and palpable pleasure, that he considers it as a proof of his wisdom to set them in decided opposition to the invisible realities of eternity.

As soon as Bragwell came in, he gayly threw the money he had received on the table, and desired his wife to lock it up. Instead of receiving it with her usual satisfaction, she burst into a violent fit of passion, and threw it back to him. "You may keep your cash yourself," said she. "It is all over—we want no more money. You are a ruined man! A wicked creature, scraping and working as we have done for her!" Bragwell trembled, but durst not ask what he dreaded to hear. His wife spared him the trouble, by crying out as soon as her rage permitted: "The girl is ruined; Polly is gone off!" Poor Bragwell's heart sunk within him; he grew sick and giddy, and as his wife's rage swallowed up her grief, so, in his grief, he almost forgot his anger. The purse fell from his hand, and he cast a look of anguish upon it, finding, for the first time, that money could not relieve his misery.

Mr. Worthy, who, though much concerned, was less discomposed, now called to mind, that the young lady had not returned with her mother and sister the night before; he begged Mrs. Bragwell to explain this sad story. She, instead of soothing her husband, fell to reproaching him. "It is all your fault," said she; "you were a fool for your pains. If I had had my way the girls would never have kept company with any but men of substance, and then they could not have been ruined." "Mrs. Bragwell," said Worthy, "if she has chosen a bad man, it would be still a misfortune, even though he had been rich." "O, that would alter the case," said she, "a fat sorrow is better than a lean one. But to marry a beggar, there is no sin like that." Here Miss Betsy, who stood sullenly by, put in a word, and said, her sister, however, had not disgraced herself by having married a farmer or a tradesman; she had, at least, made choice of a gentleman. "What marriage! what gentleman!" cried the afflicted father. "Tell me the worst;" He was now informed that his darling daughter was gone off with a strolling player, who had been acting in the neighboring villages lately. Miss Betsy again put in, saying, he was no stroller, but a gentleman in disguise, who only acted for his own diversion. "Does he so," said the now furious Bragwell, "then he shall be transported for mine."

At this moment a letter was brought him from his new son-in-law, who desired his leave to wait upon him, and implore his forgiveness. He owned he had been shopman to a haberdasher; but thinking his person and talents ought not to be thrown away upon trade, and being also a little behindhand, he had taken to the stage with a view of making his fortune; that he had married Miss Bragwell entirely for love, and was sorry to mention so paltry a thing as money, which he despised, but that his wants were pressing: his landlord, to whom he was in debt, having been so vulgar as to threaten to send him to prison. He ended with saying: "I have been obliged to shock your daughter's delicacy, by confessing my unlucky real name. I believe I owe part of my success with her, to my having assumed that of Augustus Frederic Theodosius. She is inconsolable at this confession, which, as you are now my father, I must also make to you, and subscribe myself, with many blushes, by the vulgar name of your dutiful son,

"TIMOTHY INCLE."

"O!" cried the afflicted father, as he tore the letter in a rage, "Miss Bragwell married to a strolling actor! How shall I bear it?" "Why, I would not bear it at all," cried the enraged mother; "I would never see her; I would never forgive her; I would let her starve at the corner of the barn, while that rascal, with all those pagan, popish names, was ranting away at the other." "Nay," said Miss Betsy, "if he is only a shopman, and if his name be really Timothy Incle, I would never forgive her neither. But who would have thought it by his looks, and by his monstrous genteel behavior? no, he never can have so vulgar a name."

"Come, come," said Mr. Worthy, "were he really an honest haberdasher, I should think there was no other harm done, except the disobedience of the thing. Mr. Bragwell, this is no time to blame you, or hardly to reason with you. I feel for you sincerely. I ought not, perhaps, just at present, to reproach you for the mistaken manner in which you have bred up your daughters, as your error has brought its punishment along with it. You now see, because you now feel, the evil of a false education. It has ruined your daughter; your whole plan unavoidably led to some such end. The large sums you spent to qualify them, as you thought, for a high station, only served to make them despise their own, and could do them nothing but harm, while your habits of life properly confined them to company of a lower class. While they were better dressed than the daughters of the first gentry, they were worse taught as to real knowledge, than the daughters of your plowmen. Their vanity has been raised by excessive finery, and kept alive by excessive flattery. Every evil temper has been fostered by indulgence. Their pride has never been controlled; their self-will has never been subdued; their idleness has laid them open to every temptation, and their abundance has enabled them to gratify every desire; their time, that precious talent, has been entirely wasted. Every thing they have been taught to do is of no use, while they are utterly unacquainted with all which they ought to have known. I deplore Miss Polly's false step. That she should have married a runaway shopman, turned stroller, I truly lament. But for what better husband was she qualified? For the wife of a farmer she was too idle; for the wife of a tradesman she was too expensive; for the wife of a gentleman she was too ignorant. You yourself was most to blame. You expected her to act wisely, though you never taught her that fear of God which is the beginning of wisdom. I owe it to you, as a friend, and to myself as a Christian, to declare, that your practices in the common transactions of life, as well as your present misfortune, are almost the natural consequences of those false principles which I protested against when you were at my house."[12]

[12] See Part II.

Mrs. Bragwell attempted several times to interrupt Mr. Worthy, but her husband would not permit it. He felt the force of all his friend said, and encouraged him to proceed. Mr. Worthy thus went on: "It grieves me to say how much your own indiscretion has contributed even to bring on your present misfortune. You gave your countenance to this very company of strollers, though you knew they were acting in defiance of the laws of the land, to say no worse. They go from town to town, and from barn to barn, stripping the poor of their money, the young of their innocence, and all of their time. Do you remember with how much pride you told me that you had bespoke The Bold Stroke for a Wife, for the benefit of this very Mr. Frederic Theodosius? To this pernicious ribaldry you not only carried your own family, but wasted I know not how much money in treating your workmen's wives and children, in these hard times, too, when they have scarcely bread to eat, or a shoe on their feet; and all this only that you might have the absurd pleasure of seeing those flattering words, By desire of Mr. Bragwell, stuck up in print at the public house, on the blacksmith's shed, at the turnpike-gate, and on the barn-door."

Mr. Bragwell acknowledged that his friend's rebuke was too just, and he looked so very contrite as to raise the pity of Mr. Worthy, who, in a mild voice, thus went on: "What I have said is not so much to reproach you with the ruin of one daughter, as from a desire to save the other. Let Miss Betsy go home with me. I do not undertake to be her jailor, but I will be her friend. She will find in my daughters kind companions, and in my wife a prudent guide. I know she will dislike us at first, but I do not despair in time of convincing her that a sober, humble, useful, pious life, is as necessary to make us happy on earth, as it is to fit us for heaven."

Poor Miss Betsy, though she declared it would be frightful dull, and monstrous vulgar, and dismal melancholy, yet was she so terrified at the discontent and grumbling which she would have to endure at home, that she sullenly consented. She had none of that filial tenderness which led her to wish to stay and sooth and comfort her afflicted father. All she thought about was to get out of the way of her mother's ill humor, and to carry so much of her finery with her as to fill the Misses Worthy with envy and respect. Poor girl! she did not know that envy was a feeling they never indulged; and that fine clothes were the last thing to draw their respect.

Mr. Worthy took her home next day. When they reached his house they found there young Wilson, Miss Betsy's old admirer. She was much pleased at this, and resolved to treat him well. But her good or ill treatment now signified but little. This young grazier reverenced Mr. Worthy's character, and ever since he had met him at the Lion, had been thinking what a happiness it would be to marry a young woman bred up by such a father. He had heard much of the modesty and discretion of both the daughters, but his inclination now determined him in favor of the elder.

Mr. Worthy, who knew him to be a young man of good sense and sound principles, allowed him to become a visitor at his house, but deferred his consent to the marriage till he knew him more thoroughly. Mr. Wilson, from what he saw of the domestic piety of this family, improved daily, both in the knowledge and practice of religion; and Mr. Worthy soon formed him into a most valuable character. During this time Miss Bragwell's hopes had revived: but though she appeared in a new dress almost every day, she had the mortification of being beheld with great indifference by one whom she had always secretly liked. Mr. Wilson married before her face a girl who was greatly her inferior in fortune, person, and appearance; but who was humble, frugal, meek, and pious. Miss Bragwell now strongly felt the truth of what Mr. Wilson had once told her, that a woman may make an excellent partner for a dance who would make a very bad companion for life.

Hitherto Mr. Bragwell and his daughters had only learned to regret their folly and vanity, as it had produced them mortification in this life; whether they were ever brought to a more serious sense of their errors may be seen in a future part of this history.

PART VI

GOOD RESOLUTIONS

Mr. Bragwell was so much afflicted at the disgraceful marriage of his daughter, who ran off with Timothy Incle, the strolling player, that he never fully recovered his spirits. His cheerfulness, which had arisen from a high opinion of himself, had been confirmed by a constant flow of uninterrupted success; and that is a sort of cheerfulness which is very liable to be impaired, because it lies at the mercy of every accident and cross event in life. But though his pride was now disappointed, his misfortunes had not taught him any humility, because he had not discovered that they were caused by his own fault; nor had he acquired any patience or submission, because he had not learned that all afflictions come from the hand of God, to awaken us to a deep sense of our sins, and to draw off our hearts from the perishing vanities of this life. Besides, Mr. Bragwell was one of those people who, if they would be thought to bear with tolerable submission such trials as appear to be sent more immediately from Providence, yet think they have a sort of right to rebel at every misfortune which befalls them through the fault of a fellow-creature; as if our fellow-creatures were not the agents and instruments by which Providence often sees fit to try or to punish us.

In answer to his heavy complaints, Mr. Worthy wrote him a letter in which he expatiated on the injustice of our impatience, and on the folly of our vindicating ourselves from guilt in the distinctions we make between those trials which seem to come more immediately from God, and those which proceed directly from the faults of our fellow-creatures. "Sickness, losses, and death, we think," continued he, "we dare not openly rebel against; while we fancy we are quite justified in giving loose to our violence when we suffer by the hand of the oppressor, the unkindness of the friend, or the disobedience of the child. But this is one of the delusions of our blinded hearts. Ingratitude, unkindness, calumny, are permitted to assail us by the same power who cuts off 'the desire of our eyes at a stroke.' The friend who betrays us, and the daughter who deceives us, are instruments for our chastisement, sent by the same purifying hand who orders a fit of sickness to weaken our bodies, or a storm to destroy our crop, or a fire to burn down our house. And we must look for the same remedy in the one case as in the other; I mean prayer and a deep submission to the will of God. We must leave off looking at second causes, and look more at Him who sets them in action. We must try to find out the meaning of the Providence, and hardly dare pray to be delivered from it till it has accomplished in us the end for which it was sent."

His imprudent daughter Bragwell would not be brought to see or forgive, nor was the degrading name of Mrs. Incle ever allowed to be pronounced in his hearing. He had loved her with an excessive and undue affection, and while she gratified his vanity by her beauty and finery, he deemed her faults of little consequence; but when she disappointed his ambition by a disgraceful marriage, all his natural affection only served to increase his resentment. Yet, though he regretted her crime less than his own mortification, he never ceased in secret to lament her loss. She soon found out she was undone, and wrote in a strain of bitter repentance to ask him for forgiveness. She owned that her husband, whom she had supposed to be a man of fashion in disguise, was a low person in distressed circumstances. She implored that her father, though he refused to give her husband that fortune for which alone it was now too plain he married her, would at least allow her some subsistence; for that Mr. Incle was much in debt, and, she feared, in danger of a jail.

The father's heart was half melted at this account, and his affection was for a time awakened; but Mrs. Bragwell opposed his sending her any assistance. She always made it a point of duty never to forgive; for, she said, it only encouraged those who had done wrong once to do worse next time. For her part she had never yet been guilty of so mean and pitiful a weakness as to forgive any one; for to pardon an injury always showed either want of spirit to feel it, or want of power to resent it. She was resolved she would never squander the money for which she worked early and late, on a baggage who had thrown herself away on a beggar, while she had a daughter single, who might yet raise her family by a great match. I am sorry to say that Mrs. Bragwell's anger was not owing to the undutifulness of the daughter, or the worthlessness of the husband; poverty was in her eyes the grand crime. The doctrine of forgiveness, as a religious principle, made no more a part of Mr. Bragwell's system than of his wife's; but in natural feeling, particularly for this offending daughter, he much exceeded her.

In a few months the youngest Miss Bragwell desired leave to return home from Mr. Worthy's. She had, indeed, only consented to go thither as a less evil of the two, than staying in her father's house after her sister's elopement. But the sobriety and simplicity of Mr. Worthy's family were irksome to her. Habits of vanity and idleness were become so rooted in her mind, that any degree of restraint was a burden; and though she was outwardly civil, it was easy to see that she longed to get away. She resolved, however, to profit by her sister's faults; and made her parents easy by assuring them she would never throw herself away on a man who was worth nothing. Encouraged by these promises, which her parents thought included the whole sum and substance of human wisdom, and which was all, they said, they could in reason expect, her father allowed her to come home.

Mr. Worthy, who accompanied her, found Mr. Bragwell gloomy and dejected. As his house was no longer a scene of vanity and festivity, Mr. Bragwell tried to make himself and his friend believe that he was grown religious; whereas he was only become discontented. As he had always fancied that piety was a melancholy, gloomy thing, and as he felt his own mind really gloomy, he was willing to think that he was growing pious. He had, indeed, gone more constantly to church, and had taken less pleasure in feasting and cards, and now and then read a chapter in the Bible; but all this was because his spirits were low, and not because his heart was changed. The outward actions were more regular, but the inward man was the same. The forms of religion were resorted to as a painful duty; but this only added to his misery, while he was utterly ignorant of its spirit and power. He still, however, reserved religion as a loathsome medicine, to which he feared he must have recourse at last, and of which he even now considered every abstinence from pleasure, or every exercise of piety as a bitter dose. His health also was impaired, so that his friend found him in a pitiable state, neither able to receive pleasure from the world, which he so dearly loved, nor from religion, which he so greatly feared. He expected to have been much commended by Mr. Worthy for the change in his way of life; but Worthy, who saw that the alteration was only owing to the loss of animal spirits, and to the casual absence of temptation, was cautious of flattering him too much. "I thought, Mr. Worthy," said he, "to have received some comfort from you. I was told, too, that religion was full of comfort, but I do not much find it." "You were told the truth," replied Worthy; "religion is full of comfort, but you must first be brought into a state fit to receive it before it can become so; you must be brought to a deep and humbling sense of sin. To give you comfort while you are puffed up with high thoughts of yourself, would be to give you a strong cordial in a high fever. Religion keeps back her cordials till the patient is lowered and emptied—emptied of self, Mr. Bragwell. If you had a wound, it must be examined and cleansed, ay, and probed too, before it would be safe to put on a healing plaster. Curing it to the outward eye, while it was corrupt at bottom, would only bring on a mortification, and you would be a dead man, while you trusted that the plaster was curing you. You must be, indeed, a Christian before you can be entitled to the comforts of Christianity."

"I am a Christian," said Mr. Bragwell; "many of my friends are Christians, but I do not see as it has done us much good." "Christianity itself," answered Worthy, "can not make us good, unless it be applied to our hearts. Christian privileges will not make us Christians, unless we make use of them. On that shelf I see stands your medicine. The doctor orders you to take it. Have you taken it?" "Yes," replied Bragwell. "Are you the better for it?" said Worthy. "I think I am," he replied. "But," added Mr. Worthy, "are you the better because the doctor has ordered it merely, or because you have also taken it?" "What a foolish question," cried Bragwell; "why to be sure the doctor might be the best doctor, and his physic the best physic in the world; but if it stood forever on the shelf, I could not expect to be cured by it. My doctor is not a mountebank. He does not pretend to cure by a charm. The physic is good, and as it suits my case, though it is bitter, I take it."

"You have now," said Mr. Worthy, "explained undesignedly the reason why religion does so little good in the world. It is not a mountebank; it does not work by a charm; but it offers to cure your worst corruptions by wholesome, though sometimes bitter prescriptions. But you will not take them; you will not apply to God with the same earnest desire to be healed with which you apply to your doctor; you will not confess your sins to one as honestly as you tell your symptoms to the other, nor read your Bible with the same faith and submission with which you take your medicine. In reading it, however, you must take care not to apply to yourself the comforts which are not suited to your case. You must, by the grace of God, be brought into a condition to be entitled to the promises, before you can expect the comfort of them. Conviction is not conversion; that worldly discontent, which is the effect of worldly disappointment, is not that godly sorrow which worketh repentance. Besides, while you have been pursuing all the gratifications of the world, do not complain that you have not all the comforts of religion too. Could you live in the full enjoyment of both, the Bible would not be true."

Bragwell. Well, sir, but I do a good action sometimes; and God, who knows he did not make us perfect, will accept it, and for the sake of my good actions will forgive my faults.

Worthy. Depend upon it, God will never forgive your sins for the sake of your virtues. There is no commutation tax there. But he will forgive them on your sincere repentance for the sake of Jesus Christ. Goodness is not a single act to be done; so that a man can say, I have achieved it, and the thing is over; but it is a habit that is to be constantly maintained; it is a continual struggle with the opposite vice. No man must reckon himself good for any thing he has already done; though he may consider it as an evidence that he is in the right way, if he feels a constant disposition to resist every evil temper. But every Christian grace will always find work enough; and he must not fancy that because he has conquered once, his virtue may now sit down and take a holiday.

Bragwell. But I thought we Christians need not be watchful against sin; because Christ, as you so often tell me, died for sinners.

Worthy. Do not deceive yourself: the evangelical doctrines, while they so highly exalt a Saviour, do not diminish the heinousness of sin, they rather magnify it. Do not comfort yourself by extenuation or mitigation of sin; but by repentance toward God, and faith in our Lord Jesus Christ. It is not by diminishing or denying your debt; but by confessing it, by owning that you have nothing to pay, that forgiveness is to be hoped.

Bragwell. I don't understand you. You want to have me as good as a saint, and as penitent as a sinner at the same time.

Worthy. I expect of every real Christian, that is, every real penitent, that he should labor to get his heart and life impressed with the stamp of the gospel. I expect to see him aiming at a conformity in spirit and in practice to the will of God in Jesus Christ. I expect to see him gradually attaining toward the entire change from his natural self. When I see a man at constant war with those several pursuits and tempers which are with peculiar propriety termed worldly, it is a plain proof to me that the change must have passed on him which the gospel emphatically terms becoming "a new man."

Bragwell. I hope then I am altered enough to please you. I am sure affliction has made such a change in me, that my best friends hardly know me to be the same man.

Worthy. That is not the change I mean. 'Tis true, from a merry man you have become a gloomy man; but that is because you have been disappointed in your schemes: the principle remains unaltered. A great match for your single daughter would at once restore all the spirits you have lost by the imprudence of your married one. The change the gospel requires is of quite another cast: it is having "a new heart and a right spirit;" it is being "God's workmanship;" it is being "created anew in Christ Jesus unto good works;" it is becoming "new creatures;" it is "old things being done away, and all things made new;" it is by so "learning the truth as it is in Jesus—to the putting off the old man, and putting on the new, which after God is created in righteousness and true holiness;" it is by "partaking of the divine nature." Pray observe, Mr. Bragwell, these are not my words, nor words picked out of any fanatical book; they are the words of that gospel you profess to believe; it is not a new doctrine, it is as old as our religion itself. Though I can not but observe, that men are more reluctant in believing, more averse to adopting this doctrine than almost any other: and indeed I do not wonder at it; for there is perhaps no one which so attacks corruption in its strongholds; no one which so thoroughly prohibits a lazy Christian from uniting a life of sinful indulgence with an outward profession of piety.

Bragwell now seemed resolved to set about the matter in earnest; but he resolved in his own strength: he never thought of applying for assistance to the Fountain of Wisdom; to Him who giveth might to them who have no strength. Unluckily the very day Mr. Worthy took leave, there happened to be a grand ball at the next town, on account of the assizes. An assize-ball, courteous reader! is a scene to which gentlemen and ladies periodically resort to celebrate the crimes and calamities of their fellow-creatures, by dancing and music, and to divert themselves with feasting and drinking, while unhappy wretches are receiving sentence of death.

To this ball Miss Bragwell went, dressed out with a double portion of finery, pouring out on her head, in addition to her own ornaments, the whole band-box of feathers, beads, and flowers, her sister had left behind her. While she was at the ball her father formed many plans of religious reformation; he talked of lessening his business, that he might have more leisure for devotion; though not just now, while the markets were so high; and then he began to think of sending a handsome subscription to the Infirmary; though, on second thoughts he concluded that he needed not be in a hurry, but might as well leave it in his will; though to give, and repent, and reform, were three things he was bent upon. But when his daughter came home at night so happy and so fine! and telling how she had danced with Squire Squeeze, the great corn contractor, and how many fine things he had said to her, Mr. Bragwell felt the old spirit of the world return in its full force. A marriage with Mr. Dashall Squeeze, the contractor, was beyond his hopes; for Mr. Squeeze was supposed from a very low beginning to have got rich during the war.

As for Mr. Squeeze, he had picked up as much of the history of his partner between the dances as he desired; he was convinced there would be no money wanting; for Miss Bragwell, who was now looked on as an only child, must needs be a great fortune, and Mr. Squeeze was too much used to advantageous contracts to let this slip. As he was gaudily dressed, and possessed all the arts of vulgar flattery, Miss Bragwell eagerly caught at his proposal to wait on her father next day. Squeeze was quite a man after Bragwell's own heart, a genius at getting money, a fine dashing fellow at spending it. He told his wife that this was the very sort of man for his daughter; for he got money like a Jew and spent it like a prince; but whether it was fairly got or wisely spent, he was too much a man of the world to inquire. Mrs. Bragwell was not so run away with by appearances but that she desired her husband to be careful, and make himself quite sure it was the right Mr. Squeeze, and no impostor. But being assured by her husband that Betsy would certainly keep her carriage, she never gave herself one thought with what sort of a man she was to ride in it. To have one of her daughters drive in her own coach, filled up all her ideas of human happiness, and drove the other daughter quite out of her head. The marriage was celebrated with great splendor, and Mr. and Mrs. Squeeze set off for London, where they had taken a house.

Mr. Bragwell now tried to forget that he had any other daughter; and if some thoughts of the resolutions he had made of entering on a more religious course would sometimes force themselves upon him, they were put off, like the repentance of Felix, to a more convenient season; and finding he was likely to have a grandchild, he became more worldly and more ambitious than ever; thinking this a just pretense for adding house to house, and field to field. And there is no stratagem by which men more fatally deceive themselves, than when they make even unborn children a pretense for that rapine, or that hoarding, of which their own covetousness is the true motive. Whenever he ventured to write to Mr. Worthy about the wealth, the gayety, and the grandeur of Mr. and Mrs. Squeeze, that faithful friend honestly reminded him of the vanity and uncertainty of worldly greatness, and the error he had been guilty of in marrying his daughter before he had taken time to inquire into the real character of the man, saying, that he could not help foreboding that the happiness of a match made at a ball might have an untimely end.

Notwithstanding Mr. Bragwell had paid down a larger fortune than was prudent, for fear Mr. Squeeze should fly off, yet he was surprised to receive very soon a pressing letter from him, desiring him to advance a considerable sum, as he had the offer of an advantageous purchase, which he must lose for want of money. Bragwell was staggered, and refused to comply; but his wife told him he must not be shabby to such a gentleman as Squire Squeeze; for that she heard on all sides such accounts of their grandeur, their feasts, their carriages, and their liveries, that she and her husband ought even to deny themselves comforts to oblige such a generous son, who did all this in honor of their daughter; besides, if he did not send the money soon, they might be obliged to lay down their coach, and then she would never be able to show her face again. At length Mr. Bragwell lent him the money on his bond; he knew Squeeze's income was large; for he had carefully inquired into this particular, and for the rest he took his word. Mrs. Squeeze also got great presents from her mother, by representing to her how expensively they were forced to live to keep up their credit, and what honor she was conferring on the family of the Bragwell's, by spending their money in such grand company. Among many other letters she wrote her the following:

"TO MRS. BRAGWELL.

"You can't imagine, dear, mother, how charmingly we live. I lie a-bed almost all day, and am up all night; but it is never dark, for all that, for we burn such numbers of candles all at once, that the sun would be of no use at all in London. Then I am so happy; for we are never quiet a moment, Sundays or working-days; nay, I should not know which was which, only that we have most pleasure on a Sunday; because it is the only day on which people have nothing to do but to divert themselves. Then the great folks are all so kind, and so good; they have not a bit of pride, for they will come and eat and drink, and win my money, just as if I was their equal; and if I have got but a cold, they are so very unhappy that they send to know how I do; and though I suppose they can't rest till the footman has told them, yet they are so polite, that if I have been dying they seem to have forgotten it the next time we meet, and not to know but they have seen me the day before. Oh! they are true friends; and for ever smiling, and so fond of one another, that they like to meet and enjoy one another's company by hundreds, and always think the more the merrier. I shall never be tired of such a delightful life.

"Your dutiful daughter,
"BETSY SQUEEZE."

The style of her letters, however, altered in a few months. She owned that though things went on gayer and grander than ever, yet she hardly ever saw her husband, except her house was full of company, and cards or dancing was going on; that he was often so busy abroad he could not come home all night; that he always borrowed the money her mother sent her when he was going out on this nightly business; and that the last time she had asked him for money he cursed and swore, and bid her apply to the old farmer and his rib, who were made of money. This letter Mrs. Bragwell concealed from her husband.

At length, on some change in public affairs, Mr. Squeeze, who had made an overcharge of some thousand pounds in one article, lost his contract; he was found to owe a large debt to government, and his accounts must be made up immediately. This was impossible; he had not only spent his large income, without making any provision for his family, but had contracted heavy debts by gaming and other vices. His creditors poured in upon him. He wrote to Bragwell to borrow another sum; but without hinting at the loss of his contract. These repeated demands made Bragwell so uneasy, that instead of sending him the money, he resolved to go himself secretly to London, and judge by his own eyes how things were going on, as his mind strangely misgave him. He got to Mr. Squeeze's house about eleven at night, and knocked gently, concluding that they must be gone to bed. But what was his astonishment to find the hall was full of men; he pushed through in spite of them, though to his great surprise they insisted on knowing his name, saying they must carry it to their lady. This affronted him; he refused, saying, "It is not because I am ashamed of my name, it will pass for thousands in any market in the west of England. Is this your London manners, not to let a man of my credit in without knowing his name indeed!" What was his amazement to see every room as full of card-tables and of fine gentlemen and ladies as it would hold. All was so light, and so gay, and so festive, and so grand, that he reproached himself for his suspicions, thought nothing too good for them, and resolved secretly to give Squeeze another five hundred pounds to help to keep up so much grandeur and happiness. At length seeing a footman he knew, he asked him where were his master and mistress, for he could not pick them out among the company; or rather his ideas became so confused with the splendor of the scene, that he did not know whether they were there or not. The man said, that his master had just sent for his lady up stairs, and he believed that he was not well. Mr. Bragwell said he would go up himself and look for his daughter, as he could not speak so freely to her before all that company.

He went up, knocked at the chamber door, and its not being opened, made him push it with some violence. He heard a bustling noise within, and again made a fruitless attempt to open the door. At this the noise increased, and Mr. Bragwell was struck to the heart at the sound of a pistol from within. He now kicked so violently against the door that it burst open, when the first sight he saw was his daughter falling to the ground in a fit, and Mr. Squeeze dying by a shot from a pistol which was dropping out of his hand. Mr. Bragwell was not the only person whom the sound of the pistol had alarmed. The servants, the company, all heard it, and all ran up to the scene of horror. Those who had the best of the game took care to bring up their tricks in their hands, having had the prudence to leave the very few who could be trusted, to watch the stakes, while those who had the prospect of losing profiled by the confusion, and threw up their cards. All was dismay and terror. Some ran for a surgeon, others examined the dying man; some removed Mrs. Squeeze to her bed, while poor Bragwell could neither see, nor hear, nor do any thing. One of the company took up a letter which lay open upon the table, and was addressed to him; they read it, hoping it might explain the horrid mystery. It was as follows:

"TO MR. BRAGWELL.

"Sir—Fetch home your daughter; I have ruined her, myself, and the child to which she every hour expects to be a mother. I have lost my contracts. My debts are immense. You refuse me money; I must die then; but I will die like a man of spirit. They wait to take me to prison; I have two executions in my house; but I have ten card-tables in it. I would die as I have lived. I invited all this company, and have drank hard since dinner to get primed for this dreadful deed. My wife refuses to write to you for another thousand, and she must take the consequences. Vanity has been my ruin; it has caused all my crimes. Whoever is resolved to live beyond his income is liable to every sin. He can never say to himself, Thus far shalt thou go and no further. Vanity led me to commit acts of rapine, that I might live in splendor; vanity makes me commit self-murder, because I will not live in poverty. The new philosophy says that death is an eternal sleep; but the new philosophy lies. Do you take heed; it is too late for me: the dreadful gulf yawns to swallow me; I plunge into perdition: there is no repentance in the grave, no hope in hell.

"Yours, etc.
"DASHALL SQUEEZE."

The dead body was removed, and Mr. Bragwell remaining almost without speech or motion, the company began to think of retiring, much out of humor at having their party so disagreeably broken up: they comforted themselves however, that it was so early (for it was now scarcely twelve) they could finish their evening at another party or two; so completely do habits of pleasure, as it is called, harden the heart, and steel it not only against virtuous impressions, but against natural feelings! Now it was, that those who had nightly rioted at the expense of these wretched people, were the first to abuse them. Not an offer of assistance was made to this poor forlorn woman; not a word of kindness or of pity; nothing but censure was now heard, "Why must these upstarts ape people of quality?" though as long as these upstarts could feast them, their vulgarity and their bad character had never been produced against them. "As long as thou dost well unto thyself, men shall speak good of thee." One guest who, unluckily, had no other house to go to, coolly said, as he walked off, "Squeeze might as well have put off shooting himself till morning. It was monstrously provoking that he could not wait an hour or two."

As every thing in the house was seized Mr. Bragwell prevailed on his miserable daughter, weak as she was, next morning to set out with him to the country. His acquaintance with polite life was short, but he had seen a great deal in a little time. They had a slow and sad journey. In about a week, Mrs. Squeeze lay-in of a dead child; she herself languished a few days, and then died; and the afflicted parents saw the two darling objects of their ambition, for whose sakes they had made too much haste to be rich, carried to the land where all things are forgotten. Mrs. Bragwell's grief, like her other passions, was extravagant; and poor Bragwell's sorrow was rendered so bitter by self-reproach, that he would have quite sunk under it, had he not thought of his old expedient in distress, that of sending for Mr. Worthy to comfort him.

It was Mr. Worthy's way, to warn people of those misfortunes which he saw their faults must needs bring on them; but not to reproach or desert them when the misfortunes came. He had never been near Bragwell during the short but flourishing reign of the Squeezes: for he knew that prosperity made the ears deaf and the heart hard to counsel; but as soon as he heard his friend was in trouble, he set out to go to him. Bragwell burst into a violent fit of tears when he saw him, and when he could speak, said, "This trial is more than I can bear." Mr. Worthy kindly took him by the hand, and when he was a little composed, said, "I will tell you a short story. There was in ancient times a famous man who was a slave. His master, who was very good to him, one day gave him a bitter melon, and made him eat it: he ate it up without one word of complaint. 'How was it possible,' said the master, 'for you to eat so very nauseous and disagreeable a fruit?' The slave replied, 'My good master, I have received so many favors from your bounty, that it is no wonder if I should once in my life eat one bitter melon from your hands.' This generous answer so struck the master, that the history says he gave him his liberty. With such submissive sentiments, my friend, should man receive his portion of sufferings from God, from whom he receives so many blessings. You in particular have received 'much good at the hand of God, shall you not receive evil also?'"

"O! Mr. Worthy!" said Bragwell, "this blow is too heavy for me, I can not survive this shock: I do not desire it, I only wish to die." "We are very apt to talk most of dying when we are least fit for it," said Worthy. "This is not the language of that submission which makes us prepare for death; but of that despair which makes us out of humor with life. O! Mr. Bragwell! you are indeed disappointed of the grand ends which made life so delightful to you; but till your heart is humbled, till you are brought to a serious conviction of sin, till you are brought to see what is the true end of life, you can have no hope in death. You think you have no business on earth, because those for whose sake you too eagerly heaped up riches are no more. But is there not under the canopy of heaven some afflicted being whom you may yet relieve, some modest merit which you may bring forward, some helpless creature you may save by your advice, some perishing Christian you may sustain by your wealth? When you have no sins of your own to repent of, no mercies of God to be thankful for, no miseries of others to relieve, then, and not till then, I consent you should sink down in despair, and call on death to relieve you."

Mr. Worthy attended his afflicted friend to the funeral of his unhappy daughter and her babe. The solemn service, the committing his late gay and beautiful daughter to darkness, to worms, and to corruption; the sight of the dead infant, for whose sake he had resumed all his schemes of vanity and covetousness, when he thought he had got the better of them; the melancholy conviction that all human prosperity ends in ashes to ashes, and dust to dust, had brought down Mr. Bragwell's self-sufficient and haughty soul into something of that humble frame in which Mr. Worthy had wished to see it. As soon as they returned home, he was beginning to seize the favorable moment for fixing these serious impressions, when they were unseasonably interrupted by the parish officer, who came to ask Mr. Bragwell what he was to do with a poor dying woman who was traveling the country with her child, and was taken in a fit under the church-yard wall? "At first they thought she was dead," said the man, "but finding she still breathed, they have carried her into the work-house till she could give some account of herself."

Mr. Bragwell was impatient at the interruption, which was, indeed, unseasonable, and told the man that he was at that time too much overcome by sorrow to attend to business, but he would give him an answer to-morrow. "But, my friend," said Mr. Worthy, "the poor woman may die to-night; your mind is indeed not in a frame for worldly business; but there is no sorrow too great to forbid our attending the calls of duty. An act of Christian charity will not disturb, but improve the seriousness of your spirit; and though you can not dry your own tears, God may in great mercy permit you to dry those of another. This may be one of those occasions for which I told you life was worth keeping. Do let us see this woman." Bragwell was not in a state either to consent or refuse, and his friend drew him to the work-house, about the door of which stood a crowd of people. "She is not dead," said one, "she moves her head." "But she wants air," said all of them, while they all, according to custom, pushed so close upon her that it was impossible she could get any. A fine boy of two or three years old stood by her, crying, "Mammy is dead, mammy is starved." Mr. Worthy made up to the poor woman, holding his friend by the arm; in order to give her air he untied a large black bonnet which hid her face, when Mr. Bragwell, at that moment casting his eyes on her saw in this poor stranger the face of his own runaway daughter, Mrs. Incle. He groaned, but could not speak; and as he was turning away to conceal his anguish, the little boy fondly caught hold of his hand, lisping out, "O stay and give mammy some bread." His heart yearned toward the child; he grasped his little hand in his, while he sorrowfully said to Mr. Worthy, "It is too much, send away the people. It is my dear naughty child; 'my punishment is greater than I can bear.'" Mr. Worthy desired the people to go and leave the stranger to them; but by this time she was no stranger to any of them. Pale and meager as was her face, and poor and shabby as was her dress, the proud and flaunting Miss Polly Bragwell was easily known by every one present. They went away, but with the mean revenge of little minds, they paid themselves by abuse, for all the airs and insolence they had once endured from her. "Pride must have a fall," said one, "I remember when she was too good to speak to a poor body," said another. "Where are her flounces and furbelows now? It is come home to her at last; her child looks as if he would be glad of the worst bit she formerly denied us."

In the mean time Mr. Bragwell had sunk into an old wicker chair which stood behind, and groaned out, "Lord, forgive my hard heart! Lord, subdue my proud heart; create a clean heart, O God! and renew a right spirit within me." These were perhaps the first words of genuine prayer he had ever offered up in his whole life. Worthy overheard it, and in his heart rejoiced; but this was not a time for talking, but doing. He asked Bragwell what was to be done with the unfortunate woman, who now seemed to recover fast, but she did not see them, for they were behind. She embraced her boy, and faintly said, "My child, what shall we do? I will arise and go to my father, and say unto him, Father, I have sinned against heaven and before thee." This was a joyful sound to Mr. Worthy, who was inclined to hope that her heart might be as much changed for the better as her circumstances were altered for the worse; and he valued the goods of fortune so little, and contrition of soul so much, that he began to think the change on the whole might be a happy one. The boy then sprung from his mother, and ran to Bragwell, saying, "Do be good to mammy." Mrs. Incle looking round, now perceived her father; she fell at his feet, saying, "O forgive your guilty child, and save your innocent one from starving." Bragwell sunk down by her, and prayed God to forgive both her and himself, in terms of genuine sorrow. To hear words of real penitence and heart-felt prayer from this once high-minded father and vain daughter, was music to Worthy's ears, who thought this moment of outward misery was the only joyful one he had ever spent in the Bragwell family.

He was resolved not to interfere, but to let the father's own feelings work out the way into which he was to act.

Bragwell said nothing, but slowly led to his own house, holding the little boy by the hand, and pointing to Worthy to assist the feeble steps of his daughter, who once more entered her father's doors; but the dread of seeing her mother quite overpowered her. Mrs. Bragwells heart was not changed, but sorrow had weakened her powers of resistance; and she rather suffered her daughter to come in, than gave her a kind reception. She was more astonished than pleased; and even in this trying moment, was more disgusted with the little boy's mean clothes, than delighted with his rosy face. As soon as she was a little recovered, Mr. Bragwell desired his daughter to tell him how she happened to be at that place at that time.

In a weak voice she began: "My tale, sir, is short, but mournful." Now, I am very sorry that my readers must wait for this short, but mournful tale, a little longer.

PART VII

MRS. INCLE'S STORY

"I left your house, dear father," said Mrs. Incle, "with a heart full of vain triumph. I had no doubt but my husband was a great man, who put on that disguise to obtain my hand. Judge, then, what I felt to find that he was a needy impostor, who wanted my money, but did not care for me. This discovery, though it mortified, did not humble me. I had neither affection to bear with the man who had deceived me, nor religion to improve by the disappointment. I have found that change of circumstances does not change the heart, till God is pleased to do it. My misfortune only taught me to rebel more against him. I thought God unjust; I accused my father, I was envious of my sister, I hated my husband; but never once did I blame myself.

"My husband picked up a wretched subsistence by joining himself to any low scheme of idle pleasure that was going on. He would follow a mountebank, carry a dice-box, or fiddle at the fair. He was always taunting me for that gentility on which I so much valued myself. 'If I had married a poor working girl,' said he, 'she could now have got her bread; but a fine lady without money is a disgrace to herself, a burden to her husband, and a plague to society.' Every trial which affection might have made lighter, we doubled by animosity; at length my husband was detected in using false dice; he fought with his accuser, both were seized by a press-gang, and sent to sea. I was now left to the wide world; and miserable as I had thought myself before, I soon found there were higher degrees of misery. I was near my time, without bread for myself, or hope for my child. I set out on foot in search of the village where I had heard my husband say his friends lived. It was a severe trial to my proud heart to stoop to those low people; but hunger is not delicate, and I was near perishing. My husband's parents received me kindly, saying, that though they had nothing but what they earned by their labor, yet I was welcome to share their hard fare; for they trusted that God who sent mouths would send meat also. They gave me a small room in their cottage, and furnished me with many necessaries, which they denied themselves."

"O! my child!" interrupted Bragwell, "every word cuts me to the heart. These poor people gladly gave thee of their little, while thy rich parents left thee to starve."

"How shall I own," continued Mrs. Incle, "that all this goodness could not soften my heart; for God had not yet touched it. I received all their kindness as a favor done to them; and thought them sufficiently rewarded for their attentions by the rank and merit of their daughter-in-law. When my father brought me home any little dainty which he could pick up, and my mother kindly dressed it for me, I would not condescend to eat it with them, but devoured it sullenly in my little garret alone, suffering them to fetch and carry every thing I wanted. As my haughty behavior was not likely to gain their affection, it was plain they did not love me; and as I had no notion that there were any motives to good actions but fondness, or self-interest, I was puzzled to know what could make them so kind to me; for of the powerful and constraining law of Christian charity I was quite ignorant. To cheat the weary hours, I looked about for some books, and found, among a few others of the same cast, 'Doddridge's Rise and Progress of Religion in the Soul.' But all those sort of books were addressed to sinners; now as I knew I was not a sinner, I threw them away in disgust. Indeed, they were ill suited to a taste formed by plays and novels, to which reading I chiefly trace my ruin; for, vain as I was, I should never have been guilty of so wild a step as to run away, had not my heart been tainted and my imagination inflamed by those pernicious books.

"At length my little George was born. This added to the burden I had brought on this poor family, but it did not diminish their kindness, and we continued to share their scanty fare without any upbraiding on their part, or any gratitude on mine. Even this poor baby did not soften my heart; I wept over him, indeed, day and night, but they were tears of despair; I was always idle, and wasted those hours in sinful murmurs at his fate, which I should have employed in trying to maintain him. Hardship, grief, and impatience, at length brought on a fever. Death seemed now at hand, and I felt a gloomy satisfaction in the thought of being rid of my miseries, to which I fear was added a sullen joy, to think that you, sir, and my mother, would be plagued to hear of my death when it would be too late; and in this your grief I anticipated a gloomy sort of revenge. But it pleased my merciful God not to let me thus perish in my sins. My poor mother-in-law sent for a good clergyman, who pointed out the danger of dying in that hard and unconverted state, so forcibly, that I shuddered to find on what a dreadful precipice I stood. He prayed with me and for me so earnestly, that at length God, who is sometimes pleased to magnify his own glory in awakening those who are dead in trespasses and sins, was pleased of his free grace, to open my blind eyes, and soften my stony heart. I saw myself a sinner, and prayed to be delivered from the wrath of God, in comparison of which the poverty and disgrace I now suffered appeared as nothing. To a soul convinced of sin, the news of a Redeemer was a joyful sound. Instead of reproaching Providence, or blaming my parents, or abusing my husband, I now learned to condemn myself, to adore that God who had not cut me off in my ignorance, to pray for pardon for the past, and grace for the time to come. I now desired to submit to penury and hunger, so that I might but live in the fear of God in this world, and enjoy his favor in the next. I now learned to compare my present light sufferings, the consequence of my own sin, with those bitter sufferings of my Saviour, which he endured for my sake, and I was ashamed of murmuring. But self-ignorance, conceit, and vanity were so rooted in me, that my progress was very gradual, and I had the sorrow to feel how much the power of long bad habits keeps down the growth of religion in the heart, even after the principle itself has begun to take root. I was so ignorant of divine things, that I hardly knew words to frame a prayer; but when I got acquainted with the Psalms, I there learned how to pour out the fullness of my heart, while in the gospel I rejoiced to see what great things God had done for my soul.

"I now took down once more from the shelf 'Doddridge's Rise and Progress;' and oh! with what new eyes did I read it! I now saw clearly, that not only the thief and the drunkard, the murderer and the adulterer are sinners, for that I knew before! but I found out that the unbeliever, the selfish, the proud, the worldly-minded, all, in short, who live without God in the world, are sinners. I did not now apply the reproofs I met with to my husband, or my father, or other people, as I used to do; but brought them home to myself. In this book I traced, with strong emotions and close self-application, the sinner through all his course; his first awakening, his convictions, repentance, joys, sorrows, backsliding, and recovering, despondency, and delight, to a triumphant death-bed; and God was pleased to make it a chief instrument in bringing me to himself. Here it is," continued Mrs. Incle, untying her little bundle, and taking out a book; "accept it, my dear father, and I will pray that God may bless it to you, as He has done to me.

"When I was able to come down, I passed my time with these good old people, and soon won their affection. I was surprised to find they had very good sense, which I never had thought poor people could have; but, indeed, worldly persons do not know how much religion, while it mends the heart, enlightens the understanding also. I now regretted the evenings I had wasted in my solitary garret, when I might have passed them in reading the Bible with these good folks. This was their refreshing cordial after a weary day, which sweetened the pains of want and age. I one day expressed my surprise that my unfortunate husband, the son of such pious parents, should have turned out so ill: the poor old man said with tears, 'I fear we have been guilty of the sin of Eli; our love was of the wrong sort. Alas! like him, we honored our son more than God, and God has smitten us for it. We showed him by our example, what was right; but through a false indulgence, we did not correct him for what was wrong. We were blind to his faults. He was a handsome boy, with sprightly parts: we took too much delight in these outward things. He soon got above our management, and became vain, idle, and extravagant; and when we sought to restrain him, it was then too late. We humbled ourselves before God; but he was pleased to make our sin become its own punishment. Timothy grew worse and worse, till he was forced to abscond for a misdemeanor, after which we never saw him, but have often heard of him changing from one idle way of life to another; unstable as water, he has been a footman, a soldier, a shopman, a gambler, and a strolling actor. With deep sorrow we trace back his vices to our ungoverned fondness; that lively and sharp wit, by which he has been able to carry on such a variety of wild schemes, might, if we had used him to bear reproof in his youth, have enabled him to have done great service for God and his country. But our flattery made him wise in his own conceit; and there is more hope of a fool than of him. We indulged our own vanity, and have destroyed his soul.'"

Here Mr. Worthy stopped Mrs. Incle, saying, that whenever he heard it lamented that the children of pious parents often turned out so ill, he could not help thinking that there must be frequently something of this sort of error in the bringing them up; he knew, indeed, some instances to the contrary, in which the best means had failed; but he believed, that from Eli, the priest, to Incle, the laborer, much more than half the failures of this sort might be traced to some mistake, or vanity, or bad judgment, or sinful indulgence in the parents.

"I now looked about," continued Mrs. Incle, "in order to see in what I could assist my poor mother; regretting more heartily than she did, that I knew no one thing that was of any use. I was so desirous of humbling myself before God and her, that I offered even to try to wash." "You wash!" exclaimed Bragwell, starting up with great emotion, "Heaven forbid, that with such a fortune and education, Miss Bragwell should be seen at a washing-tub." This vain father, who could bear to hear of her distresses and her sins, could not bear to hear of her washing. Mr. Worthy stopped him, saying, "As to her fortune, you know you refused to give her any; and as to her education, you see it had not taught her how to do any thing better; I am sorry you do not see in this instance, the beauty of Christian humility. For my own part I set a greater value on such an active proof of it, than on a whole volume of professions." Mr. Bragwell did not quite understand this, and Mrs. Incle went on. "What to do to get a penny I knew not. Making of filagree, or fringe, or card-purses, or cutting out paper, or dancing and singing was of no use in our village. The shopkeeper, indeed, would have taken me, if I had known any thing of accounts; and the clergyman could have got me a nursery-maid's place, if I could have done good plain work. I made some awkward attempts to learn to spin and knit, when my mother's wheel or knitting lay by, but I spoiled both through my ignorance. At last I luckily thought upon the fine netting I used to make for my trimmings, and it struck me that I might turn this to some little account. I procured some twine, and worked early and late to make nets for fishermen, and cabbage-nets. I was so pleased that I had at last found an opportunity to show my good will by this mean work, that I regretted my little George was not big enough to contribute his share to our support, by traveling about to sell my nets."

"Cabbage-nets!" exclaimed Bragwell; "there's no bearing this. Cabbage-nets! My grandson hawk cabbage-nets! How could you think of such a scandalous thing?" "Sir," said Mrs. Incle, mildly, "I am now convinced that nothing is scandalous which is not wicked. Besides, we were in want; and necessity, as well as piety, would have reconciled me to this mean trade." Mr. Bragwell groaned, and bade her go on.

"In the mean time my little George grew a fine boy; and I adored the goodness of God who in the sweetness of maternal love, had given me a reward for many sufferings. Instead of indulging a gloomy distrust about the fate of this child, I now resigned him to the will of God. Instead of lamenting because he was not likely to be rich, I was resolved to bring him up with such notions as might make him contented to be poor. I thought if I could subdue all vanity and selfishness in him, I should make him a happier man than if I had thousands to bestow on him; and I trusted that I should be rewarded for every painful act of self-denial, by the future virtue and happiness of my child. Can you believe it, my dear father, my days now passed not unhappily? I worked hard all day, and that alone is a source of happiness beyond what the idle can guess. After my child was asleep at night, I read a chapter in the Bible to my parents, whose eyes now began to fail them. We then thanked God over our frugal supper of potatoes, and talked over the holy men of old, the saints, and the martyrs who would have thought our homely fare a luxury. We compared our peace, and liberty, and safety, with their bonds, and imprisonment, and tortures; and should have been ashamed of a murmur. We then joined in prayer, in which my absent parents and my husband were never forgotten, and went to rest in charity with the whole world, and at peace with our own souls."

"Oh! my forgiving child!" interrupted Mr. Bragwell, sobbing; "and didst thou really pray for thy unnatural father? and didst thou lay thee down in rest and peace? Then, let me tell thee, thou wast better off than thy mother and I were. But no more of this; go on."

"Whether my father-in-law had worked beyond his strength, in order to support me and my child, I know not, but he was taken dangerously ill. While he lay in this state, he received an account that my husband was dead in the West Indies of the yellow fever, which has carried off such numbers of our countrymen; we all wept together, and prayed that his awful death might quicken us in preparing for our own. This shock joined to the fatigue of nursing her sick husband, soon brought my poor mother to death's door. I nursed them both, and felt a satisfaction in giving them all I had to bestow, my attendance, my tears, and my prayers. I, who was once so nice and so proud, so disdainful in the midst of plenty, and so impatient under the smallest inconvenience, was now enabled to glorify God by my activity and by my submission. Though the sorrows of my heart were enlarged, I cast my burden on Him who cares for the weary and heavy-laden. After having watched by these poor people the whole night, I sat down to breakfast on my dry crust and coarse dish of tea, without a murmur: my greatest grief was, lest I should bring away the infection to my dear boy; for the fever was now become putrid. I prayed to know what it was my duty to do between my dying parents and my helpless child. To take care of the sick and aged, seemed to be my first duty; so I offered up my child to Him who is the father of the fatherless, and He in mercy spared him to me.

"The cheerful piety with which these good people breathed their last, proved to me that the temper of mind with which the pious poor commonly meet death, is the grand compensation made them by Providence for all the hardships of their inferior condition. If they have had few joys and comforts in life already, and have still fewer hopes in store, is not all fully made up to them by their being enabled to leave this world with stronger desires of heaven, and without those bitter regrets after the good things of this life, which add to the dying tortures of the worldly rich? To the forlorn and destitute, death is not so terrible as it is to him who sits at ease in his possessions, and who fears that this night his soul shall be required of him."

Mr. Bragwell felt this remark more deeply than his daughter meant he should. He wept, and bade her proceed.

"I followed my departed parents to the same grave, and wept over them, but not as one who had no hope. They had neither houses nor lands to leave me, but they had left me their Bible, their blessing, and their example, of which I humbly trust I shall feel the benefits when all the riches of this world shall have an end. Their few effects, consisting of some poor household goods, and some working-tools, hardly sufficed to pay their funeral expenses. I was soon attacked with the same fever, and saw myself, as I thought, dying the second time; my danger was the same, but my views were changed. I now saw eternity in a more awful light than I had done before, when I wickedly thought death might be gloomily called upon as a refuge from every common trouble. Though I had still reason to be humble on account of my sin, yet, by the grace of God, I saw death stripped of his sting and robbed of his terrors, through him who loved me, and gave himself for me; and in the extremity of pain, my soul rejoiced in God my Saviour.

"I recovered, however, and was chiefly supported by the kind clergyman's charity. When I felt myself nourished and cheered by a little tea or broth, which he daily sent me from his own slender provision, my heart smote me, to think how I had daily sat down at home to a plentiful dinner, without any sense of thankfulness for my own abundance, or without inquiring whether my poor sick neighbors were starving: and I sorrowfully remembered, that what my poor sister and I used to waste through daintiness, would now have comfortably fed myself and child. Believe me, my dear mother, a laboring man who has been brought low by a fever, might often be restored to his work some weeks sooner, if on his recovery he was nourished and strengthened by a good bit from a farmer's table. Less than is often thrown to a favorite spaniel would suffice; so that the expense would be almost nothing to the giver, while to the receiver it would bring health, and strength, and comfort, and recruited life. And it is with regret I must observe, that young women in our station are less attentive to the comforts of the poor, less active in visiting the cottages of the sick, less desirous of instructing the young, and working for the aged, than many ladies of higher rank. The multitude of opportunities of this sort which we neglect, among the families of our father's distressed tenants and workmen, will, I fear, one day appear against us.

"By the time I was tolerably recovered, I was forced to leave the house. I had no human prospect of assistance. I humbly asked of God to direct my steps, and to give me entire obedience to his will. I then cast my eye mournfully on my child; and, though prayer had relieved my heart of a load which without it would have been intolerable, my tears flowed fast, while I cried out in the bitterness of my soul, How many hired servants of my father have bread enough, and to spare, and I perish with hunger. This text appeared a kind of answer to my prayer, and gave me courage to make one more attempt to soften you in my favor. I resolved to set out directly to find you, to confess my disobedience, and to beg a scanty pittance with which I and my child might be meanly supported in some distant county, where we should not, by our presence, disgrace our more happy relations. We set out and traveled as fast as my weak health and poor George's little feet and ragged shoes would permit. I brought a little bundle of such work and necessaries as I had left, by selling which we subsisted on the road." "I hope," interrupted Bragwell, "there were no cabbage-nets in it?" "At least," said her mother, "I hope you did not sell them near home?" "No; I had none left," said Mrs. Incle, "or I should have done it. I got many a lift in a wagon for my child and my bundle, which was a great relief to me, as I should have had both to carry. And here

I can not help saying, I wish drivers would not be too hard in their demands; if they help a poor sick traveler on a mile or two, it proves a great relief to weary bodies and naked feet; and such little cheap charities may be considered as the cup of cold water, which, if given on right grounds, shall not lose its reward." Here Bragwell sighed to think that when mounted on his fine bay mare, or driving his neat chaise, it had never once crossed his mind that the poor way-worn foot traveler was not equally at his ease, nor had it ever occurred to him that shoes were a necessary accommodation. Those who want nothing are apt to forget how many there are who want every thing. Mrs. Incle went on; "I got to this village about seven this morning; and while I sat on the church-yard wall to rest and meditate how I should make myself known at home, I saw a funeral; I inquired whose it was, and learned it was my sister's. This was too much for me, and I sank down in a fit, and knew nothing that happened to me from that moment, till I found myself in the work-house with my father and Mr. Worthy."

Here Mrs. Incle stopped. Grief, shame, pride, and remorse, had quite overcome Mr. Bragwell. He wept like a child, and said he hoped his daughter would pray for him; for that he was not in a condition to pray for himself, though he found nothing else could give him any comfort. His deep dejection brought on a fit of sickness. "O! said he, I now begin to feel an expression in the sacrament which I used to repeat without thinking it had any meaning, the remembrance of my sins is grievous, the burden of them is intolerable. O! it is awful to think what a sinner a man may be, and yet retain a decent character! How many thousands are in my condition, taking to themselves all the credit of their prosperity, instead of giving God the glory! heaping up riches to their hurt, instead of dealing their bread to the hungry! O! let those who hear of the Bragwell family, never say that vanity is a little sin. In me it has been the fruitful parent of a thousand sins—selfishness, hardness of heart, forgetfulness of God. In one of my sons vanity was the cause of rapine, injustice, extravagance, ruin, self-murder. Both my daughters were undone by vanity, thought it only wore the more harmless shape of dress, idleness, and dissipation. The husband of my daughter Incle it destroyed, by leading him to live above his station, and to despise labor. Vanity insnared the souls even of his pious parents, for while it led them to wish their son in a better condition, it led them to allow such indulgences as were unfit for his own. O! you who hear of us, humble yourselves under the mighty hand of God; resist high thoughts; let every imagination be brought into obedience to the Son of God. If you set a value on finery look into that grave; behold the moldering body of my Betsy, who now says to Corruption, thou art my father, and to the worm, thou art my mother, and my sister. Look to the bloody and brainless head of her husband. O, Mr. Worthy, how does Providence mock at human foresight! I have been greedy of gain, that the son of Mr. Squeeze might be a great man; he is dead; while the child of Timothy Incle, whom I had doomed to beggary, will be my heir. Mr. Worthy, to you I commit this boy's education; teach him to value his immortal soul more, and the good things of this life less than I have done. Bring him up in the fear of God, and in the government of his passions. Teach him that unbelief and pride are at the root of all sin. I have found this to my cost. I trusted in my riches; I said, 'To-morrow shall be as this day and more abundant.' I did not remember that for all these things God would bring me to judgment. I am not sure that I believe in a judgment: I am not sure that I believe in a God."

Bragwell at length grew better, but he never recovered his spirits. The conduct of Mrs. Incle through life was that of an humble Christian. She sold all her sister's finery which her father had given her, and gave the money to the poor; saying, "It did not become one who professed penitence to return to the gayeties of life." Mr. Bragwell did not oppose this; not that he had fully acquired a just notion of the self-denying spirit of religion, but having a head not very clear at making distinctions, he was never able after the sight of Squeeze's mangled body, to think of gayety and grandeur, without thinking at the same time of a pistol and bloody brains; for, as his first introduction into gay life had presented him with all these objects at one view, he never afterward could separate them in his mind. He even kept his fine beaufet of plate always shut; because it brought to his mind the grand unpaid-for sideboard that he had seen laid out for Mr. Squeeze's supper, to the remembrance of which he could not help tacking the idea of debts, prisons, executions, and self-murder.

Mr. Bragwell's heart had been so buried in the love of the world, and evil habits had become so rooted in him, that the progress he made in religion was very slow; yet he earnestly prayed and struggled against sin and vanity; and when his unfeeling wife declared she could not love the boy unless he was called by their name instead of Incle, Bragwell would never consent, saying he stood in need of every help against pride. He also got the letter which Squeeze wrote just before he shot himself, framed and glazed; this he hung up in his chamber, and made it a rule to go and read it as often as he found his heart disposed to VANITY.

'TIS ALL FOR THE BEST [13]

[13] A profligate wit of a neighboring country having attempted to turn this doctrine into ridicule, under the same title here assumed, it occurred to the author that it might not be altogether useless to illustrate the same doctrine on Christian principles.

"It is all for the best," said Mrs. Simpson, whenever any misfortune befell her. She had got such a habit of vindicating Providence, that instead of weeping and wailing under the most trying dispensations, her chief care was to convince herself and others, that however great might be her sufferings, and however little they could be accounted for at present, yet that the Judge of all the earth could not but do right. Instead of trying to clear herself from any possible blame that might attach to her under those misfortunes which, to speak after the manner of men, she might seem not to have deserved, she was always the first to justify Him who had inflicted it. It was not that she superstitiously converted every visitation into a punishment; she entertained more correct ideas of that God who overrules all events. She knew that some calamities were sent to exercise her faith, others to purify her heart; some to chastise her rebellious will, and all to remind her that this "was not her rest;" that this world was not the scene for the full and final display of retributive justice. The honor of God was dearer to her than her own credit, and her chief desire was to turn all events to his glory.

Though Mrs. Simpson was the daughter of a clergyman, and the widow of a genteel tradesman, she had been reduced by a succession of misfortunes, to accept of a room in an almshouse. Instead of repining at the change; instead of dwelling on her former gentility, and saying, "how handsomely she had lived once; and how hard it was to be reduced; and she little thought ever to end her days in an alms-house"—which is the common language of those who were never so well off before—she was thankful that such an asylum was provided for want and age; and blessed God that it was to the Christian dispensation alone that such pious institutions owed their birth.

One fine evening, as she was sitting reading her Bible on the little bench shaded with honey-suckles, just before her door, who should come and sit down by her but Mrs. Betty, who had formerly been lady's maid at the nobleman's house in the village of which Mrs. Simpson's father had been minister. Betty, after a life of vanity, was, by a train of misfortunes, brought to this very alms-house; and though she had taken no care by frugality and prudence to avoid it, she thought it a hardship and disgrace, instead of being thankful, as she ought to have been, for such a retreat. At first she did not know Mrs. Simpson; her large bonnet, cloak, and brown stuff gown (for she always made her appearance conform to her circumstances) being very different from the dress she had been used to wear when Mrs. Betty had seen her dining at the great house; and time and sorrow had much altered her countenance. But when Mrs. Simpson kindly addressed her as an old acquaintance, she screamed with surprise. "What! you, madam?" cried she; "you in an alms-house, living on charity; you, who used to be so charitable yourself, that you never suffered any distress in the parish which you could prevent?" "That may be one reason, Betty," replied Mrs. Simpson, "why Providence has provided this refuge for my old age. And my heart overflows with gratitude when I look back on his goodness." "No such great goodness, methinks," said Betty; "why, you were born and bred a lady, and are now reduced to live in an alms-house." "Betty, I was born and bred a sinner, undeserving of the mercies I have received." "No such great mercies," said Betty. "Why, I heard you had been turned out of doors; that your husband had broke; and that you had been in danger of starving, though I did not know what was become of you." "It is all true, Betty, glory be to God! it is all true."

"Well," said Betty, "you are an odd sort of a gentlewoman. If from a prosperous condition I had been made a bankrupt, a widow, and a beggar, I should have thought it no such mighty matter to be thankful for: but there is no accounting for taste. The neighbors used to say that all your troubles must needs be a judgment upon you; but I who knew how good you were, thought it very hard you should suffer so much; but now I see you reduced to an alms-house, I beg your pardon, madam, but I am afraid the neighbors were in the right, and that so many misfortunes could never have happened to you without you had committed a great many sins to deserve them; for I always thought that God is so just that he punishes us for all our bad actions, and rewards us for all our good ones." "So he does, Betty; but he does it in his own way, and at his own time, and not according to our notions of good and evil; for his ways are not as our ways. God, indeed, punishes the bad, and rewards the good; but he does not do it fully and finally in this world. Indeed he does not set such a value on outward things as to make riches, and rank, and beauty, and health, the reward of piety; that would be acting like weak and erring men, and not like a just and holy God. Our belief in a future state of rewards and punishments is not always so strong as it ought to be, even now; but how totally would our faith fail, if we regularly saw every thing made even in this world. We shall lose nothing by having pay-day put off. The longest voyages make the best returns. So far am I from thinking that God is less just, and future happiness less certain, because I see the wicked sometimes prosper, and the righteous suffer in this world, that I am rather led to believe that God is more just and heaven more certain: for, in the first place, God will not put off his favorite children with so poor a lot as the good things of this world; and next, seeing that the best men here below do not often attain to the best things; why it only serves to strengthen my belief that they are not the best things in His eye; and He has most assuredly reserved for those that love Him such 'good things as eye has not seen nor ear heard.' God, by keeping man in Paradise while he was innocent, and turning him into this world as soon as he had sinned, gave a plain proof that he never intended the world, even in its happiest state, as a place of reward. My father gave me good principles and useful knowledge; and while he taught me by a habit of constant employment to be, if I may so say, independent of the world; yet he led me to a constant sense of dependence on God—" "I do not see, however," interrupted Mrs. Betty, "that your religion has been of any use to you. It has been so far from preserving you from trouble, that I think you have had more than the usual share."

"No," said Mrs. Simpson; "nor did Christianity ever pretend to exempt its followers from trouble; this is no part of the promise. Nay, the contrary is rather stipulated: 'In the world ye shall have tribulation.' But if it has not taught me to escape sorrow, I humbly hope it has taught me how to bear it. If it has taught me not to feel, it has taught me not to murmur. I will tell you a little of my story: as my father could save little or nothing for me, he was desirous of seeing me married to a young gentleman in the neighborhood, who expressed a regard for me. But while he was anxiously engaged in bringing this about, my good father died."

"How very unlucky," interrupted Betty.

"No, Betty," replied Mrs. Simpson, "it was very providential; this man, though he maintained a decent character, had a good fortune, and lived soberly, yet he would not have made me happy." "Why, what could you want more of a man?" said Betty. "Religion," returned Mrs. Simpson. "As my father made a creditable appearance, and was very charitable; and as I was an only child, this gentleman concluded that he could give me a considerable fortune; for he did not know that all the poor in his parish are the children of every pious clergyman. Finding I had little or nothing left me, he withdrew his attentions." "What a sad thing!" cried Betty. "No, it was all for the best; Providence overruled his covetousness for my good. I could not have been happy with a man whose soul was set on the perishable things of this world; nor did I esteem him, though I labored to submit my own inclinations to those of my kind father. The very circumstance of being left penniless produced the direct contrary effect on Mr. Simpson: he was a sensible young man, engaged in a prosperous business. We had long highly valued each other; but while my father lived, he thought me above his hopes. We were married; I found him an amiable, industrious, good-tempered man; he respected religion and religious people; but with excellent dispositions, I had the grief to find him less pious than I had hoped. He was ambitious, and a little too much immersed in worldly schemes; and though I knew it was all done for my sake, yet that did not blind me so far as to make me think it right. He attached himself so eagerly to business, that he thought every hour lost in which he was not doing something that would tend to raise me to what he called my proper rank. The more prosperous he grew the less religious he became: and I began to find that one might be unhappy with a husband one tenderly loved. One day as he was standing on some steps to reach down a parcel of goods, he fell from the top and broke his leg in two places."

"What a dreadful misfortune!" said Mrs. Betty. "What a signal blessing!" said Mrs. Simpson. "Here I am sure I had reason to say all was for the best; from the very hour in which my outward troubles began, I date the beginning of my happiness. Severe suffering, a near prospect of death, absence from the world, silence, reflection, and above all, the divine blessing on the prayers and Scriptures I read to him, were the means used by our merciful Father to turn my husband's heart. During his confinement he was awakened to a deep sense of his own sinfulness, of the vanity of all this world has to bestow, and of his great need of a Saviour. It was many months before he could leave his bed; during this time his business was neglected. His principal clerk took advantage of his absence to receive large sums of money in his name, and absconded. On hearing of this great loss, our creditors came faster upon us than we could answer their demands; they grew more impatient as we were less able to satisfy them; one misfortune followed another, till at length Mr. Simpson became a bankrupt."

"What an evil!" exclaimed Betty. "Yet it led in the end to much good," resumed Mrs. Simpson. "We were forced to leave the town in which we had lived with so much credit and comfort, and to betake ourselves to a mean lodging in a neighboring village, till my husband's strength should be recruited, and till we could have time to look about us and see what was to be done. The first night we got to this poor dwelling, my husband felt very sorrowful, not for his own sake, but that he had brought so much poverty on me, whom he had so dearly loved; I, on the contrary, was unusually cheerful, for the blessed change in his mind had more than reconciled me to the sad change in his circumstances. I was contented to live with him in a poor cottage for a few years on earth, if it might contribute to our spending a blessed eternity together in heaven. I said to him, 'Instead of lamenting that we are now reduced to want all the comforts of life, I have sometimes been almost ashamed to live in the full enjoyments of them, when I have reflected that my Saviour not only chose to deny himself all these enjoyments, but even to live a life of hardship for my sake; not one of his numerous miracles tended to his own comfort; and though we read at different times that he both hungered and thirsted, yet it was not for his own gratification that he once changed water into wine; and I have often been struck with the near position of that chapter in which this miracle is recorded, to that in which he thirsted for a draught of water at the well in Samaria.[14] It was for others, not himself, that even the humble sustenance of barley-bread was multiplied. See here, we have a bed left us (I had, indeed, nothing but straw to stuff it with), but the Saviour of the world "had not where to lay his head."' My husband smiled through his tears, and we sat down to supper. It consisted of a roll and a bit of cheese which I had brought with me, and we ate it thankfully. Seeing Mr. Simpson beginning to relapse into distrust, the following conversation, as nearly as I can remember, took place between us. He began by remarking, that it was a mysterious Providence that he had been less prosperous since he had been less attached to the world, and that his endeavors had not been followed by that success which usually attends industry. I took the liberty to reply: 'Your heavenly Father sees on which side your danger lies, and is mercifully bringing you, by these disappointments, to trust less in the world and more in himself. My dear Mr. Simpson,' added I, 'we trust every body but God. As children, we obey our parents implicitly, because we are taught to believe all is for our good which they command or forbid. If we undertake a voyage, we trust entirely to the skill and conduct of the pilot; we never torment ourselves in thinking he will carry us east, when he has promised to carry us west. If a dear and tried friend makes us a promise, we depend on him for the performance, and do not wound his feelings by our suspicions. When you used to go your annual journey to London, in the mail-coach, you confided yourself to the care of the coachman that he would carry you where he had engaged to do so; you were not anxiously watching him, and distrusting and inquiring at every turning. When the doctor sends home your medicine, don't you so fully trust in his ability and good will that you swallow it down in full confidence? You never think of inquiring what are the ingredients, why they are mixed in that particular way, why there is more of one and less of another, and why they are bitter instead of sweet! If one dose does not cure you, he orders another, and changes the medicine when he sees the first does you no good, or that by long use the same medicine has lost its effect; if the weaker fails, he prescribes you a stronger; you swallow all, you submit to all, never questioning the skill or kindness of the physician. God is the only being whom we do not trust, though He is the only one who is fully competent, both in will and power, to fulfill all his promises; and who has solemnly and repeatedly pledged himself to fulfill them in those Scriptures which we receive as his revealed will.'

[14] See John, chap. ii.; and John, chap. iv.

"Mr. Simpson thanked me for my little sermon, as he called it; but said, at the same time, that what made my exhortations produce a powerful effect on his mind was, the patient cheerfulness with which he was pleased to say I bore my share in our misfortunes. A submissive behavior, he said, was the best practical illustration of a real faith. When we had thanked God for our supper, we prayed together; after which we read the eleventh chapter of the epistle to the Hebrews. When my husband had finished it, he said, 'Surely, if God's chief favorites have been martyrs, is not that a sufficient proof that this world is not a place of happiness, no earthly prosperity the reward of virtue? Shall we, after reading this chapter, complain of our petty trials? Shall we not rather be thankful that our affliction is so light?'

"Next day Mr. Simpson walked out in search of some employment, by which we might be supported. He got a recommendation to Mr. Thomas, an opulent farmer and factor, who had large concerns, and wanted a skillful person to assist him in keeping his accounts. This we thought a fortunate circumstance, for we found that the salary would serve to procure us at least all the necessaries of life. The farmer was so pleased with Mr. Simpson's quickness, regularity, and good sense, that he offered us, of his own accord, a neat little cottage of his own, which then happened to be vacant, and told us we should live rent free, and promised to be a friend to us." "All does seem for the best now, indeed," interrupted Mrs. Betty. "We shall see," said Mrs. Simpson, and thus went on:

"I now became very easy and very happy; and was cheerfully employed in putting our few things in order, and making every thing look to the best advantage. My husband, who wrote all day for his employer, in the evening assisted me in doing up our little garden. This was a source of much pleasure to us; we both loved a garden, and we were not only contented but cheerful. Our employer had been absent some weeks on his annual journey. He came home on a Saturday night, and the next morning sent for Mr. Simpson to come and settle his accounts, which were got behind-hand by his long absence. We were just going to church, and Mr. Simpson sent back word that he would call and speak to him on his way home. A second message followed, ordering him to come to the farmer's directly; he agreed that he would walk round that way, and that my husband should call and excuse his attendance.

"The farmer, more ignorant and worse educated than his plowman, with all that pride and haughtiness which the possession of wealth, without knowledge or religion is apt to give, rudely asked my husband what he meant by sending him word that he would not come to him till the next day; and insisted that he should stay and settle the accounts then. 'Sir,' said my husband, in a very respectful manner, 'I am on my road to church, and I am afraid shall be too late.' 'Are you so?' said the farmer. 'Do you know who sent for you? You may, however, go to church, if you will, so you make haste back; and, d'ye hear, you may leave your accounts with me, as I conclude you have brought them with you; I will look them over by the time you return, and then you and I can do all I want to have done to-day in about a couple of hours, and I will give you home some letters to copy for me in the evening.' 'Sir,' answered my husband, 'I dare not obey you; it is Sunday.' 'And so you refuse to settle my accounts only because it is Sunday.' 'Sir,' replied Mr. Simpson, 'if you would give me a handful of silver and gold I dare not break the commandment of my God.' 'Well,' said the farmer, 'but this is not breaking the commandment; I don't order you to drive my cattle, or to work in my garden, or to do any thing which you might fancy would be a bad example.' 'Sir,' replied my husband, 'the example indeed goes a great way, but it is not the first object. The deed is wrong in itself.' 'Well, but I shall not keep you from church; and when you have been there, there is no harm in doing a little business, or taking a little pleasure the rest of the day.' 'Sir,' answered my husband, 'the commandment does not say, thou shalt keep holy the Sabbath morning, but the Sabbath day.' 'Get out of my house, you puritanical rascal, and out of my cottage too,' said the farmer; 'for if you refuse to do my work, I am not bound to keep my engagement with you; as you will not obey me as a master, I shall not pay you as a servant.' 'Sir,' said Mr. Simpson, 'I would gladly obey you, but I have a Master in heaven whom I dare not disobey.' 'Then let him find employment for you,' said the enraged farmer; 'for I fancy you will get but poor employment on earth with these scrupulous notions, and so send home my papers, directly, and pack off out of the parish.' 'Out of your cottage,' said my husband, 'I certainly will; but as to the parish, I hope I may remain in that, if I can find employment.' 'I will make it too hot to hold you,' replied the farmer, 'so you had better troop off bag and baggage: for I am overseer, and as you are sickly, it is my duty not to let any vagabonds stay in the parish who are likely to become chargeable.'

"By the time my husband returned home, for he found it too late to go to church, I had got our little dinner ready; it was a better one than we had for a long while been accustomed to see, and I was unusually cheerful at this improvement in our circumstances. I saw his eyes full of tears, and oh! with what pain did he bring himself to tell me that it was the last dinner we must ever eat in this house. I took his hand with a smile, and only said, 'the Lord gave and the Lord taketh away, blessed be the name of the Lord.' 'Notwithstanding this sudden stroke of injustice,' said my husband, 'this is still a happy country. Our employer, it is true, may turn us out at a moment's notice, because it is his own, but he has no further power over us; he can not confine or punish us. His riches, it is true, give him power to insult, but not to oppress us. The same laws to which the affluent resort, protect us also. And as to our being driven out from a cottage, how many persons of the highest rank have lately been driven out from their palaces and castles; persons too, born in a station which he never enjoyed, and used to all the indulgences of that rank and wealth we never knew, are at this moment wandering over the face of the earth, without a house or without bread; exiles and beggars; while we, blessed be God, are in our own native land; we have still our liberty, our limbs, the protection of just and equal laws, our churches, our Bibles, and our Sabbaths.'

"This happy state of my husband's mind hushed my sorrows, and I never once murmured; nay, I sat down to dinner with a degree of cheerfulness, endeavoring to cast all our care on 'Him that careth for us.' We had begged to stay till the next morning, as Sunday was not the day on which we liked to remove; but we were ordered not to sleep another night in that house; so as we had little to carry, we marched off in the evening to the poor lodging we had before occupied. The thought that my husband had cheerfully renounced his little all for conscience sake, gave an unspeakable serenity to my mind; and I felt thankful that though cast down we were not forsaken: nay I felt a lively gratitude to God, that while I doubted not he would accept this little sacrifice, as it was heartily made for his sake, he had graciously forborne to call us to greater trials."

"And so you were turned adrift once more? Well, ma'am, saving your presence, I hope you won't be such a fool as to say all was for the best now." "Yes, Betty: He who does all things well, now made his kind Providence more manifest than ever. That very night, while we were sweetly sleeping in our poor lodging, the pretty cottage, out of which we were so unkindly driven, was burned to the ground by a flash of lightning which caught the thatch, and so completely consumed the whole little building that had it not been for the merciful Providence who thus overruled the cruelty of the farmer for the preservation of our lives, we must have been burned to ashes with the house. 'It was the Lord's doing, and it was marvelous in our eyes.' 'O that men would therefore praise the Lord for his goodness, and for all the wonders that he doeth for the children of men!'

"I will not tell you all the trials and afflictions which befell us afterward. I would also spare my heart the sad story of my husband's death." "Well, that was another blessing too, I suppose," said Betty. "Oh, it was the severest trial ever sent me!" replied Mrs. Simpson, a few tears quietly stealing down her face. "I almost sunk under it. Nothing but the abundant grace of God could have carried me through such a visitation; and yet I now feel it to be the greatest mercy I ever experienced; he was my idol; no trouble ever came near my heart while he was with me. I got more credit than I deserved for my patience under trials, which were easily borne while he who shared and lightened them was spared to me. I had indeed prayed and struggled to be weaned from this world, but still my affection for him tied me down to the earth with a strong cord: and though I did earnestly try to keep my eyes fixed on the eternal world, yet I viewed it with too feeble a faith; I viewed it at too great a distance. I found it difficult to realize it—I had deceived myself. I had fancied that I bore my troubles so well from the pure love of God, but I have since found that my love for my husband had too great a share in reconciling me to every difficulty which I underwent for him. I lost him; the charm was broken, the cord which tied me down to earth was cut, this world had nothing left to engage me. Heaven had now no rival in my heart. Though my love of God had always been sincere, yet I found there wanted this blow to make it perfect. But though all that had made life pleasant to me was gone, I did not sink as those who have no hope. I prayed that I might still, in this trying conflict, be enabled to adorn the doctrine of God my Saviour.

"After many more hardships, I was at length so happy as to get an asylum in this alms-house. Here my cares are at an end, but not my duties." "Now you are wrong again," interrupted Mrs. Betty; "your duty is now to take care of yourself: for I am sure you have nothing to spare." "There you are mistaken again," said Mrs. Simpson. "People are so apt to fancy that money is all in all, that all the other gifts of Providence are overlooked as things of no value. I have here a great deal of leisure; a good part of this I devote to the wants of those who are more distressed than myself. I work a little for the old, and I instruct the young. My eyes are good: this enables me to read the Bible either to those whose sight is decayed, or who were never taught to read. I have tolerable health; so that I am able occasionally to sit up with the sick; in the intervals of nursing I can pray with them. In my younger days I thought it not much to sit up late for my pleasure; shall I now think much of sitting up now and then to watch by a dying bed? My Saviour waked and watched for me in the garden and on the mount; and shall I do nothing for his suffering members? It is only by keeping his sufferings in view that we can truly practice charity to others, or exercise self-denial to ourselves."

"Well," said Mrs. Betty, "I think if I had lived in such genteel life as you have done, I could never be reconciled to an alms-house; and I am afraid I should never forgive any of those who were the cause of sending me there, particularly that farmer Thomas who turned you out of doors."

"Betty," said Mrs. Simpson, "I not only forgive him heartily, but I remember him in my prayers, as one of those instruments with which it has pleased God to work for my good. Oh! never put off forgiveness to a dying bed! When people come to die, we often see how the conscience is troubled with sins, of which before they hardly felt the existence. How ready are they to make restitution of ill-gotten gain; and this perhaps for two reasons; from a feeling conviction that it can be of no use to them where they are going, as well as from a near view of their own responsibility. We also hear from the most hardened, of death-bed forgiveness of enemies. Even malefactors at Tyburn forgive. But why must we wait for a dying bed to do what ought to be done now? Believe me, that scene will be so full of terror and amazement to the soul, that we had not need load it with unnecessary business."

Just as Mrs. Simpson was saying these words, a letter was brought her from the minister of the parish where the farmer lived, by whom Mrs. Simpson had been turned out of the cottage. The letter was as follows:

"MADAM—I write to tell you that your old oppressor, Mr. Thomas, is dead. I attended him in his last moments. O, may my latter end never be like his! I shall not soon forget his despair at the approach of death. His riches, which had been his sole joy, now doubled his sorrows; for he was going where they could be of no use to him; and he found too late that he had laid up no treasure in heaven. He felt great concern at his past life, but for nothing more than his unkindness to Mr. Simpson. He charged me to find you out, and let you know that by his will he bequeathed you five hundred pounds as some compensation. He died in great agonies, declaring with his last breath, that if he could live his life over again, he would serve God, and strictly observe the Sabbath.

"Yours, etc.
"J. JOHNSON."

Mrs. Betty, who had listened attentively to the letter, jumped up, clapped her hands, and cried out, "Now all is for the best, and I shall see you a lady once more." "I am, indeed, thankful for this money," said Mrs. Simpson, "and am glad that riches were not sent me till I had learned, as I humbly hope, to make a right use of them. But come, let us go in, for I am very cold, and find I have sat too long in the night air."

Betty was now ready enough to acknowledge the hand of Providence in this prosperous event, though she was blind to it when the dispensation was more dark. Next morning she went early to visit Mrs. Simpson, but not seeing her below, she went up stairs, where, to her great sorrow, she found her confined to her bed by a fever, caught the night before, by sitting so late on the bench, reading the letter and talking it over. Betty was now more ready to cry out against Providence than ever. "What! to catch a fever while you were reading that very letter which told you about your good fortune; which would have enabled you to live like a lady as you are. I never will believe this is for the best; to be deprived of life just as you were beginning to enjoy it!"

"Betty," said Mrs. Simpson, "we must learn not to rate health nor life itself too highly. There is little in life, for its own sake, to be so fond of. As a good archbishop used to say, "'tis but the same thing over again, or probably worse: so many more nights and days, summers and winters, a repetition of the same pleasures, but with less relish for them; a return of the same or greater pains, but with less strength, and perhaps less patience to bear them.'" "Well," replied Betty, "I did think that Providence was at last giving you your reward." "Reward!" cried Mrs. Simpson. "O, no! my merciful Father will not put me off with so poor a portion as wealth; I feel I shall die." "It is very hard, indeed," said Betty, "so good as you are, to be taken off just as your prosperity was beginning." "You think I am good just now," said Mrs. Simpson, "because I am prosperous. Success is no sure mark of God's favor; at this rate, you, who judge by outward things, would have thought Herod a better man than John the Baptist; and if I may be allowed to say so, you, on your principles, that the sufferer is the sinner, would have believed Pontius Pilate higher in God's favor than the Saviour whom he condemned to die, for your sins and mine."

In a few days Mrs. Betty found that her new friend was dying, and though she was struck at her resignation, she could not forbear murmuring that so good a woman should be taken away at the very instant which she came into possession of so much money. "Betty," said Mrs. Simpson in a feeble voice, "I believe you love me dearly, you would do any thing to cure me; yet you do not love me so well as God loves me, though you would raise me up, and He is putting a period to my life. He has never sent me a single stroke which was not absolutely necessary for me. You, if you could restore me, might be laying me open to some temptation from which God, by removing, will deliver me. Your kindness in making this world so smooth for me, I might forever have deplored in a world of misery. God's grace in afflicting me, will hereafter be the subject of my praises in a world of blessedness. Betty," added the dying woman, "do you really think that I am going to a place of rest and joy eternal?" "To be sure I do," said Betty. "Do you firmly believe that I am going to the assembly of the first-born; to the spirits of just men made perfect, to God the judge of all; and to Jesus the Mediator of the new Covenant?" "I am sure you are," said Betty. "And yet," resumed she, "you would detain me from all this happiness; and you think my merciful Father is using me unkindly by removing me from a world of sin, and sorrow, and temptation, to such joys as have not entered into the heart of man to conceive; while it would have better suited your notions of reward to defer my entrance into the blessedness of heaven, that I might have enjoyed a legacy of a few hundred pounds! Believe my dying words—ALL IS FOR THE BEST."

Mrs. Simpson expired soon after, in a frame of mind which convinced her new friend, that "God's ways are not as our ways."

Mrs. Jones was the widow of a great merchant. She was liberal to the poor, as far as giving them money went; but as she was too much taken up with the world, she did not spare so much of her time and thoughts about doing good as she ought; so that her money was often ill bestowed. In the late troubles, Mr. Jones, who had lived in an expensive manner, failed; and he took his misfortunes so much to heart, that he fell sick and died. Mrs. Jones retired, on a very narrow income, to the small village of Weston, where she seldom went out, except to church. Though a pious woman, she was too apt to indulge her sorrow; and though she did not neglect to read and pray, yet she gave up a great part of her time to melancholy thoughts, and grew quite inactive. She well knew how sinful it would be for her to seek a remedy for her grief in worldly pleasures, which is a way many people take to cure afflictions; but she was not aware how wrong it was to weep away that time which might have been better spent in drying the tears of others.

It was happy for her, that Mr. Simpson, the vicar of Weston, was a pious man. One Sunday he happened to preach on the good Samaritan. It was a charity sermon, and there was a collection at the door. He called on Mrs. Jones after church, and found her in tears. She told him she had been much moved by his discourse, and she wept because she had so little to give to the plate, for though she felt very keenly for the poor in these dear times, yet she could not assist them. "Indeed, sir," added she, "I never so much regretted the loss of my fortune as this afternoon, when you bade us go and do likewise." "You do not," replied Mr. Simpson, "enter into the spirit of our Saviour's parable, if you think you can not go and do likewise without being rich. In the case of the Samaritan, you may observe, that charity was bestowed more by kindness, and care, and medicine, than by money. You, madam, were as much concerned in the duties inculcated in my sermon as Sir John with his great estate; and, to speak plainly, I have been sometimes surprised that you should not put yourself in the way of being more useful."

"Sir," said Mrs. Jones, "I am grown shy of the poor since I have nothing to give them." "Nothing! madam?" replied the clergyman; "Do you call your time, your talents, your kind offices, nothing? Doing good does not so much depend on the riches as on the heart and the will. The servant who improved his two talents was equally commended by his Lord with him who had ten; and it was not poverty, but selfish indolence, which drew down so severe a condemnation on him who had only one. It is by our conformity to Christ, that we must prove ourselves Christians. You, madam, are not called upon to work miracles, nor to preach the gospel, yet you may in your measure and degree, resemble your Saviour by going about and doing good. A plain Christian, who has sense and leisure, by his pious exertions and prudent zeal, may, in a subordinate way, be helping on the cause of religion, as well as of charity, and greatly promote, by his exertions and example, the labors of the parish minister. The generality, it is true, have but an under part to act; but to all God assigns some part, and he will require of all whose lot is not very laborious, that they not only work out their own salvation, but that they promote the cause of religion, and the comfort and salvation of others.

"To those who would undervalue works of mercy as evidences of piety, I would suggest a serious attention to the solemn appeal which the Saviour of the world makes, in that awful representation of the day of judgment, contained in the twenty-fifth chapter of Matthew, both to those who have neglected, and to those who have performed such works; performed them, I mean, on right principles. With what a gracious condescension does he promise to accept the smallest kindness done to his suffering members for his sake. You, madam, I will venture to say, might do more good than the richest man in the parish could do by merely giving his money. Instead of sitting here, brooding over your misfortunes, which are past remedy, bestir yourself to find out ways of doing much good with little money; or even without any money at all. You have lately studied economy for yourself; instruct your poor neighbors in that important art. They want it almost as much as they want money. You have influence with the few rich persons in the parish; exert that influence. Betty, my house-keeper, shall assist you in any thing in which she can be useful. Try this for one year, and if you then tell me that you should have better shown your love to God and man, and been a happier woman, had you continued gloomy and inactive, I shall be much surprised, and shall consent to your resuming your present way of life."

The sermon and this discourse together made so deep an impression on Mrs. Jones, that she formed a new plan of life, and set about it at once, as every body does who is in earnest. Her chief aim was the happiness of her poor neighbors in the next world; but she was also very desirous to promote their present comfort; and indeed the kindness she showed to their bodily wants gave her such an access to their houses and hearts, as made them better disposed to receive religious counsel and instruction. Mrs. Jones was much respected by all the rich persons in Weston, who had known her in her prosperity. Sir John was thoughtless, lavish, and indolent. The squire was over frugal, but active, sober, and not ill-natured. Sir John loved pleasure, the squire loved money. Sir John was one of those popular sort of people who get much praise, and yet do little good; who subscribe with equal readiness to a cricket match or a charity school; who take it for granted that the poor are to be indulged with bell-ringing and bonfires, and to be made drunk at Christmas; this Sir John called being kind to them; but he thought it was folly to teach them, and madness to think of reforming them. He was, however, always ready to give his guinea; but I question whether he would have given up his hunting and his gaming to have cured every grievance in the land. He had that sort of constitutional good nature which, if he had lived much within sight of misery, would have led him to be liberal; but he had that selfish love of ease, which prompted him to give to undeserving objects, rather than be at the pains to search out the deserving. He neither discriminated between the degrees of distress, nor the characters of the distressed. His idea of charity was, that a rich man should occasionally give a little of his superfluous wealth to the first object that occurred; but he had no conception that it was his duty so to husband his wealth and limit his expenses, as to supply a regular fund for established charity. And the utmost stretch of his benevolence never led him to suspect that he was called to abridge himself in the most idle article of indulgence, for a purpose foreign to his own personal enjoyment. On the other hand, the squire would assist Mrs. Jones in any of her plans if it cost him nothing; so she showed her good sense by never asking Sir John for advice, or the squire for subscriptions, and by this prudence gained the full support of both.

Mrs. Jones resolved to spend two or three days in a week in getting acquainted with the state of the parish, and she took care never to walk out without a few little good books in her pocket to give away. This, though a cheap, is a most important act of charity; it has its various uses; it furnishes the poor with religious knowledge, which they have so few ways of obtaining; it counteracts the wicked designs of those who have taught us at least one lesson, by their zeal in the dispersion of wicked books—I mean the lesson of vigilance and activity; and it is the best introduction for any useful conversation which the giver of the book may wish to introduce.

She found that among the numerous wants she met with, no small share was owing to bad management, or to imposition; she was struck with the small size of the loaves. Wheat was now not very dear, and she was sure a good deal of blame rested with the baker. She sent for a shilling loaf to the next great town, where the mayor often sent to the bakers' shops to see that the bread was proper weight. She weighed her town loaf against her country loaf, and found the latter two pounds lighter than it ought to be. This was not the sort of grievance to carry to Sir John; but luckily the squire was also a magistrate, and it was quite in his way; for though he would not give, yet he would counsel, calculate, contrive, reprimand, and punish. He told her he could remedy the evil if some one would lodge an information against her baker; but that there was no act of justice which he found it so difficult to accomplish.

THE INFORMER

She dropped in on the blacksmith. He was at dinner. She inquired if his bread was good. "Ay, good enough, mistress; for you see it is as white as your cap, if we had but more of it. Here's a sixpenny loaf; you might take it for a penny roll!" He then heartily cursed Crib the baker, and said he ought to be hanged. Mrs. Jones now told him what she had done; how she had detected the fraud, and assured him the evil should be redressed on the morrow, provided he would appear and inform. "I inform," said he, with a shocking oath, "hang an informer! I scorn the office." "You are nice in the wrong place," replied Mrs. Jones; "for you don't scorn to abuse the baker, nor to be in a passion, nor to swear, though you scorn to redress a public injury, and to increase your children's bread. Let me tell you there's nothing in which you ignorant people mistake more than in your notions about informers. Informing is a lawful way of obtaining redress; and though it is a mischievous and a hateful thing to go to a justice about every trifling matter, yet laying an information on important occasions, without malice, or bitterness of any kind, is what no honest man ought to be ashamed of. The shame is to commit the offense, not to inform against it. I, for my part, should perhaps do right, if I not only informed against Crib, for making light bread, but against you, for swearing at him."

"Well, but madam," said the smith, a little softened, "don't you think it a sin and a shame to turn informer?" "So far from it, that when a man's motives are good," said Mrs. Jones, "and in clear cases as the present, I think it a duty and a virtue. If it is right that there should be laws, it must be right that they should be put in execution; but how can this be, if people will not inform the magistrates when they see the laws broken? I hope I shall always be afraid to be an offender against the laws, but not to be an informer in support of them. An informer by trade is commonly a knave. A rash, malicious, or passionate informer is a firebrand; but honest and prudent informers are almost as useful members of society as the judges of the land. If you continue in your present mind on this subject, do not you think that you will be answerable for the crimes you might have prevented by informing, and thus become a sort of accomplice of the villains who commit them."

"Well, madam," said the smith, "I now see plainly enough that there is no shame in turning informer when my cause is good." "And your motive right; always mind that," said Mrs. Jones. Next day the smith attended, Crib was fined in the usual penalty, his light bread was taken from him and given to the poor. The justices resolved henceforward to inspect the bakers in their district; and all of them, except Crib, and such as Crib, were glad of it; for honesty never dreads a trial. Thus had Mrs. Jones the comfort of seeing how useful people may be without expense; for if she could have given the poor fifty pounds, she would not have done them so great, or so lasting a benefit, as she did them in seeing their loaves restored to their lawful weight: and the true light in which she had put the business of informing was of no small use, in giving the neighborhood right views on that subject.

There were two shops in the parish; but Mrs. Sparks, at the Cross, had not half so much custom as Wills, at the Sugarloaf, though she sold her goods a penny in a shilling cheaper, and all agreed that they were much better. Mrs. Jones asked Mrs. Sparks the reason, "Madam," said the shopkeeper, "Mr. Wills will give longer trust. Besides his wife keeps shop on a Sunday morning while I am at church." Mrs. Jones now reminded Mr. Simpson to read the king's proclamation against vice and immorality next Sunday at church; and prevailed on the squire to fine any one who should keep open shop on a Sunday. This he readily undertook: for while Sir John thought it good-natured to connive at breaking the laws, the squire fell into the other extreme, of thinking that the zealous enforcing of penal statutes would stand in the stead of all religious restraints. Mrs. Jones proceeded to put the people in mind that a shopkeeper who would sell on a Sunday, would be more likely to cheat them all the week, than one who went to church.

She also labored hard to convince them how much they would lessen their distress, if they would contrive to deal with Mrs. Sparks for ready money, rather than with Wills on long credit; those who listened to her found their circumstances far more comfortable at the year's end, while the rest, tempted, like some of their betters, by the pleasure of putting off the evil day of payment, like them, at last found themselves plunged in debt and distress. She took care to make a good use of such instances in her conversation with the poor, and by perseverance, she at length brought them so much to her way of thinking, that Wills found it to be his interest to alter his plan, and sell his goods on as good terms, and as short credit as Mrs. Sparks sold hers. This completed Mrs. Jones's success; and she had the satisfaction of having put a stop to three or four great evils in the parish of Weston, without spending a shilling in doing it.

Patty Smart and Jenny Rose were thought to be the two best managers in the parish. They both told Mrs. Jones, that the poor would get the coarse pieces of meat cheaper, if the gentlefolks did not buy them for soups and gravy. Mrs. Jones thought there was reason in this: so away she went to Sir John, the squire, the surgeon, the attorney, and the steward, the only persons in the parish who could afford to buy these costly things. She told them, that if they would all be so good as to buy only prime pieces, which they could very well afford, the coarse and cheap joints would come more within the reach of the poor. Most of the gentry readily consented. Sir John cared not what his meat cost him, but told Mrs. Jones, in his gay way, that he would eat any thing, or give any thing, so that she would not tease him with long stories about the poor. The squire said he should prefer vegetable soups, because they were cheaper, and the doctor preferred them because they were wholesomer. The steward chose to imitate the squire; and the attorney found it would be quite ungenteel to stand out. So gravy soups became very unfashionable in the parish of Weston; and I am sure if rich people did but think a little on this subject, they would become as unfashionable in many other places. When wheat grew cheaper, Mrs. Jones was earnest with the poor women to bake large brown loaves at home, instead of buying small white ones at the shop. Mrs. Betty had told her, that baking at home would be one step toward restoring the good old management. Only Betty Smart and Jenny Rose baked at home in the whole parish; and who lived so well as they did? Yet the general objection seemed reasonable. They could not bake without yeast, which often could not be had, as no one brewed, except the great folks and the public houses. Mrs. Jones found, however, that Patty and Jenny contrived to brew as well as to bake. She sent for these women, knowing that from them she could get truth and reason. "How comes it," she said to them, "that you two are the only two poor women in the parish who can afford to brew a small cask of beer? Your husbands have no better wages than other men." "True, madam," said Patty, "but they never set foot in a public house. I will tell you the truth. When I first married, our John went to the Checkers every night, and I had my tea and fresh butter twice a-day at home. This slop, which consumed a deal of sugar, began to rake my stomach sadly, as I had neither meat nor rice; at last (I am ashamed to own it) I began to take a drop of gin to quiet the pain, till in time, I looked for my gin as regularly as for my tea. At last the gin, the ale-house, and the tea began to make us both sick and poor, and I had like to have died with my first child. Parson Simpson then talked so finely to us on the subject of improper indulgences, that we resolved, by the grace of God, to turn over a new leaf, and I promised John, if he would give up the Checkers, I would break the gin bottle, and never drink tea in the afternoon, except on Sundays, when he was at home to drink it with me. We have kept our word, and both our eating and drinking, our health and our consciences are better for it. Though meat is sadly dear, we can buy two pounds of fresh meat for less than one pound of fresh butter, and it gives five times the nourishment. And dear as malt is, I contrive to keep a drop of drink in the house for John, and John will make me drink half a pint with him every evening, and a pint a-day when I am a nurse."

PUBLIC HOUSES

As one good deed, as well as one bad one, brings on another, this conversation set Mrs. Jones on inquiring why so many ale-houses were allowed. She did not choose to talk to Sir John on this subject, who would only have said, "let them enjoy themselves, poor fellows: if they get drunk now and then, they work hard." But those who have this false good-nature forget that while the man is enjoying himself, as it is called, his wife and children are ragged and starving. True Christian good-nature never indulges one at the cost of many, but is kind to all. The squire who was a friend to order, took up the matter. He consulted Mr. Simpson. "The Lion," said he, "is necessary. It stands by the roadside; travelers must have a resting-place. As to the Checkers and the Bell, they do no good, but much harm." Mr. Simpson had before made many attempts to get the Checkers put down, but, unluckily, it was Sir John's own house, and kept by his late butler. Not that Sir John valued the rent, but he had a false kindness, which made him support the cause of an old servant, though he knew he was a bad man, and kept a disorderly house. The squire, however, now took away the license from the Bell. And a fray happening soon after at the Checkers (which was near the church) in time of divine service, Sir John was obliged to suffer the house to be put down as a nuisance. You would not believe how many poor families were able to brew a little cask, when the temptation of those ale-houses was taken out of their way. Mrs. Jones, in her evening walks, had the pleasure to see many an honest man drinking his wholesome cup of beer by his own fire-side, his rosy children playing about his knees, his clean cheerful wife singing her youngest baby to sleep, rocking the cradle with her foot, while with her hands she was making a dumpling for her kind husband's supper. Some few, I am sorry to say, though I don't chose to name names, still preferred getting drunk once a week at the Lion, and drinking water at other times. Thus Mrs. Jones, by a little exertion and perseverance, added to the temporal comforts of a whole parish, and diminished its immorality and extravagance in the same proportion.

The good women being now supplied with yeast from each other's brewings, would have baked, but two difficulties still remained. Many of them had no ovens; for since the new bad management had crept in, many cottages have been built without this convenience. Fuel also was scarce at Weston. Mrs. Jones advised the building a large parish oven. Sir John subscribed to be rid of her importunity, and the squire, because he thought every improvement would reduce the poor's rate. It was soon accomplished; and to this oven, at a certain hour, three times a week, the elder children carried their loaves which their mothers had made at home, and paid a half-penny, or a penny, according to their size, for the baking.

Mrs. Jones found that no poor women in Weston could buy a little milk, as the farmers' wives did not care to rob their dairies. This was a great distress, especially when the children were sick. So Mrs. Jones advised Mrs. Sparks, at the Cross, to keep a couple of cows, and sell out the milk by halfpennyworths. She did so, and found, that though this plan gave her some additional trouble, she got full as much by it as if she had made cheese and butter. She always sold rice at a cheap rate; so that, with the help of the milk and the public oven, a fine rice-pudding was to be had for a trifle.

CHARITY SCHOOLS FOR SERVANTS

The girls' school, in the parish, was fallen into neglect; for though many would be subscribers, yet no one would look after it. I wish this was the case at Weston only: many schools have come to nothing, and many parishes are quite destitute of schools, because too many gentry neglect to make it a part of the duty of their grown-up daughters to inspect the instruction of the poor. It was not in Mr. Simpson's way to see if girls were taught to work. The best clergyman can not do every thing. This is ladies' business. Mrs. Jones consulted her counselor, Mrs. Betty, and they went every Friday to the school, where they invited mothers, as well as daughters, to come, and learn to cut out to the best advantage. Mrs. Jones had not been bred to these things; but by means of Mrs. Cowper's excellent cutting-out book, she soon became mistress of the whole art. She not only had the girls taught to make and mend, but to wash and iron too. She also allowed the mother or eldest daughter of every family to come once a week, and learn how to dress one cheap dish. One Friday, which was cooking day, who should pass but the squire, with his gun and dogs. He looked into the school for the first time. "Well, madam," said he, "what good are you doing here? What are your girls learning and earning? Where are your manufactures? Where is your spinning and your carding?" "Sir," said she, "this is a small parish, and you know ours is not a manufacturing county; so that when these girls are women, they will be not much employed in spinning. We must, in the kind of good we attempt to do, consult the local genius of the place: I do not think it will answer to introduce spinning, for instance, in a country where it is quite new. However, we teach them a little of it, and still more of knitting, that they may be able to get up a small piece of household linen once a year, and provide the family with the stockings, by employing the odds and ends of their time in these ways. But there is another manufacture which I am carrying on, and I know of none within my own reach which is so valuable." "What can that be?" said the squire. "To make good wives for working men," said she. "Is not mine an excellent staple commodity? I am teaching these girls the arts of industry and good management. It is little encouragement to an honest man to work hard all the week, if his wages are wasted by a slattern at home. Most of these girls will probably become wives to the poor, or servants to the rich; to such the common arts of life are of great value: now, as there is little opportunity for learning these at the school-house, I intend to propose that such gentry as have sober servants, shall allow one of these girls to come and work in their families one day in a week, when the house-keeper, the cook, the house-maid or the laundry-maid, shall be required to instruct them in their several departments. This I conceive to be the best way of training good servants. They would serve this kind of regular apprenticeship to various sorts of labor. Girls who come out of charity-schools, where they have been employed in knitting, sewing, and reading, are not sufficiently prepared for hard or laborious employments. I do not in general approve of teaching charity children to write, for the same reason. I confine within very strict limits my plan of educating the poor. A thorough knowledge of religion, and of some of those coarser arts of life by which the community may be best benefitted, includes the whole stock of instruction, which, unless in very extraordinary cases, I would wish to bestow."

"What have you got on the fire, madam?" said the squire; "for your pot really smells as savory as if Sir John's French cook had filled it." "Sir," replied Mrs. Jones, "I have lately got acquainted with Mrs. Whyte who has given us an account of her cheap dishes, and nice cookery, in one of the Cheap Repository little books.[15] Mrs. Betty and I have made all her dishes, and very good they are; and we have got several others of our own. Every Friday we come here and dress one. These good woman see how it is done, and learn to dress it at their own house. I take home part for my own dinner, and what is left I give to each in turn. I hope I have opened their eyes on a sad mistake they have got into, that we think any thing is good enough for the poor. Now, I do not think any thing good enough for the poor which is not clean, wholesome, and palatable, and what I myself would not cheerfully eat, if my circumstances required it."

[15] See the Way to Plenty for a number of cheap recipes.

"Pray, Mrs. Betty," said the squire, "oblige me with a basin of your soup." The squire found it so good after his walk, that he was almost sorry that he had promised to buy no more legs of beef, and declared, that not one sheep's head should ever go to his kennel again. He begged his cook might have the recipe, and Mrs. Jones wrote it out for her. She has also been so obliging as to favor me with a copy of all her recipes. And as I hate all monopoly, and see no reason why such cheap, nourishing, and savory dishes should be confined to the parish of Weston, I print them, that all other parishes may have the same advantage. Not only the poor, but all persons with small income may be glad of them.'

"Well, madam," said Mr. Simpson, who came in soon after, "which is best, to sit down and cry over our misfortunes, or to bestir ourselves to do our duty to the world?" "Sir," replied Mrs. Jones, "I thank you for the useful lesson you have given me. You have taught me that an excessive indulgence of sorrow is not piety, but selfishness; that the best remedy for our own afflictions is to lessen the afflictions of others, and thus evidence our submission to the will of God, who perhaps sent these very trials to abate our own self-love, and to stimulate our exertions for the good of others. You have taught me that our time and talents are to be employed with zeal in God's service, if we wish for his favor here or hereafter; and that one great employment of those talents which he requires, is the promotion of the present, and much more the future happiness of all around us. You have taught me that much good may be done with little money; and that the heart, the head, and the hand are of some use as well as the purse. I have also learned another lesson, which I hope not to forget, that Providence, in sending these extraordinary seasons of scarcity and distress, which we have lately twice experienced, has been pleased to overrule these trying events to the general good; for it has not only excited the rich to an increased liberality, as to actual contribution, but it has led them to get more acquainted with the local wants of their poor brethren, and to interest themselves in their comfort; it has led to improved modes of economy, and to a more feeling kind of beneficence. Above all, without abating any thing of a just subordination, it has brought the affluent to a nearer knowledge of the persons and characters of their indigent neighbors; it has literally brought 'the rich and poor to meet together;' and this I look upon to be one of the essential advantages attending Sunday-schools also, where they are carried on upon true principles, and are sanctioned by the visits as well as supported by the contributions of the wealthy."

May all who read this account of Mrs. Jones, and who are under the same circumstances, go and do likewise.

ALLEGORIES

THE PILGRIMS

Methought I was once upon a time traveling through a certain land which was very full of people; but, what was rather odd, not one of all this multitude was at home; they were all bound to a far distant country. Though it was permitted by the lord of the land that these pilgrims might associate together for their present mutual comfort and convenience; and each was not only allowed, but commanded, to do the others all the services he could upon their journey, yet it was decreed, that every individual traveler must enter the far country singly. There was a great gulf at the end of the journey, which every one must pass alone, and at his own risk, and the friendship of the whole united world could be of no use in shooting that gulf. The exact time when each was to pass was not known to any; this the lord always kept a close secret out of kindness, yet still they were as sure that the time must come, and that at no very great distance, as if they had been informed of the very moment. Now, as they knew they were always liable to be called away at an hour's notice, one would have thought they would have been chiefly employed in packing up, and preparing, and getting every thing in order. But this was so far from being the case, that it was almost the only thing which they did not think about.

Now, I only appeal to you, my readers, if any of you are setting out upon a little common journey, if it is only to London or York, is not all your leisure time employed in settling your business at home, and packing up every little necessary for your expedition? And does not the fear of neglecting any thing you ought to remember, or may have occasion for, haunt your mind, and sometimes even intrude upon you unseasonably? And when you are actually on your journey, especially if you have never been to that place before, or are likely to remain there, don't you begin to think a little about the pleasures and the employment of the place, and to wish to know a little what sort of a city London or York is? Don't you wonder what is doing there, and are you not anxious to know whether you are properly qualified for the business or the company you expect to be engaged in? Do you never look at the map or consult Brooke's Gazetteer? And don't you try to pick up from your fellow-passengers in the stage-coach any little information you can get? And though you may be obliged, out of civility, to converse with them on common subjects, yet do not your secret thoughts still run upon London or York, its business, or its pleasures? And above all, if you are likely to set out early, are you not afraid of oversleeping, and does not that fear keep you upon the watch, so that you are commonly up and ready before the porter comes to summon you? Reader! if this be your case, how surprised will you be to hear that the travelers to the far country have not half your prudence, though embarked on a journey of infinitely more importance, bound to a land where nothing can be sent after them, in which, when they are once settled, all errors are irretrievable.

I observed that these pilgrims, instead of being upon the watch, lest they should be ordered off unprepared; instead of laying up any provision, or even making memoranda of what they would be likely to want at the end of their journey, spent most of their time in crowds, either in the way of traffic or diversion. At first, when I saw them so much engaged in conversing with each other, I thought it a good sign, and listened attentively to their talk, not doubting but the chief turn of it would be about the climate, or treasures, or society, they should probably meet with in the far country. I supposed they might be also discussing about the best and safest road to it, and that each was availing himself of the knowledge of his neighbor, on a subject of equal importance to all. I listened to every party, but in scarcely any did I hear one word about the land to which they were bound, though it was their home, the place where their whole interest, expectation, and inheritance lay; to which also great part of their friends were gone before, and whither they were sure all the rest would follow. Instead of this, their whole talk was about the business, or the pleasure, or the fashion of the strange but bewitching country which they were merely passing through, in which they had not one foot of land which they were sure of calling their own for the next quarter of an hour. What little estate they had was personal, and not real, and that was a mortgaged, life-hold tenement of clay, not properly their own, but only lent to them on a short, uncertain lease, of which three-score years and ten was considered as the longest period, and very few indeed lived in it to the end of the term; for this was always at the will of the lord, part of whose prerogative it was, that he could take away the lease at pleasure, knock down the stoutest tenement at a single blow, and turn out the poor shivering, helpless inhabitant naked, to that far country for which he had made no provision. Sometimes, in order to quicken the pilgrim in his preparation, the lord would break down the tenement by slow degrees; sometimes he would let it tumble by its own natural decay; for as it was only built to last a certain term, it would often grow so uncomfortable by increasing dilapidations even before the ordinary lease was out, that the lodging was hardly worth keeping, though the tenant could seldom be persuaded to think so, but finally clung to it to the last. First the thatch on the top of the tenement changed color, then it fell off and left the roof bare; then the grinders ceased because they were few; then the windows became so darkened that the owner could scarcely see through them; then one prop fell away, then another, then the uprights became bent, and the whole fabric trembled and tottered, with every other symptom of a falling house. But what was remarkable, the more uncomfortable the house became, and the less prospect there was of staying in it, the more preposterously fond did the tenant grew of his precarious habitation.

On some occasions the lord ordered his messengers, of which he had a great variety, to batter, injure, deface, and almost demolish the frail building, even while it seemed new and strong; this was what the landlord called giving warning, but many a tenant would not take warning, and so fond of staying where he was, even under all these inconveniences, that at last he was cast out by ejectment, not being prevailed on to leave the dwelling in a proper manner, though one would have thought the fear of being turned out would have whetted his diligence in preparing for a better and more enduring inheritance. For though the people were only tenants at will in these crazy tenements, yet, through the goodness of the same lord, they were assured that he never turned them out of these habitations before he had on his part provided for them a better, so that there was not such a landlord in the world, and though their present dwelling was but frail, being only slightly run up to serve the occasion, yet they might hold their future possession by a most certain tenure, the word of the lord himself. This word was entered in a covenant, or title-deed, consisting of many sheets, and because a great many good things were given away in this deed, a book was made of which every soul might get a copy.

This indeed had not always been the case, because, till a few ages back, there had been a sort of monopoly in the case, and "the wise and prudent," that is the cunning and fraudful, had hid these things from "the babes and sucklings;" that is, from the low and ignorant, and many frauds had been practiced, and the poor had been cheated of their right; so that not being allowed to read and judge for themselves, they had been sadly imposed upon; but all these tricks had been put an end to more than two hundred years when I passed through the country, and the meanest man who could read might then have a copy; so that he might see himself what he had to trust to; and even those who could not read, might hear it read once or twice every week, at least, without pay, by learned and holy men, whose business it was. But it surprised me to see how few comparatively made use of these vast advantages. Of those who had a copy, many laid it carelessly by, expressed a general belief in the truth of the title-deed, a general satisfaction that they should come in for a share of the inheritance, a general good opinion of the lord whose word it was, and a general disposition to take his promise upon trust, always, however, intending, at a convenient season to inquire further into the matter; but this convenient season seldom came; and this neglect of theirs was construed by their lord into a forfeiture of the inheritance.

At the end of this country lay the vast gulf mentioned before; it was shadowed over by a broad and thick cloud, which prevented the pilgrims from seeing in a distinct manner what was doing behind it, yet such beams of brightness now and then darted through the cloud, as enabled those who used a telescope, provided for that purpose, to see the substance of things hoped for; but it was not every one who could make use of this telescope; no eye indeed was naturally disposed to it; but an earnest desire of getting a glimpse of the invisible realities, gave such a strength and steadiness to the eye which used the telescope, as enabled it to discern many things which could not be seen by the natural sight. Above the cloud was this inscription: "The things which are seen are temporal, but the things which are not seen are eternal." Of these last things many glorious descriptions had been given; but as those splendors were at a distance, and as the pilgrims in general did not care to use the telescope, these distant glories made little impression.

The glorious inheritance which lay beyond the cloud, was called "The things above," while a multitude of trifling objects, which appeared contemptibly small when looked at through the telescope, were called "the things below." Now as we know it is nearness which gives size and bulk to any object, it was not wonderful that these ill-judging pilgrims were more struck with these baubles and trifles, which by laying close at hand, were visible and tempting to the naked eye, and which made up the sum of the things below, than with the remote glories of the things above; but this was chiefly owing to their not making use of the telescope, through which, if you examined thoroughly the things below, they seemed to shrink almost down to nothing, which was indeed their real size: while the things above appeared the more beautiful and vast, the more the telescope was used. But the surprising part of the story was this; not that the pilgrims were captivated at first sight with the things below, for that was natural enough; but that when they had tried them all over and over, and found themselves deceived and disappointed in almost every one of them, it did not at all lessen their fondness, and they grasped at them again with, the same eagerness as before. There were some gay fruits which looked alluring, but on being opened, instead of a kernel, they were found to contain rottenness; and those which seemed the fullest, often proved on trial to be quite hollow and empty. Those which were the most tempting to the eye, were often found to be wormwood to the taste, or poison to the stomach, and many flowers that seemed most bright and gay had a worm gnawing at the root; and it was observable that on the finest and brightest of them was seen, when looked at through the telescope, the word vanity inscribed in large characters.

Among the chief attractions of the things below were certain little lumps of yellow clay, on which almost every eye and every heart was fixed. When I saw the variety of uses to which this clay could be converted, and the respect which was shown to those who could scrape together the greatest number of pieces, I did not much wonder at the general desire to pick up some of them; but when I beheld the anxiety, the wakefulness, the competitions, the contrivances, the tricks, the frauds, the scuffling, the pushing, the turmoiling, the kicking, the shoving, the cheating, the circumvention, the envy, the malignity, which was excited by a desire to possess this article; when I saw the general scramble among those who had little to get much, and of those who had much to get more, then I could not help applying to these people a proverb in use among us, that gold may be bought too dear.

Though I saw that there were various sorts of baubles which engaged the hearts of different travelers, such as an ell of red or blue ribbon, for which some were content to forfeit their future inheritance, committing the sin of Esau, without his temptation of hunger; yet the yellow clay I found was the grand object for which most hands were scrambling, and most souls were risked. One thing was extraordinary, that the nearer these people were to being turned out of their tenements, the fonder they grew of these pieces of clay; so that I naturally concluded they meant to take the clay with them to the far country, to assist them in their establishment in it; but I soon learned this clay was not current there, the lord having further declared to these pilgrims that as they had brought nothing into this world, they could carry nothing away.

I inquired of the different people who were raising the various heaps of clay, some of a larger, some of a smaller size, why they discovered such unremitting anxiety, and for whom? Some, whose piles were immense, told me they were heaping up for their children; this I thought very right, till, on casting my eyes around, I observed many of the children of these very people had large heaps of their own. Others told me it was for their grand-children; but on inquiry I found these were not yet born, and in many cases there was little chance that they ever would. The truth, on a close examination, proved to be, that the true genuine heapers really heaped for themselves; that it was in fact neither for friend nor child, but to gratify an inordinate appetite of their own. Nor was I much surprised after this to see these yellow hoards at length canker, and the rust of them become a witness against the hoarders, and eat their flesh as it were fire.

Many, however, who had set out with a high heap of their father's raising, before they had got one third of their journey, had scarcely a single piece left. As I was wondering what had caused these enormous piles to vanish in so short a time, I spied scattered up and down the country all sorts of odd inventions, for some or other of which the vain possessors of the great heaps of clay had trucked and bartered them away in fewer hours than their ancestors had spent years in getting them together. O what a strange unaccountable medley it was! and what was ridiculous enough, I observed that the greatest quantity of the clay was always exchanged for things that were of no use that I could discover, owing I suppose to my ignorance of the manners of the country.

In one place I saw large heaps exhausted, in order to set two idle pampered horses a running; but the worst of the joke was, the horses did not run to fetch or carry any thing, and of course were of no kind of use, but merely to let the gazers see which could run fastest. Now, this gift of swiftness, exercised to no useful purpose, was only one out of many instances, I observed, of talents employed to no end. In another place I saw whole piles of the clay spent to maintain long ranges of buildings full of dogs, on provisions which would have nicely fattened some thousands of pilgrims, who sadly wanted fattening, and whose ragged tenements were out at elbows, for want of a little help to repair them. Some of the piles were regularly pulled down once in seven years, in order to corrupt certain needy pilgrims to belie their consciences, by doing that for a bribe which they were bound to do from principle. Others were spent in playing with white stiff bits of paper, painted over with red and black spots, in which I thought there must be some conjuring, because the very touch of these painted pasteboards made the heaps fly from one to another, and back again to the same, in a way that natural causes could not account for. There was another proof that there must be some magic in this business which was that if a pasteboard with red spots fell into a hand which wanted a black one, the person changed color, his eyes flashed fire, and he discovered other symptoms of madness, which showed there was some witchcraft in the case. These clean little pasteboards, as harmless as they looked, had the wonderful power of pulling down the highest piles in less time than all the other causes put together. I observed that many small piles were given in exchange for an enchanted liquor which when the purchaser had drank to a little excess, he lost the power of managing the rest of his heap without losing the love of it; and thus the excess of indulgence, by making him a beggar, deprived him of that very gratification on which his heart was set.

Now I find it was the opinion of sober pilgrims, that either hoarding the clay, or trucking it for any such purposes as the above, was thought exactly the same offense in the eyes of the lord; and it was expected that when they should come under his more immediate jurisdiction in the far country, the penalty annexed to hoarding and squandering would be nearly the same. While I examined the countenances of the owners of the heaps, I observed that those who I well knew never intended to make any use at all of their heap, were far more terrified at the thought of losing it, or of being torn from it, than those were who were employing it in the most useful manner. Those who best knew what to do with it, set their hearts least upon it, and were always most willing to leave it. But such riddles were common in this odd country. It was indeed a very land of paradoxes.

Now I wondered why these pilgrims, who were naturally made erect with an eye formed to look up to the things above, yet had their eyes almost constantly bent in the other direction, riveted to the earth, and fastened on things below, just like those animals who walk on all fours. I was told they had not always been subject to this weakness of sight, and proneness to earth; that they had originally been upright and beautiful, having been created after the image of the lord, who was himself the perfection of beauty; that he had, at first, placed them in a far superior situation, which he had given them in perpetuity; but that their first ancestors fell from it through pride and carelessness; that upon this the freehold was taken away, they lost their original strength, brightness, and beauty, and were driven out into this strange country, where, however, they had every opportunity given them of recovering their original health, and the lord's favor and likeness; for they were become so disfigured, and were grown so unlike him, that you would hardly believe they were his own children, though, in some, the resemblance was become again visible.

The lord, however, was so merciful, that, instead of giving them up to the dreadful consequences of their own folly, as he might have done without any impeachment of his justice, he gave them immediate comfort, and promised them that, in due time, his own son should come down and restore them to the future inheritance which he should purchase for them. And now it was, that in order to keep up their spirits, after they had lost their estate through the folly of their ancestors, that he began to give them a part of their former title-deed. He continued to send them portions of it from time to time by different faithful servants, whom, however, these ungrateful people generally used ill, and some of whom they murdered. But for all this, the lord was so very forgiving, that he at length sent these mutineers a proclamation of full and free pardon by his son. This son, though they used him in a more cruel manner than they had done any of his servants, yet after having finished the work his father gave him to do, went back into the far country to prepare a place for all them who believe in him; and there he still lives; begging and pleading for those unkind people, whom he still loves and forgives, and will restore to the purchased inheritance on the easy terms of their being heartily sorry for what they have done, thoroughly desirous of pardon, and convinced that he is able and willing to save to the uttermost all them that come unto him.

I saw, indeed, that many old offenders appeared to be sorry for what they had done; that is, they did not like to be punished for it. They were willing enough to be delivered from the penalty of their guilt, but they did not heartily wish to be delivered from the power of it. Many declared, in the most public manner, once every week, that they were sorry they had done amiss; that they had erred and strayed like lost sheep, but it was not enough to declare their sorrow, ever so often, if they gave no other sign of their penitence. For there was so little truth in them, that the lord required other proofs of their sincerity beside their own word, for they often lied with their lips and dissembled with their tongue. But those who professed to be penitent must give some outward proof of it. They were neither allowed to raise heaps of clay, by circumventing their neighbors, or to keep great piles lying by them useless; nor must they barter them for any of those idle vanities which reduced the heaps on a sudden; for I found that among the grand articles of future reckoning, the use they had made of the heaps would be a principal one.

I was sorry to observe many of the fairer part of these pilgrims spend too much of their heaps in adorning and beautifying their tenements of clay, in painting, whitewashing, and enameling them. All those tricks, however, did not preserve them from decay; and when they grew old, they even looked worse for all this cost and varnish. Some, however, acted a more sensible part, and spent no more upon their moldering tenements than just to keep them whole and clean, and in good repair, which is what every tenant ought to do; and I observed, that those who were most moderate in the care of their own tenements, were most attentive to repair and warm the ragged tenements of others. But none did this with much zeal or acceptance, but those who had acquired a habit of overlooking the things below, and who also, by the constant use of the telescope had got their natural weak and dim sight so strengthened, as to be able to discern pretty distinctly the nature of the things above. The habit of fixing their eyes on these glories made all the shining trifles, which compose the mass of things below, at last appear in their own diminutive littleness. For it was in this case particularly true, that things are only big or little by comparison; and there was no other way of making the things below, appear as small as they really were, but by comparing them, by means of the telescope, with the things above. But I observed that the false judgment of the pilgrims ever kept pace with their wrong practices; for those who kept their eyes fastened on the things below, were reckoned wise in their generation, while the few who looked forward to the future glories, were accounted by the bustlers, or heapers, to be either fools or mad.

Most of these pilgrims went on in adorning their tenements, adding to their heaps, grasping the things below as if they would never let them go, shutting their eyes, instead of using their telescope, and neglecting their title-deed, as if it was the parchment of another man's estate, and not of their own; till one after another each felt his tenement tumbling about his ears. Oh! then what a busy, bustling, anxious, terrifying, distracting moment was that! What a deal of business was to be done, and what a strange time was this to do it in! Now, to see the confusion and dismay occasioned by having left every thing to the last minute. First, some one was sent for to make over the yellow heaps, to another, which the heaper now found would be of no use to himself in shooting the gulf; a transfer which ought to have been made while the tenement was sound. Then there was a consultation between two or three masons at once perhaps, to try to patch up the walls, and strengthen the props, and stop the decays of the tumbling tenement; but not till the masons were forced to declare it was past repairing (a truth they were rather too apt to keep back) did the tenant seriously think it was time to pack up, prepare and begone. Then what sending for the wise men who professed to explain the title-deed! And oh! what remorse that they had neglected to examine it till their senses were too confused for so weighty a business! What reproaches, or what exhortations to others, to look better after their own affairs than they had done. Even to the wisest of the inhabitants the falling of their tenements was a solemn thing; solemn, but not surprising; they had long been packing up and preparing; they praised their lord's goodness that they had been suffered to stay so long; many acknowledged the mercy of their frequent warnings, and confessed that those very dilapidations which had made the house uncomfortable had been a blessing, as it had set them on diligent preparation for their future inheritance; had made them more earnest in examining their title to it, and had set them on such a frequent application to the telescope, that the things above had seemed every day to approach nearer and nearer, and the things below to recede and vanish in proportion. These desired not to be unclothed but to be clothed upon, for they knew that if their tabernacle was dissolved, they had an house not made with hands, eternal in the heavens.

THE VALLEY OF TEARS

A VISION; OR, BEAR YE ONE ANOTHER'S BURDENS

Once upon a time methought I set out upon a long journey, and the place through which I traveled appeared to be a dark valley, which was called the Valley of Tears. It had obtained this name, not only on account of the many sorrowful adventures which poor passengers commonly meet with in their journey through it; but also because most of these travelers entered it weeping and crying, and left it in very great pain and anguish. This vast valley was full of people of all colors, ages, sizes and descriptions.

But whether white or black, or tawny, all were traveling the same road; or rather they were taking different little paths which all led to the same common end.

Now it was remarkable, that notwithstanding the different complexions, ages, and tempers of this vast variety of people, yet all resembled each other in this one respect, that each had a burden on his back which he was destined to carry through the toil and heat of the day, until he should arrive, by a longer or shorter course, at his journey's end. These burdens would in general have made the pilgrimage quite intolerable, had not the lord of the valley, out of his great compassion for these poor pilgrims, provided, among other things, the following means for their relief.

In their full view over the entrance of the valley, there were written, in great letters of gold, the following words:

BEAR YE ONE ANOTHER'S BURDENS

Now I saw in my vision that many of the travelers hurried on without stopping to read this inscription, and others, though they had once read it, yet paid little or no attention to it. A third sort thought it very good advice for other people, but very seldom applied it to themselves. They uniformly desired to avail themselves of the assistance which by this injunction others were bound to offer them, but seldom considered that the obligation was mutual, and that reciprocal wants and reciprocal services formed the strong cord in the bond of charity. In short, I saw that too many of these people were of opinion that they had burdens enough of their own, and that there was therefore no occasion to take upon them those of others; so each tried to make his own load as light, and his own journey as pleasant as he could, without so much as once casting a thought on a poor overloaded neighbor. Here, however, I have to make a rather singular remark, by which I shall plainly show the folly of these selfish people. It was so ordered and contrived by the lord of this valley, that if any one stretched out his hand to lighten a neighbor's burden, in fact he never failed to find that he at that moment also lightened his own. Besides the benefit of helping each other, was as mutual as the obligation. If a man helped his neighbor, it commonly happened that some other neighbor came by-and-by and helped him in his turn; for there was no such thing as what we called independence in the whole valley. Not one of all these travelers, however stout and strong, could move on comfortably without assistance, for so the lord of the valley, whose laws were all of them kind and good, had expressly ordained.

I stood still to watch the progress of these poor wayfaring people, who moved slowly on, like so many ticket-porters, with burdens of various kinds on their backs; of which some were heavier and some were lighter, but from a burden of one kind or other, not one traveler was entirely free. There might be some difference in the degree, and some distinction in the nature, but exemption there was none.

THE WIDOW

A sorrowful widow, oppressed with the burden of grief for the loss of an affectionate husband, moved heavily on, and would have been bowed down by her heavy load, had not the surviving children, with great alacrity, stepped forward and supported her. Their kindness, after a while, so much lightened the load which threatened at first to be intolerable, that she even went on her way with cheerfulness, and more than repaid their help, by applying the strength she derived from it to their future assistance.

THE HUSBAND

I next saw a poor old man tottering under a burden so heavy, that I expected him every moment to sink under it. I peeped into his pack, and saw it was made up of many sad articles: there were poverty, oppression, sickness, debt, and, what made by far the heaviest part, undutiful children. I was wondering how it was that he got on even so well as he did, till I spied his wife, a kind, meek, Christian woman, who was doing her utmost to assist him. She quietly got behind, gently laid her shoulder to the burden, and carried a much larger portion of it than appeared to me when I was at a distance. It was not the smallest part of the benefit that she was anxious to conceal it. She not only sustained him by her strength, but cheered him by her counsels. She told him, that "through much tribulation we must enter into rest;" that "he that overcometh shall inherit all things." In short, she so supported his fainting spirit, that he was enabled to "run with patience the race which was set before him."

THE KIND NEIGHBOR

An infirm, blind woman was creeping forward, with a very heavy burden, in which were packed sickness and want, with numberless other of those raw materials out of which human misery is worked up. She was so weak that she could not have got on at all, had it not been for the kind assistance of another woman almost as poor as herself, who, though she had no light burden of her own, cheerfully lent a helping hand to a fellow-traveler who was still more heavily laden. This friend had indeed little or nothing to give, but the very voice of kindness is soothing to the weary. And I remarked in many other cases, that it was not so much the degree of the help afforded, as the manner of helping that lightened the burdens. Some had a coarse, rough, clumsy way of assisting a neighbor, which, though in fact it might be of real use, yet seemed, by galling the traveler, to add to the load it was intended to lighten; while I observed in others that so cheap a kindness as a mild word, or even an affectionate look made a poor burdened wretch move on cheerily. The bare feeling that some human being cared for him, seemed to lighten the load. But to return to this kind neighbor. She had a little old book in her hand, the covers of which were worn out by much use. When she saw the blind woman ready to faint, she would read her a few words out of this book, such as the following: "Blessed are the poor in spirit, for theirs is the kingdom of heaven." "Blessed are they that mourn, for they shall be comforted." "I will never leave thee nor forsake thee." "For our light affliction, which is but for a moment, worketh out for us a far more exceeding and eternal weight of glory." These quickened the pace, and sustained the spirits of the blind traveler; and the kind neighbor, by thus directing the attention of the poor sufferer to the blessings of a better world, helped to enable her to sustain the affliction of this, more effectually than if she had had gold and silver to bestow on her.

THE CLERGYMAN

A pious minister, sinking under the weight of a distressed parish, whose worldly wants he was totally unable to bear, was suddenly relieved by a charitable widow, who came up and took all the sick and hungry on her own shoulders as her part of the load. The burden of the parish, thus divided, became tolerable. The minister being no longer bowed down by the temporal distresses of his people, applied himself cheerfully to his own part of the weight. And it was pleasant to see how those two persons, neither of them very strong, or rich, or healthy, by thus kindly uniting together, were enabled to bear the weight of a whole parish; though singly, either of them must have sunk under the attempt. And I remember one great grief I felt during my whole journey was, that I did not see more of this union and concurring kindness—more of this acting in concert, by which all the burdens might have been so easily divided. It troubled me to observe, that of all the laws of the valley there was not one more frequently broken than the law of kindness.

THE NEGROES

I now spied a swarm of poor black men, women, and children, a multitude which no man could number; these groaned, and toiled, and sweated, and bled under far heavier loads than I have yet seen. But for a while no man helped them; at length a few white travelers were touched with the sorrowful sighing of those millions, and very heartily did they put their hands to the burdens; but their number was not quite equal to the work they had undertaken. I perceived, however, that they never lost sight of these poor heavily-laden wretches; though often repulsed, they returned again to the charge; though discomfited, they renewed the effort, and some even pledged themselves to an annual attempt till the project was accomplished; and as the number of these generous helpers increased every year, I felt a comfortable hope, that before all the blacks got out of the valley, the whites would fairly divide the burden, and the loads would be effectually lightened.

Among the travelers, I had occasion to remark, that those who most kicked and struggled under their burdens, only made them so much the heavier, for their shoulders became extremely galled by these vain and ineffectual struggles. The load, if borne patiently, would in the end have turned even to the advantage of the bearers, for so the lord of the valley had kindly decreed; but as to these grumblers, they had all the smart, and none of the benefit; they had the present suffering without the future reward. But the thing which made all these burdens seem so very heavy was, that in every one without exception, there was a certain inner packet, which most of the travelers took pains to conceal, and kept carefully wrapped up; and while they were forward enough to complain of the other part of their burdens, few said a word about this, though in truth it was the pressing weight of this secret packet which served to render the general burden so intolerable. In spite of all their caution, I contrived to get a peep at it. I found in each that this packet had the same label—the word SIN was written on all as a general title, and in ink so black that they could not wash it out. I observed that most of them took no small pains to hide the writing; but I was surprised to see that they did not try to get rid of the load but the label. If any kind friend who assisted these people in bearing their burdens, did but so much as hint at the secret packet, or advise them to get rid of it, they took fire at once, and commonly denied they had any such article in their portmanteau; and it was those whose secret packet swelled to the most enormous size, who most stoutly denied they had any.

I saw with pleasure, however, that some who had long labored heartily to get rid of this inward packet, at length found it much diminished, and the more this packet shrunk in size, the lighter was the other part of their burden also. I observed, moreover, that though the label always remained in some degree indelible, yet that those who were in earnest to get rid of the load, found that the original traces of the label grew fainter also; it was never quite obliterated in any, though in some cases it seemed nearly effaced.

Then methought, all at once, I heard a voice, as it had been the voice of an angel, crying out and saying, "Ye unhappy pilgrims, why are ye troubled about the burden which ye are doomed to bear through this valley of tears? Know ye not, that as soon as ye shall have escaped out of this valley the whole burden shall drop off, provided ye neglect not to remove that inward weight, that secret load of SIN which principally oppresses you? Study, then, the whole will of the lord of this valley. Learn from him how this heavy part of your burdens may now be lessened, and how at last it may be removed forever. Be comforted. Faith and hope may cheer you even in this valley. The passage, though it seems long to weary travelers, is comparatively short, for beyond there is a land of everlasting rest, where ye shall hunger no more, neither thirst any more; where ye shall be led by living fountains of waters, and all tears shall be wiped away from your eyes."

Now, I had a second vision of what was passing in the Valley of Tears. Methought I saw again the same kind of travelers whom I had seen in the former part, and they were wandering at large through the same vast wilderness. At first setting out on his journey, each traveler had a small lamp so fixed in his bosom that it seemed to make a part of himself; but as this natural light did not prove to be sufficient to direct them in the right way, the king of the country, in pity to their wanderings and blindness, out of his gracious condescension, promised to give these poor wayfaring people an additional supply of light from his own royal treasury. But as he did not choose to lavish his favors where there seemed no disposition to receive them, he would not bestow any of his oil on such as did not think it worth asking for. "Ask and ye shall have," was the universal rule he laid down for them. But though they knew the condition of the obligation, many were prevented from asking through pride and vanity, for they thought they had light enough already, preferring the feeble glimmering of their own lamp to all the offered light from the king's treasury. Yet it was observed of those who had rejected it, as thinking they had enough, that hardly any acted up to what even their own natural light showed them. Others were deterred from asking, because they were told that this light not only pointed out the dangers and difficulties of the road, but by a certain reflecting power, it turned inward on themselves, and revealed to them ugly sights in their own hearts, to which they rather chose to be blind; for those travelers were of that preposterous number who "chose darkness rather than light," and for the old obvious reason—"because their deeds were evil." Now, it was remarkable that these two properties were inseparable, and that the lamp would be of little outward use, except to those who used it as an internal reflector. A threat and a promise also never failed to accompany the offer of this light from the king: a promise that to those who improved what they had, more should be given; and a threat, that from those who did not use it wisely, should be taken away even what they had.

I observed that when the road was very dangerous; when terrors, and difficulties, and death beset the fervent traveler; then, on their faithful importunity, the king voluntarily gave large and bountiful supplies of light, such as in common seasons never could have been expected: always proportioning the quantity to the necessity of the case; "as their day was, such was their light and strength."

Though many chose to depend entirely on their own original lamp, yet it was observed that this light was apt to go out if left to itself. It was easily blown out by those violent gusts which were perpetually howling through the wilderness; and indeed it was the natural tendency of that unwholesome atmosphere to extinguish it, just as you have seen a candle go out when exposed to the vapors and foul air of a damp room. It was a melancholy sight to see multitudes of travelers heedlessly pacing on boasting they had light enough of their own, and despising the offer of more.

But what astonished me most of all was, to see many, and some of them too accounted men of first rate wit, actually busy in blowing out their own light, because while any spark of it remained, it only served to torment them, and point out things which they did not wish to see. And having once blown out their own light, they were not easy till they had blown out that of their neighbors also; so that a good part of this wilderness seemed to exhibit a sort of universal blindman's buff, each endeavoring to catch his neighbor, while his own voluntary blindness exposed him to be caught himself; so that each was actually falling into the snare he was laying for another till at length, as selfishness is the natural consequence of blindness, "catch he that catch can," became the general motto of the wilderness.

Now I saw in my vision, that there were some others who were busy in strewing the most gaudy flowers over the numerous bogs, and precipices, and pitfalls with which the wilderness abounded; and thus making danger and death look so gay, that poor thoughtless creatures seemed to delight in their own destruction. Those pitfalls did not appear deep or dangerous to the eye, because over them were raised gay edifices with alluring names. These were filled with singing men and singing women, and with dancing, and feasting, and gaming, and drinking, and jollity, and madness. But though the scenery was gay, the footing was unsound. The floors were full of holes, through which the unthinking merry-makers were continually sinking. Some tumbled through in the middle of a song; more at the end of a feast; and though there was many a cup of intoxication wreathed round with flowers, yet there was always poison at the bottom. But what most surprised me was that though no day passed over their heads in which some of the most merry-makers did not drop through, yet their loss made little impression on those who were left. Nay, instead of being awakened to more circumspection and self-denial by the continual dropping off of those about them, several of them seemed to borrow from thence an argument of a direct contrary tendency, and the very shortness of time was only urged as a reason to use it more sedulously for the indulgence in sensual delights. "Let us eat and drink, for to-morrow we die." "Let us crown ourselves with rose-buds before they are withered." With these and a thousand other such like inscriptions, the gay garlands of the wilderness were decorated. Some admired poets were set to work to set the most corrupt sentiments to the most harmonious tunes; these were sung without scruple, chiefly indeed by the looser sons of riot, but not seldom also by the more orderly daughters of sobriety, who were not ashamed to sing to the sound of instruments, sentiments so corrupt and immoral, that they would have blushed to speak or read them; but the music seemed to sanctify the corruption, especially such as was connected with love or drinking.

Now I observed that all the travelers who had so much as a spark of life left, seemed every now and then, as they moved onward, to cast an eye, though with very different degrees of attention, toward the Happy Land, which they were told lay at the end of their journey: but as they could not see very far forward, and as they knew there was a dark and shadowy valley which must needs be crossed before they could attain to the Happy Land, they tried to turn their attention from it as much as they could. The truth is, they were not sufficiently apt to consult a map and a road-book which the King had given them, and which pointed out the path to the Happy Land so clearly that the "wayfaring men, though simple, could not err." This map also defined very correctly the boundaries of the Happy Land from the Land of Misery, both of which lay on the other side of the dark and shadowy valley; but so many beacons and lighthouses were erected, so many clear and explicit directions furnished for avoiding the one country and attaining the other, that it was not the King's fault, if even one single traveler got wrong. But I am inclined to think that, in spite of the map and road-book, and the King's word, and his offers of assistance to get them thither, that the travelers in general did not heartily and truly believe, after all, that there was any such country as the Happy Land; or at least the paltry and transient pleasures of the wilderness so besotted them, the thoughts of the dark and shadowy valley so frightened them, that they thought they should be more comfortable by banishing all thought and forecast, and driving the subject quite out of their heads.

Now, I also saw in my dream, that there were two roads through the wilderness, one of which every traveler must needs take. The first was narrow, and difficult, and rough, but it was infallibly safe. It did not admit the traveler to stray either to the right hand or the left, yet it was far from being destitute of real comforts or sober pleasures. The other was a broad and tempting way, abounding with luxurious fruits and gaudy flowers, to tempt the eye and please the appetite. To forget this dark valley, through which every traveler was well assured he must one day pass, seemed the object of general desire. To this grand end, all that human ingenuity could invent was industriously set to work. The travelers read, and they wrote, and they painted, and they sung, and they danced, and they drank as they went along, not so much because they all cared for these things, or had any real joy in them, as because this restless activity served to divert their attention from ever being fixed on the dark and shadowy valley.

The King, who knew the thoughtless tempers of the travelers, and how apt they were to forget their journey's end, had thought of a thousand kind little attentions to warn them of their dangers: and as we sometimes see in our gardens written on a board in great letters, BEWARE OF SPRING GUNS—MAN TRAPS ARE SET HERE; So had this king caused to be written and stuck up before the eyes of the travelers, several little notices and cautions; such as, "Broad is the way that leadeth to destruction."— "Take heed, lest you also perish." "Woe to them that rise up early to drink wine." "The pleasures of sin are but for a season," etc. Such were the notices directed to the broad-way travelers; but they were so busily engaged in plucking the flowers sometimes before they were blown, and in devouring the fruits often before they were ripe, and in loading themselves with yellow clay, under the weight of which millions perished, that they had no time so much as to look at the king's directions. Many went wrong because they preferred a merry journey to a safe one, and because they were terrified by certain notices chiefly intended for the narrow-way travelers; such as, "ye shall weep and lament, but the world shall rejoice;" but had these foolish people allowed themselves time or patience to read to the end, which they seldom would do, they would have seen these comfortable words added, "But your sorrow shall be turned into joy;" also "your joy no man taketh from you;" and, "they that sow in tears shall reap in joy."

Now, I also saw in my dream, that many travelers who had a strong dread of ending at the Land of Misery walked up to the Strait Gate, hoping that though the entrance was narrow, yet if they could once get in, the road would widen; but what was their grief, when on looking more closely they saw written on the inside, "Narrow is the way;" this made them take fright; they compared the inscriptions with which the whole way was lined, such as, "Be ye not conformed to this world; deny yourselves, take up your cross," with all the tempting pleasures of the wilderness. Some indeed recollected the fine descriptions they had read of the Happy Land, the Golden City, and the River of Pleasure, and they sighed; but then those joys were distant, and from the faintness of their light, they soon got to think that what was remote might be uncertain, and while the present good increased in bulk the distant good receded, diminished, disappeared. Their faith failed; they would trust no further than they could see; they drew back and got into the Broad Way, taking a common but sad refuge in the number, the fashion, and the gayety of their companions. When these faint-hearted people, who yet had set out well, turned back, their light was quite put out, and then they became worse than those who had made no attempt to get in. "For it is impossible, that is, it is next to impossible, for those who were once enlightened, and have tasted of the heavenly gift, and the good word of God, and the powers of the world to come, if they fall away to renew them again to repentance."

A few honest, humble travelers not naturally stronger than the rest, but strengthened by their trust in the king's word, came up, by the light of their lamps, and meekly entered in at the Strait Gate; as they advanced further they felt less heavy, and though the way did not in reality grow wider, yet they grew reconciled to the narrowness of it, especially when they saw the walls here and there studded with certain jewels called promises, such as: "He that endureth to the end shall be saved;" and "my grace is sufficient for you." Some, when they were almost ready to faint, were encouraged by seeing that many niches in the Narrow Way were filled with statues and pictures of saints and martyrs, who had borne their testimony at the stake, that the Narrow Way was the safe way; and these travelers, instead of sinking at the sight of the painted wheel and gibbet, the sword and furnace, were animated with these words written under them, "Those that wear white robes, came out of great tribulation," and "be ye followers of those who through faith and patience inherit the promises."

In the mean time there came a great multitude of travelers all from Laodicea; this was the largest party I had yet seen; these were neither hot nor cold, they would not give up future hope, and they could not endure present pain. So they contrived to deceive themselves, by fancying that though they resolved to keep the Happy Land in view, yet there must needs be many different ways which lead to it, no doubt all equally sure, without all being equally rough; so they set on foot certain little contrivances to attain the end without using the means, and softened down the spirit of the king's directions to fit them to their own practice. Sometimes they would split a direction in two, and only use that half which suited them. For instance when they met with the following rule on the way-post: "Trust in the Lord and be doing good," they would take the first half, and make themselves easy with a general sort of trust, that through the mercy of the king all would go well with them, though they themselves did nothing. And on the other hand, many made sure that a few good works of their own would do their business, and carry them safely to the Happy Land, though they did not trust in the Lord, nor place any faith in his word. So they took the second half of the spliced direction. Thus some perished by a lazy faith, and others by a working pride.

A large party of Pharisees now appeared, who had so neglected their lamp that they did not see their way at all, though they fancied themselves to be full of light; they kept up appearances so well as to delude others, and most effectually to delude themselves with a notion that they might be found in the right way at last. In this dreadful delusion they went on to the end, and till they were finally plunged in the dark valley, never discovered the horrors which awaited them on the dismal shore. It was remarkable that while these Pharisees were often boasting how bright their light burned, in order to get the praise of men, the humble travelers, whose steady light showed their good works to others, refused all commendation, and the brighter their light shined before men, so much the more they insisted that they ought to glorify not themselves, but their Father which is in heaven.

I now set myself to observe what was the particular lot, molestation and hinderance which obstructed particular travelers in their endeavors to enter in at the Strait Gate. I remarked a huge portly man who seemed desirous of getting in, but he carried about him such a vast provision of bags full of gold, and had on so many rich garments, which stuffed him out so wide, that though he pushed and squeezed, like one who had really a mind to get in, yet he could not possibly do so. Then I heard a voice crying, "Woe to him who loadeth himself with thick clay." The poor man felt something was wrong, and even went so far as to change some of his more cumbersome vanities into others which seemed less bulky, but still he and his pack were much too wide for the gate. He would not, however, give up the matter so easily, but began to throw away a little of the coarser part of his baggage, but still I remarked that he threw away none of the vanities which lay near his heart. He tried again, but it would not do; still his dimensions were too large. He now looked up and read these words, "How hardly shall those who have riches enter into the kingdom of God." The poor man sighed to find that it was impossible to enjoy his fill of both worlds, and "went away sorrowing." If he ever afterward cast a thought toward the Happy Land, it was only to regret that the road which led to it was too narrow to admit any but the meager children of want, who were not so incumbered by wealth as to be too big for the passage. Had he read on, he would have seen that "with God all things are possible."

Another advanced with much confidence of success, for having little worldly riches or honor, the gate did not seem so strait to him. He got to the threshold triumphantly, and seemed to look back with disdain on all that he was quitting. He soon found, however, that he was so bloated with pride, and stuffed out with self-sufficiency, that he could not get in. Nay, he was in a worse way than the rich man just named; for he had been willing to throw away some of his outward luggage, whereas this man refused to part with a grain of that vanity and self-applause which made him too large for the way. The sense of his own worth so swelled him out that he stuck fast in the gateway, and could neither get in nor out. Finding now that he must cut off all these big thoughts of himself, if he wished to be reduced to such a size as to pass the gate, he gave up all thoughts of it. He scorned that humility and self-denial which might have shrunk him down to the proper dimensions; the more he insisted on his own qualifications for entrance, the more impossible it became to enter, for the bigger he grew. Finding that he must become quite another manner of man before he could hope to get in, he gave up the desire; and I now saw that though when he set his face toward the Happy Land he could not get an inch forward, yet the instant he made a motion to turn back into the world, his speed became rapid enough, and he got back into the Broad Way much sooner than he got out of it.

Many, who for a time were brought down from their usual bulk by some affliction, seemed to get in with ease. They now thought all their difficulties over, for having been surfeited with the world during their late disappointment, they turned their backs upon it willingly enough, and fancied they were tired of it. A fit of sickness, perhaps, which is very apt to reduce, had for a time brought their bodies into subjection, so that they were enabled just to get in at the gateway; but as soon as health and spirit returned, the way grew narrower and narrower to them; and they could not get on, but turned short, and got back into the world. I saw many attempt to enter who were stopped short by a large burden of worldly cares; others by a load of idolatrous attachments; but I observed that nothing proved a more complete bar than that vast bundle of prejudices with which multitudes were loaded. Others were fatally obstructed by loads of bad habits, which they would not lay down, though they knew it prevented their entrance.

Some few, however, of most descriptions, who had kept their light alive by craving constant supplies from the king's treasury, got through at last by a strength which they felt not to be their own. One poor man, who carried the largest bundle of bad habits I had seen, could not get on a step; he never ceased, however, to implore for light enough to see where his misery lay; he threw down one of his bundles, then another, but all to little purpose; still he could not stir. At last striving as if in agony (which is the true way of entering) he threw down the heaviest article in his pack; this was selfishness; the poor fellow felt relieved at once, his light burned brightly, and the rest of his pack was as nothing.

Then I heard a great noise as of carpenters at work. I looked what this might be, and saw many sturdy travelers, who, finding they were too bulky to get through, took it into their heads not to reduce themselves, but to widen the gate; they hacked on this side, and hewed on that; but all their hacking, and hewing, and hammering was to no purpose, they got their labor for their pains. It would have been possible for them to have reduced themselves, had they attempted it, but to widen the narrow way was impossible.

What grieved me most was to observe that many who had got on successfully a good way, now stopped to rest and to admire their own progress. While they were thus valuing themselves on their attainments, their light diminished. While these were boasting how far they had left others behind who had set out much earlier, some slower travelers, whose beginning had not been so promising, but who had walked meekly and circumspectly, now outstripped them. These last walked not as though they had already attained; but this one thing they did, forgetting the things which were behind, they pushed forward to the mark, for the prize of their high calling. These, though naturally weak, yet by laying aside every weight, finished the race that was before them. Those who had kept their "light burning," who were not "wise in their own conceit," who "laid their help on one that is mighty," who had "chosen to suffer affliction rather than to enjoy the pleasures of sin for a season," came at length to the Happy Land. They had indeed the Dark and Shadowy Valley to cross, but even there they found a rod and a staff to comfort them. Their light instead of being put out by the damps of the Valley and of the Shadow of Death, often burned with added brightness. Some indeed suffered the terrors of a short eclipse; but even then their light, like that of a dark lantern, was not put out; it was only turned for a while from him who carried it, and even these often finished their course with joy. But be that as it might, the instant they reached the Happy Land, all tears were wiped from their eyes, and the king himself came forth and welcomed them into his presence, and put a crown upon their heads, with these words, "Well done, good and faithful servant, enter thou into the joy of thy Lord."

PARLEY, THE PORTER:

SHOWING HOW ROBBERS WITHOUT CAN NEVER GET INTO A HOUSE, UNLESS THERE ARE TRAITORS WITHIN

There was once a certain nobleman who had a house or castle situated in the midst of a great wilderness, but inclosed in a garden. Now there was a band of robbers in the wilderness who had a great mind to plunder and destroy the castle, but they had not succeeded in their endeavors, because the master had given strict orders to "watch without ceasing." To quicken their vigilance he used to tell them that their care would soon have an end: that though the nights to watch were dark and stormy, yet they were but few; the period of resistance was short, that of rest would be eternal.

The robbers, however, attacked the castle in various ways. They tried at every avenue, watched to take advantage of every careless moment; looked for an open door or a neglected window. But though they often made the bolts shake and the windows rattle, they could never greatly hurt the house, much less get into it. Do you know the reason? It was because the servants were never off their guard. They heard the noises plain enough, and used to be not a little frightened, for they were aware both of the strength and perseverance of their enemies. But what seemed rather odd to some of these servants, the lord used to tell them, that while they continued to be afraid they would be safe; and it passed into a sort of proverb in that family, "Happy is he that feareth always." Some of the servants, however, thought this a contradiction.

One day, when the master was going from home, he called his servants all together, and spoke to them as follows: "I will not repeat to you the directions I have so often given you; they are all written down in THE BOOK OF LAWS, of which every one of you has a copy. Remember, it is a very short time that you are to remain in this castle; you will soon remove to my more settled habitation, to a more durable house, not made with hands. As that house is never exposed to any attack, so it never stands in need of any repair; for that country is never infested by any sons of violence. Here you are servants; there you will be princes. But mark my words, and you will find the same in THE BOOK OF MY LAWS, whether you will ever attain to that house, will depend on the manner in which you defend yourselves in this. A stout vigilance for a short time will secure your certain happiness forever. But every thing depends on your present exertions. Don't complain and take advantage of my absence, and call me a hard master, and grumble that you are placed in the midst of a howling wilderness without peace or security. Say not, that you are exposed to temptations without any power to resist them. You have some difficulties, it is true, but you have many helps and many comforts to make this house tolerable, even before you get to the other. Yours is not a hard service; and if it were, 'the time is short.' You have arms if you will use them, and doors if you will bar them, and strength if you will use it. I would defy all the attacks of the robbers without, if I could depend on the fidelity of the people within. If the thieves ever get in and destroy the house, it must be by the connivance of one of the family. For it is a standing law of this castle, that mere outward attack can never destroy it, if there be no consenting traitor within. You will stand or fall as you will observe this rule. If you are finally happy, it will be by my grace and favor; if you are ruined, it will be your own fault."

When the nobleman had done speaking, every servant repeated his assurance of attachment and firm allegiance to his master. But among them all, not one was so vehement and loud in his professions as old Parley, the porter. Parley, indeed, it was well known, was always talking, which exposed him to no small danger; for as he was the foremost to promise, so he was the slackest to perform: and, to speak the truth, though he was a civil-spoken fellow, his lord was more afraid of him, with all his professions, than he was of the rest who protested less. He knew that Parley was vain, credulous, and self-sufficient; and he always apprehended more danger from Parley's impertinence, curiosity, and love of novelty, than even from the stronger vices of some of his other servants. The rest indeed, seldom got into any scrape of which Parley was not the cause in some shape or other.

I am sorry to be obliged to confess, that though Parley was allowed every refreshment, and all the needful rest which the nature of his place permitted, yet he thought it very hard to be forced to be so constantly on duty. "Nothing but watching," said Parley. "I have, to be sure, many pleasures, and meat sufficient; and plenty of chat, in virtue of my office, and I pick up a good deal of news of the comers and goers by day, but it is hard that at night I must watch as narrowly as a house-dog, and yet let in no company without orders; only because there is said to be a few straggling robbers here in the wilderness, with whom my master does not care to let us be acquainted. He pretends to make us vigilant through fear of the robbers, but I suspect it is only to make us mope alone. A merry companion and a mug of beer would make the night pass cheerily." Parley, however, kept all these thoughts to himself, or uttered them only when no one heard, for talk he must. He began to listen to the nightly whistling of the robbers under the windows with rather less alarm than formerly, and was sometimes so tired of watching, that he thought it was even better to run the risk of being robbed once, than to live always in the fear of robbers.

There were certain bounds in which the lord allowed his servants to walk and divert themselves at all proper seasons. A pleasant garden surrounded the castle, and a thick hedge separated this garden from the wilderness which was infested by the robbers; in this garden they were permitted to amuse themselves. The master advised them always to keep within these bounds. "While you observe this rule," said he, "you will be safe and well; and you will consult your own safety and happiness, as well as show your love to me, by not venturing over to the extremity of your bounds; he who goes as far as he dares, always shows a wish to go further than he ought, and commonly does so."

It was remarkable, that the nearer these servants kept to the castle, and the further from the hedge, the more ugly the wilderness appeared. And the nearer they approached the forbidden bounds, their own home appeared more dull, and the wilderness more delightful. And this the master knew when he gave his orders; for he never either did or said any thing without a good reason. And when his servants sometimes desired an explanation of the reason, he used to tell them they would understand it when they came to the other house; for it was one of the pleasures of that house, that it would explain all the mysteries of this, and any little obscurities in the master's conduct would be then made quite plain.

Parley was the first who promised to keep clear of the hedge, and yet was often seen looking as near as he durst. One day he ventured close up to the hedge, put two or three stones one on another, and tried to peep over. He saw one of the robbers strolling as near as he could be on the forbidden side. This man's name was Mr. Flatterwell, a smooth, civil man, "whose words were softer than butter, having war in his heart." He made several low bows to Parley.

Now, Parley knew so little of the world, that he actually concluded all robbers must have an ugly look which should frighten you at once, and coarse brutal manners which would at first sight show they were enemies. He thought, like a poor ignorant fellow as he was, that this mild, specious person could never be one of the band. Flatterwell accosted Parley with the utmost civility, which put him quite off his guard; for Parley had no notion that he could be an enemy who was so soft and civil. For an open foe he would have been prepared. Parley, however, after a little discourse drew this conclusion, that either Mr. Flatterwell could not be one of the gang, or that if he was, the robbers themselves could not be such monsters as his master had described, and therefore it was a folly to be afraid of them.

Flatterwell began, like a true adept in his art, by lulling all Parley's suspicions asleep; and instead of openly abusing his master, which would have opened Parley's eyes at once, he pretended rather to commend him in a general way, as a person who meant well himself, but was too apt to suspect others. To this Parley assented. The other then ventured to hint by degrees, that though the nobleman might be a good master in the main, yet he must say he was a little strict, and a little stingy, and not a little censorious. That he was blamed by the gentlemen of the wilderness for shutting his house against good company, and his servants were laughed at by people of spirit for submitting to the gloomy life of the castle, and the insipid pleasures of the garden, instead of ranging in the wilderness at large.

"It is true enough," said Parley, who was generally of the opinion of the person he was talking with, "my master is rather harsh and close. But to own the truth, all the barring, and locking, and bolting, is to keep out a set of gentlemen, who he assures us are robbers, and who are waiting for an opportunity to destroy us. I hope no offense, sir, but by your livery I suspect you, sir, are one of the gang he is so much afraid of."

Flatterwell. Afraid of me? Impossible, dear Mr. Parley. You see, I do not look like an enemy. I am unarmed; what harm can a plain man like me do?

Parley. Why, that is true enough. Yet my master says, if we were to let you into the house, we should be ruined soul and body.

Flatterwell. I am sorry, Mr. Parley, to hear so sensible a man as you are, so deceived. This is mere prejudice. He knows we are cheerful entertaining people, foes to gloom and superstition, and therefore he is so morose he will not let you get acquainted with us.

Parley. Well; he says you are a band of thieves, gamblers, murderers, drunkards, and atheists.

Flatterwell. Don't believe him; the worst we should do, perhaps is, we might drink a friendly glass with you to your master's health, or play an innocent game of cards just to keep you awake, or sing a cheerful song with the maids; now is there any harm in all this?

Parley. Not the least in the world. And I begin to think there is not a word of truth in all my master says.

Flatterwell. The more you know us, the more you will like us. But I wish there was not this ugly hedge between us. I have a great deal to say, and I am afraid of being overheard.

Parley was now just going to give a spring over the hedge, but checked himself, saying, "I dare not come on your side, there are people about, and every thing is carried to the master." Flatterwell saw by this that his new friend was kept on his own side of the hedge by fear rather than by principle, and from that moment he made sure of him. "Dear Mr. Parley," said he, "if you will allow me the honor of a little conversation with you, I will call under the window of your lodge this evening. I have something to tell you greatly to your advantage. I admire you exceedingly. I long for your friendship; our whole brotherhood is ambitious of being known to so amiable a person." "O dear," said Parley, "I shall be afraid of talking to you at night. It is so against my master's orders. But did you say you had something to tell me to my advantage?"

Flatterwell. Yes, I can point out to you how you may be a richer, a merrier, and a happier man. If you will admit me to-night under the window, I will convince you that it is prejudice and not wisdom, which makes your master bar his door against us; I will convince you that the mischief of a robber, as your master scurrilously calls us, is only in the name; that we are your true friends, and only mean to promote your happiness.

"Don't say we," said Parley, "pray come alone; I would not see the rest of the gang for the world; but I think there can be no great harm in talking to you through the bars, if you come alone; but I am determined not to let you in. Yet I can't say but I wish to know what you can tell me so much to my advantage; indeed, if it is for my good I ought to know it."

Flatterwell. (going out, turns back.) Dear Mr. Parley, there is one thing I had forgotten. I can not get over the hedge at night without assistance. You know there is a secret in the nature of that hedge; you in the house may get over it, into the wilderness of your own accord, but we can not get to your side by our own strength. You must look about to see where the hedge is thinnest, and then set to work to clear away here and there a little bough for me, it won't be missed; and if there is but the smallest hole made on your side, those on ours can get through, otherwise we do but labor in vain. To this Parley made some objection, through the fear of being seen. Flatterwell replied, that the smallest hole from within would be sufficient, for he could then work his own way. "Well," said Parley, "I will consider of it. To be sure I shall even then be equally safe in the castle, as I shall have all the bolts, bars, and locks between us, so it will make but little difference."

"Certainly not," said Flatterwell, who knew it would make all the difference in the world. So they parted with mutual protestations of regard. Parley went home charmed with his new friend. His eyes were now clearly opened as to his master's prejudices against the robbers, and he was convinced there was more in the name than in the thing. "But," said he, "though Mr. Flatterwell is certainly an agreeable companion, he may not be so safe an inmate. There can, however, be no harm in talking at a distance, and I certainly won't let him in."

Parley, in the course of the day, did not forget his promise to thin the hedge of separation a little. At first he only tore off a handful of leaves, then a little sprig, then he broke away a bough or two. It was observable, the larger the branch became, the worse he began to think of his master, and the better of himself. Every peep he took through the broken hedge increased his desire to get out into the wilderness, and made the thoughts of the castle more irksome to him. He was continually repeating to himself, "I wonder what Mr. Flatterwell can have to say so much to my advantage? I see he does not wish to hurt my master, he only wishes to serve me." As the hour of meeting, however, drew near, the master's orders now and then came across Parley's thoughts. So to divert them, he took up THE BOOK. He happened to open it at these words: "My son, if sinners entice thee, consent thou not." For a moment his heart failed him. "If this admonition should be sent on purpose?" said he; but no, 'tis a bugbear. My master told me that if I went to the bounds I should get over the hedge. Now I went to the utmost limits, and did not get over. Here conscience put in: "Yes, but it was because you were watched." "I am sure," continued Parley, "one may always stop where one will, and this is only a trick of my master's to spoil sport. So I will even hear what Mr. Flatterwell has to say so much to my advantage. I am not obliged to follow his counsels, but there can be no harm in hearing them."

Flatterwell prevailed on the rest of the robbers to make no public attack on the castle that night. "My brethren," said he, "you now and then fail in your schemes, because you are for violent beginnings, while my smooth, insinuating measures hardly ever miss. You come blustering and roaring, and frighten people, and set them on their guard. You inspire them with terror of you, while my whole scheme is to make them think well of themselves, and ill of their master. If I once get them to entertain hard thoughts of him, and high thoughts of themselves, my business is done, and they fall plump into my snares. So let this delicate affair alone to me: Parley is a softly fellow, he must not be frightened, but cajoled. He is the very sort of a man to succeed with; and worth a hundred of your sturdy, sensible fellows. With them we want strong arguments and strong temptations; but with such fellows as Parley, in whom vanity and sensuality are the leading qualities (as, let me tell you, is the case with far the greater part) flattery and a promise of ease and pleasure, will do more than your whole battle array. If you will let me manage, I will get you all into the castle before midnight."

At night the castle was barricaded as usual, and no one had observed the hole which Parley had made in the hedge. This oversight arose that night from the servants' neglecting one of the master's standing orders—to make a nightly examination of the state of things. The neglect did not proceed so much from willful disobedience, as from having passed the evening in sloth and diversion, which often amounts to nearly the same in its consequences.

As all was very cheerful within, so all was very quiet without. And before they went to bed, some of the servants observed to the rest, that as they heard no robbers that night, they thought they might now begin to remit something of their diligence in bolting and barring: that all this fastening and locking was very troublesome, and they hoped the danger was now pretty well over. It was rather remarkable, that they never made these sort of observations, but after an evening of some excess, and when they had neglected their private business with their master. All, however, except Parley, went quietly to bed, and seemed to feel uncommon security.

Parley crept down to his lodge. He had half a mind to go to bed too. Yet he was not willing to disappoint Mr. Flatterwell. So civil a gentleman! To be sure he might have had bad designs. Yet what right had he to suspect any body who made such professions, and who was so very civil? "Besides, it is something for my advantage," added Parley. "I will not open the door, that is certain; but as he is to come alone, he can do me no harm through the bars of the windows: and he will think I am a coward if I don't keep my word. No, I will let him see that I am not afraid of my own strength; I will show him I can go what length I please, and stop short when I please." Had Flatterwell heard this boastful speech, he would have been quite sure of his man.

About eleven, Parley heard the signal agreed upon. It was so gentle as to cause little alarm. So much the worse. Flatterwell never frightened any one, and therefore seldom failed of any one. Parley stole softly down, planted himself at his little window, opened the casement, and spied his new friend. It was pale starlight. Parley was a little frightened; for he thought he perceived one or two persons behind Flatterwell; but the other assured him it was only his own shadow, which his fears had magnified into a company. "Though I assure you," said he, "I have not a friend but what is as harmless as myself."

They now entered into serious discourse, in which Flatterwell showed himself a deep politician. He skillfully mixed up in his conversation a proper proportion of praise on the pleasures of the wilderness, of compliments to Parley, of ridicule on his master, and of abusive sneers on the BOOK in which the master's laws were written. Against this last he had always a particular spite, for he considered it as the grand instrument by which the lord maintained his servants in their allegiance; and when they could once be brought to sneer at the BOOK there was an end of submission to the lord. Parley had not penetration enough to see his drift. "As to the BOOK, Mr. Flatterwell," said he, "I do not know whether it be true or false. I rather neglect than disbelieve it. I am forced, indeed, to hear it read once a week, but I never look into it myself, if I can help it." "Excellent," said Flatterwell to himself, "that is just the same thing. This is safe ground for me. For whether a man does not believe in the BOOK, or does not attend to it, it comes pretty much to the same, and I generally get him at last."

"Why can not we be a little nearer, Mr. Parley," said Flatterwell; "I am afraid of being overheard by some of your master's spies. The window from which you speak is so high; I wish you would come down to the door." "Well," said Parley, "I see no great harm in that. There is a little wicket in the door through which we may converse with more ease and equal safety. The same fastenings will be still between us." So down he went, but not without a degree of fear and trembling. The little wicket being now opened, and Flatterwell standing close on the outside of the door, they conversed with great ease. "Mr. Parley," said Flatterwell, "I should not have pressed you so much to admit me into the castle, but out of pure disinterested regard to your own happiness. I shall get nothing by it, but I can not bear to think that a person so wise and amiable should be shut up in this gloomy dungeon, under a hard master, and a slave to the unreasonable tyranny of his BOOK OF LAWS. If you admit me, you need have no more waking, no more watching." Here Parley involuntarily slipped back the bolt of the door. "To convince you of my true love," continued Flatterwell, "I have brought a bottle of the most delicious wine that grows in the wilderness. You shall taste it, but you must put a glass through the wicket to receive it, for it is a singular property of this wine, that we of the wilderness can not succeed in conveying it to you of the castle, without you hold out a vessel to receive it." "O here is a glass," said Parley, holding out a large goblet, which he always kept ready to be filled by any chance-comer. The other immediately poured into the capacious goblet a large draught of that delicious intoxicating liquor, with which the family of the Flatterwells have for near six thousand years gained the hearts, and destroyed the souls of all the inhabitants of the castle, whenever they have been able to prevail on them to hold out a hand to receive it. This the wise, master of the castle well knew would be the case, for he knew what was in men; he knew their propensity to receive the delicious poison of the Flatterwells; and it was for this reason that he gave them THE BOOK of his laws, and planted the hedge and invented the bolts, and doubled the lock.

As soon as poor Parley had swallowed the fatal draught, it acted like enchantment. He at once lost all power of resistance. He had no sense of fear left. He despised his own safety, forgot his master, lost all sight of the home in the other country, and reached out for another draught as eagerly as Flatterwell held out the bottle to administer it. "What a fool have I been," said Parley, "to deny myself so long!" "Will you now let me in?" said Flatterwell. "Ay, that I will," said the deluded Parley. Though the train was now increased to near a hundred robbers, yet so intoxicated was Parley, that he did not see one of them except his new friend. Parley eagerly pulled down the bars, drew back the bolts and forced open the locks; thinking he could never let in his friend soon enough. He had, however, just presence of mind to say, "My dear friend I hope you are alone." Flatterwell swore he was—Parley opened the door—in rushed, not Flatterwell only, but the whole banditti, who always lurked behind in his train. The moment they had got sure possession, Flatterwell changed his soft tone, and cried in a voice of thunder, "Down with the castle; kill, burn, and destroy."

Rapine, murder, and conflagration, by turns took place. Parley was the very first whom they attacked. He was overpowered with wounds. As he fell he cried out, "O my master, I die a victim to my unbelief in thee, and to my own vanity and imprudence. O that the guardians of all other castles would hear me with my dying breath repeat my master's admonition, that all attacks from without will not destroy unless there is some confederate within. O that the keepers of all other castles would learn from my ruin, that he who parleys with temptation is already undone. That he who allows himself to go to the very bounds will soon jump over the hedge; that he who talks out of the window with the enemy, will soon open the door to him: that he who holds out his hand for the cup of sinful flattery, loses all power of resisting; that when he opens the door to one sin, all the rest fly in upon him, and the man perishes as I now do."

THE GRAND ASSIZES, ETC.;

OR, GENERAL JAIL DELIVERY

There was in a certain country a great king, who was also a judge. He was very merciful, but he was also very just; for he used to say, that justice was the foundation of all goodness, and that indiscriminate and misapplied mercy was in fact injustice. His subjects were apt enough, in a general way, to extol his merciful temper, and especially those subjects who were always committing crimes which made them particularly liable to be punished by his justice. This last quality they constantly kept out of sight, till they had cheated themselves into a notion that he was too good to punish at all.

Now it had happened a long time before, that this whole people had broken their allegiance, and had forfeited the king's favor, and had also fallen from a very prosperous state in which he had originally placed them, having one and all become bankrupts. But when they were over head and ears in debt, and had nothing to pay, the king's son most generously took the whole burden of their debts on himself; and, in short, it was proposed that all their affairs should be settled, and their very crimes forgiven (for they were criminals as well as debtors), provided only they would show themselves sincerely sorry for what they had done themselves, and be thankful for what had been done for them. I should, however, remark, that a book was also given them, in which a true and faithful account of their own rebellion was written; and of the manner of obtaining the king's pardon, together with a variety of directions for their conduct in time to come; and in this book it was particularly mentioned, that after having lived a certain number of years in a remote part of the same king's country, yet still under his eye and jurisdiction, there should be a grand assizes, when every one was to be publicly tried for his past behavior; and after this trial was over, certain heavy punishments were to be inflicted on those who should have still persisted in their rebellion, and certain high premiums were to be bestowed as a gracious reward upon the penitent and obedient.

It may be proper here to notice, that this king's court differed in some respect from our courts of justice, being indeed a sort of court of appeal, to which questions were carried after they had been imperfectly decided in the common courts! And although with us all criminals are tried (and a most excellent mode of trial it is) by a jury of their peers, yet in this king's country the mode was very different; for since every one of the people had been in a certain sense criminals, the king did not think it fair to make them judges also. It would, indeed, have been impossible to follow in all respects the customs which prevail with us, for the crimes with which men are charged in our courts are mere overt acts, as the lawyers call them, that is, acts which regard the outward behavior; such as the acts of striking, maiming, stealing, and so forth. But in this king's court it was not merely outward sins, but sins of the heart also which were to be punished. Many a crime, therefore, which was never heard of in the court of King's Bench, or at the Old Bailey, and which indeed could not be cognizable by these courts, was here to be brought to light, and was reserved for this great day. Among these were pride, and oppression, and envy, and malice, and revenge, and covetousness, and secret vanity of mind, and evil thoughts of all sorts, and all sinful wishes and desires. When covetousness, indeed, put men on committing robbery, or when malice drove them to acts of murder, then the common courts immediately judged the criminal, without waiting for these great assizes; nevertheless, since even a thief and murderer would now and then escape in the common courts, for want of evidence, or through some fault or other of the judge or jury, the escape was of little moment to the poor criminal, for he was sure to be tried again by this great king; and even though the man should have been punished in some sense before, yet he had now a further and more lasting punishment to fear, unless, indeed, he was one of those who had obtained (by the means I before spoke of) this great king's pardon. The sins of the heart, however, were by far the most numerous sort of sins, which were to come before this great tribunal; and these were to be judged by this great king in person, and by none but himself; because he alone possessed a certain power of getting at all secrets.

I once heard of a certain king of Sicily, who built a whispering gallery in the form of an ear, through which he could hear every word his rebellious subjects uttered, though spoken ever so low. But this secret of the king of Sicily was nothing to what this great king possessed; for he had the power of knowing every thought which was conceived in the mind, though it never broke out into words, or proceeded to actions.

Now you may be ready to think, perhaps, that these people were worse off than any others, because they were to be examined so closely, and judged so strictly. Far from it; the king was too just to expect bricks without giving them straw; he gave them, therefore, every help that they needed. He gave them a book of directions, as I before observed; and because they were naturally short-sighted, he supplied them with a glass for reading it, and thus the most dim-sighted might see, if they did not willfully shut their eyes: but though the king invited them to open their eyes, he did not compel them; and many remain stone blind all their lives with the book in their hand, because they would not use the glass, nor take the proper means for reading and understanding all that was written for them. The humble and sincere learned in time to see even that part of the book which was least plainly written; and it was observed that the ability to understand it depended more on the heart than the head; an evil disposition blinded the sight, while humility operated like an eye-salve.

Now it happened that those who had been so lucky as to escape the punishment of the lower courts, took it into their heads that they were all very good sort of people, and of course very safe from any danger at this great assize. This grand intended trial, indeed, had been talked of so much, and put off so long (for it had seemed long at least to these short-sighted people) that many persuaded themselves it would never take place at all; and far the greater part were living away therefore, without ever thinking about it; they went on just as if nothing at all had been done for their benefit; and as if they had no king to please, no king's son to be thankful to, no book to guide themselves by, and as if the assizes were never to come about.

But with this king a thousand years were as a day, for he was not slack concerning his promises, as some men count slackness. So at length the solemn period approached. Still, however, the people did not prepare for the solemnity, or rather, they prepared for it much as some of the people of our provincial towns are apt to prepare for the annual assize times; I mean by balls and feastings, and they saw their own trial come on with as little concern as is felt by the people in our streets when they see the judge's procession enter the town; they indeed comfort themselves that it is only those in the prisons who are guilty.

But when at last the day came, and every man found that he was to be judged for himself; and that somehow or other, all his secrets were brought out, and that there was now no escape, not even a short reprieve, things began to take a more serious turn. Some of the worst of the criminals were got together debating in an outer court of the grand hall; and there they passed their time, not in compunction and tears, not in comparing their lives with what was required in that book which had been given them, but they derived a fallacious hope by comparing themselves with such as had been still more notorious offenders.

One who had grown wealthy by rapine and oppression, but had contrived to keep within the letter of the law, insulted a poor fellow as a thief, because he had stolen a loaf of bread. "You are far wickeder than I was," said a citizen to his apprentice, "for you drank and swore at the ale-house every Sunday night." "Yes," said the poor fellow, "but it was your fault that I did so, for you took no care of my soul, but spent all your Sabbaths in jaunting abroad or in rioting at home; I might have learned, but there was no one to teach me; I might have followed a good example, but I saw only bad ones. I sinned against less light than you did." A drunken journeyman who had spent all his wages on gin, rejoiced that he had not spent a great estate in bribery at elections, as the lord of his manor had done, while a perjured elector boasted that he was no drunkard like the journeyman; and the member himself took comfort that he had never received the bribes which he had not been ashamed to offer.

I have not room to describe the awful pomp of the court, nor the terrible sounding of the trumpet which attended the judge's entrance, nor the sitting of the judge, nor the opening of the books, nor the crowding of the millions, who stood before him. I shall pass over the multitudes who were tried and condemned to dungeons and chains, and eternal fire, and to perpetual banishment from the presence of the king, which always seemed to be the saddest part of the sentence. I shall only notice further, a few who brought some plea of merit, and claimed a right to be rewarded by the king, and even deceived themselves so far as to think that his own book of laws would be their justification.

A thoughtless spendthrift advanced without any contrition, and said, "that he had lived handsomely, and had hated the covetous whom God abhorreth; that he trusted in the passage of the book which said, that covetousness was idolatry; and that he therefore hoped for a favorable sentence." Now it proved that this man had not only avoided covetousness, but that he had even left his wife and children in want through his excessive prodigality. The judge therefore immediately pointed to that place in the book where it is written, he that provideth not for his household is worse than an infidel. He that liveth in pleasure is dead while he liveth; "thou," said he, "in thy lifetime, receivedst thy good things, and now thou must be tormented." Then a miser, whom hunger and hoarding had worn to skin and bone, crept forward, and praised the sentence passed on the extravagant youth, "and surely," said he, "since he is condemned, I am a man that may make some plea to favor—I was never idle or drunk, I kept my body in subjection, I have been so self-denying that I am certainly a saint: I have loved neither father nor mother, nor wife nor children, to excess, in all this I have obeyed the book of the law." Then the judge said, "But where are thy works of mercy and thy labors of love? see that family which perished in thy sight last hard winter while thy barns were overflowing; that poor family were my representatives; yet they were hungry, and thou gavest them no meat. Go to, now, thou rich man, weep and howl for the miseries that are come upon you. Your gold and silver is cankered, and the rust of them shall be a witness against you, and shall eat your flesh as it were fire."

Then came up one with a most self-sufficient air. He walked up boldly, having in one hand the plan of a hospital which he had built, and in the other the drawing of the statue which was erecting for him in the country that he had just left, and on his forehead appeared, in gold letters, the list of all the public charities to which he had subscribed. He seemed to take great pleasure in the condemnation of the miser, and said, "Lord when saw I thee hungry and fed thee not, or in prison and visited thee not? I have visited the fatherless and widow in their affliction." Here the judge cut him short, by saying, "True, thou didst visit the fatherless, but didst thou fulfill equally that other part of my command, 'to keep thyself unspotted from the world.' No, thou wast conformed to the world in many of its sinful customs, thou didst follow a multitude to do evil; thou didst love the world and the things of the world; and the motive to all thy charities was not a regard to me but to thy own credit with thy fellow-men. Thou hast done every thing for the sake of reputation, and now thou art vainly trusting in thy deceitful works, instead of putting all thy trust in my son, who has offered himself to be a surety for thee. Where has been that humility and gratitude to him which was required of thee? No, thou wouldest be thine own surety: thou hast trusted in thyself: thou hast made thy boast of thine own goodness; thou hast sought after and thou hast enjoyed the praise of men, and verily I say unto thee, 'thou hast had thy reward.'"

A poor, diseased, blind cripple, who came from the very hospital which this great man had built, then fell prostrate on his face, crying out, "Lord be merciful to me a sinner!" on which the judge, to the surprise of all, said, "Well done, good and faithful servant." The poor man replied, "Lord, I have done nothing!" "But thou hast 'suffered well:'" said the judge; "thou hast been an example of patience and meekness, and though thou hadst but few talents, yet thou hast well improved those few; thou hadst time, this thou didst spend in the humble duties of thy station, and also in earnest prayer; thou didst pray even for that proud founder of the hospital, who never prayed for himself; thou wast indeed blind and lame, but it is no where said, My son give me thy feet, or thine eyes, but Give me thy heart; and even the few faculties I did grant thee, were employed to my glory; with thine ears thou didst listen to my word, with thy tongue thou didst show forth my praise: 'enter thou into the joy of thy Lord.'"

There were several who came forward, and boasted of some single and particular virtue, in which they had been supposed to excel. One talked of his generosity, another of his courage, and a third of his fortitude; but it proved on a close examination, that some of those supposed virtues were merely the effect of a particular constitution of body; the others proceeded from a false motive, and that not a few of them were actual vices, since they were carried to excess; and under the pretense of fulfilling one duty, some other duty was lost sight of; in short, these partial virtues were none of them practiced in obedience to the will of the King, but merely to please the person's own humor, or to gain praise, and they would not, therefore, stand this day's trial, for "he that had kept the whole law, and yet had willfully and habitually offended in any one point, was declared guilty of breaking the whole."

At this moment a sort of thick scales fell from the eyes of the multitude. They could now no longer take comfort, as they had done for so many years, by measuring their neighbors' conduct against their own. Each at once saw himself in his true light, and found, alas! when it was too late, that he should have made the book which had been given him his rule of practice before, since it now proved to be the rule by which he was to be judged. Nay, every one now thought himself even worse than his neighbor, because, while he only saw and heard of the guilt of others, he felt his own in all its aggravated horror.

To complete their confusion they were compelled to acknowledge the justice of the judge who condemned them: and also to approve the favorable sentence by which thousands of other criminals had not only their lives saved, but were made happy and glorious beyond all imagination; not for any great merits which they had to produce, but in consequence of their sincere repentance, and their humble acceptance of the pardon offered to them by the King's son. One thing was remarkable, that whilst most of those who were condemned, never expected condemnation, but even claimed a reward for their supposed innocence or goodness, all who were really rewarded and forgiven were sensible that they owed their pardon to a mere act of grace, and they cried out with one voice, "Not unto us, not unto us, but unto thy name be the praise!"

THE SERVANT MAN TURNED SOLDIER; OR, THE FAIR-WEATHER CHRISTIAN

William was a lively young servant, who lived in a great, but very irregular family. His place was on the whole agreeable to him, and suited to his gay and thoughtless temper. He found a plentiful table and a good cellar. There was, indeed, a great deal of work to be done, though it was performed with much disorder and confusion. The family in the main were not unkind to him, though they often contradicted and crossed him, especially when things went ill with themselves. This, William never much liked, for he was always fond of having his own way. There was a merry, or rather a noisy and riotous servants' hall; for disorder and quarrels are indeed the usual effects of plenty and unrestrained indulgence. The men were smart, but idle; the maids were showy but licentious, and all did pretty much as they liked for a time, but the time was commonly short. The wages were reckoned high, but they were seldom paid, and it was even said by sober people, that the family was insolvent, and never fulfilled any of their flattering engagements, or their most positive promises; but still, notwithstanding their real poverty, things went on with just the same thoughtlessness and splendor, and neither master nor servants looked beyond the jollity of the present hour.

In this unruly family there was little church-going, and still less praying at home. They pretended, indeed, in a general way, to believe in the Bible, but it was only an outward profession; few of them read it at all, and even of those who did read still fewer were governed by it. There was indeed a Bible lying on the table in the great hall, which was kept for the purpose of administering an oath, but was seldom used on any other occasion, and some of the heads of the family were of opinion that this was its only real use, as it might serve to keep the lower parts of it in order.

William, who was fond of novelty and pleasure, was apt to be negligent of the duties of the house. He used to stay out on his errands, and one of his favorite amusements was going to the parade to see the soldiers exercise. He saw with envy how smartly they were dressed, listened with rapture to the music, and fancied that a soldier had nothing to do but to walk to and fro in a certain regular order, to go through a little easy exercise, in short, to live without fighting, fatigue, or danger.

O, said he, whenever he was affronted at home, what a fine thing it must be to be a soldier! to be so well dressed, to have nothing to do but to move to the pleasant sound of fife and drum, and to have so many people come to look at one, and admire one. O it must be a fine thing to be a soldier!

Yet when the vexation of the moment was over, he found so much ease and diversion in the great family, it was so suited to his low taste and sensual appetites, that he thought no more of the matter. He forgot the glories of a soldier, and eagerly returned to all the mean gratifications of the kitchen. His evil habits were but little attended to by those with whom he lived; his faults, among which were lying and swearing, were not often corrected by the family, who had little objections to those sins, which only offended God and did not much affect their own interest or property. And except that William was obliged to work rather more than he liked, he found little, while he was young and healthy, that was very disagreeable in this service. So he went on, still thinking, however, when things went a little cross, what a fine thing it was to be a soldier! At last one day as he was waiting at dinner, he had the misfortune to let fall a china dish, and broke it all to pieces. It was a curious dish, much valued by the family, as they pretended; this family were indeed apt to set a false fantastic value on things, and not to estimate them by their real worth. The heads of the family, who had generally been rather patient and good-humored with William, as I said before, for those vices, which though offensive to God did not touch their own pocket, now flew out into a violent passion with him, called him a thousand hard names, and even threatened to horsewhip him for his shameful negligence.

William in a great fright, for he was a sad coward at bottom, ran directly out of the house to avoid the threatened punishment; and happening just at that very time to pass by the parade where the soldiers chanced to be then exercising, his resolution was taken in a moment. He instantly determined to be no more a slave, as he called it; he would return no more to be subject to the humors of a tyrannical family: no, he was resolved to be free; or at least, if he must serve, he would serve no master but the king.

William, who had now and then happened to hear from the accidental talk of the soldiers that those who served the great family he had lived with, were slaves to their tyranny and vices, had also heard in the same casual manner, that the service of the king was perfect freedom. Now he had taken it into his head to hope that this might be a freedom to do evil, or at least to do nothing, so he thought it was the only place in the world to suit him.

A fine likely young man as William was, had no great difficulty to get enlisted. The few forms were soon settled, he received the bounty money as eagerly as it was offered, took the oaths of allegiance, was joined to the regiment and heartily welcomed by his new comrades. He was the happiest fellow alive. All was smooth and calm. The day happened to be very fine, and therefore William always reckoned upon a fine day. The scene was gay and lively, the music cheerful, he found the exercise very easy, and he thought there was little more expected from him.

He soon began to flourish away in his talk; and when he met with any of his old servants, he fell a prating about marches and counter-marches, and blockades, and battles, and sieges, and blood, and death, and triumphs, and victories, all at random, for these were words and phrases he had picked up without at all understanding what he said. He had no knowledge, and therefore he had no modesty; he had no experience, and therefore he had no fears.

All seemed to go on swimmingly, for he had as yet no trial. He began to think with triumph what a mean life he had escaped from in the old quarrelsome family, and what a happy, honorable life he should have in the army. O there was no life like the life of a soldier!

In a short time, however, war broke out; his regiment was one of the first which was called out to actual and hard service. As William was the most raw of all the recruits, he was the first to murmur at the difficulties and hardships, the cold, the hunger, the fatigue and danger of being a soldier. O what watchings, and perils, and trials, and hardships, and difficulties, he now thought attended a military life! Surely, said he, I could never have suspected all this misery when I used to see the men on the parade in our town.

He now found, when it was too late, that all the field-days he used to attend, all the evolutions and exercises which he had observed the soldiers to go through in the calm times of peace and safety, were only meant to fit, train and qualify them for the actual service which they were now sent out to perform by the command of the king.

The truth is, William often complained when there was no real hardship to complain of; for the common troubles of life fell out pretty much alike to the great family which William had left, and to the soldiers in the king's army. But the spirit of obedience, discipline, and self-denial of the latter seemed hardships to one of William's loose turn of mind. When he began to murmur, some good old soldier clapped him on the back, saying, Cheer up lad, it is a kingdom you are to strive for, if we faint not, henceforth there is laid up for us a great reward; we have the king's word for it, man. William observed, that to those who truly believed this, their labors were as nothing, but he himself did not at the bottom believe it; and it was observed, of all the soldiers who failed, the true cause was that they did not really believe the king's promise. He was surprised to see that those soldiers, who used to bluster and boast, and deride the assaults of the enemy, now began to fall away; while such as had faithfully obeyed the king's orders, and believed in his word, were sustained in the hour of trial. Those who had trusted in their own strength all fainted on the slightest attack, while those who had put on the armor of the king's providing, the sword, and the shield, and the helmet, and the breast-plate, and whose feet were shod according to order, now endured hardship as good soldiers, and were enabled to fight the good fight.

An engagement was expected immediately. The men were ordered to prepare for battle. While the rest of the corps were so preparing, William's whole thoughts were bent on contriving how he might desert. But alas! he was watched on all sides, he could not possibly devise any means to escape. The danger increased every moment, the battle came on. William, who had been so sure and confident before he entered, flinched in the moment of trial, while his more quiet and less boastful comrades prepared boldly to do their duty. William looked about on all sides, and saw that there was no eye upon him, for he did not know that the king's eye was everywhere at once. He at last thought he spied a chance of escaping, not from the enemy, but from his own army. While he was endeavoring to escape, a ball from the opposite camp took off his leg. As he fell, the first words which broke from him were, While I was in my duty I was preserved; in the very act of deserting I am wounded. He lay expecting every moment to be trampled to death, but as the confusion was a little over, he was taken off the field by some of his own party, laid in a place of safety, and left to himself after his wound was dressed.

The skirmish, for it proved nothing more, was soon over. The greater part of the regiment escaped in safety. William in the mean time suffered cruelly both in mind and body. To the pains of a wounded soldier, he added the disgrace of a coward, and the infamy of a deserter. O, cried he, why was I such a fool as to leave the great family I lived in, where there was meat and drink enough and to spare, only on account of a little quarrel? I might have made up that with them as we had done our former quarrels. Why did I leave a life of ease and pleasure, where I had only a little rub now and then, for a life of daily discipline and constant danger? Why did I turn soldier? O what a miserable animal is a soldier!

As he was sitting in this weak and disabled condition, uttering the above complaints, he observed a venerable old officer, with thin gray locks on his head, and on his face, deep wrinkles engraved by time, and many an honest scar inflicted by war. William had heard this old officer highly commended for his extraordinary courage and conduct in battle, and in peace he used to see him cool and collected, devoutly employed in reading and praying in the interval of more active duties. He could not help comparing this officer with himself. I, said he, flinched and drew back, and would even have deserted in the moment of peril, and now in return, I have no consolation in the hour of repose and safety. I would not fight then, I can not pray now. O why would I ever think of being a soldier? He then began afresh to weep and lament, and he groaned so loud that he drew the notice of the officer, who came up to him, kindly sat down by him, took him by the hand, and inquired with as much affection as if he had been his brother, what was the matter with him, and what particular distress, more than the common fortune of war it was which drew from him such bitter groans? "I know something of surgery," added he, "let me examine your wound, and assist you with such little comfort as I can."

William at once saw the difference between the soldiers in the king's army, and the people in the great family; the latter commonly withdrew their kindness in sickness and trouble, when most wanted, which was just the very time when the others came forward to assist. He told the officer his little history, the manner of his living in the great family, the trifling cause of his quarreling with it, the slight ground of his entering into the king's service. "Sir," said he, "I quarreled with the family and I thought I was at once fit for the army: I did not know the qualifications it required. I had not reckoned on discipline, and hardships, and self-denial. I liked well enough to sing a loyal song, or drink the king's health, but I find I do not relish working and fighting for him, though I rashly promised even to lay down my life for his service if called upon, when I took the bounty money and the oath of allegiance. In short, sir, I find that I long for the ease and sloth, the merriment and the feasting of my old service; I find I can not be a soldier, and, to speak truth, I was in the very act of deserting when I was stopped short by the cannon-ball. So that I feel the guilt of desertion, and the misery of having lost my leg into the bargain."

The officer thus replied: "Your state is that of every worldly irreligious man. The great family you served is a just picture of the world. The wages the world promises to those who are willing to do its work are high, but the payment is attended with much disappointment; nay, the world, like your great family, is in itself insolvent, and in its very nature incapable of making good the promises and of paying the high rewards which it holds out to tempt its credulous followers. The ungodly world, like your family, cares little for church, and still less for prayer; and considers the Bible rather as an instrument to make an oath binding, in order to keep the vulgar in obedience, than as containing in itself a perfect rule of faith and practice, and as a title-deed to heaven. The generality of men love the world as you did your service, while it smiles upon them, and gives them easy work and plenty of meat and drink; but as soon as it begins to cross and contradict them, they get out of humor with it, just as you did with your service. They then think its drudgery hard, its rewards low. They find out that it is high in its expectations from them, and slack in its payments to them. And they begin to fancy (because they do not hear religious people murmur as they do) that there must be some happiness in religion. The world, which takes no account of their deeper sins, at length brings them into discredit for some act of imprudence, just as your family overlooked your lying and swearing, but threatened to drub you for breaking a china dish. Such is the judgment of the world! it patiently bears with those who only break the laws of God, but severely punishes the smallest negligence by which they themselves are injured. The world sooner pardons the breaking ten commandments of God, than even a china dish of its own.

"After some cross or opposition, worldly men, as I said before, begin to think how much content and cheerfulness they remember to have seen in religious people. They therefore begin to fancy that religion must be an easy and delightful, as well as a good thing. They have heard that, her ways are ways of pleasantness, and all her paths are peace; and they persuade themselves, that by this is meant worldly pleasantness and sensual peace. They resolve at length to try it, to turn their back upon the world, to engage in the service of God and turn Christians; just as you resolved to leave your old service, to enter into the service of the king and turn soldier. But as you quitted your place in a passion, so they leave the world in a huff. They do not count the cost. They do not calculate upon the darling sin, the habitual pleasures, the ease, and vanities, which they undertake by their new engagements to renounce, no more than you counted what indulgences you were going to give up when you quitted the luxuries and idleness of your place to enlist in the soldier's warfare. They have, as I said, seen Christians cheerful, and they mistook the ground of their cheerfulness; they fancied it arose, not because through grace they had conquered difficulties, but because they had no difficulties in their passage. They fancied that religion found the road smooth, whereas it only helps to bear with a rough road without complaint. They do not know that these Christians are of good cheer, not because the world is free from tribulation, but because Christ, their captain, has overcome the world. But the irreligious man, who has only seen the outside of a Christian in his worldly intercourse, knows little of his secret conflicts, his trials, his self-denials, his warfare with the world without; and with his own corrupt desires within.

"The irreligious man quarrels with the world on some such occasion as you did with your place. He now puts on the outward forms and ceremonies of religion, and assumes the badge of Christianity, just as you were struck with the show of a field-day; just as you were pleased with the music and the marching, and put on the cockade and red coat. All seems smooth for a little while. He goes through the outward exercise of a Christian, a degree of credit attends his new profession, but he never suspects there is either difficulty or discipline attending it; he fancies religion is a thing for talking about, and not a thing of the heart and the life. He never suspects that all the psalm-singing he joins in, and the sermons he hears, and the other means he is using, are only as the exercise and the evolutions of the soldiers, to fit and prepare him for actual service; and that these means are no more religion itself, than the exercises and evolutions of your parade were real warfare.

"At length some trial arises: this nominal Christian is called to differ from the world in some great point; something happens which may strike at his comfort, or his credit, or security. This cools his zeal for religion, just as the view of an engagement cooled your courage as a soldier. He finds he was only angry with the world, he was not tired of it. He was out of humor with the world, not because he had seen through its vanity and emptiness, but because the world was out of humor with him. He finds that it is an easy thing to be a fair-weather Christian, bold where there is nothing to be done, and confident where there is nothing to be feared. Difficulties unmask him to others; temptations unmask him to himself; he discovers, that though he is a high professor, he is no Christian; just as you found out that your red coat and your cockade, your shoulder-knot and your musket, did not prevent you from being a coward.

"Your misery in the military life, like that of the nominal Christian, arose from your love of ease, your cowardice, and your self-ignorance. You rushed into a new way of life without trying after one qualification for it. A total change of heart and temper were necessary for your new calling. With new views and principles the soldier's life would have been not only easy, but delightful to you. But while with a new profession you retained your old nature it is no wonder if all discipline seemed intolerable to you.

"The true Christian, like the brave soldier, is supported under dangers by a strong faith that the fruits of that victory for which he fights will be safety and peace. But, alas! the pleasures of this world are present and visible; the rewards for which he strives are remote. He therefore fails, because nothing short of a lively faith can ever outweigh a strong present temptation, and lead a man to prefer the joys of conquest to the pleasures of indulgence."

Hannah More was born on February 2nd, 1745 at Fishponds in the parish of Stapleton, near Bristol. She was the fourth of five daughters of Jacob More, a schoolmaster. He was originally from a family of Presbyterians in Norfolk, but had become a member of the Church of England to pursue a career in the Church. After losing a lawsuit over an estate he had hoped to inherit, he moved to Bristol, becoming an excise officer and later a teacher at the Fishponds free school.

The City of Bristol, at that time, was a centre for slave-trading and Hannah would, over time, become one of its staunchest critics.

The More's were a close family and all the sisters were educated at first by their father who taught them Latin and mathematics. Hannah was also taught French by her elder sisters. Her conversational French was improved by time spent with French prisoners of war from the Seven-Year's-War in Frenchay, then a small village near Bristol.

She was keen to learn, possessed a sharp intellect and was assiduous in studying and, according to family tradition, began writing at an early age.

In 1758 Jacob established his own girls' boarding school at Trinity Street in Bristol for the elder sisters, Mary and Elizabeth, to run. Hannah became a pupil there when she was 12. Jacob and his wife moved to Stony Hill in the city to open a school for boys.

Hannah became a teacher at her sister's school and it was here that she produced her first literary efforts. These were prompted by trying to find material suitable for her young charges to act in. Her first, written in 1762, was The Search after Happiness (by the mid-1780s some 10,000 copies had been sold).

In 1767 Hannah gave up her share in the school to become engaged to William Turner. After six years, with no wedding in sight, and Turner reluctant to move forward, the engagement was broken off. It was now 1773 and by all accounts Hannah suffered a nervous breakdown and spent some time recuperating in nearby Uphill. Turner then bestowed upon her an annual annuity of £200. This was enough to meet her needs and set her free to pursue a literary career. With that ambition London was her next stop. She travelled there in the winter of 1773/74 together with her sisters, Sarah and Martha.

She had previously written some verses on a production of King Lear staged by the famous actor David Garrick and this led to a lasting friendship with him and a pivotal introduction to the London Literary society. Now she met and charmed Samuel Johnson, Joshua Reynolds and Edmund Burke. Johnson is quoted as saying to her "Madam, before you flatter a man so grossly to his face, you should consider whether or not your flattery is worth having." He would later be quoted as calling her "the finest versifatrix in the English language".

Hannah also became a leading member of the Bluestocking group of women who met to further literary and intellectual pursuits. Here she met women who were to become life-long friends; Elizabeth Montagu, Frances Boscawen, Elizabeth Carter, Elizabeth Vesey and Hester Chapone (Hannah later wrote a celebration of this circle in her 1782 poem The Bas Bleu, or, Conversation, published in 1784).

Her first play, The Inflexible Captive, was staged at Bath in 1775. It was based on the opera, Attilio Regulo, by the Italian Pietro Metastasio (1698-1782) whose works she admired.

Her theatrical career was now in full swing. David Garrick himself produced her next play, Percy, in 1777 as well as writing both the Prologue and Epilogue for it. It was a great success when performed at Covent Garden in December of that year. Her next play, Fatal Falsehood, was staged in 1779, shortly after the death of Garrick. It was less successful but still admired.

With David Garrick now passed (January 20th, 1779) Hannah came to view the theatre as both morally wrong and not where her ambitions now lay. She now began to spend her time advancing her interests in other areas.

In 1781 she first met Horace Walpole, man of letters art historian and Whig politician and now corresponded regularly with him.

A friendship with James Oglethorpe, who had long been concerned with slavery as a moral issue and who was working with Granville Sharp in an early abolitionist capacity, started to awaken Hannah's social conscious.

Hannah turned to religious writing, beginning with her Sacred Dramas in 1782; it rapidly ran through nineteen editions. These and the poems Bas-Bleu and Florio (1786) mark her gradual transition to a more serious and considered view of life and are fully expressed in her Thoughts on the Importance of the Manners of the Great to General Society (1788), and An Estimate of the Religion of the Fashionable World (1790).

In Bristol, in 1784, she discovered the poet Ann Yearsley, the so-called 'poetical milkmaid of Bristol'. With Yearsley destitute, Hannah raised a considerable sum of money for her. Lactilia, as Yearsley was known, published Poems, on Several Occasions in 1785, earning about £600. Hannah and Elizabeth Montagu held the profits in trust to protect them from Yearsley's husband. However Ann wished for the capital to be made over, and made insinuations of stealing against Hannah. The money was released and Hannah felt her reputation had been tarnished.

With the death of Samuel Johnson in December 1784, Hannah moved, with her sister Martha, in 1795, to a cottage at Cowslip Green, near Wrington in rural Somerset, "to escape from the world gradually".

In the summer of 1786, she spent time with Sir Charles and Lady Margaret Middleton at their home in Teston in Kent. Among their guests was the local vicar James Ramsay and a young Thomas Clarkson, both of whom were central to the early abolition campaign against slavery.

In 1787, she met John Newton and the 'Clapham Sect' (a group of wealthy evangelical Christians who lived near Clapham and met at Henry Thornton's house). The group was strongly opposed to the Slave Trade. William Wilberforce was a member of the group and he and Hannah became firm friends.

Hannah contributed much to the running of the newly-founded Abolition Society including, in February 1788, her publication of Slavery, a Poem which has long been recognised as one of the most important poems of the abolition period. The poem dramatically described a mistreated, enslaved female separated from her children and severely questioned Britain's role in the Slave Trade.

Her relationship with members of the society, especially Wilberforce, was close. She spent the summer of 1789 holidaying with Wilberforce in the Peak District, planning for the abolition campaign, which, at the time, was at its height.

Her work now became more evangelical. In the 1790s she wrote several Cheap Repository Tracts which covered moral, religious and political topics and were both for sale or distributed to literate poor people. This coincided with her increasing philanthropic work in the Mendip area.

Beyond any doubt, Hannah was the most influential female member of the Society for Effecting the Abolition of the African Slave Trade.

Hannah wrote many ethical books and tracts: Strictures on the Modern System of Female Education (1799), Hints towards Forming the Character of a Young Princess (1805), Cœlebs in Search of a Wife (only nominally a story, 1809), Practical Piety (1811), Christian Morals (1813), Character of St Paul (1815), Moral Sketches (1819). She was a rapid writer, and her work is consequently discursive, animated and without a rigorous structure.

However the originality and force of Hannah's writings perhaps explains her extraordinary popularity. At the behest of Beilby Porteus, Bishop of London and a leading abolitionist, Hannah wrote many spirited rhymes and prose tales, the earliest of which was Village Politics, by Will Chip (1792), intended to counteract the doctrines of Thomas Paine and the influence of the French Revolution.

The series of Cheap Repository Tracts, eventually led to the formation of the Religious Tracts Society. The Tracts were produced at the rate of three a month between 1795 and 1797.

The most famous is perhaps The Shepherd of Salisbury Plain, describing a family of incredible frugality and contentment. Two million copies of these rapid and telling sketches were circulated, in one year, teaching the poor in rhetoric of the most ingenious homeliness to rely upon the virtues of content, sobriety, humility, industry and reverence for the British Constitution, hatred of the French, trust in God and in the kindness of the gentry.

Several of the Tracts oppose slavery and the slave trade, in particular, the poem The Sorrows of Yamba; or, The Negro Woman's Lamentation, which appeared in November 1795 and which was co-authored with Eaglesfield Smith. However, the tracts have also been noted for their encouragement of social quietism in an age of revolution.

In 1789, she purchased a small house at Cowslip Green in Somerset. Wilberforce encouraged Hannah to set up a Sunday school in Cheddar, where poor children could be taught to read. Soon she and her sisters had set up similar schools throughout the Mendip villages, despite fierce opposition.

She was instrumental in setting up twelve schools by 1800 where reading, the Bible and the catechism were taught to local children. Hannah also donated money to Bishop Philander Chase for the founding of Kenyon College, and a portrait of her hangs there in Peirce Hall.

John Scandrett Harford of Blaise Castle was a prodigious benefactor to More's schools in the 1790s, and Hannah modeled the idealised hero and heroine in Cœlebs in Search of Wife (1809) on Mr and Mrs Harford.

However it cannot be said that Hannah was a staunch supporter of Women's rights. She refused to read Mary Wollstonecraft's Rights of Women, saying "so many women are fond of government... because they are not fit for it. To be unstable and capricious is but too characteristic of our sex". She was also shocked by the movement for female education in France, saying "they run to study philosophy, and neglect their families to be present at lectures in anatomy". She is also said to have turned down an honorary membership of the Royal Society of Literature because she considered her "sex alone a disqualification".

The More sisters also met with a good deal of opposition in their philanthropic works: the farmers thought that education, even to the limited extent of learning to read, would be fatal to agriculture, and the clergy, whose neglect she was making good, accused her of Methodist tendencies.

She continued to oppose slavery throughout her life, but at the time of the Abolition Bill of 1807 (which outlawed the slave trade, but not slavery itself), her health did not permit her to take as active a role in the movement as she had done in the late 1780s, although she maintained a correspondence with Wilberforce and others Abolitionists.

In her later life, she continued to dedicate much of her time to religious writing. Nevertheless, her most popular work was a novel, Cœlebs in Search of a Wife, which appeared in two volumes in 1809 (and which ran to nine editions in 1809 alone).

In 1816, Hannah was still at odds with the French. Following Waterloo she is quoted as saying that 'peace with France is a worse evil than war', and refused to allow a French translation of Cœlebs.

Her last few years were spent at Clifton, people from all parts came to visit her even though her health was fading and she was writing less often.

She lived just long enough to see the act finally abolishing slavery. In July 1833, the Bill to abolish slavery throughout the British Empire passed in the House of Commons, followed by the House of Lords on August 1st.

Hannah More died on September 7th, 1833. She is buried at Church of All Saints, Wrington. In her will she left more than £30,000 to charities and religious societies, the equivalent today of many millions.

www.ingramcontent.com/pod-product-compliance
Lightning Source LLC
Chambersburg PA
CBHW072050170626
46813CB00004B/1288